CW01149323

FROM THE ASHES

Published books by Amos Keppler

Your Own Fate
Night on Earth
Dreams Belong to the Night
Alarums of Reality
Black Dragon
Thunder Road - Ice and Fire
Season of the Witch
Fangs and Claws of the Earth

The Nine series:

Falling
Forsaken
Fallen
Afterglow Dust
Afterglow Rain
Afterglow Fire

Anthology: Red Shadow and Other Stories

The Janus Clan series:

The Defenseless
The Slaves
Birds Flying in the Dark
At the End of the Rainbow
Lewis of Modern York
The Werewolf of Locus Bradle
The Valley of Kings
Eyes in the Sky
ShadowWalk
Phoenix Green Earth book 1 and 2

Poetry:

Amos Keppler: Complete Poems 1989 – 2003
Secrets - Descriptions of what cannot be described

From the Ashes

by

Amos Keppler

Midnight Fire Media
2024

Midnight Fire Media

http://midnight-fire.net/mfm
For more about From the Ashes and The Janus Clan:
http://midnight-fire.net/sw

E-Mail:
Amos13@midnight-fire.net
manofhood@yahoo.com

Cover, text, design, premedia, art and photos Amos Keppler

Copyright © Amos Keppler/Ståle Olsen 2024
All rights reserved

ISBN 978-82-91693-39-2

«If anyone should give a truthful account of humanity's thoughts about godhood, we must acknowledge that the word «gods» to a large degree has been used to express the hidden, distant and unknown causes to the effects we have observed. We must further acknowledge that this word has been used when we no longer fathom the cause of known and natural phenomena. The moment we lose sight of causes, or no longer can follow causation, we solve this quandary and put on hold the search for causality by explaining them by the existence of gods… Therefore, when we claim that the gods are responsible for certain phenomena, what else are we doing than to conceal the darkness in our own mind by views we have been used to look at with reverence and awe».
Paul Heinrich Dietrich, Baron von Holbach
System de la nature, London 1770

«The world isn't just stranger than we believe, but stranger than we can imagine».
J. B. S. Haldane

«This fool wants to turn astronomy upside down. But the holy book says that Joshua commanded the sun to stand still, not the earth».
Martin Luther about Nikolai Copernicus

«Ceux qui ont apparlè notre vie á une songe ont eu de la raison... nous veillons dormants et veillants dormons»
«Those who have compared our lives to a dream were right... We sleeping wake, and waking asleep».

Michel Eyquem De Montaigne 1533 - 1593

Part one: ashes

Chapter 1

A shadow sat in a deep chair, in a dark room, staring into the fire. The hair did look red - red like fire. He saw the fire dance, saw flashes, images there. Closing his eyes, keeping them open, it was all the same. He remembered.

– There is fire in you, the old woman told him. – There is that in us all, but more so in you than in almost anyone else. Fire is everything. It was there at the beginning, and will be there after the End. Learn to move fire, and you may move existence itself.

There was a fjord somewhere, a fjord inside a fjord inside a fjord in The Big Fjord. The mountains here were steeper than any other place, blacker than the darkness sneaking in everywhere. The shadow world of the Earth was close this night. The world so few people would admit existed, but everyone knew about. Down in the deep well of the small valley six fires reached for the sky, making the black mountains even blacker. Five of them burned at the five points of a star, a smoldering star painted on the ground, a star surrounded by an equally smoldering circle.

– This is a Pentacle, the woman told him in-between her chanting, – A tool of the Witch to breach borders between worlds and to the depth of human existence.

Before the sixth and biggest stood a young man, turned towards the fire at the center of the Pentacle. It was hard guessing the age of the young face, because there were lines there of longing, fatigue and hatred not present not long ago. He stood straight and completely nude. Lines of colors covered the body and face. He had long hair and bristled beard. And the color was fire, and it burned in the wind. He stood unprotected before the smoldering heat. The hairs on his skin crouched and oozed, the skin itself turning slowly red.

He looked at the mountains. They seemed to lean outwards, to the point that he got the impression of being in a giant cave. To one who had grown up by the coastline, who had been used to seeing the Sun sink in the ocean every day, this impression was even stronger. His eyes slid down the black rock, beyond the Fire, to the older woman dressed in her cloak and hood. He saw glimpses of gray hair, but with her, too, the age was difficult to determine. The face didn't have that many wrinkles. The body glimpsed under the cloak wasn't that weakened by age, if weakened at all. She stood a bit crouched on the opposite side of the center fire, revealed and hidden off and on by the flames. It was like a ghost was standing there, a spirit of fire and shadow, one without soul, skin and eyes. She regularly threw a powder at the fire, making the flames burst and shriek, chanting in a language long dead.

There was late fall and there was a full moon. The night wind was surprisingly warm and countered the cold moonlight. It was a special night, one that for ages had been consecrated to nature's old gods. The servants of the new White Christ called it All Hallows' Eve.

The youth knew that, naturally. He had, himself been raised as one of them.

– Fire was first, she cried, – and we are its Shadow.

He suddenly understood her words, even though he felt confident that she had not changed the tongue of her chant, the one rocking the very mountains.

She felt so familiar to him, in ways he didn't understand, but kept wondering about. He kept staring at her as she ended her chant, her ceremony, her litany of fire. She sagged a bit, clearly spent, her advanced age taking its toll.

– Your ways are strange, he said aloud. – I do not understand them.

– Your ways are strange, she grinned, – and becoming stranger still.

He looked around him, at everything he could see. It wasn't much now. Nothing outside the circle, the Pentacle. Nothing, except for the full moon, and it seemed much farther away - or much closer. In one moment, there was one truth, in the next the other. Everything shifted and changed. The old one straightened. The young man realized with absolute certainty that the small fires slowly burned out, while the big only grew bigger, as if it fed off the others. He stood close to it, but yet he didn't feel the heat. He couldn't hear it burning, and was able to look straight into the intense flames.

– The time grows close. The old one stated. – I ask you one more time: Are you ready?

A hesitant nod. Then another, forceful.

– My time grows close, she said. – *He* will find me soon. If not tomorrow, then the day after tomorrow. I still don't know who he is, no more than I know who you are, or I am, or you know who you are… but I know *what* he is, what we are. So will you. This will prepare you for him, and perhaps more. There are those who are better suited for the task, but they are not available now. They will be, into the far future. Until then you are alone.

He blinked, catching a glimpse of an older man with gray hair, and a ponytail going far down his back. And for the first time, the first time he could remember anyway he shivered down his spine.

– Remember what will happen if you don't remember what you have learned or are not «worthy». Then I will gain a substantial sacrifice on my way to the Other World.

The boy nodded again, nodded fiercely.

– I have chosen, he said. – I will take my changes.

– The burden is yours, the Witch said. – Until we meet again.

He saw his companion reach above her head. She began chanting once more in her ancient, long dead tongue. He once more saw the five small fires shrink much faster than they should have. The recent past repeated itself. It was like they were in a cave. The darkness reflected the light as a ceiling. He stared down at his palms. There was a sharp pain, and they started bleeding. Blood flowed from him. Life fled from him. The fires in the five points, in the circle had shrunk to a point where there were hardly flames left. The huge fire virtually reached the moon. The chanting stopped.

– SAMHAIN, GATHERER OF THE CONDEMNED, she cried, – ACCEPT OUR SACRIFICE, TAKE US INTO YOUR LAP OR AID US IN OUR LABORS.

It turned quiet, deadly quiet. Now, for the first time, it truly looked like a cave, like another world.

– Now! A voice so hoarse that it hardly resembled a voice anymore. – NOW!

He watched her then, saw her fade away, as the ghost she was, into the shadows and the darkness. He feared for her, feared for himself. He couldn't deny that. He didn't want to. He had been told repeatedly that it was natural, that it could even be useful… if he didn't let it overwhelm him. His feet… a sea of blood boiled and flowed around his feet. Just one moment, and it seemed to go on forever. One moment was forever. One tiny moment he stood there, hesitant, and then… He jumped into the searing heat.

And all the tiny fires disappeared.

2

BERGEN, WESTERN NORWAY 1970 CE (Common Era)

It was dark. Darkness swirled around all the blinking lights. Carousels, a rollercoaster, wheels of fortune, gaming halls, an arena with tiny, electric cars, performers with fire flowing from their mouths. A traveling Tivoli, a fun fair had come to town. Wide-eyed children, accompanied by their parents arrived from all over the district to have fun, fun, fun.

It never turned completely dark during summer this far north, but the twilight seemed to darken when confronted by all the bright, electrical currents.

The visiting fair was an annual occurrence. But this year was still special. This year the celebration seemed to have spread throughout the town.

– You remember last year, don't you children? A mother said to her daughter and son.

– Yes, last year was *fun*.

Seven-year-old Axel brightened some more.

– But it is bigger now, five-year-old Lillian said, wrinkling her smooth forehead. – Isn't it, mother?

The mother and father exchanged glances, smiling a bit uncertain.

– It is indeed, my children. This year we're celebrating our proud city's nine hundredth anniversary. It was founded in the year of our Lord 1070, by King Olav Kyrre, one of Norway's first and finest christians.

– THOUSAND YEARS' RESISTANCE, a man shouted from a kind of temporary stage just outside the fair's limits. – ONE THOUSAND YEARS' RESISTANCE TO THE DANK, OPPRESSIVE CHRISTIAN YOKE.

Axel and Lillian's parents hurried past him, into the fair's guarded area.

The brother and sister didn't look much alike. He was fair-haired and with just a hint of the dark skin dominating her features. She had dark curls and while he was quite robust, she seemed a bit frail, and her searching eyes never rested. They led and were alternately led by their parents to the fair's various amusements.

The smoldering summer heat encouraged light clothing and heavy passions. The Tivoli stood by a water. Many older citizens scowled at young boys and girls, dipping naked feet in it, and generally were a very tight group.

Lillian watched it. She watched it all, sucking up everything in a way only a child could do. She saw people in strange clothes. The boys had long hair and beard. They could be mistaken for girls from behind. Her stern father looked even more so when being close to any of them. The fair people also looked weird, but they were more… dressed up. She had seen actors on television, hiding under the couch when her parents thought she was sound asleep.

The fair was fun. Both children laughed and grinned wildly during the rollercoaster ride, while the parents held hard in the thick safety pole. They pulled Lillian and Axel quickly past a tent with many blinking machines, muttering to themselves about «sin».

– This is fun, daddy, Lillian said, – why don't you have fun?

– Be quiet, young lady, he replied. – There are things you're too young to understand.

Growing used to be rebutted and reprimanded by her parents, the girl didn't take it too bad or too seriously, but continued on her own, private journey of discovery. There was so much to see, so much to experience, especially with a child's extreme curiosity. Held by both her father and mother she turned her head, and moved her eyes constantly. She took in the sight of the firebreathers, marveling at the young girl, dark like herself winning a teddy bear at the Wheel of Fortune, breathing deeply when watching a boy and a girl doing acrobatics on the tarmac, the hard and cold tarmac.

And then she saw him, a man with long red hair. They were about to leave. They had been here for hours, she knew that, but she still felt cheated somehow, brushed off by her parents' aloofness. When they left, she cast her eyes behind her for one last look. Her head froze in that position. She saw him stand at the gate, looking at her. And… she met his eyes.

She had a sense of vertigo, and clung to her mother's hand.

He didn't really look that much different from the other strange men in the city. He didn't have a beard, like most of the others. But the real difference was how he made her feel. She wrestled in her mother's grip. Her lips formed a name. A heat stronger than the Sun and a cold colder than ice erupted inside her. She wanted to run to him, but her mother held her back.

– What's the *matter* with you? Mother said incredulous.

– Let go of me, mother. It's the boy I see in my dreams. I *must* go to him.

He had turned away, and was on his way back inside the fair.

– Who…? Mother asked.

– He was there, the girl pointed, and jumped up and down. – I saw him, I saw him!

– Those fantasies of yours. Her mother slapped her on her cheek. – They must stop soon, or we will be forced to do something about it, you hear. Besides, it wasn't the man you saw. It couldn't have been. How many times must I tell you that dreams are not real?

– And that man, her father said shocked. – Those flower children are so *indecent*.

And they dragged her off. She didn't fight it. Tears formed in the corners of her eyes.

– THE TIME CALLED THE SIXTIES HAS ENDED, the man on the self-made stage cried. – AND ALL GOOD PEOPLE ARE CELEBRATING.

Mother and father speeded up further, their expression turning even a bit grimmer.

Little Lillian stubbornly dried her eyes. She often turned her head and looked behind her on her way home, but didn't see the boy man again. The following day she went and played in the mud, mudding herself profoundly, grinning wickedly.

– Till we meet again, she sang happily. – Meet again, meet again.

But the catching in her throat remained hard and sore.

3
BERGEN 1985 CE

It was January, supposedly winter in Bergen. Slush and ponds of water warred for dominance in the gray, colorless streets. Long lines of cars wrestled with the rush hour's limitation on traffic. People walking along the cars coughed and shook as they attempted, in vain to breathe normally in the bad air.

Lillian ran. She ran through the Nygård Park in the central parts of the city, crossing a small bridge, where she almost fell on the slippery ground of slush and ice, but kept herself on her feet, and kept running, keeping up with her high, supple steps in the quicksand soup of snow and water. The rain poured from the gray, foggy skies. One could hardly see the mountains surrounding the city because of the low clouds. The runner picked up speed, running flat out up the steep hill, pumping, pumping, her feet hammering the ground. Finally, halfway up she started having problems. The steps turned shorter and not so supple. She was close to slipping and falling several times in the slush, but she kept going. She had done this for some time, now, and had developed quite a resistance to fatigue, but today, because of the wet snow everywhere was worse. She struggled hard, and was virtually totally spent, to the brink of exhaustion when reaching the top. She kept going, slowly regaining a resemblance of a run. She forced herself further on her trail. There was hardly any thought anymore, just the need to put one foot in front of the other, beyond the old houses, reaching the three-story apartment blocks.

Soon. *Soooon...*

She found herself outside her block, and the moment she became consciously aware of that fact all her remaining reserves of strength seemed to leave her. With her hands resting on her knees, she stood there heaving for breath, slowly, slowly regaining some ability to move. She rushed back to the nearest green area, and started beating and kicking the closest tree, making bark fly. The pain in her hands and feet felt good. Her sight darkened to a red haze, darkening further as she kept at it. There was still strength left in her body, and she kept hammering the tree, hammering herself, until she even more exhausted stumbled back to the block entrance. She rushed through the gate, and inside the ground floor, crawled up the stairs to the top of the building, attempting to wring some water out of the clothes, but it did no good. Water kept flowing on the floor when she reached her wonderfully warm apartment. Closing the door behind her, she slowly, painfully removed her clothes, leaving them on the floor by the front door. She started the stretching and bending thing, making sure all her muscles were somewhat soft and supple before running into the shower, the shower with the warm, warm water. She turned on so much heat she could handle. Lovely. Wonderful. The numbness the cold had visited upon her faded slowly. Sore muscles softened. The shaking stopped. She felt like she was floating. Everything seemed light, hazy. She turned the knob back to a more normal level. Her mind cleared. The hot rain on the skin purified not just her body, but her mind as well.

Eyes closed. The water against the skin was so pleasant. The monotone hammering against the skin made her so relaxed and so sleepy. She hardly registered that she was leaning against the wall, the soft and warm wall. The dream came to her again, even in this half-awake state. It had happened so often lately that it didn't alarm her anymore.

Faces danced before her, a long row of faces. She stood in a field of flowers by a forest, glancing at an eagle, or rather a huge bird of an unknown species flying by. It had wings in red and shadow, and each time it flapped those wings it battered her like a storm. They looked like fire in the sunset, in the dusk the land had become.

She blinked a few times before her eyes remained open. Nausea almost overwhelmed her. She quickly turned off the water and hurried out of the cabinet. Steam filled the room, covered the mirror. In the mirror, she could still see the dancing faces, and only just about glimpse her own anxious expression. She was breathing hard again, as if she had just finished running.

Humming a bit strained, she grabbed a towel and jumped the two steps out in the hallway. There was another mirror there. She stopped in front of it, drying her hair, while looking, looking at her brown skin and dark hair. There was just her there, in the mirror, and nothing else. She passed it briefly, on her way to the living room.

The heat from the central heating hit her. She usually thought of it as too hot, but now it felt kind of pleasant, as the strange kind of cold persisted in riding her.

The radio overwhelmed her humming. It was the tune from the movie Ghostbusters by the same name. She shook her head. The girl sharing the apartment with her, Tove Hegtun noticed, as she was covering most of the floor in her exuberant dance.

– You should learn to enjoy this one, she grinned. – It's Wild.

– I don't like it, Lillian replied. – I didn't enjoy the movie, and I don't care for the music.

She stopped before the window, staring into the night, at her indistinct image, as she kept rubbing dry her tall and big and athletic body.

The music ended, and the news came on. There had been a murder. A young girl had been killed by a sharp object, and left on the cold sidewalk in a less traveled part of the city.

– Hey, nigger bitch, Tove joked rather cruelly. – You're doing it again, exposing yourself to the panting dogs across the street.

Lillian studied herself further, as if she wanted to burn the image of herself into memory. She wasn't really black, but rather a multicultural mix of her Scandinavian, southern and eastern ancestry. Her oriental eyes stayed a prominent part of the face.

– I'm one eight Moorish Spanish Asian or something, she said with a distant look in those prominent eyes. – But Axel has fair skin and hair and no tilted eyes, and my mother is like him, even though she's one generation closer. I must have inherited all my great grandmother's genes.

There it was, another face in the window, in the misty painting revealed to her.

– Or perhaps it isn't all the panting dogs you're displaying yourself for? Tove said teasingly. – But only a certain sweet redhead?

Lillian blushed and instantly covered herself. Tove laughed thrillingly.

– I am quite shameless am I not?

Lillian began dressing, well before she had dried properly.

– Hey, if you've got it, flaunt it, her friend shrugged. – I don't mind. And you're entitled. And you need to learn to relax, anyway, the way you've worked your butt off lately, with both your studies and long hours at work and beyond hard exercise *to boot*. I can't, for the love of me understand how you can do it all.

– I must, Lillian said quietly, subdued.

– I know, sweetie, Tove nodded. – I know.

Lillian, with that remote expression intact returned to the window, and stared outside some more. But she didn't see the gray buildings and streets. The image and sensations from the field of flowers and green grass kept haunting her. The scent of spring and summer lingered in her nostrils. She blinked in confusion.

– No matter, I will do you the favor of joining you in the celebration tonight, Tove declared. – You're only twenty once, you know.

– It's only three days since New Years' Eve, Lillian objected. – I did the celebration then, really.

– It didn't look like that to me, girl. You didn't celebrate much of anything. You used to play around, but that night, you behaved pretty much like a nun.

– Well, I did break away from a strict, christian upbringing and surroundings, Lillian pointed out. – Most of those play around a lot before settling down. I'm actually quite the average girl in this matter.

– Nice try, her friend grinned. – But a warm-blooded female like you is nothing like that. My prediction is that you will never settle down, with anything.

Lillian sighed, and her friend's words brought inevitable pride. She relented with a smile, and walked to the kitchen and fetched the steaming kettle. They had dinner. Lillian fed like a wolf.

– You've always been hungry, Tove whispered, – so very hungry.

– Feeding right after hard exercise is the right thing to do, Lillian munched. – You build muscle mass, not fat.

– You've got answers for everything, don't you…

Lillian made no verbal reply. She kept devouring the food.

The plate was empty. The kettle was empty. She looked astonished at both.

She walked to the closet and picked up the white dress, the one she had saved for so long to buy. There were two white dresses, a matching set. Tove had bought hers the same day. She could afford it, afford such spontaneous decisions.

They stood before the mirror and admired themselves.

– You're so big and curvy and athletic, Tove said, sounding very jealous. – I wish I had meat on my bones like that.

– No, you don't Lillian snorted.

That brought a good chuckle from both girls.

Tove called for a taxi, a necessity in this weather. Lillian felt both gratitude and shame because she knew her friend would pay for it, like she paid for most of their excesses.

The taxi brought them from door to door. It had the heater on. The chill touched their bare legs and arms only briefly as they rushed the few steps from the door to the car. It was Friday night and packed everywhere. They had to drive past two places until they found one without a long queue outside. Tove paid the driver. They rushed once again through the moist chill. The heat of the disco welcomed them.

– Bergen is finally getting the entertainment quality it deserves, Tove said, – It would have been hard to find places like this that weren't packed on Friday night just a few years ago.

– You're the expert, Lillian said brightly.

– You're funny, her friends giggled. – Do you know that?

They found a table. Tove rushed to the bar to procure drinks. She would pay for them, pay for all of them. Lillian looked glum at her back.

Tove returned with drinks before Lillian got even remotely bored.

– Cheers! Her friend cried.

– Cheers! Lillian responded.

Both raised their glasses. Glasses met and parted. Both drank.

– I keep hearing that this is a decent place, Tove said, – that you can leave your handbag at the table and expect it to still be there when you return.

Lillian felt the first hints of a headache. Loud music and a pounding beat did that. She ignored it. The two of them had the second, or the third or fifth toast. Both emptied their glasses and rushed out on the dance floor. They moved, surrounded by flickering lights and pounding beat.

Her feet, her body moved to the rhythm in an effortless manner on the crowded floor. A smile touched her face. Her feet moved faster on the floor. The smile widened. She... let go.

The lights flickered around her. The drum thundered in her ears and mind. She gasped in a way not connected to her being physically tired or anything. Half closed eyes opened wide. She chuckled when she and Tove left the floor.

– You certainly enjoyed yourself, her friend remarked.

– I've always enjoyed dancing, Lillian marveled, – but not so much the sledgehammer beat of the disco, but now, it didn't seem to matter that much.

Tove studied her, like she always did when Lillian had behaved strangely. Even that didn't ruin Lillian's good mood.

They returned to the table. Their handbags were still there. Tove rushed to the bar to fetch two more drinks. Lillian sat there, and imagined that all her senses were going into overdrive. It was the strangest feeling. She studied the details caught by her eyes, the faces, the shadows, the flashing lights.

Tove returned with four glasses, breaking the spell. Lillian shook her head. She grabbed her glass when Tove grabbed hers. They had another toast.

– It was like I was levitating, floating, she confessed to her friend later. – It was the strangest thing.

She held back. Tove clearly wasn't interested. She didn't enjoy talking about or even contemplating anything outside normal, average.

– You're dreaming yourself away again, Tove remarked.

– But isn't it funny? Lillian giggled. – These places are designed to kill young people's ability to think and imagine, but I'm thinking and imagining more than ever.

It suddenly seemed hilariously funny. She laughed out loud. People by several neighboring tables glanced at her. She laughed even louder.

They danced some more. Lillian reveled in it. Tove didn't. Lillian couldn't say she didn't enjoy that reversal of fortunes. She danced face to face with a boy. He was clearly inexperienced and pulled back because of her aggressive courting. She enjoyed that, too.

The two girls followed the flow to a nightclub. That was a different, quieter scene. There was more drinking, more adult courting. She began the subconscious selection process, not really finding any good candidates, and certainly not among fellow students. She relented and focused on enjoying herself. Both girls became intoxicated, looking at the world through hazy eyes.

The nightclub closed, too. They followed the flow further to a nachspiel with mostly students, both fellow history students and from other faculties. Most of them, including Tove had become piss drunk. Lillian hadn't been drinking that much, setting out to remain somewhat sober.

A redhead handed her a drink. She accepted it reluctantly.

– My name is Gunnar, he said. – What's yours?

– Lillian, she replied sweetly, eye-flirting with him.

There was something about the man making her interested. She resisted it, but it persisted. He offered her a second glass. They had another toast. Her sweet smile faded.

– You don't need to make me drunk, she stated with a deliberate shrug.

He looked both pleased and peeved, not appreciating being found out. He grabbed her, quite rough. She wanted to pull herself free, but relented, unable to help herself. He kissed her on the lips, and chuckled when she responded. Something about him made her attracted to him. She wondered if it was his rough, callous behavior. He began fondling her. She became aroused. It was sudden and notable. She gasped, unable to keep it contained. His smug grin didn't keep that from happening. She chastised herself, in vain. He pulled her with him to the top floor. They walked through a hallway filled with doors. She heard loud sounds from almost every room.

– We won't be bothered, he stated.

– That's good, she heard herself say.

He brought her to a large room, with a large bed, and closed and locked the door. He began undressing her promptly, pulling the dress over her head. She helped him by raising her arms, and lifting her feet, and writhing in his arms.

– I knew it, he spat. – You're such an eager bitch, walking around half nude like that.

He sounded angry, confirming her opinion of him.

– What's the matter, you don't like eager females?

He slapped her on the cheek. She didn't react that much. Her need kept growing. She offered her lips to him. Lips met. He kept roughing her up. She hardly felt it, and worked on removing his clothes. He grabbed her and held her.

– You're such a firecracker, such a juicy cunt. I like that, love that…

His dirty talk made her even more needy.

– Stand still, he bid her, giving her another slap.

She obeyed, being a good girl. She watched him undress, revealing his hard and strong body. He took his time. His knowing grin revealed that he knew how that affected her. He had finally completed the process. He grabbed her and mangled her with lips and hands. The loud moan didn't seem to come from her at all. He chuckled pleased.

They tumbled down on the bed. She choked when he penetrated her, and started moving in response immediately. He moved on top of her, back and forth, back and forth. Each new thrust brought a stronger need.

– Children will just roll out of you with those hips, he grunted.

He sounded… sounded like her father.

He emptied himself in her and she erupted in pleasure, screaming her heart out in anger and shame and joy.

She had to take the brunt of his weight for a few seconds before he rolled off her and onto his back.

– That's my girl.

He petted her like he would a cat.

– It was good for you, I presume?

She nodded subdued.

– I did come, she acknowledged, – did come hard.

His laughter echoed in her ears. He pulled her close and kissed her on the cheek. She crouched in his arms for a while. All of it felt very awkward, and she was glad.

She pulled free and left the bed. He made a half-hearted, failed attempt to hold her back. She picked up her shoes and clothes from the table.

– Hey, he said indignant. – Where are you going?

– I need to get home, she said, – but I will have a shower first.

– Do you need some company? He grinned.

– No, thank you, I can manage.

The grin didn't leave his face. He was so stupid.

She left the room. There was no one in the hallway. She heard water flowing from several showers. Relief flooded her when she found an available bathroom almost at the end of the hallway. She rushed inside and closed and locked the door behind her. She put the clothes on the bench and stepped into the shower. Her hand turned the knob, and the warm water hit her. She rubbed herself hard everywhere. There was no hint of arousal. She soaped and rinsed and cleaned herself twice. She dried herself in front of the steamy mirror, glimpsing her face, imagining that it changed again.

The hallway looked strange, more like a tunnel than a hallway, but there was certainly no light at in the end of the tunnel.

The living room had turned more or less quiet. There was some low-keyed conversation. Most partygoers slept in more or less impossible positions. Tove did as well. She crouched under the long table with other heavy sleepers. A bunch of people in an adjacent room argued about the value of money.

– Money is the only true currency, a student from the Norwegian School of Economics sniveled, clearly more honest than he would have been sober.

But there are countless ways of obtaining them, a medical student pointed out. – A good education, and you've got it made.

– Work within the oil-sector is still good, another argued. – It will be good for a long time.

– There are infinite possibilities, the economy student agreed, – for anyone not screaming about the end of the world and shit.

Lillian mixed herself another drink. She emptied the glass in one go, silencing the buzz from the ants pissing in her veins. The students in the other room turned silent, too, their snoring joining that of the rest. She hesitated a bit before making another drink straight up. She walked, somewhat composed to the room, to the economy student and emptied the glass on his head. There was no notable reaction.

She heard steps behind her and turned around. Redhair had stopped three steps away.

– That's my naughty girl, he said. – I take it, you don't care much for this assembly. Shall we take our leave?

– Yes, Gunnar, she said subdued.

It had just started brightening in the horizon when they walked to his sleek car, his expensive Porsche.

– You didn't drink anything…

– I don't drink alcohol, he said, very patronizing.

She nodded to herself. He didn't notice, or pretended not to notice. He held the door open to her. She sat down in the passenger seat. He sat down in the driver's seat, and drove off. Gray streets soaked in water and slush passed before her eyes. She hardly noticed. He held her hand and handled the wheel with one hand. It wasn't that far. The streets blurred in her eyes.

She hardly noticed any substantial details until the end of the drive. He stopped outside the iron gate.

– Thank you, she said sweetly and kissed him on the cheek. – You're a lifesaver.

– Aren't you gonna invite me in? We could do another nachspiel.

He was so very dominating, so confident.

– No! She replied curtly, attempting to joke a bit. – Even bitches in heat need their beauty sleep.

– I would say they need it even more, he boasted in his arrogant manner. – I'll be seeing you, little beauty.

She opened the door and stepped outside. She slammed the door shut and waved to him. He drove off. She wanted so much to curl her hands into fists, and had trouble holding onto the key and push it into the keyhole. She managed and rushed inside. Well home, she had feared she had trouble breathing. She wasn't little, in any meaning of the word, and he knew that, of course. He was just being a patronizing jerk again.

She undressed as she walked to the bedroom, dropping the precious white dress on the floor, dog-tired, all of a sudden, hardly able to keep her eyes open. She walked to the bed and dropped down on it, asleep before her head missed the pillow.

4

The dream was always the same, with variations. She twisted back and forth on the bed, soaked in sweat, never really staying still. There were the big white birds resembling seagulls flying above her. She stood on a pier and looked at herself in the water mirror. She had fair hair and long braids. The birds flew into the darkness with the many campfires. In the glow from one of them, she spotted a face, a man's face framed by red hair, the face indistinct in the darkness and shifting light. She stood with him in the field of flowers. He stared at the bay, at the many boats returning home with lots of fish. The dream had no sound. They didn't speak with a verbal voice, but they could still hear each other. He turned, she turned, and they stood face to face. He spoke to her. She knew he did. His lips moved. But she couldn't hear anything. She looked distressed at him.

He repeated his words, more insistent. It dawned on her that she still couldn't see his face. She saw no distinct features, only a blurry bundle of flesh.

She woke up with hammering heart and a scream caught in her throat. There had been more, but she could not recall it except in tiny glimpses fading quickly in the light of day. She realized that she had thrown off the blanket and sat up in bed. Her hair blocked her sight. She pushed it back on her head with a lingering panic.

The weather hadn't changed. The day remained dark and wet. She rose from the bed and picked up her purse. Hands found the set of pills there, morning after pills. She picked one and swallowed it without water. The purse dropped from her weak hand. She stepped out in the hallway. The door to the other bedroom stayed ajar. Tove slept the sleep of the just. Lillian started making breakfast, taking her time, reckoning that her friend would wake up in time to share it with her, which she did, just a little worse for wear. They sat there and enjoyed the food and drink,

– You did it, didn't you? I didn't imagine that, did I?

– Nope, the tall dark girl shrugged.

– I heard you all the way to the living room, Tove mused. – It must have been something, the way you screamed.

– He was one more skilled arsehole, Lillian said subdued. – He did what he was supposed to do.

Tove put a hand on top of her friend's.

– Why do I only get it with shitheads? Lillian asked her friend.

– We all have that problem, honey, Tove drawled and joked.

– I can't seem to say no to them, Lillian despaired.

Tove hugged her and cuddled her.

– The thing is, Lillian said with anger in her voice, – I never saw myself as a weak, codependent person. I gained self-confidence emerging from my domestic hell, not the opposite.

– You are strong, her friend stated. – But it isn't far-fetched that your father and mother's machinations have rubbed off on you. You just must keep fighting to liberate yourself from it, that's all.

Lillian dried a few tears.

– Thank you, she sniffed.

– Don't mention it, Tove grinned. – Hey, why don't we stay at home and rent Conan the Barbarian tonight?

Lillian looked nonplussed at her.

– But you hate that movie.

– But you love it, so, what do I know...

They laughed together. That always felt good.

– Let's take a walk, Lillian suggested, – just walk.

– No exercise today?

– No! A headshake. – I've set myself back at least two weeks after last night's alcohol revels, anyway.

They dressed in thick, protective clothes, and stepped outside, into the moist winter air. In spite of the temperature being above zero, there was a notable chill in the air. And wind, icy wind. Lillian was well used to spending time outdoors during far worse conditions than this, and handled it well. Tove wasn't and didn't.

There were lots of people in town, as was usually the case on Saturdays. They walked on the cobblestones. Lillian frowned after just a few steps. She had become the girl with the long braids. She walked through a street looking completely different, but was still the same. When she looked at Tove, she didn't see her, but a completely different girl. She suddenly had trouble breathing.

– Are you alright? Tove asked concerned.

Tove had become Tove again. The street had become the modern street again.

– I am! Lillian assured her friend. – Nothing is wrong.

– You looked really weird for one moment there, Tove chuckled.

Tove didn't understand. Lillian realized that even better than before in that very moment.

– I don't mind, her friend shrugged. – You are weird. I like it!

Lillian wanted to speak up, to really make an attempt at explaining it to her, but relented.

They walked through the City Park with lots of other people, and also birds around them. The birds screamed in Lillian's ears in a way she doubted that they did in other humans.

– I've always had sharp senses, she said spontaneously. – I tested myself once. My hearing is distinctly above average.

– You're Supergirl, Tove chuckled.

A large birds passed over them, one Lillian would swear was an eagle. She knew Tove didn't see it. No one else did either.

Eagles had been extinct in these parts for a long time.

She glimpsed red hair and turned to take a closer look, but it was a woman. She sighed in frustration.

They had sandwiches and coffee at a cafeteria.

– Running, hard exercise is such a pleasure, Lillian said with blushing cheeks. – I feel so light on my feet, even during ordinary walk that I imagine I can fly.

– You get so easily excited, Tove said enviously.

– I am immediate, Lillian grinned. – I know! I love it!

She spotted a frown on her friend's brow, one occasionally appearing when the other girl felt she had overstepped her bounds. The grin widened.

Lillian Donner noted that moment, for some reason, unable to understand why. The two of them ended their lunch. They stood up and left. Lillian shook her head, unable to shake a feeling of… of dread. The chill in the air entered her body, her bones.

They rented Conan the Barbarian at the closest video rental store, and went home without further ado. It was still fairly bright outside, as bright as it would be in the twilight day of winter at this latitude. The day lasted only six hours. Impatiently, they covered the windows with thick, dark blankets. Lillian looked good-humored at her friend.

– I love the movie, too, Tove said. – Sue me!

Lillian grinned.

They sat down in the sofa. Tove had popcorn. Lillian didn't. Tove offered several times. Lillian refused.

The movie began. The heavy drums. Mako's voice. The boy growing up in the forest with the swordmaker father. The brutal assault. The boy and many others taken away, bound for slavery. The young man fleeing from his chains, let go by the slaver. The man, the thief meeting the female warrior, his beloved. His beloved killed. The burning on the hill. Conan having his vengeance.

Lillian had popcorn. She never removed her attention from the screen, just reached out a hand, and grinning Tove offered again.

Lillian realized that her face was soaked in tears. The skin just grew wetter as the credits flashed on the small TV-screen.

– The screen seemed to fill the wall, she frowned. – It was like I was watching the movie in the theater again.

Tove dried her tears.

– I just love that movie, Lillian said.

She shook her head, overwhelmed by emotion, the chill in her bones deeper than ever.

5

The studies took all their time. Sometimes Lillian despaired, fearing they took absolutely everything from her. Human history immersed itself on her. She dreamed about it, dreamed even more about it than before. A battle happened before her eyes. She didn't take part in it directly, but was one of the countless women tending the wounded and the dying, swearing to herself that she could smell the blood and the rot of dead bodies.

The sword flashed brightly, blinding her. She walked between tents on a rainy day. The sword still flashed brightly, as if reflecting a bright light.

The scene shifted. She couldn't tell the exact moment it did, but found herself on her back on a table of some kind in a room with dry air and thick smoke. She wanted to move her arms and legs, but they had put bracelets around her wrists and ancles, chained her to the table. Several men, clearly priests surrounded her. They didn't speak. She had half expected them to do so, but they stayed silent. One of them squeezed her cheeks, forcing her mouth open and to stay open. They pushed the water funnel into her mouth and poured on the water. She started coughing and imagined that it never ended. It seemed to go on for hours, for eternities. The fireplace burned. She saw that clearly, knowing what would happen. The water torture finally ended. One man brought a hot poker from the fireplace. He pushed the hot iron at her skin, and more desperate screams caused by the horrible, horrible pain mixed with the men's cruel laughter.

She screamed her throat raw, noticing only after a while that she sat on her bed, and that Tove attempted to hold her, calm her down. Another eternity passed until Lillian finally did. She sat there, unable to stop shaking.

– I experienced a battle, one so brutal that any current such pales in comparison. She dried herself around the lips. – I was being t-tortured by members of the... the inquisition. They used the infamous water funnel, making me admit my «guilt» of being a witch, a servant of Satan. Then, they b-burned me with an iron poker. They did many other similar acts. It felt even worse, even more horrible and brutal than all the stories about it.

– Too much history lessons for you, Tove joked or attempted to joke.

Lillian hardly heard her friend or even sensed her surroundings. Everything had turned into one, continuous blur.

She went through the motions that day, and the coming days. She expected the visions to return to her during the day, or/and in the night, but for some reason, they didn't. They stayed vivid in her mind, but she didn't reexperience them. She focused even harder on her studies, acknowledging the foolhardiness of that. She ran, ran flat out, faster and longer than ever before, burying her head in the books when she didn't. It made her dog-tired, able to fall asleep the moment her head touched the pillow. She had suffered some trouble doing that.

Her ancle hurt. She had overdone the running and training. The ancle stayed tender after several days of relative rest and recuperation. She had to suspend the exercise for a while.

She remembered February 18. Tove wanted to go to a waterhole for a drink or ten, but Lillian strongly suggested they went to watch Dune at Forum movie theater instead. Tove relented.

– I've been looking forward to this one for a long time, Lillian said, unable to hide her excitement, giving Tove pointers, not caring one bit. – It's David Lynch. It's one of the more notable novels ever published.

She glanced around and frowned. The entrance hall was almost empty. They walked into the large theater. There were almost no people anywhere. The two of them had no trouble taking possession of the best, elevated seats, with a direct, horizontal line of sight to the screen.

– This movie won't stay on for long, Tove said, – not with this sorry attendance.

Lillian had to give her right. She waited for more people to arrive, but no one did.

Then, she forgot about that, forgot distractions, directing her full attention at the large screen.

The movie lasted for two hours and seventeen minutes. It felt like moments to Lillian.

They stood in the entrance hall afterwards. She noticed with blushing cheeks how she was breathing, how every breath felt like it filled her lungs to full capacity.

– I didn't think I would be disappointed, but I didn't think it would be this great either. It was nothing short of *amazing*. We lived the lives of the characters. I don't understand how people can deliberately allow themselves to miss this. I don't understand that at all.

She noticed a large man, a bear of a man with red hair by the ticket office. She turned absolutely still, feeling like she was unable to breathe.

– I enjoyed it, too, Tove acknowledged. – It was great!

Lillian was distracted, giving her a brief, annoyed glance.

When she turned her attention back to the ticket office, the man was gone. Lillian rushed outside, but the man wasn't there either.

She returned to the entrance hall and walked straight to one of the guards. The second performance of the evening was about to start. There were even fewer people on their way in.

– I forgot my umbrella, she told the guard. – Can I go inside and look for it? I'll be right back out.

He nodded reluctantly. She rushed through the short hallway. There were only a few people there. None of them were him. She walked to the seats she and Tove had inhabited.

– I forgot my umbrella, she said, keeping up the pretense.

She walked back out.

– Someone must have stolen it, she told the guard. – Thanks, anyway.

She walked down the stairs to the toilet, the men's toilet. She stepped inside. She checked all the stalls. There was no one there. People stared when she returned upstairs. The stairs to the women's toilet were at the other side of the hall.

They walked back to town. It wasn't far. Tove didn't pry. Lillian appreciated that.

– It won't last a week, Lillian said. – We need to watch it again no later than Thursday.

The program changed on Fridays.

She brimmed with impatience the next couple of days. She could hardly contain herself. She did a light run on Wednesday, and changed the route to include the cinema. She arrived well before the doors opened. No one with red hair entered the building.

Thursday finally arrived.

– You're even more obsessed than usual, Tove remarked. – What gives?

Lillian didn't reply. She glanced constantly around her, studying every single somewhat tall and big person they encountered. No one looked even remotely similar to the large bulk of a man with red hair she had seen at the cinema.

They arrived. There were more people tonight. The place was almost half full. Lillian didn't see the man she was looking for. They didn't get the best seats tonight. It hardly mattered. She did become immersed in the movie again, drawn into the story and the motion. That she had watched it once before, and knew what was gonna happen only added to her enjoyment. She tore herself away occasionally to seek the man with red hair.

The credits rolled across the screen again. Lillian sat in the seat with fiery thoughts surging through her mind.

The two friends returned to the lobby. Lillian looked directly at the ticket office.

She didn't see the giant with red hair anywhere.

Chapter 2
BJORGVIN, NORWAY 1070 CE

The seagulls began filling the sky early in the morning, while there was no rain. They kept coming during the heavy showers later and stayed when sunshine followed the dark, dreary weather. They were flying all over the large coastal valley and the bay, along the steep mountains surrounding it.

– They're always here on such occasions, a man said. – They know when the boats arrive.

And more and more people arrived with the birds, growing more and more excited. The first, smaller fishing boats appeared between Fenring the island and Bjorgvin the mainland. There were two quays. The largest belonged to the king. Both were filled with excited people.

The first smaller boats reached the shore. They were filled with herring. That didn't really make people that excited. The small boats were usually filled to capacity. But the fishermen's expression and wild cries did make the excitement spread like wildfire among the awaiting people.

– The sea is boiling, a man stepping off a boat shouted. – I've never experienced anything like it.

He was one of the older, experienced seafarers, and had caught fish since he was a boy.

The bigger boats entered the bay between the island and the small, nebulous town. The people standing on land, closer to the boats started shouting. The stories about the massive catches had begun circulating early that day, but people had just shaken their head good humored. Those stories were just too wild to be believed. Now, they were confirmed.

– The herring practically fought to get into the nets, the old-timer marveled and shook his head, not in denial, but in astonishment.

This had been a scarcely populated and fairly insignificant trading settlement until it had caught the king's interest. Olav Kyrre, son of King Harald Hardråde had founded the town this year and called it Bjorgvin «the green meadows among the mountains». He already had his own royal farm, his own royal anything already. He clearly planned on staying. People had had mixed feelings about that at first, but now, they figured he brought luck and prosperity.

Everyone was caught in the growing euphoria.

– I've never even heard about it happening anywhere else, another man chuckled in gathering anticipation. – If it had, it must have been when the gods walked the land.

The legends, the oral stories spoke about the god kings many generations back, in an ancient time shrouded in mist and shadow.

The larger ships grew bigger in the horizon, visible to all. The chilly northern wind brought the stench of fish to people's nostrils. People waved from the shore as the boats made their way to the quays. The tough guys onboard returned the waves reluctantly, fearful of appearing unmanly. A minute or two later, they didn't care. They stood to their knees in fish, and kept jumping up and down, in spite of falling several times.

One of the largest boats had only a crew of five, all of them exhausted. A tall and big beardless youth crouched in the bow. He stared at the sky, at the seagulls, listening to their screeches. The long, red hair was so wet that it hardly moved in the wind. No matter how much rainwater he used to clean his face, he failed at getting rid of the salt.

– Hey, Kjell the Red, one of the fellow crewmembers shouted at him, – aren't you happy Thor blessed our catch today?

A tired smile touched the worn, young face.

– Be careful with who you give thanks, another barked at the man, – if you want to enjoy your catch.

The old gods had become a touchy subject. The king worshiped White Christ. The hearty laughter had a notable touch of uncertainty.

The boats reached the shore. The quays didn't have nowhere near the capacity to handle them all simultaneously. Some practically crashed their boats on land, not really caring in their perpetual euphoria. A few ran from their catch, not bothering to leave a guard. One man held up one single herring. He kept kissing it. The people who had been waiting and those who had been catching fish ran together to the houses. Women, men, children, rich and poor danced in the streets and the yards. This day would be remembered for a long time.

And it didn't stop there. The boats returning to the sea in the coming weeks kept catching insane amounts of herring. The rumors about the riches in the ocean spread fast and throughout the land, spread beyond the time and the place. It seemed clear that this day would never be forgotten.

The sun set on a day several weeks later. The full moon that had already shown itself above the mountains turned bright on the dark sky. It was the spring equinox, where the day and the night were equal. New and old citizens of Bjorgvin celebrated harder than ever this year. People drank mead in enormous quantities, like only Vikings could. And they stuck to the high-quality stuff. None bothered with the sour, simpler version this night.

The fishing had returned to normal eventually, but the excitement prevailed. Trade remained beyond excellent. All possible goods were traded.

People kept talking and whispering about the impossible, what they had never dared voice before.

Many campfires reached for the sky. People gathered around the dancing flames, close enough to burn themselves. Kjell «The Red» Gudmundson sat on a rock a good distance from the celebration. The light from the fires and from the moon fought for dominance in the red hair that had given him his additional name.

He had climbed the tallest mountain this morning, joined the eagles, the proud eagles up there. He had watched them fly, and felt free, too.

His clansman, Erling Arneson stumbled towards him, stopping just one step away, clearly in a foul mood.

– Not drinking our mead, are you?

There was no kindness or sense of kinship in his voice and appearance.

– Not tonight, with better stuff available, no, Kjell grinned.

That didn't exactly improve Erling's mood. He turned abruptly and left again.

Kjell hardly noticed, more or less ignoring him, as he usually did. They had never seen eye to eye in anything.

A motion caught his attention. He spotted the lone old woman moving between the fires. People here knew her as Stine. No one Kjell knew could tell if that was her true name. She looked worn, both in body and face and appeared feeble-minded, with visible signs of a harsh life painted in her features. But she lived alone in that small, derelict cabin in the mountains, and handled herself well enough. He knew of her. So did most others around here. She… touched something in him. It was as if he knew her from somewhere. He thought that, even as he knew it couldn't be true. She survived by treating people for various illnesses, curing what no one else could cure. People knew that, and visited her in the cabin in the mountain valley concealed by darkness, by night. It was ridiculous how many needed her, but wouldn't acknowledge it in public. He chuckled a bit.

Kjell fought himself up, a bit unsteady on his feet. He walked among the tall fires, feeling the heat on all sides of his body. He spotted blood from sacrifices several places. That did comfort him. He wasn't certain how he felt about the old ways, but he knew he favored them over the new. People declared themselves followers of White Christ in front of trustworthy witnesses by day, but kept sacrificing to the old gods by night. That made him chuckle quite a bit, making him unable to hold it back

– You bring light to the world of men, Stine told him.

He remembered that she had told him that once, out of the blue, while buying fish from him. He had looked incredulous at her. But she had just walked on with a remote expression in her eyes, lost to this world.

He joined his kin eventually, finally, after a long time denying himself the pleasure. They treated him like they always treated him; like a pebble stuck in their throat. He sat down among the men. They were so drunk, now, that they were unable to offer him the usual show of contempt. A cup was stuck in his hand. Gudrun smiled sweetly to him. He feared he was too intoxicated to decide whether or not the smile was real, or a figment of his imagination.

– So, Kjell Gudmundson, she joked. – Is it your intention to become just as good at handling the sword as the fish?

She was sweet and open, a happy girl not yet ruined by men or gods.

– Far better, he insisted courageously and emptied the cup in one go.

All the mead seemed to hit his stomach simultaneously. He coughed hard. She giggled a bit, and her teasing him became apparent when he looked deep into her eyes. He coughed so hard that his eyes filled with tears, and he didn't see her leave, but she was gone when his eyes cleared, and he felt overwhelmed by loneliness again.

He pulled back to his small, drafty cabin. It didn't improve his mood. It never did.

Something made him turn and cast a glance behind him. Arne Einarson, with his oldest son, Erling walked with other wealthy and influential citizens of Bjorgvin towards Bjorgvin Farm, looking suspiciously sober and steady on their feet. Kjell turned ten steps from the door to his humble abode and followed them at a distance. He didn't bother with keeping them in his line of sight all the time. They had their full attention forward, anyway. He recognized two of the king's men, managers of Alrekstad, the king's farm and of Bjorgvin itself. Kjell grew even more curious.

The men rushed inside and closed the door behind them. Kjell walked straight to the door and stopped there. The men spoke a lot and very loud. He had no trouble getting everything they said. He had no trouble picturing them in his overly active mind, their faces well known to him.

– Great things are afoot, Arne Einarson declared in his pompous manner.

Another man responded. Kjell recognized the voice of the Alrekstad manager.

– My friends, good things are waiting for us, if we dare taking advantage of it. People already come from far away to trade with us, giving us silver for our fish and fur. Bjorgvin can become a trading place to benefit our children and children's children many generations ahead.

– We still need the king's support, though, another man stated nervously.

– We already have it, young Erling stated triumphantly. – Our man at the king's table says so, and there's no reason for doubting him. He also states categorically we will get even more when the king arrives. They claim with confidence he's quite fond of our beautiful place.

Kjell no longer felt the chilly morning air. He was furious. The wrath within felt powerful enough to burn for generations. He had earned a lot during the fishing, and allowed Arne and the sons to sell it. He now knew why they had grinned even wider and treated him with even more contempt than they usually did. The day all this became known, everything here would become more valuable. It wouldn't surprise him if they had stored much of the catch themselves.

At sunrise, he found himself high up in the mountains. The first, modest sunrays made his blood boil. The blade of his sword was neither smooth nor sharp, but it still flashed when he wielded it against invisible foes. He felt clumsy and awkward, but kept training, his rage and obsession making him unable to feel the chill in the air. The rage both distracted and spurred him on. He imagined he made great progress up there, in the mountain that morning.

The misery clung to him like a wet blanket, making it hard for him to move, to even breathe. He kept moving until the sun boiled his blood and mind, and there was hardly any thought worth having left anywhere.

2

The longships sailed into the bay in front of countless others in the heat of spring. People had gathered on both sides of Vågen to watch the spectacle. King Olav Kyrre had come to Bjørgvin to formally found a trading place, aiming to make it a city worthy of envy across the kingdoms of Europe. On the king's right hand stood Skule Kongsfostre. His last name meant «fostered by the king». He had accompanied him from England in 1067. On his left hand, there was the future Bishop in the new Bjørgvin diocese.

The main longship docked with those belonging to the important men and chiefs accompanying the king. Olav stepped down on the wharf. His Guard had set out to brave the way, but there was no need for that. People had stepped aside, showing both wisdom and good will. Olav was known as a benevolent ruler compared to his father, Harald Hardråde. That didn't take much, though. Daring souls kept telling stories about Harald's cruelty. His taken last name meant «harsh rule». He had earned that name.

Olav Kyrre was still young, hardly more than twenty years of age. He had been only sixteen when he had become king. He had shared the position with his older brother Magnus, until Magnus had died last year.

The local delegation welcomed the king and his Guard and Court. The king rubbed his beardless jaw.

– Welcome, Good King, the manager at Alrekstad stepped forward and greeted him. – Everything is ready for you, Your Grace.

Olav rubbed his jaw again, hiding the silent snarl of contempt. There would be bootlicking, lots of bootlicking. He had been prepared for that. It still ailed him.

He would give them everything they dreamed about and more, but he would make them sweat for it.

– Our best horses stand ready to serve you, Good King, Arne Einarson declared. – We can set course for Alrekstad immediately.

– Thank you for that generous offer, Olav said graciously, – but I and my Court have brought our own horses. Give them to my Guard, so they can keep up.

Arne Einarson had turned speechless. It was a moment to remember to those knowing him.

Skule grinned and joined the king on horseback. The fifteen-year-old boy carried both axe and sword. In spite of his youth, he was already taller and bigger than most. He looked at his adoptive father with pride in his eyes.

They rode up Stretet, a broad passage between the houses, the only one resembling a street on this place. They left the gathering of houses behind. Skule had stared at the mountains when they approached land. Now, he stared even more. Everything had been more or less flat when he ran around in the many streets of London.

The king's farm remained visible from far away, at the deeper part, narrow part of the cove isolating it from the rest. The mountain rose behind it, seemingly touching the sky. That, too impressed Skule. He had been raised as a warrior, but he imagined that he had a bit of the bard in him as well. He could see the idyllic in the landscape surrounding them.

The local servants welcomed Olav and his fellow travelers. Their bowing and excessive politeness got to the king and his mood turned notably foul.

– Return to the vultures, he bid Skule. – Tell them that the offerings have been postponed until tonight. They better get it.

Skule rode away good-humored, well used to the king's shifting mood. Olav rode alone to the two cliffs, taking in as much as possible of the impressive landscape.

– I'm king, he said aloud, – but I'm only a man.

He was uncertain whether or not anyone heard him, and he didn't care.

The offerings, sacrifices to the gods began at dusk. The northerners had not given up their traditional practices. The bishop to be frowned, but kept his mouth shut. He was a patient man.

Kjell fumed, very much like the king, intensely disliking the pervasive hypocrisy of the gathering. In a downright strange, eerie way, it seemed to focus, heightening his problems. The patronizing looks sent his way burned his back, and made him hot around his ears. He carried his sword outside the cardigan. No one grinned openly at him. That did please him.

He had arrived with his kin early. He left not long afterwards, disregarding proper conduct and politeness. That act pleased him, too. He passed Stine's worn cabin on his way back, realizing that he had chosen the scenic route. She always made him feel weird, without really doing anything, anything at all to make it happen.

It was still daylight when he had walked far into the mountains. He could no longer see the houses, or any sign of being in a populated area. The sun kept hovering above the horizon. The sea devoured it slowly, enjoying its meal. The boy imagined he had stepped into another land, the wasteland between realms, the realms of the gods, no matter how familiar the wild, untouched landscape appeared to him.

Arne, true to form had presented Gudrun to the king in the hope of forming allegiances. The king had clearly appreciated the sight of the lovely, obedient creature, but hadn't shown interest beyond that. Word said that Olav was well pleased with his Ingerid. There was clearly obvious truth in this. Arne's efforts had been frustrated yet again.

Kjell pictured the girl in his mind. Even that hurt, or seemed to hurt. He could not stop thinking about her. When the other young males talked about females, they focused on a given person's qualities as a future wife. They hardly considered her emotions or desires at all.

Strange thoughts came to him in moments like this. He imagined himself to be at other, warmer places he had a hard time believing existed. He saw Gudrun, but she had a strange, dark skin and dark hair.

He reached the place he considered his favorite spot, a depth in the ground, a hollow. The wind blew when he entered the hole, but stopped blowing a few steps down. Smoke still rose from the ashes of last night's fire. He glimpsed motion down there. It dawned on him that it was a human being. He recognized Stine.

– How could you be here? He asked, feeling very silly.

The eyes in the worn face stared at him. A chill passed through him. He no longer felt silly.

– You're asking the wrong question, Kjell Gudmundson.

He wanted to ask what the right question was, but stayed quiet.

– Let's sit face to face, tryout Phoenix.

Kjell kept wondering what the old woman meant, and what… what her game was.

– It's an ancient tale, she stated, – about a bird that is human, a human that is a bird, a godlike creature dwarfing any god.

He joined her at the depths, struggling with the apparent contradiction of her statement. He waited for her to elaborate, but no explanation was forthcoming They sat down face to face. Her face looked even more enigmatic closeup. The wind picked up above. Black clouds covered the sky.

– We're alone here, the old woman assured him, in another strange statement.

As if they were in danger. He realized startled that she was afraid. Her attention drifted, her eyes glanced up, as if she feared someone would come. She had wanted to assure both of them.

His curiosity got the best of him.

– Where do you come from? He asked her. – You arrived here just a few years ago. No one here knows you.

– Everywhere and nowhere, she replied. – I've traveled far and wide.

She spoke the local tongue well enough, even though he caught an occasional distinct variation in some words.

A draft seemed to rise from the very land surrounding them. He glanced around, notably alarmed. She seemed instead to dream herself away, probably reexperiencing her past.

– This place holds nothing for you, she stated, suddenly very astute again.

He stared stunned at her.

– You shouldn't care that your father was born a thrall, she stated. – You should care that your mother was ostracized for bonding with him, though. That is definitely something you should care about.

She gathered dry wood and made a heap without moving much. She lit the fire effortlessly. It rose between them. He watched as the flame danced in the air, and the shadows shifted on her face. She nodded, confirming something to herself.

– Olav the Cruel wanted to kill me, wanted to catch me, and sacrifice me to his God, to White Christ, but he never could.

She sniffed a bit.

– He hunted us, hunted us relentlessly, and caught many of us or killed or sacrificed us one by one. Only a few are left. I left them because I became a burden to them, to our purpose, to our very survival. We will meet again.

– Olav the Cruel is dead, Kjell pointed out. – His body turned to rot at Stiklestad. His god didn't save him. White Christ might have made his hair grow, but couldn't make him stand up and walk.

– That does give me some limited comfort, she sniffed.

And she chuckled in pride, and there was something in that laughter making him choke, something so very familiar.

The laughter stopped, seemingly by itself.

– He and his army came to our village, she said. – We refused to become White Christ's thralls. He chopped off the heads of all adult males, made all females thralls and made the boys join his growing army. I crouched in hiding for hours, fearing I would get caught, wanting to get caught, so the torture of watching my kin and tribe be tortured and abused would end. I finally ran away, a young girl fleeing in panic, joining up with his enemies, with others of our kind. We fought back and struck him down. It was glorious, but too late. White Christ's power in Norway has become rooted, dominant. They've gained a stranglehold, a crucial foothold. We lost.

Shivers of heat and cold passed through him.

– «Our kind»? He prompted her.

She just gave him her roguish smile. He shivered again.

– You know what I'm talking about, she said curtly, – know it in your very bones. Your father's legacy, his inheritance to you was far more than his thralldom.

His inheritance. Kjell nodded.

– Just as you know that if anyone ever found out about me, about my presence here, we would both be in mortal danger.

He didn't doubt her words, didn't doubt them at all.

– Why did you come here? He asked abruptly.

– Why? That's a strange question. Why not? It's just as good a place to hide in plain sight as anywhere else in Norway, and I wanted to stay. I don't have enough years left in me to go galvanizing in distant lands. I came here for several reasons. Meeting up with you was one.

Impatience ravaged him, but he saw that she had more to say, and stayed quiet.

– There is a mountain not that far east of here, she mused, – did you know that? I came here for a specific reason, and I found what was I was looking for. You have no idea how long I've sought.

She looked at the boy, and he felt thoroughly scrutinized. He couldn't interpret the strange expression in her eyes.

– None of this makes sense, he cried.

– You're used to think like that, aren't you, Kjell Gudmundson, trained by your dumb and dull kin to follow the herd and not question that rather silly conviction?

He could almost guess what she was talking about then.

– We've sat here too long on empty stomachs, she decided. – You should hunt us some food, young warrior.

– You sound like the queen, he snarled, – so full of yourself.

She chuckled pleased. He rose abruptly and ran off with the bow in his hands, and an arrow on the string. Emerging from the deep hollow felt like emerging from Hel or something, like life itself surged through him. She had done that, brought forth his fire with just a few, well-placed words. She reminded him... of his mother.

He found tracks fast and traced them across the mountain. Tracking prey had never presented significant problems to him. It had become natural from his first hunt. His kin had been thoroughly disappointed. They had expected to enjoy themselves at his expense. The memory still brought heat and fire to his bones.

He chased along a shore of a pond, glimpsing himself in its mirror. He saw himself with... with horns, strange protrusions on his forehead. More strange impressions and sensations surged through his feverish mind.

Distractions faded. He spotted the fat buck ahead. Thought and action become one. He let go of the arrow. The arrow penetrated the buck's heart. It jumped away, attempting to flee. It reached only a few steps before collapsing, dropping to the ground, dying with each breath.

He carried the dead animal on his shoulder and returned to the old woman... to the sorcerer. That thought startled him yet again.

– The Hunter brings a feast, she declared.

Her pronunciation was a little off. It sounded distinctly different when she spoke it.

They roasted the meat. She started devouring it before he did, as if she had been starving for days. He knew that wasn't true. He had watched her. She had no trouble getting enough food for herself. She probably hunted, too. She had still made him hunt. His eyes narrowed ever so slightly.

– White Christ has vanquished the old gods, she munched, – not just here, this far north, but others, far south. I've listened to sad and horrible tales of his exploits for many years.

– He's more powerful than them? Kjell wondered, casting anxious glances around him.

– He's certainly craftier. My guess is that they were unprepared for him, for someone like him.

A shiver passed down Kjell Gudmundson's spine. He couldn't help it. Fear touched him, and he could hide it from her.

– You're wise to fear him. I do, too. But remember that he has been at my tail my entire life, and neither he nor his agents have caught me. He works by proxy, even though I would guess that he takes direct part, too occasionally.

– You talk like a commander, he snorted, – like a chief.

– Thank you, she said, attempting to embrace herself, to give herself even more heat than the campfire could provide.

White Christ did frighten her, but the fear rekindled the fire instead of extinguishing it. Kjell nodded exalted to himself.

Then, amazingly, she grinned.

– The fair-haired girl... you like her, don't you?

Kjell started sweating. The heat from the campfire hadn't really bothered him before, but now, it was like the sun had descended between them. Sweat suddenly covered his entire body. He nodded, unable to voice a verbal reply.

– You don't just want a good mate, a mother of your offspring. You want her.

He looked into the mist and the rain again.

– It's like I know her, he cried incredulous, – know what's on her mind and how she feels.

He looked close to exhausted at the old one.

– But that doesn't really matter. Erling has been promised her, and he will get her, like she's nothing more than a donkey being traded and sold.

Stine didn't speak, as if she knew he appreciated silence right now.

They sat there a bit longer. He spotted Stine's frown when she looked at him, as if she had trouble determining her thoughts on him as well.

He started yawning at some point, and once he had started, he couldn't stop. He lay down on his side and fell asleep, just like that, as if someone, probably her had snapped her fingers and made it so. She was gone when he reopened his eyes at dawn. He watched as the eagles flew out of the night. The fire had been reduced to tiny embers in the ashes. He slid up on his feet, doing so remarkably easy concerning his uncomfortable «bed». He felt wide awake, as if he hadn't just emerged from sleep at all.

Every sound in the deep hollow seemed to grow stronger as it reached him. His senses kept working overtime. He stood there and marveled for a long time.

He finally picked up the bow and the arrows, and the remains of the roasted meat, and started on the long walk back to his cabin.

3

The sun shone with unmitigated cruelty at all the bloated faces, those having successfully reached the yard before the mead erupted from their sore throats. Many had fallen asleep and writhed in discomfort and their awakening would definitely become a painful process.

The king had enjoyed his usual morning bath, first in the ocean, and then in a large tube filled with just as cold water from the river. He looked far better than his guests when he met them around the long table. They were all pale and queasy, so sick that they hardly could sit upright. No one felt compelled to speak much. Skule gritted his teeth while attempting a grin. The king seemed quite eager. This was his most commonly used tactic to test people's mettle before important decisions were made.

White Christ's priest, the bishop to be slid unsteady but dignified forward. He dumped into the chair at the king's left side. It was supposed to be the right. He realized his mistake, but was unable to correct it. He sighed in despair.

Everyone that would ever be there that morning was. The meeting began.

– The most important task for us at present, the king cut to the chase, – is to build White Christ's church, one we can be proud of, and an equally dignified farm to our friend the Bishop. We don't want him to live in the barn, now, would we. No, we wouldn't…

Everyone groaned silently. This would cut deep into their supply of silver, and they knew this was only the modest beginning of what he would demand of them.

Gudrun and the other girls serving food and water all looked amazingly bright and fresh. They dressed light on this hot summer day. Skule lent forward in a useless attempt to hide a hardon. A mere glimpse of her had done that. It turned worse by the moment.

Her fair hair had been tied in braids reaching far down on her curvy and strong body. She held her head high, drawing envious stares from the other girls. He wanted her, but she clearly had her interest elsewhere, and therefore, he kept his interest to himself.

The «negotiations» continued the entire day and several days beyond that. The king, visibly frustrated, released the carrot early on and reinforced the stick. It worked. He cut out plots from a limited part of his properties to a selection of the important men in the area. They grew extremely excited. Those not included in the king's generosity less so, even though everyone seemed beyond pleased when the meetings ended. When everyone set the course home, one man declared that Bjorgvin's future looked bright. Loud declarations of agreement accompanied his words.

When Arne and his sons returned to their abodes, they could finally release their pent-up frustrations. They looked with dismay around them, at the place looking downright poor compared to Alrekstad.

– That aloof, arrogant…

Arne stopped there, with an effort.

– Giving all the best plots to his chiefs. The rest of us is only allowed to rent them one year at the time. And don't get me going about the Christ-houses. We will struggle, even with what we earn on the rented properties. It's more important than ever to gain complete control over all... values within the family.

He looked outside, at Gudrun talking with Kjell.

– I'll deal with it, father, Erling grinned in anticipation.

– That's good, son, the father nodded. – The rest of you aid him as much as you possibly can, keeping others away.

The other two, Tore and Torstein nodded serious-minded.

– The importance of this can't be overestimated, Arne stressed. – Bjorgvin might become the most important trading town in the northern lands. Goods from both near and far away may come our way. We will share the spoils, if we don't spoil our mead, if we do not fuck up.

The three nodded solemnly. Their father looked at them with unmitigated pride and faith. Four souls stayed aligned to perfection.

4

Kjell worked so hard that he became soaked in sweat. He expanded and improved his cabin. He had done so for months, and been close to completing the process several times, but he never got satisfied enough to stop the work. It never got anywhere near good enough in his eyes. He had used stone on the expansion, and had removed bushes and roots. People kept telling him that his home could compare to those owned by several people of better breeding. He kept working.

The old woman had on this fine day made one of her rare visits down here, to the densely populated area. She entertained the children with magick tricks and stories. Kjell sent her many an irritated glance.

Gudrun picked flowers and enjoyed the heat from the sun. She had always enjoyed the sun. Her mother had always told her that the night and the darkness belonged to dark powers and vengeful spirits. The girl recalled how she, as a little girl had crouched in bed at night, and waiting for the night terrors to come and claim her. Yes, she enjoyed the day and the bright light.

She walked through the field, the bed of flowers and picked the biggest and most beautiful. The cheerful tune rose from her throat. It just came to her, seemingly from nowhere.

Erling watched her. His cold, calculating eyes rocked her being.

Kjell heard Stine's voice rise loud and clear across the field. She told the children a story.

– Once upon a time lived a bird, a giant bigger than any other, bigger than the biggest dragon, dwarfing the serpent enclosing Midgard. It had golden wings with a touch of the rarest red. They called it Phoenix. And nothing was beyond its reach, because it couldn't die.

Kjell had ceased all motion. He stood like that for a long time. When he emerged from his trancelike state, he realized that the shadows had moved quite a bit on the ground.

He walked off, not really in doubt where he was heading. He reached another field, one concealed from the populated areas with a heap of soil and rocks. He spotted Gudrun at the center of the flowers. His strong emotions grew even stronger, impossible to withstand. He walked to her filled with determination.

She had sat down on the ground. She rose and smiled when she spotted him. He returned the smile, unable to help himself. He fumbled with the sword handle without really being aware of doing so, revealing his anxiety. She glanced around with anxious eyes. She was tall for a woman, reaching him to the jaw. Her broad shoulders could match that of a man. He met eyes blue as the ocean.

– I knew I would find you here, he began the conversation, unable to conceal his coarse voice.

– I've been expecting you, she teased him. – I didn't believe you would come, now, when you've become a rich man.

– I would have come even if I was a king, he said, – or only a traveler without a single piece of silver in my possession.

She reddened, unable to hide it, unable to speak, to give a clever response.

They had played here as children, wild and free, unfettered by kin and obligation. They had made offerings to the moon, to Mani, but they had pictured a woman, a female in their buzzing mind, almost able to make out her features, becoming fearful of angering the male deity. But nothing had happened, and they had embraced their fledgling worship of the hunter's moon.

– I know I should have gone to Arne, he said, – know that this is… uncustomary, out-letting, but I don't care. I want to wed you, bond with you, and I would have wanted it even if White Christ, Thor and Odin all had come as suitors simultaneously, if you had been the highest queen or the lowest thrall.

She turned a deeper shade of red. He knew he frightened her, but that he also excited her. It was all so very evident in her blushing, shifting face wrecked with doubt.

– We can leave, of course, he said casually, – leave behind both obligation and fortune, travel on the wings of eagles to places we've never heard of, and no one has heard of us.

– No, we can't, she responded spontaneously. – The world outside the valley is dangerous and uncertain. We would be in the willful hands of the fates and might suffer horribly. And we will bring eternal shame on our kin, both the living and the dead.

He wanted to shake her, even as her words made sense to him, even as he rejected them.

– Is that how the snake has raised you? He snapped. – To be a good thrall? Is that who you are?

– Please, Kjell, she begged him. – I can't.

– Yes, you can. He grabbed her hard and pulled her close. – You will!

He kissed her so hard on the lips that she whimpered. She resisted, but was helpless in his strong grip. He felt the strong, but sensual body against his and grew eager. She turned soft, and stopped struggling, reacting pretty much like the thrall belonging to the blacksmith at Alrekstad. The condescending thought shamed him, but didn't stop him.

Then, it did. He held her at arms' length. But she smiled sweetly to him.

– Yes, you are my mate, she whispered, – you and no one else. We will leave together, challenge the fates.

Lips sought lips without thought, without reluctance.

– It's our secret, she cautioned him. – No one can know.

– No one can know, he agreed.

They parted company reluctantly. He walked off with fast, angry steps. He chuckled and choked simultaneously. It was funny. He had just gained everything he had ever wanted.

Stine stood on the side of the road behind the heap and waited for him. It was something sinister about the dark woman. Kjell didn't slow down, but walked in a large half circle around her, without acknowledging her further.

– It doesn't matter what you want, or I want, she said. – You will come to me.

What is her game, the boy thought. What does she want with me?

He wasn't certain if he wanted to know the answer.

He feared the answer, feared it with a deep chill in the gut.

5

Arne Einarson laughed so hard that he shook. He struck his knees repeatedly until he finally straightened and looked at the boy with utter contempt and disregard.

– So, you want your inheritance and what's due you?

– I do, Kjell replied calmly.

– You ungrateful worm, Arne spat. – The answer is no, a thousand times. This is the thanks we get for feeding you, for holding out with your whining for so long. Get out, before we throw you out, you pathetic whelp.

These people had been his kin. The boy realized startled that he had believed that until this very moment. They were in truth his mortal enemies.

– I want what's due me, Kjell the Red stated firmly, and found himself grinning. – Make no attempt at stopping me. Consider the law for once. And remember how happy the other greedy bastards will be to support me, and strike at you.

Arne turned furious. He had only been patronizing earlier. Now, he had become angry enough to burst.

– You will have what's due you, he snarled, – all of it.

It was an amazing statement, so ambiguous and crystal clear both.

Kjell boiled over within, cold and warm and alive and dead simultaneously. Just as he left the house for the final time, he and Erling's eyes met in boiling contact. They had been enemies since they first opened their eyes. It was an amazing realization. Kjell almost turned and attacked them. His temper had always threatened to get the best of him. He imagined that he had never had bigger trouble controlling himself than in that very moment.

He set out on a long walk then, one where he quickly lost the sense of time and any kind of measurement. Kjell the Red roamed the mountains, the wilderness so close and so far away from the population center below. He walked along a steep slope. There was a cliff ahead. He had been there before. He reached it in his mind well before he reached it in fact. The valley appeared to him. The waves struck the cliffs down there, making the sea rise high into the air. The wild sight impressed him. The houses down there seemed to fade away in his mind, leaving only the waves striking the shore.

Another man approached from the opposite side. Kjell recognized Skule. The two nodded to each other.

– I discovered this place by a coincidence, Skule started speaking, his voice still sounding somewhat boyish. – It's a nice place to ponder important matters.

Kjell felt strange in the boy's company. It wasn't just that he had a conversation with a runt that did it.

– Some people hardly think at all, Skule remarked.

He threw a coin to Kjelle. Kjell grabbed it and looked incredulous at the boy. The metal had an inscription: Olavr Kunukr - Olav King. Kjell wanted to tell Skule that he didn't need charity, but something made him stay quiet.

– This is a special coin. There aren't many of them. They are the longarm of the king. Anyone carrying one enjoys special powers. The king shared them equally between his Holiness the Bishop and me, since he knows we can't stand the sight of each other. It suits him well that the town is split between two camps. Divide and conquer, you know.

He seemed to catch himself.

– He has changed. He wouldn't have done anything like that before.

When Kjell looked at the cliff later, he thought of Skule and remembered the ambiguous features.

Kjell kept mostly to himself within or right outside his home the next few days. He no longer enjoyed working on it, but he kept going still, just to have something to occupy himself. Strange and unfamiliar thoughts kept roaming his head.

Tore and Torstein arrived with his goods and property. It pleased him to look at them, at their boundless frustration and rage. But the good mood left him as he carried it inside. There would always be more than enough room here, if he stayed and ended up using it at all.

He fetched his horse, doing so with a very determined expression on his face, picturing Gudrun in his mind. He would fetch her, and they would go to Stine together, and the three of them would all leave this cursed place.

The time had come.

6

Her kin returned from yet another festivity. Kjell hadn't joined. That didn't surprise her. She had never seen him as a part of the family. That fact pleased her, even as she stretched her aching back. She had stayed here and worked the entire day. She had been under guard every single moment of it, not allowed to go anywhere without company.

Four huge warriors followed her to the barn and watched her closely while she was milking the goats. She was the only one doing it, even though there was work for three or four more. The pain in her back grew worse. She kept her mouth shut. She had already been given a slap on the cheek for speaking out. Her left eye had become swollen and sore. The buckets full of milk was heavy. She was strong and carried one in each hand across the yard and into the main building. The women there, her kin looked at her with disdain. There was no love lost there. She was as much an outcast as Kjell.

She returned to the barn, and milked the cows as well, filling the buckets again. It felt like an endless process. She feared the sun hadn't moved at all when she crossed the yard the next time. Or the next time after that.

And sometime during the late afternoon, when she stood and froze outside the house, she feared the sun didn't reach her at all. The family had returned half an hour earlier, and she didn't want to go inside. She spotted Erling in the half-open door. He studied her with hard, possessive eyes.

The sun set and it just turned too cold, and she reluctantly walked inside. There was no warmth between them and her. There never had been, not even between her and the women. They had nothing in common.

They were content with being part of their men's house and home, and their loyalty belonged to them, that. She twitched her lips in a contemptuous silent snarl.

She sought to the fireplace, and its heat. The flames danced before her eyes. It was like they… spoke to her, a constant whisper she could almost fathom. The flames seemed to change, becoming wings… and a face. One moment, she believed it to be a trick of the light, the next she didn't, and the next she did again.

It startled her, even as it piqued her curiosity. Something resembling memories assaulted her, and she zoned in on them, attempting to bring them into focus, in vain.

A dizziness approaching nausea struck her, and she almost fell. The others in the room didn't notice a thing. She curled her lips again.

Frøydis, one of her cousins approached her. It made her sigh in further despair. She had been about to dream herself away from this horrible place.

– You shouldn't despair, you know, her cousin said in a very reprimanding manner.

– Oh, why is that?

– You are desired. Your inheritance makes you a well-sought bride.

Gudrun curled her lips again.

– My inheritance is more like a curse than anything else. I imagine I've received it from Loki himself, or Lucifer, the Fallen or any other malignant god out there.

There was something about the way she spoke those words and names, a faint sense of bravery that sounded instantly appealing to her.

Frøydis pulled back in horror, and left her disgruntled cousin alone. Gudrun breathed a sigh of relief.

She spent her time there, in her corner, as she often did. They left her alone.

Everyone gathered around the dining table later, and she felt compelled to join them. There was a mood of sick anticipation around the table she didn't much care for, but she was hungry and miserable and lonely, and didn't really care where she found herself.

She devoured the food and drink in silent suffering. Time passed, but she didn't mark its passing.

– You will wed Erling soon, Arne declared.

A haze rose from the fireplace, and seemed to cover her eyes, making her surroundings blurry.

– I would rather wed a horse, she heard herself say, and rejoiced.

Arne slapped her on the cheek. She gasped in shock more than pain.

– You will do as your told, he said curtly. – I am responsible for you until you're wed. Once you are, Erling will be. He will be strict with you, like any husband.

Arne's rage frightened her. The other women crawled into the corners, Even Gyda, Arne's wife that usually had lots to say in and outside the household, seemed to shrink down to nothing. Gudrun bowed her head.

There was some commotion outside then. She heard loud screams of pain from the sentries and raised her head. One body struck the wall. They heard bones break. Wild hope surged through her.

It turned quiet, both outside and inside. Someone opened the door, and kicked it fully open. Gudrun recognized Kjell through tears. She watched as he rushed inside with his sword raised.

– You will lose every limb you move, he snarled.

No one moved.

She rushed to his side, and turned towards the others.

– This is the man I will wed, she proudly declared, – a warrior born and bred. I say this before these witnesses, and any other.

They backed away towards the door. He stayed alert, keeping his sword in both hands. She looked where he didn't look. They imagined they had become one person. She opened the door. Both gasped and kept gasping, as the blood kept boiling in their veins. She stepped outside, into the dark, spotting no one, no one moving there. He joined her, slamming the door behind him. They did make haste away from there. The door didn't open. No one gave chase. They heard loud, angry voices from within.

She looked up on him with a blushing face.

– Everything I have is yours, she said humbly.

– Everything I have is yours, he insisted.

He grabbed her hand, and squeezed lightly. She squeezed back, unable to keep it soft.

They walked on the dark trail, the dark path, the angry voices behind them fading into the night.

7

Lillian knew she was dreaming. She knew she wasn't supposed to know that she did that, but she did. In the movie, on their safe, dull home planet, before the departure to the dangerous Dune, the father told his son:

«Without change, something sleeps inside us, and seldom awakens. The sleeper must awaken».

She sat on the bus and slept with open eyes, and didn't understand why she rode the bus. The pollution had never quite ripped into her nostrils like it did this very moment. She longed for warm weather and green trees, for the green meadows among the mountains, and the very notion startled her, stunned her.

The young girl woke up in her bed in the apartment, unable to stop the shaking. She didn't understand. It had been a happy dream.

She imagined herself to be back in the theater, hearing the same phrase repeated again and again.

THE SLEEPER MUST AWAKEN
THE SLEEPER MUST AWAKEN
THE SLEEPER MUST AWAKEN
THE SLEEPER MUST AWAKEN
THE SLEEPER MUST AWAKEN

Chapter 3
BERGEN, NORWAY 1985 CE

She left the university early on Monday. The walls smothered her, practically strangled her. The subsequent random street walk brought little or no relief. She returned to the empty apartment, knowing Tove wouldn't be home for hours. Her butt hit the floor. She sat down at the center of the living room. A hand reached up on the table and grabbed the remote. She turned on the TV. They were still covering the «Sword killer», a perpetrator that had kidnapped, raped and killed three women in the new year.

Two people, the news anchor, and a so-called expert sat in the studio and had a conversation about the grim case.

– The execution is unusually brutal, the female expert said. – One of the victims was killed on the spot, but the other two were viciously beaten during the abduction, and raped and further ill-treated for days before they were finally killed. Something has clearly set it off, but I can't imagine what that can be. Norway has so far been spared the works of serial killers, but this bears all the markings of one. I fear we haven't seen the end of it.

Lillian turned it off, and threw the remote away. She fell on her back and stared at the light gray ceiling. Patterns began forming there. She saw a man with a sword. His clothing and mannerism looked completely different from any man she had ever encountered. He looked… looked like a savage.

The pattern seemed to crack in countless nightmarish, indecipherable images. She remained on the floor, crouching there, and the shakes started up again, and just like before, she couldn't make it stop.

Tove found her like that much later, comforting her with a kind of compassionate detachment typical of her.

– Your claustrophobia has taken a turn for the worse lately, she mused. – Perhaps a therapist can…

– No therapist, Lillian snapped. – Absolutely not.

– I know, the other girl said softly. – They stink.

She rubbed the dark girl on the head, rocked her in the lap like she would a newborn.

– The murders are making it worse, somehow, Lillian sniffed. – I actually dream about a man with a sword.

– No wonder that, Tove joked. – You're into swords.

– I am, Lillian stated. – I always have been, long before I started practicing with one.

She straightened and rose on her feet. It happened effortlessly, in one smooth motion. The act itself brought a smile to her face. Tove looked clumsy in comparison.

– It's like I've forgotten something, Lillian pondered, – something important. No matter how hard I try, I can't remember. Perhaps I'm trying too hard?

The despair faded. She noticed it as it happened. The sun broke through the clouds and brightened the living room. She looked incredulous at it.

They had dinner. Lillian stayed distracted, and had a little trouble engaging with her friend. She hummed a melody without being consciously aware of doing it.

– You hum your melody again, Tove remarked. – It's such a strange tune. It gives me the creeps.

Lillian grew aware of her surroundings again. She even stopped eating for a while.

– I started humming it in early childhood, she mused. – I can't remember where I first heard it. It has always comforted me. Mother made me stop doing it. She called it a heathen song. My great grandfather beamed at me. He said I had inherited his wild heart. He has certainly been one his entire life, never really settling down anywhere. The only reason the rest of the family tolerates him is the vast fortune he one day will leave behind.

She looked at herself in the hallway mirror later. The padded training gear looked strange on her. The big, muscular body looked even bigger. She pictured herself with braids, pale skin, and fair hair, losing herself in her imagination. It dawned on her that she had actually made braids.

Her hand reached out to the phone on the table. She grabbed the receiver and dialed a number. A man answered.

– I can't work today, she told him. – I can work tomorrow instead, if you like.

She worked afternoons and evenings at a suburban shopping mall, if there was work.

He said something. She didn't really register consciously what he actually said, but wrote something down on the pad in front of her.

FOUR O'CLOCK

She ran through the dark streets, hesitating only momentarily before she entered the park. Drug dealers held sway here during the evenings according to establishment media. The local newspapers made certain to inform people about that almost every day. She spotted a group of people her mother would have called dodgy individuals, but that was it. The park was mostly empty.

Running always felt good. The rhythm spread from her soles to her entire body. The sword was the connection, the key to the grisly events haunting the modern city. She pictured a man, not a woman penetrated by a dirty sword, the first vision she had while awake.

The loud sound of breaks and whining tires and horns woke her from her trance-like state. She stopped abruptly half a step into the street with wide-open eyes, staring at the car that had almost hit her. The cars behind had more scowling drivers blowing their horns at her. She stared at the frightened expression of herself in the store window, imagining that the braids made her more vulnerable. She returned in a rush to the sidewalk, and the horns finally ceased tormenting her.

The long row of cars moved like snails up the street in the afternoon peak hours. Cars dominated the city center after most of the stores had closed. Lillian spotted only a few people. She imagined she moved through a ghost town.

She started running again, faster now, focusing on staying astute, fighting the relaxing, hypnotic rhythm of the running. The sound of fast, light steps reached her ears. She frowned, wondering how she could catch that over the heavy sound of her running feet. Her hearing, her senses had always worked well, but this was… impossible. She glanced around her, doing it so much that it impaired on her run. She spotted no other people, not in the entire street.

It appeared unlikely that the killer would come for her, of all the people, all the young girls in town, but the silent voice kept whispering in her head. The victims had probably entertained similar, rational thoughts.

She slipped and fell outside the gym. The chill from the snow and the ice numbed her thigh and belly in what she imagined happened in an instant. The chill still felt worse on her back. She feared she would freeze to a statue, and be unable to fight the specter chasing her.

The hand on her shoulder froze her completely. She started trembling as she awaited her cruel fate.

– Didn't I tell you to buy spiked shoes, a male voice teased her.

– Don't listen to him, he's a jerk, a female snorted.

Lillian recognized her. It was Elisabeth, her friend.

She knew them both. They were two of her gym buddies. Both helped her up, Ronny a bit more eager. They entered the gym, showing their cards at the reception, and walked deeper into the building, where the weights and workout machines waited for them.

They began working out immediately, sweaty and malleable from the run. Lillian hardly noticed the soaked clothes anymore. She had softened her limbs and were ready, primed for further hard exercise.

51

She and Elisabeth, Lisbeth looked like a great fit together, both dark-skinned and darkhaired, with an inheritance clearly not ethnic to this country, a notable contrast to the others in the room. When Lillian glanced at her friend, studied her, it was clear she was totally at ease with that, with herself. Lillian looked enviously at her.

The two young women aided each other, taking turns at watching over the other during the final stages of pushing and lifting heavy and potential harmful weights. Lillian noticed that Ronny was studying them, and a moment later, Lisbeth noticed it, too. They giggled.

– He's looking at me, Lisbeth noted.

– You can have him, Lillian shrugged.

– I wouldn't mind fucking him, Lisbeth mused. – He looks quite capable.

– I wouldn't mind either.

Lillian said.

– We can both have him, Lisbeth grinned.

Lillian stared at her. She experienced the first stirrings of interest and desire. The hard training turned even harder, as she put even more into it, practically exhausting herself.

– You will pay for this overreach when you wake up tomorrow, Lisbeth said with another wicked grin.

The exhaustion brought a hazy vision. She could hardly see Lisbeth. The rest of the room and the people there turned completely blurry. She gasped for air as she fought to hold the weight a bit longer. She almost lost her hold on it. Lisbeth helped her put it back on its place, like she was supposed to do. Lillian still felt a notable disappointment.

She had completed her ambitious program. The fencing club held house just across the street. They both ran there, hardly feeling the chill. They just picked up the swords and started the practice. Lillian's sword hand shivered a bit. She fought to keep it under control. The two of them were well matched, and had a hard time outmaneuvering each other. When they took a break later, none of them had gained an advantage.

– We're the perfect fit, Lisbeth declared, – a match made in heaven.

They shared a bottle of water. Lillian drank a lot in one swallow, and felt guilty.

– An acquaintance of mine told me he was disappointed with the swords, Lisbeth said. – They didn't really look like much in his eyes, not like the flashy and shiny blades in the movies at all. I told him that this was pretty much how those used by the Vikings looked. The poor guy turned downright miserable before my eyes…

Lillian listened to her, but stayed lost in thought. She found it a remarkable feat that she could function at all, the way she dreamed herself away while awake.

– Something is up with you, isn't it?

– Huh? She looked confused at her friend.

– I've been watching you. You're hardly here anymore. What's up with you? You can tell me.

– I don't sleep well, Lillian confessed. – I sleep, but not well. I've bad dreams…

And good dreams, she thought.

… and have no idea where they're coming from.

– And you won't even consider a therapist, Lisbeth nodded.

– I dream about a girl, several girls, and it's like looking at myself. They're all me, somehow.

– You know, that sounds extremely exciting, Lisbeth joked, – but I can see why it bothers you as well. I get those girls didn't exactly live pleasant lives?

Lillian shook her head.

– But it feels real, doesn't it?

– It does, Lillian replied empathically.

– I have such dreams, too, Lisbeth said.

– You d-do?

– I have. I've read that most people have them, but discard them as dreams… instead of memories. But my guess is that yours are a bit more intense, for some reason.

The girl's face was glowing in excitement. She was no longer joking. Lillian suddenly felt an even stronger connection to her.

They hit the shower early, for once, both filled with both great eagerness and urgency. It was the usual drag getting out of the wet clothes, but even that didn't feel that difficult. They showered side by side, and Lillian imagined she could see the other from the front, both the front and the side. It felt quite disconcerting, but not as much as it would have before the chat.

She realized that she would always think of their brief conversation between swordfights as «the chat».

Everything looked different when they hit the streets again. The light had changed. So had the colors and the shadows. They sat at an Irish pub later, devouring their first pint of Guinness.

– I saw footage of Inverness in Scotland, Lisbeth mused. – I had never set my foot there, or even heard about the city before, but I recognized the streets, as if I had grown up there, spent my entire life there. And as it turned out, I had. I traveled to the city the moment I was able and met my mother, my previous mother. She looked beyond my appearance, recognized me immediately, and broke into tears. I can't even begin to describe how that made me feel. I am me, but I am also her daughter. We keep in touch. We always will.

Her passion, conviction burned Lillian. It set off more impressions and sensations within.

– Are you certain? She asked subdued.

– I understand why you ask, don't think I do, Lisbeth replied. – I guess no one can ever be absolutely certain of anything. It can be projection on my part, or a number of other explanations. But yes, within reasonable confidence I am.

Lisbeth rushed to get the second load of Guinness. It took, stole a bit of time from their urgent conversation. The foam tended to fill the glass, and the glass had to be almost completely refilled after a while. Lillian waited impatiently, looking at the ghost lights in the pub. Once again, mists and shadow seemed to fill her vision. Lisbeth returned with the two glasses, with only one centimeter of foam at the top.

The two girls had a toast and drank.

– There's a lot of fraud here, Lisbeth shrugged, – like there is in all paranormal areas. Many people claim to have been famous, powerful people, but fifty people can't have been Napoleon, right. So, they expose themselves.

That made them chuckle a bit. They had another toast, another deep swallow.

– I'm tortured, Lillian whimpered. – Priests of the inquisition do the water funnel shit and call me a witch and Satan's whore, and make me admit it, and then they b-burn me, the tortured, broken woman at the stake. A man holds me prisoner in a dank room, and call me his wife, and brags about how no one is going to help me.

Lisbeth hugged her and rubbed her back, comforting her.

– We've found each other, Lisbeth said, – found a great truth together. Everything will be fine, now.

Lillian nodded, apprehensive and excited. They walked to the northern parts of the city center together. Lillian went to bed later, apprehensive and excited. She stayed on her back, staring at the shifting pattern in the ceiling. A few cars passed by outside. The sound of them rose and faded, rose and faded in a seemingly endless flow. She rolled over on the side, staring at the shifting pattern on the wall. Closing her eyes didn't help. She didn't get tired.

She needed to pee and stumbled to the bathroom. The act of peeing didn't really distract her from her roaming thoughts. She paced back and on forth on the floor a bit. She sat down in a chair. That did work. She got sleepy and returned to bed. Her open eyes stared at the ceiling, at the wall, at the other wall. She turned again. Staying on her back usually helped making her sleepy. She stared at the ceiling. She turned on the side. Her eyes slid shut.

Her eyes opened. The morning light flooded the bedroom. She had had a dreamless sleep. Yesterday's celebration didn't really make its mark on her. She suffered no notable negative effects, no headache or fatigue. A quiet smile met her in the bathroom mirror.

– You look disgustingly healthy and happy, Tove remarked in the kitchen. – You had a good time, I gather.

– Lisbeth and I had a heart to heart, Lillian said. – We had… fun.

She wanted to share it all with her friend. She held back.

– She's into weird stuff, and so are you, Tove shrugged.

That brought another smile to Lillian's face. It lingered as she left the apartment, and walked through the city to the University. She experienced a growing sensitivity as she moved, as people passed her on all sides. The walk didn't last long, but she experienced it like it did. Her fingertips quivered. She recalled when she had been a child, when they had also done that.

She imagined she was slipping through the crowd, instead of walking. This didn't seem like one of her dreams or visions, but something different altogether. It seemed physical, not a thing of the mind, or at least not fully such.

The day passed slowly. She couldn't concentrate on her studies, and gave up after a short while, and started fraternizing with other idle students instead. She enjoyed that, enjoyed letting go, the temporary forgetting.

Someone played Over the Wall by Echo and the Bunnymen on a Walkman. She heard it extremely well, and could actually hum to it, and keep the beat with her foot. The dark tune appealed to her mood, her general mood. A boy spoke to her, courted her. She had a halfhearted conversation with him.

She turned curious, wondering what hid behind his pleasing façade. She imagined she was moving several miles, there, in the chair.

He reached out with hand and rubbed her cheek.

– Don't touch me, she said icily.

And that was that. He was gone a moment later.

A… shadow manifested at the edge of her vision. When she turned her head, there was no one or nothing there, only the shade of the sunlight shining through the window. There were quite a few people, students in the room, in the study hall. All of them looked perfectly normal to her. Her own thoughts on the matter made her frown. Those strange notions had always been there. They grew more distinct with the years, never really fading into the obscurity of memory.

Her eyes focused, pretty much by themselves at the exit. She spotted the red hair and froze. It happened, no matter how much she wanted to conceal it. She rose and met Gunnar halfway, as he made his way to her.

– What are you doing here? She asked him, making it pretty clear she didn't appreciate his presence.

– I'm a cop, he grinned, brimming with arrogance. – Didn't I tell you that? I'm here in a work-related matter.

– No, you didn't tell me that, she said curtly. – What do you want?

– We should speak in private, he said. – I have my warm car parked outside.

Outside, where cars were not allowed to park. He grabbed her arm and led her outside. She let him do it, detesting his confidence.

The black Porsche seemed to draw all light from the surrounding air. The engine was running. He opened the passenger door to her with his patronizing grin. It was warm inside. She turned cold, so cold. Gunnar drove off without dignifying her with a glance. He drove through the city center and headed north on Bryggen, the old German waterfront architecture. She looked deliberately, demonstratively out of the window, at the people waiting for the buses.

– So, you're a cop?

– I am, indeed, he shrugged, –. and right now, I'm working homicide.

That pretty much confirmed to her, at least to some degree what this was about. There was no standing homicide division in this city.

– So, why talk to me? I'm not a suspect, am I?

He didn't give any visible immediate response. She looked enraged at him. He turned off the main road with a relaxed swing of the wheel, and stopped a bit later, outside Eidsvåg post office. There were no other people there, and looked quite remote to Lillian.

– You wouldn't have been able to swing that sword with sufficient strength no matter how long time you spent in that health studio, he said with his patronizing «flair». – No, you aren't a suspect. The reason I made contact is quite the opposite. I'm here to protect you…

He reached out a hand, aiming for her jaw. She pulled back to the door, until she couldn't pull back any longer without leaving the car. His hand touched, teased her jaw.

– Please, tell me what you mean, she whimpered.

He pulled back the hand.

– We attempted to keep a lid on it, he said, – conceal the fact that all the murders had the same modus operandi and the nature of the victims, but I guess it was too sensational to stay hidden for long. All the victims had multicultural origin or genetics. Note that they weren't immigrants, but children and children's children of them, or of mixed blood in one way or another. The number of potential victims dropped significantly.

She frowned. There was something about the way he spoke, the way he phrased it that made her wonder.

– He has killed three women, and you guys haven't caught him yet?

– We will catch him, he assured her, supremely confident. – Don't let it bother your pretty head. I'll protect you.

He kissed her, and began fondling her, just like that. She wanted to resist, to make a loud protest. She stayed quiet and compliant. He pulled her close and kissed her neck.

She pushed open the door and jumped outside, landing on her feet, before looking back at him. He sat calm and collected in the seat, showing his police credentials. She had no trouble reading them. The cold got to her, practically paralyzing her.

– Let me take me to my apartment, he said. – You don't want to be alone right now.

– You rat! She spat at him.

He seemed completely uncaring. She returned to her seat in a rush of motion. He kissed her on the lips again. She returned the kiss, kicking herself in contempt.

– I like that you don't have thin sticks as upper arms and thighs.

He drove on. She stared at the road with empty eyes.

She knew how this would end. She didn't need a crystal ball to know the obvious.

2

He was gone when she woke up shivering in fear in his bed the next morning. She had had the dream again, or some dream or part of it she didn't quite remember. She glanced around her with anxious eyes. The room remained empty, no matter how many times she looked around her in the bright-lit surroundings. She rose from the bed, picked up her clothes and left the bedroom. The entire apartment was empty of people. She found a note on the kitchen table.

THIS IS A SAFE PLACE
THERE IS PLENTY OF FOOD
YOU SHOULD STAY

It pleased her when she curled her lips in anger. She dressed without showering or cleaning herself, and left the house. Her eyes kept wavering, moving constantly from side to side, keeping an eye on the terrain as she started running.

The chill got to her, no matter how much she was used to it. She realized that it wasn't a physical cold, but one originating within. His revelation had done that. She speeded up, pushing herself even harder than usual. It was quite the stretch into town. She ignored that thought, like she ignored most others, running flat out long after she started getting exhausted.

She ran all the way back to her apartment, totally exhausted when she closed and locked the door behind her. She went through the motions after that, automatically performing the exercise needed to keep her limbs from turning stiff like wood by the time she woke up the next morning. She kept going for a considerable time before sitting down on the floor.

Tove found her staring at the wall during the late afternoon twilight. She related her experience to her friend with an ongoing remote expression in her eyes.

– That scumbag, Tove swore. – He wanted to scare you as much as possible.

– He's a typical misogynist and racist in one package, Lillian said subdued. – I don't understand how I can keep fucking him, or tolerate his presence in my space, in any way.

– He's gotten under your skin, Tove said, – and like all abusers, he uses that for everything it's worth.

Lillian nodded and sniffed. That made sense, made very much sense.

She stayed at home, and mostly in bed for the rest of the day, Tove made dinner, made tea, and fuzzed over her to the point of embarrassment. Lillian told herself she had enough of this, this lethargy and indecision and fought to stand up from the bed, but she couldn't, just couldn't. She just kept staring straight ahead with empty eyes.

– I have a date tonight, Tove said, – but I should just cancel it.

– No, don't do that, Lillian made a feeble protest. – Please, don't do that.

Her friend touched her cheek in a comforting gesture.

– Will you be alright? Please, tell me you will be alright.

– I will be, Lillian assured her.

Tove kissed her on the cheek and left. Lillian heard her in the hallway for a few moments. Then, it turned quiet. She stayed in bed, writhing in bed, unable to fall asleep, fearful of doing so.

A male voice, a snarl reached her from the darkness.

– You're mine. You will always be mine.

She walked through a long, dark hallway, realizing she was dreaming. The very memory of the snarl, the triumphant hiss made her shake harder. It sounded so familiar. She couldn't attach any face to it, but it was still there, invisible in the darkness.

She woke up shaking and scared the next morning, the first time the dream had had such an impact on her. The room lit by the bright morning light looked dark and gloomy. The cold sweat kept soaking her skin. The air itself seemed threatening.

It took minutes until she could pull herself together and get out of bed. She moved as quietly as she possibly could, in an effort to not wake Tove. It had fallen quite a bit of snow during the night. She looked at the street outside through a slit in the curtain. Several cars had become completely covered by snow. The sidewalks had still not been cleaned. People walked in the middle of the road. Drivers did not exactly use the horn sparingly. It looked like a chaotic mess out there.

She had a shover. It did feel good standing under the warm flow. She had breakfast, going through the motions, feeling disconnected to just about everything around her. It helped when she fought herself forward through the wet snow, when she struggled with each new step in the deep, wet snow.

It's good exercise, she thought.

It seemed to her like she wasn't really in such a good shape, after all. She kept gasping for breath, fighting herself forward through the streets drowning in the thick white sheet, the wet soup making it an effort to move forward, making even a single step hard exercise. She had turned sweaty and was pretty much exhausted well before she reached the slope leading up to the Heights and her faculty. The top of the hill looked like an immense distance away.

She stumbled into the hall outside the reading room with a happy, triumphant smile on her face. It felt good to remove the thick jacket. It felt good to reach her destination and not really feel any significant muscle fatigue.

– You looked spooky in that hood, a well-groomed girl and student said pointedly.

Lillian didn't care that much about her opinion. She hardly revealed that she had heard the girl at all.

She buried herself in the books. Pure information and the pleasure of gaining it took the place of anxiety and sneaking, chilling horror in her mind and self. The day passed and she hardly noticed.

They were hanging out at the Student Center, an official cross-faculty community building only a short stretch from the History Faculty later. She joined a group around the table at the cafeteria, fighting to not reveal her intentions.

She noticed immediately how they noticed that something was off with her, convinced they could smell her sweat. Their eyes flickered when they glanced at her.

– Are you okay, dear? A girl said, clearly patronizing.

– I'm having bad dreams, Lillian confessed, prompting the conversation in the direction she desired, – and I have trouble sleeping.

She got the desired results immediately.

– Freud and Jung's theories are still pretty much valid, Jonathan Mover, an English exchange student said. – Dreams don't have to mean anything, have any notable reason, but they can be a result of past experiences, a relief played out in the subconscious mind.

– Some call the subconscious «The Other Mind», Marianne said eagerly.

She studied biology, Jonathan psychology. They were a perfect match.

– Nonsense, Kurt Movinkel, a physics student snorted. – Everything is pure chemical reactions. The brain is merely reacting to outer stimuli.

Lillian couldn't help enjoying herself. She had done this, put them together, with just a few small manipulations.

– I want to do a ritual of divination, she said, taking the plunge.

They looked at her with a mix of doubt and interest that was quite remarkable.

– So, you're into that, are you? Kurt said, sounding even more personally insulted.

– We don't really know what the mind is, Jonathan said, – and certainly not how it works. It remains one of the biggest mysteries of modern science. We don't know much of what works and what doesn't work.

The last sentence was clearly a stab at the physicist…

Lillian couldn't quite hold back her interest when looking at him.

Jonathan was clearly the person to speak to, face to face.

– Humanity used to see dreams as messages from the gods, she mused, – and night terrors as warnings. The mere act of interpreting the will of perceived higher beings made them insane.

– It's making us insane, a boy sighed.

The statement made them laugh a bit, a brittle laughter underlying the general mood around the table, one Lillian couldn't help but noticing.

That was it, really. The conversation changed to more common, daily life subjects. Students weren't really that much different from most people, preferring the casual to the deeper stuff.

She wanted to talk more with people in private, where they didn't have to pretend so much. Most didn't grant her that opportunity, staying flock animals. But she finally got her wish when Marianne sought her out ten minutes after they had left the table, clearly with something on her mind.

– The conversation, setting felt familiar, she frowned, – as if I have experienced it before.

Another powerful sense of Déjà Vu surged through Lillian.

– I felt it, too, she nodded.

– You did? Wow!

Marianne pondered the issue further. She seemed upbeat, bright.

– The place looked different, the building really old, she mused, – and we were wearing different clothing.

Lillian wanted very much to say something, when the girl kissed her on the cheek, and left.

– Well, see you around, huh? Don't tell people that I said what I said, okay?

If only she had known that everyone talked about her «weirdness» already.

Lillian returned the wave, a little hesitant. She had wanted to speak more with the other girl, but Marianne was already gone. Lillian began looking for Jonathan instead, but didn't see him anywhere. She walked out in the hall.

– Have you seen Jonathan? She asked a girl.

– Who?

– The English guy.

– He left.

Lillian nodded, and made herself ready to leave as well. She did a couple of minutes later, walking off campus one more day without catching much of the planned education. The snow hadn't been removed. She still walked knee-deep through some streets. Each move seemed to suck strength from her limbs. She looked for Jonathan at the usual haunts, but didn't find him, and pondered visiting him in his apartment. The very notion made her blush.

She couldn't believe her shyness, and struck her thigh with her flat hand, doing so hard enough for it to hurt, and that burst of frustration stunned her as well. The shaking began almost immediately. Once again, she wondered what was wrong with her.

Her feet moved. She didn't really. Two old women moved cautiously on the icy sidewalk. Someone had removed the snow, but forgotten about the ice. Huge chunks of it also fell from the roof, making it a hazardous proposition to stay close to the house. Everyone walked on the road. Drivers used their horns and shouted insults. The pedestrians pretty much ignored them. Lillian enjoyed that.

The strange, very recognizable feeling shook her again. She easily recognized it. Her head turned without a conscious decision on her part. She spotted redhair, not Gunnar. She watched him as he disappeared around a corner.

– Hey, STOP, she shouted. – Don't leave me AGAIN.

It was such a strange thing to say. She started running, not really pondering it anymore. She reached the corner, but couldn't see him anywhere. She kept running, checking out every direction he possibly could have moved, in vain. She followed one particular track of prints, not really convinced it was the right one. It dissolved into many before long.

She stopped, out of breath, imagining that minutes passed until she got it back. Then, her eyes grew wide. Jonathan walked towards her like the most natural things in the world. She walked towards him with a spontaneous smile on her lips.

– Hi, she grinned, – funny meeting you here.

The frown accompanied his smile. She could understand why. They were pretty close to the university area. It wasn't unfeasible that they would meet by chance. She discarded her doubt, and threw all caution to the wind.

– You have access to the sleep laboratory, right?

– I do, he said, looking uncertain at her.

– I need to use it, she stated. – It would be so great if you could help me doing it.

She found herself flirting with him. It clearly helped. She watched as his doubt faded. Her smile widened. The sense of urgency prevailed.

– I believe we can make that happen, he said.

– That's so kind of you, she said softly. – Thank you.

She spent the evening with him. They had a chat, not more than that. The evening passed without notable events. There was little or nothing she could point to or recall of interest. She started yawning at some point. She remembered that. It signified that the evening ended, and the evening truly began.

– I've never felt more excited when growing tired, she said sweetly.

They made their way to the laboratory. She walked with him through quiet, dim hallways. The quiet seemed… loud in her ears. She noticed the strange or seemingly strange mood, making her wonder if it was the place or her.

He inserted the keys in the lock. It sounded insanely high in the pervasive silence. The laboratory was steeped in darkness. He fumbled on the wall for the light switch. She found it at her first attempt. The light flooded the room. He cast her a grateful smile.

– It will take some time setting up everything, he remarked. – I need to check if everything works the way it's supposed to.

– I don't mind waiting, she grinned, feeling very generous.

The sense of urgency persisted.

He made the machinery ready for use. She watched him as he worked, not really bored, finding it very interesting. He chose one bench in the dark room, and connected the wires to that.

– You could probably get a better result if you went the official path through your physician, he said.

– I don't want anything registered anywhere, she said. – I trust you.

She lay down on the bench in the dark room. The darkness didn't frighten her. She had always been a creature of the night. That brief thought brought elation, not fear. He strapped her arms and feet and body to the bench, tightening the straps so hard that she had trouble moving.

– It's a safety procedure, he said, – just in case anything happens. It sometimes does.

She gave him another smile, concealing her sense of vulnerability. He attacked the wires to her head, and other spots on her body. She felt like a lab rat, no matter how much she had prepared herself for this, for the feeling of being trapped.

– Everything is set, he said in his dry, formal way. – As you requested, nothing will be recorded.

He gave her a confident smile. She kept felling vulnerable, shitty when he moved her braids away from the wires.

– I can give you something to make you sleep, he said.

– There is no need, she replied. – I am dead tired. I haven't really been sleeping well lately.

She had slept, but she still woke up tired.

He left the room and closed the door, leaving her in the darkness. He turned off all the lights. The room turned completely dark. She knew he could see her through the infrared cameras.

– The machines will read your brainwaves and body functions, he said. – I will monitor it, and attempt to interpret it as we go, compensating for the lack of recording.

It turned quiet again. He had turned off his microphone. She couldn't hear the sound of the machines. This time, she wanted it, wanted the dream to come. Perhaps she had always wanted it, but been afraid to admit it to herself. She closed her eyes.

Lillian slept. Even asleep, it was as if she could glimpse the laboratory and the boy, feel the shape of instruments, walls, ceiling, floor, doors. A door opened. She imagined she was swept through it, even as she remained in the room. She knew she was dreaming or was asleep and could steer it according to her desires and determination. The room and its confines dissolved slowly. The ceiling changed to a sun and blue sky and white clouds, large white birds circling in large flocks. She wondered if they were seagulls, but couldn't tell. They didn't look like any birds she had ever seen. The walls grew to tall mountains. She knew these mountains well. But the landscape between them and the ocean were strangely unfamiliar and familiar simultaneously. The bench turned to the pier her feet were standing on. The floor turned to the ocean and to green grass. Everything kept flowing, shifting. She couldn't fathom how the grass could be green while the snow still covered most of the ground. It was such a fine day, one that would never be forgotten, so full of hope and promises. She knew that, without knowing how she knew it.

The girl with the fair hair and braids wasn't alone on the pier and on the shore in general. Many other excited people waited with her. The girl's father did, too. She tried to not think about him, but the unpleasant memories of childhood kept surfacing. He had not sired her, and he never let her forget it, with his stick and tongue. He and his sons were dishonorable men, and everyone would know them as such if their dishonorable behavior became known. Other men in the valley were not like them at all. Hard, yes, but not like those she had learned to know intimately within the household.

Two younger males looking very much like him stepped up by his side. One of them had a stupid grin around the mouth, and a large blade penetrating his chest. The ghastly sight told her something, but she couldn't tell what.

She returned her attention to the ocean. Anticipation and fear surged through her. She imagined she could see the large boy with the red hair out there, on one of the ships growing bigger as they approached the shore. She stared with longing at the face framed by the long red hair in the glow from the dancing campfire. The great day of riches from the sea was celebrated all over the valley, and the surrounding areas. But there was despair in the glances the boy and the girl exchanged.

The grand ship and the man in expensive clothing arrived with the spring. A large cross accompanied the royal travelers. The strange woman surrounded by ravens granted her a rare smile. Gudrun imagined she knew her, and recognized her sideshow of dark birds. She searched her thoughts for illumination, but no illumination was forthcoming, even though her thoughts in the dream seemed so clear, so much clearer than what the simple Viking girl had been able to do.

The boy, her chosen mate approached her in the field of flowers. She hummed soundlessly on the strange song she had learned never to forget. She recalled that he had made an effort at not stamping on the flowers, doing it for her. A tear gathered at the edge of her eye. They approached each other, exchanging kisses and affectionate touches even before they got close, their union already set in their feverish mind.

A deep, dark divide grew between them and devoured all the flowers.

Time passed. A very long time passed. She couldn't tell in which direction of time's arrow. Only the mountains remained the same. The place had to be Bergen before the later growth of the population. She knew that. In the dream she knew. She cheered. She had returned to the field of flowers. But now the hair was dark. There seemed to be something like a grid in front of her, but she discovered that she could easily slip through that, as if it wasn't there. He stood there unmoving, still staring at the sea. He couldn't get to her, she knew that, too. Something, an unsurmountable hurdle kept them apart.

The scene shifted again. She found herself in a tall tower in an old building, a castle. Large beasts patrolled the ground, predatory birds the air. No one could climb that wall. She still imagined how it would be to use a strong rope and descend all the way to the ground, fighting off the birds and beasts with her sword and strong arm. The forest, the wilderness both frightened and fascinated her. Then the master of the castle came and took her, brought her deep below the ground. She turned into a helpless victim, completely in his power, bound by chains so heavy that she could hardly move.

Her eyes opened wide, and didn't blink. She stared at the ceiling. Her body shook in the straps. She was sweating, but remained somewhat calm. She made no attempt at freeing herself. Jonathan stood by the table. He looked visible confused. Her eyes had clearly been open for a while, since he didn't react.

– I'm awake, she said calmly.

The confused, rigid expression stayed on his features, his movements looking mechanical, robotic or something when he removed the wires and the straps.

Lillian sat up and stepped out on the floor. She fixed her hair without really being conscious of it or the smile appearing on her sweaty face. The dream had been extremely vivid and detailed. She remembered almost all of it, the bars between her and redhair. Everything floated towards her on a soft wave of both bad and good impressions. She found it remarkable that the good remained dominant. The frost and heat kept battling for possession of her mind. She had been wrong. It wasn't she who was prevented from coming to him, but he who was prevented from coming to her. She had to go to him.

– So, what are your conclusions? She asked excited, unable to contain the growing joy.

– I… don't know if I can tell you anything that matters, he said, clearly apprehensive.

– Tell me everything, she prompted him.

He started pacing the floor.

– Your readings don't make sense, he said. – At least not to me. You've been… dormant, for lack of a better word, for four hours. That means you should have experienced at least three REM-stages, but you didn't experience any. There is no mistake. The machines don't lie, and I have triple-checked the connections. Everything checks out.

She kept watching him with a calm interest. It was quite the fascinating observation.

– The REM-stage is quite distinct, he said, calming himself with an effort. – The dreamer breathes irregularly, and the brain activity is at the very least as strong as in an awake person.

He scrutinized her even harder.

– I presume you had the usual dream? He asked, with notable aggression in his voice and pose.

She nodded patiently. She couldn't believe her patience.

– You were sleeping, at least for a little while. The first, initial stage proceeded normally. But the REM-sleep, the second stage never appeared, not for a moment.

– So, what you're saying is that I wasn't really dreaming? She wondered.

– You weren't dreaming, he stated. – You didn't sleep, but weren't awake either. Your brain and body functions didn't resemble anything… sane. Your brain projected alpha-waves, similar to what we do during death. I was really scared for a while, until I realized that you weren't dying. I had no idea what to do. I have no idea what should be done, now, for that matter. I've got no idea what's wrong, if anything is wrong.

She experienced a strong sense of euphoria. It almost made her start laughing.

– It's different, she shrugged. – Let's leave it like that.

She grabbed her jacket in an eager motion. He kept looking at her with obvious hesitation. She prompted him again.

– There is something…

She nodded, getting a bit impatient.

– It isn't accepted knowledge, not even close to it, but it might be close to an explanation. It's well known in fringe circles that ASC, Altered State of Consciousness makes the brain produce alpha waves. It is common during meditation, and is also supposed to be during telepathy and other forms of paranormal activity.

He looked very flustered at her, expecting her to laugh at him. She didn't. Her euphoria grew stronger.

Reincarnation, she thought. Rebirth into another body after the death of the previous. Rebirth from the ashes. She suddenly had trouble breathing properly.

– You don't need to be here while I clean up, he said. – It won't take long. Too bad I couldn't help you much.

– But you did. She kissed him on the cheek. – More than you can know. Have you ever experienced anything like this?

He shook his head, sad because he had nothing to share with her.

– My path is so much clearer now, she stated passionately.

He just kept scrutinizing her. She headed for the door.

– One more thing, he said, still hesitating.

She stopped and turned around.

– You told me you have ordinary dreams as well.

– I do, she replied, – but they become rarer as this one becomes common, dominant.

– I was afraid of that, he said, clearly concerned. – You see… we don't really know much about dreams, the reason we have them or anything, but one thing seems clear. They act as a relief, necessary for keeping a kind of equilibrium in daily life. People that for some reason has had the REM-sleep reduced or had it taken away over time have without exception suffered mental problems. You may not, for some reason, but I wanted to caution you just to make sure, and make you better prepared if it happens. As stated, I don't know.

– You have helped me, she stated. – I want you to know that.

She waved as she rushed down the hallway. He returned the wave. The door between them closed. She started doing cartwheels without effort, and without getting near the wall. She chuckled as she rushed into the storm, as February ended with icy, slippery streets.

The dark-skinned girl looked at herself in the mirror of indistinct store windows with sparse lighting. She muttered under her breath, swore to herself.

– I will find you, she stated. – You won't look the same. I certainly don't. I must look for other things, look beneath the surface to the real you. I will find you, even if I need to use many lives.

The wind hardly touched her. The storm felt like a tiny draft. The inner fire burned so hot that she hardly noticed the icy air striking her from the north.

Chapter 4
BJORGVIN, NORWAY 1070 CE

Kjell and Gudrun moved into her mother's house. No one had lived there since her mother had died. Gudrun was the heir. It was her house. It looked worn. No one had helped her keeping it in order. The two of them started fixing it together.

– I'm used to hopeless causes, he joked.

She looked endeared at him.

Doing it together made them feel even better about it. The past didn't vanish, but did fade a bit into the general background of their daily experience.

One day, the old woman just showed up, seemingly out of nowhere.

– Kjell, Gudrun said anxiously.

– It's good, he grinned. – Her name is Stine. She's a friend… I think.

Not exactly confident that would comfort his mate.

Stine looked anxious, too, but determined. She looked lucid, now, as if she had awakened from a deep dormancy.

– I'm not certain I should do this, she said, – but I decided to throw caution to the wind.

Gudrun looked curious at her, giving her the same scrutiny as Kjell had once done, experiencing the same strange emotions while doing so.

Stine joined them on the roof, showing great skill performing the restoration.

– I think I perhaps was supposed to do this, she pondered.

And they suspected she didn't necessarily say what they initially believed she was saying.

– She's a very strange woman, Gudrun said shyly, during a break in the hard work, when they had dinner, and found themselves alone for a moment.

They sat outside, around the campfire the three of them in the evening. Stine basically told Gudrun the same story about her life she had told Kjell. Gudrun's eyes grew wide at some point.

– You are a warrior? She said startled.

And the girl glimpsed herself as she raised her sword and struck down a male, looking so different from her perception of herself.

– I am! The old woman replied with a pride she couldn't contain.

– You fought the invaders and their lackeys, Gudrun stated awestruck. – That's glorious.

– I did, Stine said, – but I couldn't stop the twisted flow more than any of the others.

She looked beaten, downtrodden, even as they knew that her inner fire kept burning.

They could both sense it, deep down, beyond the senses. Strange notions kept returning to their surface thoughts. Elation kept surging through them.

– The three of us belong together, Stine nodded. – We can all sense it.

Her words sounded true. Something passed between them that couldn't be denied. Gudrun started shaking.

– This life is not meant for you, Stine said. – Something will happen to put a stop to it.

She paused a bit, as her features softened.

– I know such matters well.

They studied her with dismay and anxious eyes, but she revealed nothing more of significance.

She spent the day and early evening with them, staying for the dinner, working just as hard as they did in the restauration work. They watched her as she walked off, and briefly turned and waved to them.

– I always found her strange, he said. – That doesn't change, no matter how long we spend in each other's company.

– She isn't like the rest of us, Gudrun said. – She's… free.

– And she wears it like a cloak, he said, – hiding, but not really hiding. She's amazing.

He looked at the maiden, giving her his affection, fearing she would take offence when he expressed admiration for another woman, but he had no reason to worry. She returned his smile.

– She makes me shake in my bones, Gudrun said.

They nodded to each other, as if sharing a secret.

The shaking was so deep that it stunned them. There didn't seem to be any… sensible reason for it.

They resumed the work on the dwelling and its surrounding, working together, finding it quite enjoyable. He watched her. She clearly excelled in the hard exertion. He could hardly believe how great that made him feel.

– One king wants us to worship the old gods, he mused, – another the new.

– It's… confusing, Gudrun said with a notable frown on her brow.

He nodded, understanding, sharing her bewilderment.

– Stine isn't confused, she stated. – She isn't exactly boasting it, but she is… confident in her choice.

He nodded to her, to himself.

Her voice and her show of independence seemed to echo deep within him, and he didn't understand it, understand that either.

They did interact with the rest of the town. It was a small town, after all. The interaction with their closest family remained strained, very strained. They exchanged curtly nods, and hardly that. He noticed how she put up a brave front hiding the shivering leaf beneath. He had no trouble understanding that.

They made parallel plans for their wedding, also doing preparations for following the ancient custom and rites. Fortunately, most couples did that, even though it was well known that the king frowned at the practice. They faced bigger problems finding people to stand up for them, to join in on the preparations and execution, also because tradition was that everyone wed on Friday, on Frigga's Day. Kjell felt like he practically had to threaten males with a drawn sword to get them to agree to it. The process felt endless and hard, far worse than all the fishing and physical labor he had done in his young life.

It helped that Gudrun was of good breeding. There was no stain on her line. It certainly helped that she had inherited her parents' fortune. No wonder Arne wanted his son to bond with her. Arne, in his greed, always looked for a way to gain more wealth.

Kjell imagined that the old man was staring at him, even when they were too far away for that to happen. There was something fundamentally wrong in that stare. A deep chill of fear and a fiery heat of rage warred within the young man.

The halting, hesitant preparations made progress somewhat, no matter how much Arne and his side of the family attempted to sabotage it all. Kjell watched Gudrun as she laughed happily. Anticipation kept surging through him.

– She's so full of life, Stine mumbled.

He jumped in shock. He hadn't heard her approach. She was like a shadow in the night, invisible until she stepped into the light. He imagined he knew her, knew every line in her face, every single tiny movement and gesture she made. It wasn't quite like the attachment he felt for Gudrun, but very much there.

When he looked at her, he saw a much younger woman.

He dreamt about them both, a dream within a dream also showing him disturbing impressions and sensations he didn't understand.

– There is… comprehension, Stine stated, – but it's muted, difficult to grasp.

And he imagined that he actually knew what she was talking about just then, in his feverish dreams.

The musicians began their task, helping create the mood for the big day.

Arne and sons mumbled even more among themselves. Kjell and Gudrun looked in delight at the growing celebration. The one, dark cloud couldn't stop the anticipation for the upcoming happy event.

Some people cried caustic, patronizing remarks at Kjell, but for the first time in his life, the bullying didn't really take. Snarling beasts with fireeyes still haunted him in his dreams. She comforted him through the shaking he suffered through the long dawn.

– I dream about them, too, she whispered. – They both scare me and attract me. Both the male and the female do. They're so free.

And he realized startled that he agreed with her.

– I can't stop dreaming about them, Stine said. – and I don't want to.

She pondered her words a bit.

– I dream about the whitehaired man with the braid, she whispered, – and it chills me to the bone.

– But that isn't strange, Gudrun pointed out. – You've actually encountered him. I would imagine he scared the young girl you were out of your wits. Whether White Christ is a god or man, he is fearsome beyond words.

The old woman had told them the story with a stubborn, determined look in her eyes. Their respect for her had only grown.

– I killed Olav the Cruel, Stine had cried in triumph. – I struck him down with my sword, and White Christ couldn't protect him.

– You are so brave, Gudrun said stricken. – I could never have done that, or anything like that.

– I believe you are mistaken, the old woman had said, – but you must discover that on your own, find the strength within yourself to be yourself, a shield maiden standing out among countless shield maidens I've also seen in countless dreams.

Kjell watched Gudrun as she choked with incredulity and strong emotion.

He imagined that his memory, his sense of events switched back and forth, and that he had no control over it.

Stine watched him, and made no secret about it.

– Our experience can be confusing, even riveting and difficult to handle, she said to them both. – You must teach yourself to deal with it, to endure and prevail, remember what you have forgotten, no matter what.

She encouraged… respect. Her advanced age didn't seem to weaken her at all.

Kjell noticed her flickering eyes, though, her constant anxiety, how she kept turning her head and glancing at her surroundings.

– She has lived a hard life, Gudrun mused when the two of them were alone with each other again. – She's entitled. I would guess that some of her enemies or at least their kin are still breathing.

She hesitated a bit before blurting out with it.

– White Christ is her enemy.

– He's our enemy, Kjell heard himself say from far away.

And with that realization, that startling and horrible perspective, so much turned clear to them.

– If only the king knew, Gudrun chuckled nervously. – I imagine he wouldn't treat us kindly, then.

Hands grabbed hands and eyes met eyes.

– It's our secret, she stated. – No one must know.

He nodded. They kissed lips to lips, with a hunger and desperation they could hardly handle. The abyss opened beneath them, and they clung to each other with closed fists where the knuckles turned white.

– I will be yours, she whispered, – and our union will honor the old gods and old ways of our people.

The last word sounded strange in his ears, and then he knew she had pronounced it in a strange, special manner. Even her voice had changed, had sounded completely different compared to how it usually sounded. She sounded like a stranger, stranger than Stine, stranger than anyone he, Kjell Gudmundson had ever encountered.

He realized then that he was thinking about himself as a person outside himself, an eerie notion that wouldn't let go.

The special day, the special Frigga's day approached. The old ways would be observed. The king was not averse to that. An anxious joy and anticipation filled the youths. A group of women arrived at the old, derelict house to fetch Gudrun. She would spend the night away from what would be her home as a wed woman. Some of the women were not kin, while some were, but not closely related to Arne and his clan. Gudrun turned deep red when she waved, and they led her away.

He felt the loneliness as he prepared to spend the night alone in his house. The silence overwhelmed him, as all kinds of thoughts roamed his conscious mind.

There was a knock on the door. He grabbed his sword and walked to the modest entrance in his beyond modest domain. A group of men stood outside. He recognized his fellow fishermen from his boat. They carried mugs of mead in both hands.

– Kjell Gudmundson, the old-timer said. – We would keep you company in your night of seclusion.

Kjell wasn't certain he was happy about this, but he certainly felt the catching in the throat.

– Enter and be welcomed, he bid them.

They took him up on it. He did notice a bit awkward mood at first, but it quickly faded with the consummation of mead taking off. He had participated in some nights of seclusion before, and he noted with satisfaction that this one didn't shame itself compared to those. The mead flowed freely. Voices grew loud, and shouts echoed across the valley. He feared he would grow emotional, but he didn't. The night flew away, and he did, too.

The talk flowed freely, unceremoniously back and forth. He didn't feel awkward in their company, and appreciated that.

– Kjell is a great fisherman, the old-timer cackled. – We just had to rescue him from drowning ten times or so…

They laughed a lot about that. Kjell smiled politely.

The cheers, the glass of mead consumed grew numerous, too numerous to count. The night flew away.

He woke up alone to the stench of vomit the next morning. There was no hangover, not even the slightest touch of it. He felt fresh and aware, like after a cold bath. The grin stayed frozen on his face. He stumbled outside and had a pee. The brisk air filled his lungs, sharpened his senses further. The anticipation was like a hunger within. He could hardly stand still.

She seemed to be standing in front of him, smiling sweetly. He could hardly contain himself, and could certainly not stop the catching in his throat.

He had a bath in the river, screaming in delight and anticipation, enjoying himself immensely. One twist of the body, and he pushed himself deep below the surface. He swam with open eyes, and studied the pattern of the riverbed. It made him dizzy, and more strange sensations surged through him. The water was cold. It didn't matter. He imagined he spotted her face on every smooth rock. The chill in the air when he returned to shore hardly bothered him at all. He returned to the empty hut, and started preparing himself, making the final preparations that didn't really matter. It wasn't that much to do, really. He didn't own much more than that one change of clothes. But soon he would. He discarded that traitorous thought without really pondering it.

The short walk had started some time ago. He couldn't tell exactly how long time had passed. His thoughts drifted off into the rising fever of his mind.

His eyes focused on the small house ahead. He had his complete attention directed on it. Smoke rose from its roof. They had lit the ceremonial fire inside. He caught its stench in the wind. It brought even more positive associations to the forefront of his mind.

A woman stumbled out of the door. He recognized Tora. She collapsed after a few steps. He froze in stricken paralysis, and never made a conscious decision to move. He just did, running so hard that he could hardly catch his breath after just a few moments of his forwards leaping.

He reached her after what seemed like a moment's run. The details of her face burned itself into him. Someone had struck her. Blood flowed from a wound on her brow. She fought to focus, and he saw that she recognized him, even in her dizzy state.

– They took her, she gasped, or rather choked.

He didn't ask any questions.

– I know who and I know where, he snarled, choked. – I don't need to know more.

He was very happy that he had brought his sword, for ceremonial purposes. The woman reached out a hand. He gave her time enough to squeeze her hand, and then he was gone.

All kinds of thoughts raced through his head while he raced up the mountainside. He couldn't recall a single one. The horse worked under him. He couldn't recall having jumped on its back either.

He forced himself to slow down when he approached the top of the steep slope, and left the very visible trail, and sought higher up in the terrain. He stopped himself from circling in on the hut ahead too fast by an act of will. His hand hurt. He clutched the sword hilt hard. His hand burned. He even imagined he smelled the smoke of burned skin.

His body jumped off the horse, landing on steady feet. He tied the horse at the pole nearby and rushed on.

The hut appeared in the rain and the mist, in the haze covering his eyes. His feet wanted to move faster again. He kept them from doing that. He focused on the closed door. He saw no one in the one window. He reached the wall and looked inside through the square opening. He saw Einar and Gudrun.

– You will wed me, Erling swore.

– I would rather wed a goat, she shouted loud and proud.

Einar slapped her, and the red rage overwhelmed Kjell. The enraged boy tore the door open and rushed inside. Han glimpsed her frightened visage, and her mouth and entire being preparing to shout a warning.

I forgot Torstein. I'm an idiot, an...

The big man struck him on the head from behind. He managed to twist his body so much that the strike didn't quite hit the mark, but it still paralyzed him, made him go down. He crouched on the floor and a boot stamped on his hand. It made him scream and let go of the sword.

His vision cleared for a moment. He glimpsed four shadows above him, the moment before the kicks and strikes hammered him. They abused him with loud laughter erupting from their snarling gaps. They wanted to humiliate him as much as possible, play with him before they finished him off. The strikes and kicks continued, but they didn't really hurt much, or they just hurt. He discovered to his amazement that the slow abuse didn't really affect him, not deep inside, where the fire burned strong. Gudrun's gasp echoed in his ears and her stricken face flashed crystal-clear in his hazy vision. He watched her as something turned in her, and she threw herself at Erling with fiery rage painted on her pale features. She pushed his body and head hard into the wall, and one or more ribs cracked. Blood flowed from his head. He dropped to the floor. The three standing men froze incredulous. Kjell reached for the sword in one single desperate motion. The hilt filled his hand, and he shouted in triumph. He fought himself up on his knees and rammed the blade into the chest of the charging Tore, so deep that it didn't budge when he attempted to pull it back out. All motion, the world itself seemed to slow down. He and Gudrun exchanged glances, glimpsing understanding and an extreme, horrible clarity in each other's eyes. Kjell let go of the sword and rushed at the exit. Tore dropped to the floor with a persistent incredulous expression in the face.

– RUN! Kjell heard the girl shout. – Never forget me. LEAVE!

He did, obeying her stark, stunning decree. Everything had happened so fast, making him act, not think. His ears caught the cry of pain from the girl from the fist hitting her, and the hammering feet on the floor inside the hut, as the three men still alive rushed to fetch their swords. He slipped in the wet grass, but managed to stay on his feet, and ran off the fastest he was able. The pain within felt worse than any physical pain he had ever experienced. He cast a glance back at the hut. The three men rushed out of the hut with their swords drawn, even as they realized how stupid that was and sheathed them again, as they went for their horses, set to chase the tall redhead. He reached his horse long before they did, pulling the rope from the pole, and jumped on the back of the four-legged animal. He rode hard down the steep mountainside, risking the health and feet of the horse more than once. Thinking remained hard. The numb pain and desolation kept surging through him in waves. So did his growing hatred, the ashes burning within him like the worst imaginable horror. He kept acting, not thinking, not consciously acknowledging what had happened, what was happening. He reached the lowland. That also failed at prompting real, tangible thoughts. He caught a brief glance of the ruin that had been his home, the ruin that had been his life, where he stored his few riches, before riding on.

– Take everything, he shouted. – It will avail you nothing but grief. I give you my oath on that.

Kjell Gudmundson... he would call himself that with pride from now on. They would fear that man.

He rode off, into a perceived darkness he could hardly see the end of.

His body hurt all over. He feared there was true damage somewhere in that hammered frame. He kept riding hard, turning often and scouting for those chasing him. His position on the horse grew tenuous. He feared he would fall off several times, and suspected only the glowing hatred kept him going. A long time passed. He couldn't tell how long. Everything seemed like one, torturous moment stretching on forever. He noticed, somewhat, when he turned and looked back that there was no one chasing him. When he stopped, he couldn't hear any sound of hooves hitting the ground, and he knew he would have, if they were within reasonable range.

He sniffed the air, frowning at some imperceptible notion. Anxiety grabbed him. He didn't understand that either. He kept pushing forward, heading towards something he couldn't identify. Then, he stopped, or as he suspected, the horse stopped on its own. Something formed in the very air in front of them. They both saw and sensed it. He knew that much. The horse rose on two legs and threw him off. He landed hard on the ground, having the air pushed from his lungs. He spotted the black bird, a blurry sight in the twilight, in the chilly, chilly night. A strange sense of elation surged through him. A wide range of emotion flooded him, longing, rage, putrid hatred. The horse stood its ground. A woman on a horse approached the two of them. He recognized Stine. She wore her armor, and carried her sword by the hip. He hardly recognized her. He did recognize her, on a level he couldn't name.

He dropped unconscious to the ground, and everything turned black, like the black bird still haunting his thoughts and dreams.

2

Gudrun, Daughter of Halvard crouched on the wet bed, the bed stinking from a wide range of body juices. The stench made her sick, sicker. She wore only a thin cover, hardly covering her at all. Her mouth shivered constantly, like the beak of a terrified bird. Her entire body hurt of the countless lacerations. Her huge, scared eyes never looked away from the door. The stench of cooked food added itself to her woes.

Erling entered the room a good while after that.

– Good morning, Gudrun.

She frowned, wondering briefly if it was morning.

– Good morning, Erling, she responded subdued, humbly.

She had no trouble spotting the stick in his right hand, and the bowl of soup in his left.

– Sit up, he bid her.

She obeyed, while whimpering and wailing, unable to release the involuntary sounds of suffering. She saw no mercy in his cold, hard eyes.

– You may eat.

She accepted the bowl. It shook in her hands. She started eating, feeding. The soup had a bad taste. She suspected it had been made several days ago. It tasted worse. She kept eating. He commanded. She obeyed.

He had dragged her here after her hair, and made her stay here. She couldn't tell for how long.

She kept holding the spoon and the bowl after she had cleaned the bowl, kept doing so until he nodded, until he, in his generosity granted her permission to put it down. He smiled in wicked triumph. He had enjoyed himself a lot lately.

– Tomorrow is the wedding, he said pleased. – You do want to wed me, right?

– Yes, Erling, she whispered.

He made a motion with his hand. She didn't need any stronger incentive to pull the cover over her head.

– I'm such a kind and generous man, he noted. – Look at you, slave, you are downright ugly.

She bowed her head in shame and fear.

– But your face is pretty again. We don't want any blemishes in the pretty face. You will be an obedient and loyal wed woman, I trust.

– Yes, Erling, she replied with a dull voice and empty eyes.

He rubbed a breast and squeezed a nipple. The nipple turned hard in his hand. She didn't really react, one way or another.

– This will be one more strict instruction, he boasted, – one more that will show you once and for all what happens to disobedient wenches, if they should ever be disrespectful again.

The light would never return to the pretty eyes of Gudrun, Daughter of Halvard.

3

The wind was blowing. The wind filled the sails of the small boat. It made good speed and would reach the destination well before schedule.

The destination… thoughts, impressions, sensation, all that and more flashed before his inner eye.

Kjell Gudmundson sat at the helm. The late autumn wind chilled his back. The old shield maiden stood straight in the bow, not bowing her head for the elements. Even during the most powerful gusts, he saw no sign of wobbliness. Kjell gritted his teeth, well aware of how stupid it was to compare himself to the old lady.

He had woken up from a long dormancy in a bed she had placed close to the mountain wall, one well concealed from the surroundings. In the light from the open door, it was like he saw the worn warrior for the very first time. She looked distinctly different, as if she had thrown off an old coat.

She turned towards him, well aware of him having woken up, and he couldn't say that surprised him.

– Your injuries were far more severe than you believed, she informed him. – Death has touched you. Very good.

She wore a different set of clothes. The dirty gray hair didn't fall down in her face. Her very appearance seemed to have changed. She didn't hide herself anymore.

– They have started on the Little Christ church on Holmen, she related to him. – Queen Ingerid has joined King Olav Kyrre of Norway in their new home. Gudrun is carrying Erling's child. She's rarely seen in the public. The rumors speak of a nasty illness. I can imagine that rumor is quite convenient for good old Erling, Son of Arne.

Kjell's rage rose with his calm. It was the strangest thing. He could hardly breathe, but his heartrate stayed even.

– You will return, she stated, – but if you do so unprepared, you will fail gloriously, and nothing will be won. You killed a man without paying repatriation. You're an outlaw. You need to grow bigger than that before you can even think of returning.

The nod, the acknowledgement sort of forced itself on him. He rose from the bed, finding it surprisingly easy. The pain had become faint, an old, forgotten memory. His entire nude body had been covered in ointment. The lacerations had become close to invisible. He had more or less healed already. Strength surged through his physical being. His mind struck back at him with a vengeance.

– Who are you? He exclaimed.

– I don't really know, she hesitated, – no more than you do. I know I've spent a life fighting and bleeding, and that it's just one more in an endless row.

He sensed the strange connection with her. He had done so before as well, but not this strong.

– Your words don't make sense, he stated.

– They will!

She served him breakfast, but didn't really serve him. She was certainly nothing like that. He devoured the food. She started speaking, telling him more of her exploits, her triumphs and tragedies. It was a strange thing to observe her expressive face, both excited and subdued.

– We fled from Olav the Cruel's overwhelming forces, but we didn't retreat, except as a tactical act, and we finally struck back, and took him down, but it was too late. White Christ's teaching had gained the necessary undue advantage in Norway. We lost even as we won.

The frustration, the sense of triumph and tragedy remained in her hoarse voice even now. She was such a great storyteller. He could practically visualize the scenes, the small and major battles.

– I feel like an empty well, he said slowly, – and you fill me to the brim.

– Soon, you will fill yourself up, she stated, – and there will be no limit to your knowledge.

He wondered every time she hinted at what she had planned for them, for him.

The shadows grew long, and the night fell. The campfire brightened the inside, but not the wall of darkness outside. Outside and inside were the very same. He glimpsed images on the wall, in the horizontal well of darkness on his left. They moved like people would. He even imagined that they were looking at him. He imagined he was studying himself in a mirror, studying his mirror image, his… Other Self, and he shook in excitement and anxiety.

He fell asleep like that, dreaming himself away, even before he realized he was dreaming, even before he realized he was awake, and both felt equal…

The same.

He had an ice-cold morning shower under a tiny waterfall. The cold made him shake and heave, but he stayed on the spot. The shield maiden studied him with a cruel grin on her expressive face, waiting for him to quit. Kjell waited until she signed for him to quit, until she finally took pity on him, and bid him to approach her. He returned to the more or less dry ground, shaking in cold. She looked good-humored at his exposed body. He turned red, and suddenly very hot around the ears.

– You do need to toughen up, and even if you do, there are no guarantees. I do feel something in you, something I haven't felt in any other, but I'm drawing from dreams and visions I can't properly recall. I do feel how important this, all this is, though. The… the conviction burns within me.

He shook again, and not from the cold.

She had caught game, as the proficient hunter she clearly was. They devoured it raw. He had done that before, but this still seemed different, profoundly different. That particular sensation brought a number of others, unidentifiable and strange and eerie.

– We're on a quest, she said. – We're about to awaken the forces of the world itself, and we need to be prepared. We need to be at our very best.

They moved on on foot, on what was increasingly twilight days. There were mountains around them on all sides, and no sun. The darkness lingered all around them. He shook again. She led on, light on her feet. He had some trouble keeping up with her. She speeded up, and he started struggling in earnest. Then, she speeded up even more, and doing so in the middle of a steep slope. Kjell dropped to his knees, completely exhausted.

She towered above him, like an unreachable Goddess. He could hardly see her through the red haze his vision had become.

– I believed I was in good shape, he gasped through a sore, sore throat.

– This is merely the modest beginning, she teased and patronized him. – You have a long way to go, boy.

He kept his sore eyes on her, while fighting himself on his feet. She moved on. He kept stumbling in her shadow.

Her Shadow.

Outside all trails, up and down what seemed to him like an endless number of mountainsides. He glimpsed the sun in his fever visions, or believed he did. Everything had turned into one, torturous march.

– Get going, boy.

She walked behind him, and struck him on the butt with a stick. Anger surged through him, giving him the energy to keep walking. It felt like a remarkable boost for a while. It worked for a while, until he returned to the same, dull mindset.

He sat on the wet ground. Stine went hunting. He supposed she did. She returned with a buck. They had another large piece of raw meat. He had forgotten how many. Blood filled his mouth. He knew it to have a bitter taste, but this didn't. This had a full, sweet taste.

– Blood is the life, she stated. – Life is the blood.

Those words sounded so right. He nodded in something approaching euphoria.

The feeding strengthened him. He knew that, even though he hardly noticed. The meal seemed to last only a moment, and then they were walking again.

– Your strength is growing with each step, and so are you.

His gasps had become continuous. There was no longer any pause between them. He couldn't tell whether or not he was breathing in or out. The cramps in his legs grew worse with each new step, and between the steps, and…

– Do I hear the screams of fighting men?

– You probably do, she frowned. – I hear them all the time. I can't stop hearing them.

His nod, agreement was involuntary, instinctive.

He frowned again.

– Do you hear the music?

– I do, she said excitedly, happy on his behalf. – I DO!

The music didn't seem to come from any side, but it sounded close, close to either of his ears. He started humming a melody, and she joined in.

She speeded up even more, he knew she did. He chased after her like a rabid dog. It dawned on him that he didn't feel the cramps in his legs and thighs anymore. He watched her, in a moment of clarity, and it dawned on him that she was slowing down just as they had started down yet another mountainside. She pulled to a full stop not long after that, and turned towards him with a teasing smile.

– Join me on the hunt.

He looked incredulous at her again. She rushed off, and he followed her, chased her across the valleys and the mountains, the peaks covered by snow. The light reflected from the shiny white substance made tears fill his eyes, but he had no trouble seeing. He registered with razor sharp vision every motion the old shield maiden walking in front of him made.

She, and thereby he, slowed down at a juncture. She signed for him to stand still, and he obeyed in an instant. He heard the sound of what he had learned to recognize as a four-legged run. Stine drew her bow and put an arrow on its string. The deer appeared around a turn below. She let go of the arrow. It was a difficult, downward shot. The arrow hit the deer straight in the heart. It dropped to the ground and laid still after just a few moments of shiver.

– Gather wood, Stine bid him.

It didn't even occur to him to disobey the command. He rushed around in the terrain, and picked the driest branches he could find. He made the fire where she brought the dead deer. The fire burned, reaching for the sky. It was the strangest feeling to eat roasted meet again. It wrangled through his system to the point of him fearing it would never reach its destination.

– Fire was first, she stated, – and we are its Shadow.

That sounded so right as well. He nodded to her, to himself.

His sleep, his waken time both stayed filled with vivid dreams, in the hours and days on the path to their destination. He joined her, really joined her on the hunt, practically learning it all from scratch again, or so it felt when the arrow hit the game, when his knife sliced it open, and he fed on its blood. His vision revealed a field of yellow flowers, and he both choked in pain and gasped in joy. He followed something akin to invisible tracks to that destination seemingly so far ahead.

– Do you see that river? Stine asked him with a strange excitement in her voice.

– I do, he confirmed.

He looked nonplussed at her, wondering what she was getting at. He had excellent eyesight.

– I remember it like it once was, she said, – when there was hardly any valley here. The water in the river has dug ever deeper into the rock, until this very moment.

It sounded plausible, even before the sight shifted in his vision, and revealed the same that she saw.

They relaxed after one more ravenous feeding. The old woman looked calm, almost serene, but the boy could hardly sit still.

– I feel the anxiety, too, she remarked. – I've just learned to control it, channel it better. You will, too.

She finally took pity on him and started walking again. He rushed to join her at her side. She granted him a bright, so very familiar smile. He watched her turn somber again.

– The music does sound like a discord, she said solemnly, – but that's just because we're so far removed from ourselves that we can hardly see the forest for the trees. We will once again do so. I know that!

She was Deep. She always had been, for as long as he had known her, but never more than right now.

They reached an open stretch with one single house at the end. He watched her grin.

– Three horny females live here, she said. – They throw themselves at every male paying them a visit.

He wanted to turn and walk past it, but she chuckled and pushed him back on the right course. The three women, worked in the small garden. They waved unafraid to the two travelers. Stine returned the wave. Kjell didn't. Five small children of various age rushed from the house to greet the approaching man and woman. The women joined them. Stine handed them the buck. The biggest of the women held it easily. The travelers were well received, like relatives, Kjell as a returned husband and Stine like his mother or something.

The seductive smiles made him hot as burning rock.

The children served food and drink, while their mothers sat with the guests. He didn't need much imagination or thought to see the interest and need in the three young females.

– They're all yours, boy. They long for your touch, your hot seed.

The oldest rose and posed for him, smiling seductively. The other two joined her. They didn't speak much. He appreciated that.

– You need to unwind, boy, the old woman told him. – Grab what life offers you. Gudrun won't begrudge you doing that. You know she won't. She wants you to live your life, no matter what happens to her.

He writhed in discomfort, as the women smothered him in affection. They noticed his reluctance, but didn't seem bothered with it. They kept their hungry eyes on him, working their magic. He turned hot and uncomfortable. The oldest pushed herself at him, and fondled him, patient, persistent.

She touched his hard thing below, and he couldn't hide himself anymore. Her eyes turned hazy. The others started breathing faster. He remained reluctant. The oldest rubbed his cock, squeezing it ever so little. They began removing their clothes and his in quite a coordinated manner. He grabbed one of the younger. She turned limp in his arms. He kissed her. She moaned in joy and anticipation. He wanted to stay, wanted to go outside and work off his unrest. He stayed.

Exposed skin touched exposed skin. They tumbled down on the bearskin. He realized stunned that three had turned four. Stine removed her clothing in a fast, fiery motion. One casual look told him that she was excited, too. The three became competitive, pushing each other a bit. They wanted… wanted to be first.

– They know you've got experience, Stine grinned sweetly. – They can tell. They want a man, not a bungling young boy.

She looked fabulous. He wanted to tell her that, but couldn't make his voice work. The body had battle scars, but still looked just as enticing as those of the other three females surrounding him with eager, impatient moves. He grew to full size. A collective moan rose from four throats. All of them were wet and warm. Their stench ripped into his nostrils. All four had a distinct smell he could easily separate from each other. He couldn't believe how astute he had become.

They placed themselves on all fours, with their butts pointing at him. They rubbed them against him, against his crotch and hardness. Thoughts faded. He grabbed one set of hips and pushed himself hard into the warm and wet place. The oldest sister screamed in joy and pain, in desperate need. He heard words coming from her mouth, but didn't understand them. They sounded like gibberish to him. Only the moaning and grunting made sense.

He shifted to another sister, without having emptied himself. The oldest seemed to accept that as a part of the act. She still got anxious when the moves speeded up in intensity, and she practically pushed her sister away, and recaptured her place. They did have some kind of hierarchy. The movement grew even more intense fast. She shook harder, and grew louder with every push he made. Her moans seemed to fill his entire consciousness. He emptied himself in her with hard, potent pulls and pushes. Her wretched stench filled his nostrils. They collapsed on the bearskin.

She smothered him in grateful kisses and fondling, before pulling back a little in regret, and leaving him to the other three. They started working on him without delay, impatient to get him ready again. Their skill was unmistakable. Stine kissed him on the lips and rubbed her muscular butt at him, teasing him. He started hardening immediately. The other women looked at her with respect, and bowed their heads.

All of it seemed almost ridiculous to him. He felt detached from it, not really there, even at the height of the mindless motion. He had the other two. They dropped on the now soaked bearskin, the pleased sounds echoing in his ears. He had emptied himself in all three, and felt completely exhausted.

Stine crouched before him, giving him her seductive smile. She squeezed and rubbed his soft cock between her feet. He looked incredulous at her.

– We learned to please each other hard and fast between the battles, she whispered. – Some of use even claimed that it worked better than ever.

It started twisting. The irresistible itch had returned. Her smile grew wide. She pushed herself into his arms and kissed him on the lips, pushing a tongue into his mouth. It roamed and played in there.

She climbed on top of him, rocking up and down on him, making his straining cock grow and harden some more. She rubbed it back and forth, clearly impatient.

– We need to be close, she gasped, – close as a hair.

She impaled herself on him. He pushed at her, like she pushed at him, and he penetrated the shield maiden's wet and warm hole.

– Do you see the shadow on the wall? She panted.

He turned his head and cast his attention at where she had briefly cast hers. A man with a ponytail appeared. A deep chill passed through him. He nodded.

– Very good, she nodded, too.

She gasped then, and started moving faster, harder.

– I need you, warrior. I need you so much.

She clearly did, right now, but he suspected there was more, a double meaning to her statement. She was like that.

His loins burned, like hers clearly did. She started moaning in loud, needy noises. Her face looked distinctly different, unwrinkled, young.

– You see the past, see the future, she moaned happily. – The two of us together… are magickal.

The last word came as another loud moan of pleasure, as she stopped talking, as she couldn't speak anymore, as she rocked even harder on him. The pain grew unbearable. They both shouted as the overwhelming pleasure engulfed them and rocked them to no end, and in the aftermath, he felt both joy and shame.

– Don't feel shame, warrior, she whispered in his ears. – You should never be ashamed of your powerful desires. We live and die by them.

The other three presented themselves again to him with blushing cheeks. The endless night continued, and when they finally sighed and fell asleep one by one, feverish dreams continued to haunt him. The memories of the pleasures mixed with the horror of Gudrun moving in distress and need under Erling's muscular body.

He took a turn at improving the little garden outside the next morning. The feverish dreams and night terrors continued, no matter how awake and aware he became. He imagined they were actually growing in intensity and texture.

Stine stepped outside, fully dressed, ready to depart. She still had that look of deep satisfaction on her features, on her pleased grin. Things would never be the same between them.

– It's such a beautiful morning is it not?

The other three also stepped outside to bid the other two farewell. He saw no regret in their eyes. The young man and the old woman continued on their journey.

– Strength, will and thought are all equally necessary, essential, she mused. – Do you understand, warrior?

She never called him «boy» again. He felt quite pleased because of that.

One day and one night passed. Kjell Gudmundson ran flat out the next morning. He followed the old woman with ease, or so it felt. And the mind kept up. Everything within grew to an unimaginable level. He ran with her to the top of the mountain, and it cost him nothing. Pain tore at his muscles and his throat, and he didn't really feel it.

– You're a brother of eagles, Stine cried like a young girl, – and you ride on their wings.

Each flap of the wings touched him. Each step felt like a leap. The Earth spoke to him. When he carried a large tree on his shoulder, and sweat covered him from toe to head, he sensed life at his fingertips.

– You believe you wouldn't have discovered who you were if you hadn't met me. You would.

Hatred still surged through him like a storm. That hadn't changed.

– You want vengeance. That's good. You need motivation, something making you move forward.

Rush forward like the wind, at the danger awaiting him in the distance. In a forest mist at the shore of the long fjord many days later, he chased a deer. He heard/sensed a wolf chasing its prey. He breathed with the wolf, moved with the wolf, even though they were far apart. He heard the flapping of eagle wings, and imagined he flew with each light step. Everything alive seemed close to him. The mysteries and dreams of reality were his to play with as he pleased, and he knew this was merely the start of his journey.

He jumped at the deer from a tree, pushing the blade of the sword into its back, feeling its life, its death in a euphoria he could hardly believe. He drank its blood and devoured its flesh as it breathed its last breath.

– You've grown so much, Stine breathed. – I can't believe how much you've grown.

She stood there, to the left of him, like a spirit, unfathomable like a mask, but now he imagined that he could at least guess her motivation, and grasp the dangerous, enticing ritual she wanted to perform.

They sat around the campfire in another misty forest days and nights later, devouring flesh from another still warm animal.

– Can you see them?

The shadows, spirits gathering around the fire watching them with curious and sinister eyes. He didn't nod. That felt totally redundant.

They rode the sailboat deep into the fjord. She stood straight in the hard, cold wind, still ahead, still tougher than him. The chill touched his bones. He forced himself to stand straight as well. Later, much later, he felt cold as a statue. The storm had turned calm, the tall waves reduced to no more than small ripples on the water. The wind was just strong enough to fill the sails at the center of the fjord.

– We make good speed, Stine said, eager like a girl. – We will have a week to make the final preparations. We will succeed in our daring venture.

Sensations, impressions, anticipation surged within them both.

Kjell had his eyes at a point far ahead, one visible just above Stine's left shoulder. It kept shifting in his vision, just like her features, like her name changed in his ears, his memory. She had had so many names, this being just the last in a long row. Kjell glanced up. The sun hid even longer beneath the mountains. He looked at the far shore, at the naked trees. The night had long since become dominant. The fall had come in earnest.

Chapter 5
BERGEN, NORWAY 1985 CE

Lillian woke up soaked in tears. There was no fear this time, only a deep sadness. That particular emotion followed her throughout the day, latching itself to her back like a leech.

She joined the other students in Intermediate History on a guided tour around Bergen. The professor brought them to various important historical sights.

– Bergen is indeed a massive source of historical sites, he lectured them with his dry voice and demeanor. – This is a more thorough look than the one you did earlier. We will take a closer look at everything.

Lillian fought hard with herself, fought to focus on the matter at hand.

She was at the end of her second year. The first autumn, she had done the required preparatory study, and then introductory history. She hadn't done the latter as thorough as she would have wanted because she wanted freedom to choose if she changed her mind.

She hadn't, and in that very moment, she realized that she never would.

Her interest in history had always been there. She could remember it from before she started school, could no longer recall a moment when she hadn't been interested. It had become a passion. She nodded to herself.

Intermediary students could choose between before and after 1800. She had never been in doubt which, and had also chosen a special study of the Middle Ages. The Dark Middle Ages, she thought, positively uplifted.

This was in the middle of April, but with no spring in sight. Everyone had, through solemn agreement dressed for winter. Lillian looked at the sky, at all the gulls circling just below the low clouds. The sight prompted yet another surge of strange notions in her distracted mind. She shook her head in simultaneous wonder and distress.

They visited King Håkon's Hall. That didn't really bring her any particular emotion either way, and she wondered why. The professor's dry voice kept penetrating her distracted mind, and that pleased her, somehow. They wandered around through the ancient halls and hallways. She was confident she caught more than her fellow students of the mood here. It didn't take much, really. They looked to her like they weren't there at all. She watched how they took notes, but weren't really present. It seemed like just one more unimportant excursion to them. She did take notes, and did listen to the professor. She didn't have to try, here, inside living history.

– Håkon Håkonson built the first parts of this in the thirteenth century, after he had his coronation in the boathouse during one of the worst rain-summers in living memory. I guess he didn't think that was worthy of a king.

Lillian imagined she heard whispers in the cold northern wind, heard the sound of the workers doing the building. One of her teachers at compulsory public school had told her she had «a lively imagination». The woman had been quite insistent about it. Lillian shook her head, dismissing the memory as unimportant.

– Norway was never mightier than under Håkon Håkonson, Professor Ronaldsen, an easily distracted academic said. – Our country possessed areas like Greenland, Iceland, The Orkney Islands and parts of Sweden. Håkon made Bjorgvin even more important and widely known. There was talk about making him German-Roman Emperor. He was the king of Norway for forty-six years. Norway became a wealthy country.

He sounded quite proud on Norway's behalf.

Lillian made extensive notes. She did manage to focus on the lecture, and not be distracted by her inner unrest.

The point of her pencil broke. She swore loud and angry. The others looked stunned at her. The professor didn't quite know what to do with himself. She found another pencil. The professor resumed his lecture, notably hesitant.

He brought them to the museum. They took a good look at the various artifacts. He kept lecturing them with his dry voice, and equally dry «personality». Distracted again, her attention stayed glued on a sword. It seemed to draw her to itself, to draw her in, into what suddenly seemed like its more or less shiny surface. She wanted to reach out and grab it, touch the hilt, the metal wet with blood, with screams and anguish…

But she lost her nerve, and pulled back, notably embarrassed.

– You looked like you wanted to steal the sword, a boy joked later.

She gave him the sweetest of smiles. He sounded a bit uncertain, as if he wasn't quite certain he was joking. She lost interest and turned back to the girl she had been talking to.

A few of them walked together out of the hall and the fortress to its north side. She remained distracted. That seemingly lasting personality trait had grown even stronger since her unofficial visit to the dream laboratory. She studied every redhead male she encountered. There weren't that many of them, but enough to make her fear she had developed an obsession with them.

They reached the northern point of the estate. She cast her attention at the Island, At Askøy, *Fenring*, which was its old name, at the eastern and western narrow ocean passages where ships arrived and left the city. She recognized the view at a glance. This was the spot the girl with the braids had looked for the arriving fishing ships, she and everyone else living in what had then been hardly more than a village.

Lillian heard the professor's voice again, recaptured it in her mind.

– «Holmen» was one of Olav Kyrre's many properties in the area. After his father Harald Hardråde had succumbed in the battle by Stamford Bridge in the year 1066, Olav sailed north to Orkney Islands and further on to Norway. It's likely that this was the way he first arrived in Bjorgvin, and found that he enjoyed it there. He had to travel to many key sites around the country to be crowned king, but he kept returning here…

Lillian began writing again, writing a more extensive text than she had done when he had spoken. Her hands shook. Her mouth began forming words. She realized that she was adding to his story, adding what no one had never told her.

She looked astonished at the latest added content in her notebook.

They called him Kjell «The Red» Gudmundson. He was my hero since we were children. He pushed for me and other maidens to play with the boys, to actually train as shield maidens with them. The two of us met at the field covered by yellow flowers. He grabbed me and kissed me, and it made me feel so funny, and so good.

Lillian turned hot and queasy. She had to stop reading for a while.

There was more, on the next page, and that gave her completely different associations, gave her a deep, deep chill.

Erling hit me again today. He hits me and punishes me every day and night. He has broken me, made me sickeningly compliant long ago, but he's never content. Why don't you *come for me*? You must *hurry*.

Lillian managed only with an effort to constrain herself, to keep the others from seeing how troubled she had become. She had learned playacting early in life, learned to hide her true self from her father, but this was different.

A small group of students walked together through the busy afternoon streets. She pretended again, pretended to enjoy their company, until it was natural for her to turn left when they turned right. They said their casual goodbyes, and she could walk alone.

She watched movies alone, visited the theaters alone that day and evening. The multiplex cinema Konsertpaleet didn't have many visitors on the matinee presentation. She had her attention part ahead and part on her surroundings, studying every single person there, even the females. No sense of recognition presented itself. She didn't see the red-haired man from the modern times, didn't see any redhead at all. Frustration kept riding her. She imagined she was clutching the bar of a cage, and didn't get anywhere. The inside of the building brought no illumination either. She watched the Never

Ending Story, and could enjoy that, in spite of it hardly being more than a glorified children story.

– It's the first time I'm grateful for Norwegian age limitation and censorship rules, a boy whispered to his girlfriend. – If this didn't have a twelve-year minimum age, the speech would have been dubbed, and I absolutely hate that. It would have been unwatchable.

He sounded quite passionate about it. Lillian nodded to herself, finding herself agreeing with him.

This movie also brought tears to her eyes. She couldn't help it, even though she suspected it wasn't or wasn't just due to the content of the movie.

She spent some time outside, after the movie, as usual, breathing, filled with emotion, scouting for the redhead. The couple walked off. She studied them briefly, debating whether or not she should tail them, choosing not to do so.

Her feet moved her in a different direction. She glanced at her watch, confirming to herself that she didn't need to rush anything. There was a considerable distance to the Forum Theater. She decided on a whim to walk, anyway. April had finally brought warm and dry air. She left the central part of the city, and headed south, up the long, almost straight stretch to the other cinema. Her eyes kept studying the strangers on her path. It had almost become a habit. The daylight hadn't faded, and she knew it would pretty much remain for the rest of the evening, especially tonight, when there was bright sunshine. She passed the Nygård Park, and looked at the people there as well, as they passed through the open iron gate in both directions. A crowd of youths laughed aloud. It echoed pleasantly in her ears.

She walked on the sidewalk along the main road, with lots of cars stuck in the late afternoon queue on their way south. The exhaust burned in her throat. She couldn't stop coughing. More tears flowed, this time because of the hard coughing. She spotted the huge message with red letters on the white message board.

2010 - THE YEAR WE MAKE CONTACT

The title was in truth 2010 - Odyssey Two, but she translated the Norwegian text automatically in her mind.

She walked straight to the ticket booth, and bought the ticket, figuring in a moment of sober thought that he would show up if he wanted to do so. He had circled around her like a fly for months, now, at least that. A flare of irritation surged through her.

The dark theater welcomed her. The advertising had started, telling her that she hadn't had that much time, after all. She ignored the dumbing down commercials, distracting herself deliberately with what others probably would call flimsy thoughts. Closing her eyes made her see it all again. She still couldn't quite catch it, as it replayed itself on the white canvas of her mind.

The movie began, with Thus Spoke Zarathustra, the classic music from the first movie, showing the sunrise and all the radio telescopes, the Very Large Array in Socorro County, New Mexico, United States. She breathed the name Zarathustra, forming it with her lips. The name seemed… familiar to her, and she didn't understand that either, of course. A number of unidentifiable emotions touched her on a deeper level.

She had watched the first movie and easily returned to the story, now. The mood was way different, lacking Stanley Kubrick's clinical approach, and was thereby far more engaging. The strange name of… of the prophet echoed through her head, but didn't really distract her from the movie. She could do more than one thing at the time, could do multitasking. She had always been able to do that. She wondered about herself again, where all her strange thoughts came from, if it was only memory of the… the ages, or if there was something even stranger.

The mood grew in the story the moment it moved into Space. She had no true reference points there, but she still immersed herself in the story, and not the least its beyond great and explosive end and payoff following an equally great buildup. Jupiter blew up and became a new sun, changing the life of everyone on the planet. Emotions exploded in her boiling brain, one not fading the slightest after the movie ended.

She stepped outside again, into the still bright evening, and she stepped right back inside, and watched the movie for the second time, knowing beyond knowing she would watch it several more times during her lifetime. The music lingered in her ears, and in her excited mind.

Thus Spoke Zarathustra, she thought.

She recalled the start of the first movie, when the thinking ape picked up its first tool. Excitement surged through her when she returned to the slightly darker evening. Her light steps seemed to bring her wherever she wanted to go in mere moments. She used the phone in the cinema reception area, and called Lisbeth on the spur of the moment, realizing that the thought had boiled in her mind for quite a while.

They met in the deep corner of a pub in downtown, a place where candles and shadows flickered, and Lillian was confident that they both felt right at home.

– I doubt… less, now, Lillian offered. – All of it seems more convincing the more I ponder it. But it's also like a storm, a growing obsession.

– You experience your awakening, the other girl mused. – That's always a harrowing process.

– Harrowing, yes…

They grinned self-consciously and had another toast. They drank. The alcohol brought the numbness of the skin and the enthusiasm of early drunkenness.

– I know he doesn't have to have red hair or even be anywhere near this place in this life, Lillian said, – but I feel him, feel him every day. I've also seen him, even been able to take a good look at him between the various glimpses. He does exist. The question is if he is who I believe him to be. I mean, he could have made contact on numerous occasions, but hasn't. That doesn't sound like an age-old spirit seeking me, right?

– Right, Lisbeth nodded.

– It does feel good talking about this with you, Lillian stated. – I feel like I can talk to you about anything.

She touched the other girl's hand, and let her own linger there for a moment. She couldn't believe her own courage. Eyes met eyes.

– You weren't kidding when you said you wanted to join in on a three-way?

Lisbeth shook her head. Lillian promptly joined her on the couch. They kissed. Lips met lips and lingered. Lisbeth's touch was both harder and softer than the males Lillian had made out with.

– You're sweet, Lisbeth said, blushing a bit.

The taste of her lips stayed on Lillian's, mixing with that of the lipstick. They moved closer again. Lisbeth, clearly more experienced in this cupped a breast in her hand, making the nipple turn hard and Lillian gasp in surprise.

– Yes, we dykes know how to treat a girl right, Lisbeth chuckled.

– This is pleasant, Lillian frowned. – I didn't believe I would enjoy it, but I do.

Everyone stared at them. Lillian experienced their stares like daggers on the skin.

– Don't mind them, Lisbeth shrugged. – They're just clueless.

Lisbeth jumped on her feet and headed for the bar. Lillian found herself watching her, studying her… her butt and casual motion. She couldn't help blushing. Lisbeth returned with two drinks, and put one glass in front of Lillian.

– Cheers, her friend cried.

Glasses met and parted. They drank.

Lisbeth touched her jaw with a featherlight touch.

– We'll take it slow, okay, giving you time to adapt.

Lillian masked her irritation. She didn't need a chaperone. She forced a smile, a sweet, sweet smile, and feared she was overdoing it.

– Cheers, she said.

They drank again, drank the glasses empty. Lillian jumped on her feet.

– I'll fetch.

She rushed to the bar. Faces seemed to float in the air before her as she made her way there. They all looked twisted, constantly shifting in her vision, as if they were all different people.

– Do I know you? She asked a woman promptly, not having considered it at all before she did it.

The woman shook her head, quite timid, not really seeing Lillian's interest as a positive thing.

Lillian finally reached the bar. She bought two drinks and hurried back. The two friends sat there for a while longer. Lillian noticed that Lisbeth studied her, noticed the frown.

They stepped outside in the chilly spring evening, just a little unsteady. They walked side by side for a while, keeping the low-keyed conversation going. Both stopped simultaneously at the corner, set to go their separate ways.

– See you tomorrow, Lisbeth said.

– See you tomorrow, Lillian echoed.

Lisbeth frowned.

– Is anything wrong? I didn't insult you or anything, did I?

– Not at all, Lillian replied. – I've had a great evening. Thank you.

She kissed the other girl on the lips.

They parted company, waving to each other from a distance.

Lillian walked straight back to the apartment. She remained a bit unsteady. The slight intoxication had affected her balance, like it had turned her fingertips numb. It never turned into a problem. She returned home. Tove sat in front of the television, but turning and greeting her with a smile.

– Ah, there you are. You look like you've had fun.

– I did, Lillian said, and faked a smile, her slightly paralyzed tongue and lips making her sniffle just a little.

She sat down in a chair, joining Tove in front the television. She did make an attempt at watching whatever was on, but had to give up fast.

A tear fell from her eye. Soon, many more joined it. The water just kept flowing.

– Ah, you did not have a good time. I rather thought so. I know you so well.

Tove moved closer to her, and comforted her. It did help a bit, just a bit.

Lillian dried her tears.

– Thank you, but I have to pull myself together. It's long overdue.

Her determination did get through to Tove, and Tove nodded relieved.

Lillian turned sleepy fast, and she kind of welcomed that. She drank a glass of orange juice, brushed her teeth and went to bed, removing her clothes on her body the last few steps before she reached the soft nest. She pulled the blanket over her and closed her eyes.

There were no dreams, only the visions, time and time again, on repeat. The twisted face hovered above her, and the stick fell again and again on sore skin, and her silent scream echoed in the void.

She woke up nauseous, sick, shaking like a leaf. From that moment, and far into the day, she went through the motions, not really registering anything around her. She recalled having breakfast, recalled Tove speaking to her, recalled her replying, recalled the two of them crossing the town to the university.

Today, she and her fellow students of ancient history returned to ordinary library studies and lectures. Their lecturer was professor Ronaldsen. He had clearly returned to familiar ground, sounding and appearing more confident. Lillian fought to catch the words, to actually understand what he was saying behind the dry, boring narrative. She gave up, and took extensive notes, in the hope that she would be able to fathom it later. He did a slide presentation. All of it looked like a soup of nothing to her.

The presentation ended. The lecture ended. Lillian rose with the other students, and headed for the exit.

– One more item, Ronaldsen called out and made them stop in their tracks. – I have exciting news.

He, true to his credo sounded as excited as a rock.

– We've managed to catch the services of a true capacity in older European history. His name is Martin Keller.

– *That* Martin Keller, a girl gasped.

Her astonishment was shared by most of them, including Lillian.

– That Martin Keller, the professor said, very pleased with himself. – The infamous and highly untraditional Martin Keller, if I should be so bold. I'm certain that it doesn't come as a surprise to you that not all board members at the faculty supported his tenure, no matter how temporary. I, however, will definitely recommend his series of lectures. I don't support some of his wildest theories either, but he will give you a fresh approach to your studies, and I know how important that is…

If Lillian hadn't known better, she would have sworn that the professor was joking, *joking*.

The students were visible excited as they left the building.

– I've heard so much about him, the girl, Eve said. – He's supposed to have been present, or at least nearby when the tomb of Tutankhamun was unveiled…

– That was his grandfather by the same name, of course, Ronny pointed out.

– Of course, the girl mumbled embarrassed.

– But he, like his grandfather and father has certainly blazed a trail no one can deny him, Ronny lectured them, very full of himself, set to benefit from his added knowledge as much as possible.

– He has already moved here, another boy said. – They interviewed him in the papers three months ago.

Ronny looked quite vexed. The others chuckled wickedly.

– I heard his mother was Norwegian, another girl said. – He certainly spoke Norwegian fluently on TV.

They reached the cafeteria at the Student Center. Tove sat by a table there. Lillian joined her, but she noted that Ronny and bunch sat down by a table nearby. She could easily listen in.

– You look upbeat, Tove remarked.

– We got a piece of good news today, Lillian shrugged. – A… capacity has joined the staff at the faculty as a guest lecturer.

Her ironic taint couldn't hide her excitement. Tove looked closer at her.

– Martin Keller, the man in question, has traveled the world and visited various archeological sites, Lillian told her friend. – He's a real-life Indiana Jones.

Those at the neighboring table heard her, too.

– If he is such a notoriety, why haven't I and others outside the field heard about him? Tove wondered with notable doubt in her voice.

– He's a reclusive, Ronny pointed out from the other table. – He's hardly seen in public when he isn't visiting some dig or another.

– He has traveled the *world*, Lillian said with blushing cheeks.

It dawned on her the moment she spoke the words how much importance she placed on that particular information. She also noticed easily that the others studied her with a curiosity they couldn't contain. For some reason, they had made her the center of the crowd. She didn't experience it as a bad thing, but she found herself reddening just a little. Some of the faces shifted, revealing others she couldn't identify. She shook imperceptibly.

The informal break ended, and they set out to return to their respective studies. She heard Eve and Ronny having a conversation as they removed themselves from her company.

– What is it about Lillian lately? He wondered. – She keeps acting strange.

He cast a glance behind him, fearing that Lillian had heard him. Lillian pretended that she hadn't.

– Lillian? Eve chuckled, and exposed her shiny white row of teeth. – That isn't a mystery, not a mystery at all. I've seen many like her, sweet boy. She's as easy to read as an open book. She's in love…

Both Ronny and Lillian turned deep red. She lost sight of the other two. Her blushing face kept giving off heat as she made her way across the Heights. She attempted to meditate as she moved, to cool herself down. It remained a glorious failure. The powerful sense of embarrassment and epiphany kept haunting her, and she was helpless to make it go away.

2
BJORGVIN, NORWAY 1135 CE

King Harald Gille's men celebrated, celebrated a lot during the long period of Christmas in Florvåg, on the island Fenring, ingesting mead enough for a major army. They puked their guts out after several massive drinking bouts, and were thus totally unfit for war. The king found it wise to wait for the official end of the holy days, the «Christmas Peace» before going to war.

The fleet of warship finally set course for Bjorgvin on the early morning of January 7, while it was still completely dark outside.

– It's the right time, an old veteran snorted to his men. – King Magnus can hardly keep his forces together. Armed men leave him in droves.

Cheers, both on that boat and those surrounding it, accompanied his bold statement.

King Magnus, the current acknowledged king of Norway resided in Bjorgvin. He and Harald Gille had been at odds with each other for quite some time, and now, soon, they would erupt into open warfare. Unrest haunting the kingdom of Norway since the time of Harald Hardråde approached its preliminary culmination.

A very young-looking man, Kjell «The Red» Gudmundson with fiery red hair and green eyes ignored the prattle of his fellow warriors. The name remained infamous in Norway. Everyone assumed that this man was the grandson of the first carrying the name.

He ignored the icy wind from the north. The others pulled the thick coats tighter around their bodies. He didn't. He ignored it. His hand sharpened the sword. It was a grateful, easy task. He could do it with his eyes closed.

His eyes opened wide. He directed his attention at the mainland town…

Almost sixty-five years had passed since the special All Souls Night. He had awoken the next morning in an ash still hot. The five smaller fires had all turned cold. The old shield maiden was gone, was nowhere to be seen. He recalled seeing her, in a memory true or false wave goodbye to him from the mountaintop.

Standing up didn't feel hard at all, but like a smooth flow of motion. A few steps, and he imagined the walk down to the water flowed even easier. He studied himself in the water mirror, unable to discover a single notable change. The change flowed from within, a fire rising from cold, cold ashes. It spread from his flesh and spirit to the entire visible landscape surrounding him.

He stayed in the area throughout the winter, one not truly fazing him. The chill in the air, the heat from the campfire seemed like the same. He hunted and trained with the sword. The sword felt alive in his hands, his strong, strong hands. There was no comparison to the bungling youth he had once been. He left the boat behind and headed west on foot right after the first melting of the snow in the spring. It seemed like a short walk to him, even though he knew days and weeks passed. The ocean, the town and valley eventually appeared below him like a toy model from his position at the top of the eagle mountain. He made his way down the slippery slope. The treacherous walk brought no challenges. His footing stayed firm and confident.

The valley and township had changed notably compared to his memory of it. Several new structures had been raised to honor the king and his White Christ. Smoldering rage returned to the young man. His newfound confidence and strength moved him forward across the field. It didn't make him careless. He stayed in the shadows during the last light of day and in the darkness during the late evening. A young woman stepped out from a house. He recognized her as one of the bridesmaids. He couldn't recall her name.

Something puzzled him about her, but he couldn't catch the thought roaming beneath the surface of this thoughts. He got a lot of that.

She caught sight of him and froze. He prepared himself to act, but there was no need. She left the relative safety of the yard, and sought into the darkness. He followed her there. She dried her tears in what he recognized as deep sorrow as she faced him.

– Gudrun is dead, she choked. – She died giving birth to a boy, Erling's boy. She suffered, suffered horribly in his cruel hands.

He didn't need to know more. A deep chill, a cold rage turned his bones and blood cold.

– Swear to me, Kjell Gudmundson, she spat. – Swear by the old gods that you will make Erling pay.

The desired words came easy.

– I swear!

The next moment, she had vanished, faded away like a dream.

He did, too, pulling back, further into the darkness, removing himself from the valley, but staying close, revisiting now and then, staying hidden from mortal eyes.

That word echoed in his thoughts. Disbelief and belief kept warring within him. Something had turned within him, he knew that. The ritual of fire and ashes had brought it forth.

Seasons passed. He couldn't believe how patient he had become. No one spotted the shadow lurking in the darkness, the eagle watching them from the mountaintop. He watched the boy as he started crawling, as he started walking on two feet. The shadow, the eagle sneaked into Gudrun's house, now Erling's house one dark night. Erling was snoring. Kjell touched the hilt of his sword, keeping himself from slaughtering them all with an effort.

Too easy, he mumbled quietly.

He took the boy, and left. The boy stayed asleep. The man brought him far away, far into the mountains, beyond any place they would search for him. He returned to the three sisters. They welcomed him with smothering passion, and displayed proudly the three redhead infants. He explained his situation to them, and they took it in stride and set out to comfort him in even stronger ways. They welcomed the boy, too, without hesitation.

The days and nights passed by. He did look out for his enemies to find him during the first weeks and months, but no one came. The sisters did receive other visitors now and then. He always stayed hidden then. The visits didn't faze him, one way or another. He did return to Bjorgvin at uneven intervals, and ravaged his enemies' houses and valuables, destroying their lives as much as he possibly could. He killed Arne and Erling's men and male siblings one by one. They prepared themselves for him. It did them no good. Bjorgvin grew big and prosperous, while his enemies fell into poverty and destitution.

He spent twenty years with the sisters, and taught the children, all the children the wisdom of the ages that Stine the Sorceress had taught him, doing so with an urgency that he couldn't deny. They eventually knew everything he knew, about himself and the world. He noticed that the sisters began casting him curious glances, and he knew why when he looked at himself in the water mirror. That face didn't look like it had aged a day, and neither did his body. It remained young and vital.

One day when he bid them farewell, both he and the women knew deep down that it was final. He turned and waved a single time on the western rise above the house.

One day, when Erling had grown old and poor, and lived alone, Kjell

Gudmundson rode openly to the derelict cabin. He jumped off the horse and walked with light steps inside. Only a single tallow candle lit the single room. Erling crouched in a corner in a useless attempt at protecting himself against the outside chill. The worn and mothballed skins did no good.

– You will not die in battle, Kjell spat. – Valhalla will deny you.

The old man looked puzzled at him, not recognizing, or not realizing it was him. Kjell moved closer and sat down right in front of him. The dull eyes cleared, and the pathetic creature started shaking.

– It is you, he said with an equally shaking voice. – Not your son or grandson. You.

– I didn't need any help to take on a rat like you, Kjell snarled. – Not from my offspring and not from yours, the boy hating your entrails.

– We searched for years, Erling whimpered. – We never found him, not a trace. When the accidents started, I knew it was you, that you had taken him. We became so disgraced that we were practically outlaws, even more than you. You turned people against us. From what hell did you gain your aid?

A shimmering form appeared in front of him. Kjell recognized the bridesmaid. Erling shook even harder.

– You ruined many lives, Erling Arneson, she wailed. – In this life and others, you have been a horror visited upon humanity. Your suffering won't end with your death.

She sent Kjell a grateful smile, and faded away again. Clarity grabbed him like sharp hooks. He turned his attention back to Erling.

– You destroyed Gudrun piece by piece, Kjell spat. – I trust she wasn't the only one. I hope the spirit speaks true. I hope you suffer for a thousand years. I hope you will call for pity, and none will be given, that all the old gods will despise you like the Loke you are.

He jumped on his feet in a smooth motion.

– But, no, this will have to do. Know that your son despises you. I told him in detail what you had done to his mother. I told him that I was his father. If I hadn't told him I had already killed you, he would have raced me to do so. Perhaps you will realize what a disgusting man you are before you die, but I doubt it. At least I can spit on your grave as long as it exists.

He turned and set out to leave the dark place, but something stopped him. He turned and watched Erling again. Death touched the old man, but he didn't die. His skin seemed to glow, and Kjell glimpsed the creature, the shadow Stine had called it, beneath the skin. The old man had trouble breathing, but when he spoke, the voice sounded surprisingly strong.

– You feel great, now, in your triumph, in your paltry belief in your triumph.

He suddenly sounded and looked different, like another person altogether.

Erling was more than he seemed, too. His hatred made him strong, even as his flesh crumbled to dust. His voice turned ghostly, ghoulish.

– I will sit at the side of the One God and laugh at your long grief. If you were patient, I am far more so. I will be waiting, waiting for the right moment, and then I WILL COME FOR YOU. Even if I must travel a thousand times through the gate of death, down the Dark River, I will come for you…

Kjell found himself back in the boat years later, just as much chilled to the bone as he had been that night. The sword had slipped from his hand, and he stood there with his hands drawn into fists.

Erling had died that very moment, and Kjell had caught the sight of his spirit as it left the body, and in that very moment, he had also caught a glimpse of what the human being truly was.

Harald Gille held a rousing speech, and his men struck the swords at the shipside, shouting for blood.

Kjell stood in the boat packed with Harald Gille's men, and felt anticipation. When they shouted in rage and bloodthirst, he shouted, too. His rage endured. It needed an outlet, any outlet. He welcomed the coming battle.

The warships had the powerful northern wind at their back as they made good speed to the growing township Olav Kyrre had made. His son Magnus Barefoot had made it grow even more in size and importance. It had become a true city, a coveted prize.

The direct access to the city was blocked by large and heavy poles and chains placed in the seaways on both sides of Nordnes. The war party rowed north and went to shore in Hegravik. The men ran back south across the «hills» like a black and soon to be red armada. Rumors ran high. Men from the army supporting King Magnus had started defecting, doing so well before the first skirmish, before the actual battle began.

– Magnus' men are indeed leaving him, a man in front shouted. – Bjorgvin is ours. We just need to do a little CLEANUP first.

Cruel laughter echoed his words.

The two armies met, but it could hardly be called a battle. The attackers made deep sweeps into the defending army during the first minutes of the fighting. The remains of King Magnus's army dissolved into disarray not long after that. Kjell The Red ran in front with the loudest and most aggressive warriors, cutting and stabbing with his sword without pause. Harald's army hardly slowed down on its brutal forward run.

Magnus called retreat. He and his few remaining loyal men jumped on the boats, but they didn't get far. Their own poles and chains blocked their escape. They and others on land begged for GRID (mercy). It was granted very few. Magnus was captured and taken to Harald. King Harald gave no mercy. Magnus was mistreated, mutilated, castrated and blinded to loud, cheerful shouts of scorn and triumph. He would be known as «The Blind», and would spend the last four years of his life in total darkness.

The exuberant festivities began. The wives and daughters of the losing army were more or less forced to entertain the victorious men inn all ways. The men still alive were chained and forced to watch.

Kjell Gudmundson stopped in his tracks. A powerful nausea stuck in his throat. He pulled into the darkness, away from the festivities. His eyes stared at nothing. He tried throwing up, in vain. The darkness… beckoned him. He entered it. The night didn't really impede on his movement. He walked through familiar territory, the area he had played as a boy… with Gudrun.

He thought about her deliberately, pulling her features from memory. The image of his house appeared, too, the two of them there, and then, he stood right in front of it.

– This was your grandfather's house. It should be yours.

The voice came from the left and behind him. He turned slowly, ready to raise the sword.

A man stood there, a man still covered in blood, just like Kjell himself.

– Some people doubt that, but I knew him. I was only a little boy, but we played close to this house, and he shared his food with us. No one else did that. You did well during the battle. I'm confident no one would object to you moving in. They might even help you rebuild. The people living here in this valley treated your grandfather dishonorably. They should treat you right.

– Thanks, Kjell said, – but I won't stay. I followed King Harald here, and I will leave with him when he travels around the country to be crowned king. Thank you for your kind words.

He returned to the darkness. But the old man wasn't done.

– There are other, persistent rumors I don't really pay any heed. They claim you are the same Kjell «The Red» Gudmundson…

Kjell pushed on, into the night.

The next morning dead and alive bodies were still steaming in red snow. The fallen had not been moved. Torn and cut off limbs had been distributed unevenly everywhere.

Many of the chained men, placed far from the bonfires had frozen to death during the night.

Kjell cleaned his sword meticulously. The red spots stuck to the otherwise shiny metal. He grabbed a handful of snow, and used it to clean his face. His clothes were soaked in blood, a lost cause.

The spirit appeared to him again.

– You will get rid of me soon, she grinned. – Everyone that mistreated and killed me has died, and suffered hard in the bargain. Thank you. It's time to move on.

– I will, too, he stated. – This isn't my home. It never was.

She waved goodbye, and faded away in the air, in the ether he could just about glimpse with his sharper senses.

The pervasive nausea stuck in his throat, but no matter what he did, he couldn't make himself throw up.

3

– I think you should go to Lisbeth's birthday party, Tove told Lillian early in the day. – I don't understand why you won't. It isn't like you have double-booked or anything.

– I just don't feel like it, Lillian said, notably defensive. – It's only a birthday, anyway.

– Only a… Tove looked even more exasperated. – You're something else, do you know that?

– Thank you, Lillian grinned.

The doorbell rang.

Saved by the bell, Lillian thought glumly.

She walked down the hallway to the door, and opened it. Axel, her brother stood there. She hadn't seen him since she had moved out from their parents' house. They hugged.

– Come in, she said happily. – Come in and have a look.

He stepped inside and followed her into the living room.

– Alex, this is my roommate Tove. Tove, this is my brother Axel.

– Hello, Tove greeted him sweetly.

– H'lo, he mumbled.

Lillian knew that Tove measured him from top to toe, and noticed the striking differences between them, his fair skin and hair, contrary to her dark, southern and eastern complexion.

– Axel resembles our parents, Lillian said. – I don't. I have gotten all the genes from a long-dead ancestor no one will talk about.

He took offence, and looked at her with his dog eyes. She ignored him.

– He's the good son, she pushed him. – I'm the wicked daughter, the bad company.

Tove giggled darkly. Lillian joined her, enjoyed seeing how his weakness and insecurity was displayed in full measure.

I am a wicked, wicked girl.

She reached out and touched him, rubbing his cheek, not certain whether or not that made it worse.

– This is a nice place, he remarked, in an obvious attempt at changing the conversation.

She let it pass. They sat down, she on the couch, he in the chair, face to face.

– How are your studies going?

Dry, she despaired, the conversation is dry as desert sand. She giggled darkly again, before sobering.

– Most excellent, she shrugged. – I'm learning so much great stuff, things I might have never even considered otherwise. I even read and learn outside the studies. My mind keeps expanding, opening up constantly to new and different thoughts and perceptions. I live in *sin*, in more ways than one. You should try it.

He let it pass. He always did.

– They want you to come home, he said quietly.

And then she got it.

– Ah, you were sent here, weren't you?

He wouldn't meet her eyes, and looked even more awkward than he usually did.

– So, they want that, do they? Her voice rose slightly. – Well, messenger, you can return and convey my reply: No, I'm never going back to that prison.

– You must, he insisted. – It's for your own good.

– If you just had said a single time what you thought, and not just mindlessly repeating their words and opinions, I might have considered it…

She spat at him. He rocked under the onslaught of her rage. It pleased her.

– Don't be mad, he whimpered in his weakness. – I just want what's best for you.

– Of course, I'm mad, she snarled. – You don't want what's best for me, just what's best for you, and our oppressive parents.

He practically shook then.

Tove served food with a mediating smile. It sort-of worked. Both siblings relented and started digesting the light meal.

– Eat and you shall no longer be hungry, she joked.

They sat there, making small talk. It proceeded in a fairly relaxed manner, the way it had for a long time, when they didn't touch a touchy subject.

Lillian chuckled silently.

– I exercise, too, she said excitedly. – I've become so strong and fast and enduring, and I do swordplay. That is twice satisfying in a way. The sword becomes an extension of your body, your reach. It's such a great, such a beyond great experience.

He didn't comment verbally on it, only by his frozen features, and she realized she had overstepped her bounds again. She resisted the urge to raise her voice again, and just shrugged.

The meal and cookies were done, were consumed in the dull frenzy of the strained mood. She watched him, watched him readying himself for the departing.

– I will return with you for a visit, she stated calmly. – I will give them a piece of my mind. I guess I didn't really do that the last time.

He looked even more awkward and unsettled, but also giving off a kind of sick, abundant joy making her even more suspicious of his motivation.

She joined him when he left. He had parked his car nearby. There was no parking ticket on the windshield. He hadn't spent that much time in the apartment. They drove across the city to the ferry quay. She didn't speak, and he didn't either. The quay was half full of cars. The ferry hadn't arrived yet. Lillian watched it as it approached the quay. The ferry docked. Only a few cars drove ashore. Not many cars used the ferry during the early afternoon. They drove onboard with the rest of the cars waiting on the quay. The crew directed the drivers with a hard hand. They turned quite vexed if a given driver didn't follow their directions.

– They say the bridge is in the planning stages, he said brightly.

She grinned at him. It was a good joke.

– It has been in the planning stages for thirty years, she remarked.

She looked closer at him.

– You can be funny, she joked. – Just half a day away from the patriarch, and you start making jokes. You should consider making the absence permanent.

He looked like he would say something then, but he didn't.

They stopped on the deck. Every car was safe onboard. The ferry left the quay, and moved out on the bay. Lillian stepped outside and directed her attention at the island.

Askøy, she thought.

The current name.

Fenring, she thought.

The ancient name.

That name echoed in her mind. It was pronounced in a special way. She knew that at the tip of her tongue.

She shivered in the warm sunshine.

Sensation, impressions, slowly flashing images lingered just below the surface. She had learned to keep herself hidden when this happened, and reminded herself of the importance of doing that when she returned to her parent's house.

The ferry reached the island. They drove off the ferry and headed westward on the narrow road to Strusshamn, the most religious population center on Askøy. Her parents and her siblings lived here. She shuddered involuntarily, and knew her brother noticed. They passed a statue of the pietistic «hero» Hans Nielsen Hauge. A very conscious expression of contempt revealed itself on her face. Axel definitely noticed that.

– Everything would have been better if you had put your faith in God, Axel insisted.

She looked at him, just looked at him, and it pleased her that it made him shudder to his bones.

– You mean that imaginary shitty friend of yours? She said sweetly.

He clammed up.

The old elegant, but worn estate appeared after the next turn. She couldn't help it. It elicited all kinds of contradictory emotions in her. She imagined the building towering above them, long before he drove into the extensive yard.

He parked in front of the main entrance, along lots of other expensive cars. They stepped outside. He took her hand and led her into the hallway.

– Let's go into the living room, he bid her.

– I'm staying here, she said. – Right here.

She looked around her, at the expensive interior. Her father had spared no expenses.

– It's looks even worse than I remember it, she remarked. – His flock must have been particularly generous lately.

Their father was a preacher with his own TV-channel, and «his flock» was quite generous with the donations.

Their mother appeared. She was one of those invisible women, those not making their mark anywhere. She was in her forties, but looked much older.

– There you are, she said. – It's so great that you have come home, and just in time for dinner.

– I haven't come home, Lillian responded curtly. – The only reason I'm here is to tell you what I think about the disgusting trick you used by sending Axel to me. It might have worked if you had done it early on, just after I moved out. I was more vulnerable then, hardly even sentient in my distress.

– It's for your own good, Mrs. Donner said softly. – You don't know what's best for you.

Lillian quelled the sting of pity when looking at the ruined woman.

– Everyone keeps saying that, for some reason, Lillian grinned darkly. – One thing is certain, I know it far better than you guys do. Don't contact me again, you damn fake…

– GO TO YOUR ROOM THIS INSTANT

Karl Donner also seemed older than he was, but contrary to his invisible wife, he conveyed great wrath and authority. The impressive giant in the doorway made Lillian shake in atavistic fear. All the memories from her unpleasant childhood and adolescence resurfaced.

– We will straighten you out, her mother said softly. – We talked with the nice policeman, and he promised to help us.

– Gunnar? Lillian spat. – What the fuck was his business here?

The invisible woman cringed by that one word.

– He's such a nice man, Mrs. Donner said. – He told us how you spent your time in sin.

– I don't fucking believe you guys, Lillian said exasperated. – We won't live in the days of the inquisition. You can't harass people like this. You also might have asked the «nice man» who I was sinning with, but I guess men are allowed to play around.

She expected them to keep up the verbal assault, but it didn't happen. They exchanged glances, and their eye started flickering. It dawned on her that something else was happening. Her sensitivity and analyzing mind had no trouble picking up on it. It was like they were… hiding something from her.

– Wait a minute, she brightened. – Why are you suddenly so eager to make me return? One reason is certainly your desire to control me, but… there is more.

She stared at Axel. He lowered his eyes that very instant.

– Great grandfather doesn't have long left to live, and he has changed his will. He has given everything he can of his fortune to you.

Lillian nodded to herself. Norwegian law forbade grossly selective testaments. All children and descendants would get something, but half of a given fortune could be given to persons of choice. She was that person here, and the rest was left with crumbs on the table of riches. Heat and triumph surged through her.

– Grandaunt spoke to him, her mother said, clearly frustrated, actually showing some emotion for once. – That… woman has no idea how much damage she has inflicted on this family.

Her grand aunt that had affectionately called Lillian a wild heart.

– Hypocrites, she swore enraged.

She turned towards Axel.

– You DAMN HYPOCRITE, she shouted at him. – You're no longer any better than they are.

– You aren't merely a rude girl with a rebellious streak anymore, Donner snarled. – You've sold your soul to Satan. I see now we should never have given you all those liberties.

– Liberties? She scowled incredulous at him.

– Your very tongue is cursed. Women shall be quiet in public gatherings, and by the help of God you will be.

– You don't LISTEN, she shouted. – I don't live here anymore. I'm over eighteen. You've got no hold over me anymore. I'm *done* with you.

Donner rushed her. Lillian turned fast as lightning and kicked him in the balls. An initial howl turned into a wail. He hit the floor, and crouched there, unable to move.

She bent down, her face close to his.

– Hopefully, you won't be able to fuck for quite some time. You've enjoyed the service of the choir girls and boys for way too long, with no regard for how it would affect them.

She pulled back toward the exit.

– Witch, he gasped. – Whore. You will get your deserved punishment eventually, get it tenfold.

– Go to hell, daddy, she snarled.

She rushed out the door. It slammed close behind her. She breathed in stark relief, sick to her stomach. He was a powerful man. He could have her declared insane and have her locked up at a hospital. She started on the long walk to the ferry, started out in earnest…

… on the freedom road.

Chapter 6

I must be careful, she told herself. I must be ready, ready for anything.

She appreciated the walk. It helped her cool down, or at least to master her raging emotions. She made fists, deliberately picturing Karl Donner in her mind.

It wasn't that long to the quay, half an hour walk, tops, even though it felt longer. She stayed antsy, glancing around her every ten second or so, looking for people coming for her. Sweat soaked her entire body, and it wasn't that hot. It wasn't like she had made a run for it or anything. The bus passed her. She didn't care. Waiting at the stop not that far from the house had never been an option.

She finally reached the quay. It was a busy place. Buses from all over the island drove people here, to the only place they could travel to the mainland. The ferry hadn't arrived yet. She walked through the embarking tunnel and out on the pier, and joined all the other passengers. No one looked closer at her. She was quite certain of that. The waiting still got to her. She had never been very patient, and certainly not at this spot, waiting for the ferry.

The ferry arrived. She joined the other passengers onboard. Her temper flared off and on. It had always been there, a raging beast hiding right beneath the surface.

The crossing of the bay proved uneventful. She left the ferry, left the quay, and walked across town to the police station. She paused a bit outside, before stepping inside and inquiring about Gunnar at the reception.

– He's with KRIPOS, on a case, the man behind the desk replied with a lewd grin. – I can tell him that you've been here if you want.

KRIPOS was the central Norwegian crime investigation unit.

– No, that's okay, she shrugged deliberately. – I'll encounter him soon enough. Thank you very much.

She turned and left, imagining she had his eyes in her back as well. The relief flooded her outside to the point of weakness. She had to lean against the wall. Glimpses of the dream revisited her. They had become more frequent and more intense, and supplanted more and more of her ordinary dreams, pretty much like Jonathan had predicted and feared.

I'm losing it, she thought.

She glanced at her watch, pleased that she hadn't wasted much time during her brief, final visit «home». Her stomach rumbled. A sense of urgency grabbed her. There was no valid reason for her growing restlessness, but it still made her hurry through the streets. People turned blurry around her. They looked like murky shadows in her eyes. She caught an early southbound bus, and found herself shaking with relief.

The bus ride proved eventful. At first, she experienced it like just one more tedious timespan spent in the company of yapping commuters. A couple spoke with reverence about the latest TV-show, embracing the current fad. Their shiny eyes made it absolutely clear to her that they were caught in the trap of absolute normality.

The traffic slowed down, slowed down to a crawl. All the passengers glanced bewildered at each other.

– There has been a grave accident ahead, the driver informed them. – There might be a serious delay. Sorry for the inconvenience.

That did rock the commuters out of their complacency. They began raising their voices in agitated incredulity. Lillian sort of enjoyed that, even as she, too, began glancing anxiously at her watch, at the racing clock. They passed the site of the accident. The bus driver hadn't been kidding when he called it a grave accident. Ambulances and police cars had arrived. People were still trapped in their wrecked vehicles. Lillian watched a driver with blood flowing down his face. The scene… troubled her on a deeper level. Pale colors dominated the view. Only the blood stayed deep red. Death had arrived at this place. She imagined she saw the face of the man flickering, as if there were two of him, as if a shadow had surrounded his body. Then, that shadow rose, departed from his body, and she knew he was dead, and she wondered what she had seen.

The bus drove on. It finally picked up speed. She arrived at her destination only a short time before she was supposed to begin work.

Gunnar waited for her at the entrance. The mere sight of him made her simultaneous rage and anxiety return.

– Dinner? He asked, at his most charming.

– You know I'm gonna work, right? She replied curtly.

– After work, of course, he said patronizing, as if speaking to a child. – Genuine Norwegian food at a restaurant?

He was into that, too, detesting «foreign food». It fit with the rest of him.

– No, she replied just as curtly.

– What's the matter? I heard you had asked for me at the precinct.

– Just to tell you it's over, if it ever began. How dare you speak to my parents about me?

– Because it's necessary, little one. You can't cut it alone. You aren't exactly a picture of harmony, you know.

She looked incredulous at him, struggling to stay somewhat calm.

– I'm so harmonic anyone can be in this society packed with patronizing assholes, she said icily. – I don't need protection, and I don't need you. I don't want you. Is that clear enough? And let me add that if you don't stay away, I'll file charges against you for harassment, and I doubt I'll be the only one.

He looked really pissed then behind his fake smile. She turned her back to him, and stepped into the store.

She watched him walk to his car through the window, not exactly looking like an image of harmony. It pleased her to see him riled up like that.

– You're late.

She turned and faced the store manager.

– The bus was late, she shrugged. – There was a grave accident blocking the traffic. I'm confident you've heard about it.

He wanted to say more, wanted it very much, while she changed to the standard working uniform in use at this particular chain of stores. She enjoyed watching him while he held himself back.

She sat down by a cashier. Her workday began. She sat there the entire time and pushed codes on the cashier, received money, returned change in an endless flow of repetitive motion. Today was Thursday. The store stayed open longer, and there was a seemingly endless queue. Her back started hurting. It grew steadily worse. Her mood soured to zero.

An older marine in full uniform rushed forward. She watched him as he stopped at the back of the queue, and a deep frown appeared on his brow. She focused on the other customers, or at least made the attempt doing so.

– The store should hire more people, he remarked, – enough for all the unused cashiers.

His frown grew deeper when everyone looked angry at him, and not at the employees.

– Some people are more patient, the girl at the other cashier remarked.

Lillian chuckled, unable to hold herself back.

The marine, visibly reddening reached the till. He held groceries in both hands, one full basked in one and one glass bottle of sweet and thick lemonade in the other. He attempted to hold on to the bottle while pulling his wallet from the pocket, and lost the bottle. It hit the floor and broke. The sticky fluid spread across the floor, and also hit shoes and legs. People kept staring at the man with notable indignation. He grew even more upset.

– You pushed me, young lady, he lied in a very arrogant manner, clearly not able to face up to himself as fallible.

– I most certainly did not, Lillian said incensed, – and you fucking know it.

The lie, the glaringly fake accusation was so preposterous that it almost made her mute with disgust. Almost.

– You fucked up, she said, attempting to calm herself. – It can happen to anyone. You shouldn't feel bad about it. I presume you will pay for that.

– HOW RUDE, the guy belched. – Not only does this store suffer from horrible service. It also employs the typical bad-mannered youth. I weep for today's generation. They've got no respect for elders. They…

Lillian opened one of the milk cartoons and poured the content on his head. The incessant word-flow ceased abruptly. He stared absolutely stunned at her.

– Don't fret, tin soldier, she said curtly. – This one is on me…

There was some milk left in the cartoon. She emptied it on his belly. Everyone stared at the event. They enjoyed themselves, but could hardly believe their eyes.

The manager reached the cashier, notably out of breath. He stared at the calamity with horror in his bulging eyes.

The marine reached for the girl, but she pulled back and avoided his hand easily. Coincidentally, he also pushed the man behind him, the man who hadn't been able to pay, and who had grown very impatient. That man pushed back. A chaos without peer ensued. Several others involved themselves. People snarled insults at each other, more than ready to exchange blows. A hard-sweating manager finally managed to calm down the agitators, and everything seemed to turn calm and quiet.

– You employ a very defiant girl, my good man, the marine snorted at the manager.

– Lillian, my dear, the manager said sweetly. – I want you to tell this gentleman that you're sorry.

The move wasn't exactly unexpected, but she still looked incensed at him.

– I will accept his apology, she snorted with visible pride, … if the prick licks my shoes first…

– You have a choice here, the manager said, still very calm. – The apology or being fired.

– I quit, she spat, – saving you the bother.

She removed the uniform and dropped it right down in the sticky lemonade and milk. She rushed to the storage and picked up her jacket and headed for the exit. Just as she reached the door, she turned and gave them the finger.

– You will no doubt have great success, boss, she said perfectly calm. – The customer is indeed always right in your store, except when they've got a real reason to complain.

The manager could not stop drying his brow. She turned and stepped outside, laughing herself silly. The chuckle kept making its way up her throat as she crossed the road to the bus top.

Aretha Franklin sang FREEDOM FREEDOM FREEDOM blasting from giant speakers in her head.

The laughter turned loud and full.

2

She woke up the next day filled with conflicting emotions. The sounds reached her from the kitchen. She could imagine Tove's energetic moves. Awareness struck her, her thoughts sharp and clear. She had awoken wide awake, without cobwebs in her eyes.

The smile grew on her face. She stretched and enjoyed the pleasant sensation of the warm, warm bed. Tove opened the door to the bedroom.

– Breakfast will be done the moment you leave the shower, she said brightly.

Lillian rose from bed. Tove had already turned and returned to the kitchen, such an efficient beast. Lillian walked to the shower and switched on the water. The warm rain hit her body. She lost sense of time, and imagined she spent forever in the small, enclosed space.

She dried herself by the window. People passed by outside. Some of them looked up, not certain they saw what they saw. The reflection in the window obscured the nude girl, but not completely. Lillian found herself shrugging in indifference.

Tove had really made a production out of it today. Everything was indeed ready. Lillian could just sit down and start devouring the sandwiches.

– Your appetite remains uncanny, Tove noted. – Yesterday seems to sit well with you. What do you plan for an encore?

Lillian grinned self-consciously, and continued eating, feeding. The sustenance flowed down her throat.

Tove kept studying her when they dressed later.

– Wow, you certainly go to great lengths to look your best today…

Lillian had chosen her most expensive clothing.

– There's no need to save them for a rainy day anymore, Lillian stated.

– Great grandfather has terminal cancer. He will die soon and leave me loaded. All the family's efforts at making him change the will again has failed gloriously. Grandaunt stays with him all the time, guarding him like a lioness from the two-legged predators that might devour him.

A giggle rose from her throat again.

– Eva is quite correct, Tove stated pointedly. – You are in love.

In love, Lillian thought.

There was a knock on the door.

– They're actually on time for once, Tove said incredulous. – What's gotten into people today…

She rushed to open the door. Eva, Ronny and Lisbeth stood outside.

– We'll be ready in a moment, she told them. – You guys just sit tight.

She closed the door in their faces.

The two made the final preparations. Lillian took her time in front of the mirror, too. She actually spent more time than her flat mate there, a fact speaking volumes. That acknowledgment did make her blush. They joined their friends outside, and started on their walk across town.

– This is a great day, Ronny said, – one we've anxiously awaited.

Lillian nodded to herself. He was correct. The chilly air couldn't keep her excitement from manifesting. She pulled her jacket tighter around her body, but didn't really need to do that. Her pervasive inner heat made that act totally redundant.

– I heard about your excursion to your childhood home yesterday, and the subsequent great quitting at the store, Lisbeth said in a somewhat private moment, where they walked five steps behind their friends. – Are you okay?

Everyone had, it seemed.

– He has always brought out the worst in me, always, Lillian replied, pondering her own reaction to the question. – He's my father, and he treats me like shit. I can't remember a time when he hasn't. I am okay. I actually feel better than in a long time. I needed to go there, one last time.

Lisbeth rubbed her on the cheek, not more than that.

– The stranger has red hair, Lillian added promptly.

Lisbeth nodded, knowing that she had changed subject.

– He has lived in town for a while, Lillian said breathless. – It is quite conceivable that it was him I encountered.

Sudden doubt riled her.

What am I saying?

She saw the ships sail into Vågen again with their catch of the riches from the sea. It briefly overpowered the sight of the streets in her eyes. Lisbeth noticed, but not the others. The two of them exchanged secretive smiles.

A rhythmic song played in a passing car brought on the memories of a dance she and other young girls had performed in a forest glen, a wild dance lacking pretense and shyness. She found herself on the table in the torture chamber again, and the chief torturer put the water funnel down her throat.

Ronny and Eva glanced at her. She gave them her best smile.

The cats' mating meows, the birds in the trees, the birds in the air, everything made an impression on her, excited her. She made yet another attempt at clearing her head, and find out what she was really feeling, but failing spectacularly.

They arrived at the destination, the auditorium where the lecture would commence. Jonathan arrived with Marianne from another side of the plaza. She waved to them, and they returned the wave.

There was already a queue, and still half an hour until the start of the program.

– It's a good thing you insisted on us being early, Jonathan said to Lillian.
– The hall will be packed in minutes. By the looks of it, many will have to leave and return tomorrow.

They reached the auditorium as one of the first.

– The front row, Lillian said breathless.

They managed that as well, and Lillian grinned in relief. Something made her turn. She glimpsed Gunnar and Axel just as they sat down on one of the remaining seats on the fifth row.

– Don't worry, Lisbeth assured her. – We will deal with them if they make a move, or if they even look at you the wrong way.

Lillian sent her a grateful smile.

A man, one of the professors made a brief introduction of the main speaker today. Lillian's feverish brain didn't really catch a single word of what he said.

– And then, without further ado, I give you Martin Keller.

A door opened and Lillian could swear she could hear her own heartbeat when she spotted the man entering the hall. It was him, the tall man from the cinemas. Heat and cold flowed simultaneously through her body. She saw his face clearly for the first time, and could study him carefully. He was young, twenty-five or so, just as his profile said. She couldn't take her eyes off him.

– He's such a character, Ronny said enviously, – both controversial and treasured. A professor has stated publicly that he doesn't support his tenure, and several students are boycotting it, but look at this crowd.

Lilian didn't listen to him. Her entire attention was directed at the man on the podium.

– He doesn't look much like a professor, Tove giggled.

He didn't. Lillian studied the face shifting in shadow in the bright-lit hall, and realized immediately that only she saw that. He had clean-cut hair combed to the side. That looked strange to her. His United States football sweatshirt and the wide slacks both did and didn't. He looked more like an actor than an academic, really. She watched him as he placed himself behind the dais, and seemed to be towering on the platform, looking far taller and bigger than he was, a savage giant among men.

Her feverish thoughts made her frown again.

She kept watching him. He just started talking, without a further introduction.

– I can confirm that this won't be anything even close to a traditional lecture. My task, as I see it is to educate people in matters beyond the mundane, and that is what you will get tonight. I agree with the scientist and astronomer Carl Sagan when he says that science can't be separated from general human activity. We are both anti-elitists. But the similarities in our worldview pretty much end there. He's firmly attached to the modern world and its perceived rational, superficial explanations, while I'm firmly grounded in true antiquity, in a reality far from the narrow perception of establishment science. A true scientist seeks truth and share it with others even if it's unpleasant and controversial, also if it turns his own beliefs upside down. Johannes Kepler did that. So did Copernicus, Oppenheimer, J.B. Rhine, Alam Hynek, Darwin, Galilei and John Locke, to mention a few. They weren't all anti-establishment like we would say today, but they all had and have something separating them from most others.

The auditorium stayed quiet, in spite of the occasional outburst from the captivated audience. His voice, his very demeanor seemed to penetrate deep within them all.

Them all, Lillian thought.

He didn't use any kind of aid, tool. It was just him and his mesmerizing voice.

– Humanity was once nomads, hunter-gatherers, constant travelers of unspoiled nature. They lived with nature, not against it. It was a natural part of their daily life. Today, we get our necessities far more indirectly. Our killing is done by proxy. We no longer need to kill animals in person to gain access to food. A major part of humanity exists in a state of deep disharmony with both itself, and the wilderness. We've abandoned the true wilderness and entered one far worse. The wilderness has never truly left us, not in our hearts and souls, but us attempting to leave it has led to untold suffering. A friend of mine told me that to him the entire modern society, civilization itself is just an illusion, a cruel deception, a shell hiding deeper emotions, thoughts, needs, desires. Human beings were once hunters and gatherers and travelers. They wandered the Earth in a constant struggle to find good hunting grounds. It was a constant struggle, but free from today's twisted existence. Most of what you have read and heard about it is nothing but pure propaganda, in my eyes. Those societies could be quite different from each other, a true abundance of variety, but they had in common that they were societies of equality, both between the sexes and in general. And yes, there are evidence, are recent archeological discoveries backing it up. The departure from that started in earnest with the coming of the first cities. One of the earliest cities known to current humanity is Catal Huyuk on the Konya plains in present-day Turkey. What is called level twelve in archeology is determined to be approximately 9000 years old. A notable development can be seen there by comparing older and younger graves. In the older graves there are no visible differences between those buried there, no signs of rich and poor. But in the younger graves, there are. The proof of social differences becomes notable. In the younger city of Catal Hoyuk, the hunter/gatherer had virtually lost its importance as provider for the population. Agriculture had grown extensive. The inhabitants got their meat from «animals not running away». Organized trade developed. The population specialized their skills, moving away from the previous all-purpose tribe members into craftsmen, slaves, priests, politicians… Humanity had taken the first, crucial steps away from the living planet.

He held up a fork made of bone. They got a good look at it, really. He sent it around. Everyone could look at it closeup.

– Human beings started worshiping symbols, a practice quickly growing in importance. It was systemized and extended. It spread like wildfire into something extremely unhealthy. People began trusting the gods more than themselves. The possibility of a good life became dependent on the good will of the gods. Human societies became hierarchal, like pyramids with the few at the top and the many at the bottom. These convictions have dominated and poisoned human existence all the time since.

Someone handed Lillian the fork, the piece of bone. She touched it, and it tingled so pleasantly in her hand. A buzz rose briefly in her mind.

– Yes, it spread like a plague, and reached and turned inherent, also in more enlightened societies, like China five thousand years ago, Jonia in ancient Greece 2500 years ago and in the Netherlands in the seventeenth century, to mention a few. The elitist mindset saying that slavery wasn't just acceptable but natural infested the emerging civilization everywhere. The kings were descendants of the gods. After Christianity emerged, he received his authority from the one God…

Lillian shivered even harder in her bones.

– I will start the official part of my lecture now…

He elicited laughter from a grateful, captivated audience. His features burned in her mind. She had trouble breathing properly.

– Scientific surveys in Vågen, the cove leading to the old town of Bjorgvin tell us that they dumped waste beyond ordinary agriculture as early as the eighth century, revealing pre-city activity. But Bjorgvin didn't grow to a trading place of importance, with its specific rules and regulations until Olav Kyrre arrived, and set his plans in motion. He arrived an unknown number of years after the battle of Stamford Bridge. As you know, we've got only «silent sources» from this time period. The written sources were second or even third hand. The tales of the time before 1130 aren't viewed as actual sources. Snorre Sturlason used several geographical names, for instance from his own lifetime, centuries later. So, we don't know the exact year of Bjorgvin's formation. We can safely assume that 1070 is wrong, and that the anniversary was celebrated the wrong year…

They appreciated his flippant comment.

– Olav Kyrre founded the city, though. He put it on the map. But it was his son Magnus that started its expansion in earnest. It grew to become old Norway's capital in more than name. People actually came to that remote place from what was seen as all over the world at that time to trade.

– He sounds like he was there, Lisbeth whispered in Lillian's ear.

She wanted to give her a brazen response, but had lost her voice.

– The civil wars erupting in 1130 stemmed from an unrest that had been there since Olav Kyrre's father had reigned. Harald Gille's victory over King Magnus didn't really bring a resolution. Harald reigned for less than a year before he was killed. The wars continued.

He spoke for some time. The hall remained quiet. It was safe to say that everyone in the hall was paying attention. When it ended, it didn't really end. He did receive muted, but prolonged applause.

– Thank you for coming, he said after it turned quiet again. – During the upcoming lectures, I'll cover the various events in more detail, and I'll accept questions from the audience.

He pulled back, and left through the same door he had appeared. His departure brought more applause.

When Lillian's friends rose, she remained seated. Eva grabbed her shoulder, and shook her.

– Far, far away, Eva hummed.

Lillian shook, but the remote expression in her eyes remained.

– I'll see you guys, she mumbled and rushed off.

She attempted to cheat, to move forward in the queue outside, but had to give up, and endure the slow, slow progress. She started running the moment she reached the hallway, and pushed people out of her way.

The air outside seemed sharp and cold. The human beings around her had excited conversations, but she felt far more excited. Her feet seemed to move by themselves. She caught sight of him, Martin Keller just before he turned a corner somewhat ahead. She gave chase, keeping her distance at approximately twenty meters. The buildings blurred around them. He didn't turn his head a single time, even though he seemed tempted to do so at least once.

She followed him down from the Heights, and further through town. In one way, she didn't really think or analyze much, but in another, her mind was buzzing with thoughts and theorems and registering the details of her surroundings. She followed him across town, the city center. He was headed towards the mountainside. She realized that he could just as well be on his way to her house. That thought brought another nervous giggle.

He did head for the mountainside, a fact pretty clear well before he actually started on the steep climb. She experienced some trouble keeping up with him. He seemed to be flying up the mountain. At least, she imagined he did, as her breathing turned labored. He walked up the stairs past the houses covering the mountainside as if he was on a Sunday stroll. She couldn't believe how effortless he moved.

There was a road up here, but he hardly used that, except between the stairs. She had heard he lived up here, a rumor clearly having merit. He moved faster. She fought even harder to keep up, and wondered if he was in a hurry.

She reached the top of yet another steep staircase. Her calves burned, and she was sweating. She cursed herself, muttering under her breath.

The white-painted house seemed to appear from nowhere. It seemed to be right in front of her, just across the road, surrounded by trees on both sides, and only a short driveway with no car. She caught him in her vision just as he stepped inside… and left the door ajar. She looked incredulous at the scenery, and realized that he had known about her following him for quite some time, probably from the start outside the university.

All kinds of thoughts surged through her, none of them viable. She crossed the road, feeling strong, alive. The reflection of the setting sun burned in the windows, and in her eyes. She stepped unhesitating through the open door.

The entrance hall cast in a dim light reminded her of something. It took her a while to get it, but then the smile broke on her face.

– This place reminds me of the last Dracula movie, with Frank Langella, she said brightly.

He stood at the base of the stairs, and looked at her with a very expressive face. She could hardly believe how expressive. The green eyes burned her. She grew dizzy when she stared into their depths.

– I've been waiting for you, Lillian, he greeted her with a voice that should have shaken, but didn't. – You've got no idea for how long.

She had some idea. That very thought made her even dizzier. She closed the door behind her. The light turned even dimmer. He nodded slowly.

They met in the middle space between the stairs and the door.

– You own so many nice things, she mumbled, glancing briefly at all the antiques in the room.

– They're just things, he said.

Their fingers entwined, like the most natural act in the world. Palm pushed against palm. The sensitivity of her skin seemed to have increased tenfold. She smiled with shivering lips at the closed face.

– You're so cold, she whispered. – Even when you smile, you don't reveal yourself.

– It's became ever harder to me, he said.

She pushed herself at him, as she felt how her legs turned weak with desire, and she had trouble standing. She kissed him from the neck up with wet lips. He was unresponsive at first, but when she reached his lips, he responded so hard that she lost her breath. She experienced in full his strength, his power, how he struggled with himself, struggling with holding back, and she knew he wasn't cold at all.

– The bedroom, she moaned.

He hesitated.

– We've waited long enough, she mumbled with her lips close to his.

He grabbed her and held her in his strong arms, carrying her up the broad staircase. She kept rubbing herself at him, seducing him with a yearning she could not possibly control. He let her down after a few steps upstairs and pushed her at the wall. She writhed in his arms. He fondled her with his endlessly roaming hands. They stumbled on down the hallway. She saw no closed door. All the rooms had just an easily accessible opening, in a long row from the stairs. He carried her to the last room at the end before letting her down again. They stumbled into a bright bedroom. The sunshine made the red hair glow in her blurry vision. The bed was one more antique.

They undressed, both themselves and each other. Two pair of hands seemed like one. The gasp grew to a moan and then to a wail. The burning below grew potent and irresistible. She wanted to go to the bed, but her legs refused to carry her. They dropped down on the bed, entangled in mutual need. Fear touched her one moment, leaving her far behind the next. She climbed on top of him, and kissed him in what seemed to her like vicious bites. The taste of blood, real or imaginary in her mouth turned her wild. He grabbed her and put her down on her back. He mounted her, pushed himself into her. Beasts, she thought feverishly. We're beasts mating in the wilderness. She pushed her hips against his, and he pushed back. She wanted to speak. Her lips moved, but there were no words, only the loud moans growing to screams. Fire and shadow danced on their skin. The dark flames didn't hurt, but they did burn. Green eyes glowed. She felt their heat. The heat below grew unbearable. Yes. YES

YES.

The dark flames engulfed them completely.

3
FRANCE 1785 CE

Peter Hardy and his fiancé Collette Dalle stood on a cliff at the French side of the channel. The western wind made midwinter much warmer than usual. A crowd had gathered at the place, along a coastline up and down from there. Everyone stared at the ocean, stared west.

Earlier that day, a big balloon with two people in the basket below had taken flight from Dover, England. Carrier pigeons had given word of a successful start. The hope, the aim of the venture was that it, aided by the crucial western wind, would levitate across the channel, and land on the French side.

– What makes this… craft float? A notably skeptical man wondered.

– Hot air, Collette enlightened him, very helpful. – The fire made by burning tar makes the air inside the balloon lighter than the one outside it.

Peter was distracted. He had spotted a familiar face in the crowd.

Collette shook him lightly. She wanted him to continue her narrative, to support her.

– They can't steer, he related. – The balloon is at the mercy of the wind. They needed the western wind to succeed. There's nothing mysterious about it.

The other man left, muttering something about «dangerous teaching». His focus stayed on Collette until he faded away in the crowd.

– He probably fears female intellectuals, she spat. – What an awful man.

– Too bad, we can't ignore such people, he said lightly.

– Don't worry, she stressed. – I will not end up like Inez.

The memory of a woman burned at the stake revisited him again. It always did, by the slightest prompting.

Many excited eyes kept scouting the channel and its western horizon. Low and dark, heavy clods made the sea and the sky interchangeable.

– I'm so grateful you brought me here, Collette said sweetly. – Thank you.

– You're welcome, he said. – This reminds me of my time in the

Netherlands, with more or less free thought and inquiry. They had a hunger for knowledge surpassing virtually anyone, kept seeking liberation after they gained their freedom from the Spanish Empire. They also accepted refugees from all over Europe.

Her eyes widened. They always did when he spoke of his past and travels.

– And they became a world power, she breathed, – gaining the bounty for their generosity and open-mindedness.

She lowered her voice.

– And you met John Locke, Spinoza, Rembrandt and Christiaan Huygens, she said awestruck.

– I learned about distant lands, he marveled, – and worlds beyond our globe.

She brightened again. She loved him, to the point of obsession.

The mumbling picked up. People with binoculars began raising their voice. Collette jumped on his shoulders, her well-trained and well-shaped body having no trouble standing steady there.

– I SEE THEM, she shouted.

Those with binoculars directed them in the direction she pointed. Peter didn't use binoculars. His sight had always been above average, and he had trained himself to gaze across vast distances since childhood.

What had first appeared like a dot in the horizon turned into a spot with spots, and quickly grew bigger from that point. The western wind brought the craft quickly to the shore. Too fast, in many people's eyes. A loud sigh of disappointment rose from the gathering surrounding Peter and Collette when they realized that the balloon would eventually land far from their position. The observers could see the two passengers well, see how they fought to liberate the craft from the final sandbags and anything that could make it land prematurely. It looked like they would collide with the cliff. They dropped the last sandbag, and even the technical equipment. The balloon only scratched the rocks with that final effort, and floated downhill inland. Ten more seconds, twenty passed until they landed softly on French soil.

The cheers rose at the sky. People ran from all over the place to the craft. Peter ran slow enough for Collette to keep up with him.

One of the groups had truly struggled to reach the landing site first. They carried swords and pitchforks. Everyone realized quickly that those people didn't share their happiness.

Peter ran faster, and reached the balloon as one of the first, and could thereby give a warm welcome to the pitchfork people. He hadn't felt this enraged in a long while.

He attacked them with his hammering fists. Their confidence quickly turned to shock and fear. He beat them soundly, striking them to the ground and kept up the momentum, giving those he struck to the ground brutal kicks, taking out most of them before they even managed to raise their hands and weapons in defense. The two remaining attempting to cut and stab him. He avoided the first easily. The second impaled the other man when he missed Peter. He beat them up like the rest, screaming at them like a wild man or a demon. They ran from him in terror. They showed sign of slowing down, but speeded up again when he pretended to give chase.

Kjell Gudmundson calmed himself without effort. Those standing closest applauded him.

– We give you our thanks, a man connected to the balloon crew said. – Not many would be willing and able to do what you did.

– They weren't proficient fighters, Kjell said, – but they certainly could have done much harm if they hadn't been stopped.

The two from the balloon approached him, and shook his hand.

– Allow us to join the others in our thanks, sir, one practically roared. – My name is John Jeffries, and this is Jean Blanchard. Cooperation across borders, you see.

He spoke French with a horrible British accent.

– A pleasure to meet you, both, Peter Hardy said.

– Your fighting was a delight to behold, Blanchard said. – The way you handled those thugs was as well. You handled everything in the best possible manner in my eyes. Only a few drops of blood were lost. There would have been far more if you hadn't interfered. You are more than welcome to join the festivities, of course. Please do.

The couple did, without really pondering much. They and others in the gathering kept their guard up, scouting for potential trouble, even as it slowly dissolved in the joy of the moment.

– I don't really get drunk, of course, Kjell told Collette in a sober moment. – I used to attend parties making this a civilized revelry in comparison.

She giggled in his arms.

– I love it when you speak like that, she slurred. – I love you. I want to spend eternity with you.

That made him sober up even more, even as he made an effort at concealing his reaction from her.

A solemn expression touched her face.

– Inez was a witch, a true witch?

He read the burning curiosity inherent in her question. She wanted to know, not just asking lightly, as others might do, during a casual, lighthearted conversation.

– She was, he replied. – She proved that to me several times.

He read gratitude in her eyes, then, because he had leveled with her, answered her urgent query.

They were dancing, dancing tight, and it kind of amazed him that they were hardly the only couple doing that. This was indeed a liberated crowd.

Lights and shadows and fire flashed in his eyes. He sensed it, in a way he hadn't done for quite some time. She felt it, too, and her eyes grew wide and wet.

The two balloon farers definitely had fun, and went downright overboard in their celebration. Most of the gathering did, or was about to.

– Lots of children will enter the world nine months from now, Collette whispered in his ear.

Loud cheers echoed through the smoke-filled room.

– Let's find a room, the amorous female in his arms gasped. – There must be one available in this large house.

Peter spotted the face in the crowd again, and this time he couldn't quite conceal his reaction. Collette looked curiously at him, knowing something was up. It didn't make her sensual smile disappear.

He spotted Rupert Thorn's face in the crowd again. This time, the man approached them. Collette didn't spot him before he stopped right in front of them, and she shook in stunned surprise.

– Collette Dalle, Peter presented. – This is Rupert Thorn. Rupert, this is Collette.

She studied Thorn closely, almost as hard as he studied her.

– You are… old friends, I take it?

– We met the first time during the Black Plague, Peter said casually, as if he was speaking about the weather. – We've encountered each other several times since.

She nodded to herself.

– How did you know… know that…

– We walked around in a city where dead bodies rotted in the streets without getting sick, Thorn said curtly. – That was our first, decisive clue. We realized later that we had recognized each other in a different kind of way as well.

She looked at Peter again, imploring him.

– We had a sense of each other, he explained. – We knew deep down that we were… were the same, and learned to recognize that in both each other and others.

She didn't ask the natural follow-up question. There was no need for that.

Both Pete rand Thorn nodded pleased, and she turned flustered by their appreciative gaze.

– You exposed yourself, Thorn said. – You shouldn't do that.

Peter found it amazing that he had waited this long to give him a piece of his mind.

– You're probably right, he conceded. – I just find such people so damn infuriating.

Thorn nodded, somewhat pleased with his response.

Collette blinked, and looked at them both.

– Infuriating? She said with a dull voice.

He could see she was seething inside. He had no trouble seeing that.

– I guess I can see why you should hide yourselves, she said, – hide who you are, but there should be a limit.

It was a scolding. Peter felt very much like a wet dog. He fought to keep himself from grinning.

– The two of you, all of you, who can do more than anyone to change the world hide like children, skulking in the shadows?

– It isn't that simple, Peter corrected her. – We aren't all of one mind and one inclination, and we are few, so very few.

– You have centuries to plan your conquests, she stated.

He watched her passion, watched how she reined it in.

– I don't feel like it tonight, she stated calmly.

And left them.

It wasn't the first night she had denied him, but it always left him bewildered.

– I like her, Thorn said.

Peter looked stunned at him.

– You do?

– Sure. You've probably not noticed, but I prefer females with a brain, and their own mind.

Peter shook his head in wonder.

Two sweet young birds made their ways to them with shiny eyes.

– You did such a great deed, Monsieur, one of them said huskily. – Is your friend of the same… caliber?

They were clearly aroused. There was no doubt what their desire was.

Thorn, in his usual brusque manner wasted no time. He grabbed her and started fondling her. She looked startled at him, but whatever resistance she might have possessed faded fast. A haze covered her eyes. She started writhing in his grip, surrendering fast to his rushed advances.

The other smiled sweetly to Peter. When he grabbed her, she sighed happily and started writhing impatiently in his grip. His thoughts crossed briefly Collette, but then he shrugged and filed the very thought of her away.

– You're such a take charge man, Monsieur…

– I love your eyes, he said.

They were green. He almost boiled over with the sense of familiarity.

– Thank you. You speak French well, monsieur.

Well, he had spoken French longer than anyone.

He pushed her at the wall. She gasped.

– This girl loves strong men, she breathed.

He could tell. His rough treatment turned her on even more. He smelled her stench. She attempted to free herself from his grip in her growing impatience, but he handled her easily. A soft life had made her physically unfit.

The needy moan rose from her throat and through her open mouth. He had a sense of carrying her, but that was long after he had immersed himself in it all. She clung to him, whispering low words in his ear.

– Please, Monsieur. Please.

He searched for a room, or any somewhat secluded place, but in the end, he just gave up, and settled down in the hallway packed with mating couples. He undressed her, undressed himself, and placed her on all fours and pierced her from behind.

Moans and grunts filled the air from all around him. There was no telling where each vocal sound originated from. He ravaged her, hardly holding back at all. A flow of words and sounds erupted from her wide-open mouth. He caught some of it at first, but then everything drowned in the mighty buzz flooding his mind, his entire consciousness. He emptied himself in her. She collapsed on the floor, and so did he.

He was leaning against the wall. The young woman leaned on him on his left, the wide grin and joy frozen on her features.

There was a draft. He noticed such things, noticed the smallest variations in the air.

Collette stood there. He noticed her wet groin. She kept rubbing herself a bit with a remote look in her wet eyes, seemingly not noticing what she was doing.

– I was unreasonable, she said softly.

She slipped down on him, into his lap.

– Let me make it up to you, My Lord. Please allow your bitch to serve you.

The hoarse voice spoke with clarity about her state of mind. He grabbed her and drew her close, and she sighed in happiness. She put her hand around his cock, and started petting it. There was no need, really. It had turned semihard again already. But he enjoyed her fuzzing over him.

She started moving up and down on his lap, while keeping up the petting. He regained his full strength. She sighed in anticipation. He roamed the enticing body with his hands.

– Yes, beloved, she moaned. – Yes, do it to me. Ravage your eager whore.

He grabbed her hips and penetrated her from below. Her moaning grew louder with each new thrust. He squeezed her breasts. She didn't notice, except as even more unending pain and pleasure. They both shouted when pleasure erupted through their synapses.

She rested content in his arms.

– You've been with so many females, she meowed, – and it shows. How many offspring have you sired?

– I've lost count.

She knew it wasn't an empty boast, and didn't take offense.

The other girl rested in at the other side of him. He wasn't positive she had fallen asleep yet, but she was close.

He fell asleep eventually, too, long after both Collette and the girl had. He dreamed of home, his childhood's home.

Peter and Collette bought tickets for the crossing of the channel the next morning, and had no trouble getting a cabin, quite the big-sized cabin.

– This is bigger than the house I used to live in, she said brightly.

She sobered a bit, but kept the light tone.

– I liked Thorn by the way. He didn't try to «protect my feelings», made no attempt at sheltering the «weak sex». I like that.

She walked to Peter and put her arms around his neck, and kissed him on the lips.

– You aren't gods, she stated. – You can't snap your fingers, and change the world. Not on a whim. It takes hard work over generations.

He stood by the window, staring out at the eternal sea. A different kind of scent reached his nostrils. She was making tea. She had a great knack for it.

– Am I a witch? She asked abruptly. – Can you recognize them, even if they don't know themselves?

– You aren't immortal, he replied, – but, yes, you are a witch by birth, and have the potential to develop it further if you truly desire it.

– It's what drew you to me, wasn't it?

– If it was, it wasn't the only thing…

She was blushing.

They spent most of the crossing in their cabin. It was the same western wind, making the crossing slow, but they hardly noticed. He had long since gained a strong patience, but she, too, had a kind of mindset not caring about the passage of time. He found that twice amusing. They could relax and do whatever they wanted, and they did.

– I'm confident you will pump me up, sooner, rather than later. We will have many redhaired offspring.

The ship finally approached Dover.

– I'm always surprised how flat everything is here, he mused.

– Flat? Don't you see the white cliffs?

– You should see the place I grew up, he chuckled. – What you would see there is true «cliffs»…

They left the harbor with many others. Collette glanced around.

– I half suspected that Thorn would be here in stealth mode, she said. – He didn't say goodbye.

– We don't do that, he said. – We know we will meet again soon enough. A «goodbye» is nothing more than an unnecessary gesture.

They traveled with the coach and horses to London. The coach was packed and downright uncomfortable. Peter pondered stepping off at the next stop and ride the rest of the way, but put it out of his mind.

The coach and horses stopped at the shuttle station on Strand. The two of them stepped off, and walked down the long, wide street with the warm evening sun at their back. They walked the short distance to their house in the quiet street. Four old oaks surrounded the buildings. The house was old but large, more than large enough for them to run the pub «Four Oaks» on the ground floor, and still have lots of room.

– I enjoy seeing people come and go, he stated unprompted.

– I… understand, she said and squeezed his hand.

He unlocked the door, removed the CLOSED sign, and stepped inside. It always looked like another world to him. His eyes caught sight of *Systéme de la Nature* by Paul Heinrich Dietrich on the floor. It had somehow fallen off the shelf. He picked it up and inspected it, but spotted no damage. They didn't light any lamps, but walked straight up to the upper floor, to their big, combined living room and bedroom and lit the lamps there. He put the book on the night table.

– Your homeland… how is it like?

– I honestly don't know or care, he replied without anger in his voice. – I left it in 1135, and don't think I'll ever return.

She walked to him, and they touched each other affectionately for a while. They walked to the window and watched the sunset together. It was like he had surmised. She didn't have the sense of time passing like others adopted more and more with the major introduction of small, easily portable timepieces two hundred years ago. It had become quite common «already».

He brushed a black lock from her brow. She had dark hair and dark skin and green eyes, too, and that observation prompted even more analysis in his observant, pondering mind. His light inspection made her smile softly. It turned her on. That never took much. He kissed her, kissed her hard on the lips.

– So, you didn't get enough the last two days either, *mon cherie*, she chuckled. – You're such a stud. Fortunately, your frail companion is such a horny bitch.

They both knew it would happen, in its own time and at a time of their choosing. It felt pleasant, so very, very pleasant.

– I guess we forgot to lock the door again, she sighed, a bit frustrated.

– Let them try a break in and robbery, he grinned. – It's just as much fun every time.

He grabbed her hand.

– Let's head downstairs. The paying guests will return once they know we're back.

She brightened some more. He loved it when she did. They walked down the stairs. He imagined how the place brightened with lamps and people, long before the day turned to evening.

He no longer had to remind himself why he loved the night.

Chapter 7

She pictured a bird of fire and shadow. To call the picture forth in her head didn't feel hard at all. One blink, and a shift of focus, and it was there.

It faded only slowly in the bright morning light. She stretched lazily in bed, smiling sweetly at the tall, muscular man studying her, displaying herself to him.

– It's such a great morning.

The memories of the night with him returned to her. She couldn't recall how many times they had done it, only that it had been many. She felt spent, content. The mere thought threatened to turn into a blush. She pushed herself at him and kissed him on the lips.

– I feel great. I've never felt anything close to this before.

She smiled self-consciously.

– But I've never had my brains fucked out before either…

He looked at her with a pointed stare, not really taking his eyes off her. It stunned her that she didn't lose her brazen courage, and kept displaying herself to him. One thought, one moment later she had stepped out on the floor. She watched as his green eyes lit up like fire, and her smile widened to a deep, deep divide.

– I need to call my roommate, she grinned, – or she might be seriously worried.

They could joke together. It felt so great to be with him. A catching formed in her throat. She walked nude downstairs and called Tove. She couldn't remember the words, only that Tove sounded a bit peeved. Lillian didn't fault her for that. She had vanished without telling anyone. Tove and the guys were right to be worried, to be angry with her.

She returned upstairs. She inspected the insides of her thighs. They were covered in dry body juices. The feverish memories of the night returned, and she blushed again.

Time flowed like lightning, and she couldn't catch its breath.

They walked further up the mountainside, to the top of Mount Fløyen. Hours passed, as they walked long into the mountain plains. Her cheeks gained a healthy color.

– You look great, he said cheerfully. – You are great.

– Thank you, good sire, she straightened proudly. – It's great to be appreciated.

She frowned. Her speech had changed just for a moment there.

It had been some trip. She had become soaked in sweat, while he hadn't even broken any.

– I believed I was in great shape, she despaired, – but not compared to you.

– I've exercised hard on numerous archeological sites, he grinned. – You have no idea how many.

Something doesn't feel right, she thought, seemingly unprompted.

She pondered it further, but was unable to discern the reason.

He kept leading on their walk, looking very much like he knew where he was going.

– You do look very familiar with the terrain, with the area in general, she said lightly. – Perhaps there is something to the rumor that your mother was Norwegian, and that you grew up here.

It was entirely possible, she concluded. Perhaps they never had been far apart, just been unaware of each other.

She didn't really react that strongly when he didn't respond to her joking. Her thoughts kept turning in her head.

When he turned around, and headed back the same way they had come, it dawned on her that they had only walked half the way, and had a long way left to walk, and that she was already exhausted. She wanted to speak up. She didn't want to speak up. She stayed silent.

It turned into an ordeal. She realized that at some point she couldn't quite pinpoint. He was clearly walking, but she had to run occasionally in order to keep up with him, and that seemed to happen more often the longer time the long, long walk lasted.

– You're testing me, she said aloud, or imagined she said aloud.

He didn't respond in a notable way to that statement either. Her conviction turned into a certainty.

She gritted her teeth, and kept going, kept trailing him.

Something strange and amazing happened. Everything seemed to become easier, not harder. She suddenly had no trouble keeping up with him. Even when he broke into a run, she had no trouble keeping up. A happy chuckle rose in her sore throat.

They reached the edge of the mountain, and it happened far sooner than she had expected. He stopped, and a happy smile broke on her face.

– And believe me when I say you've hardly even approached your true potential, he told her.

She rushed into his arms, laughing euphorically.

– Why haven't I experienced this before? She asked incredulous.

– You were held back by your upbringing, he said. – I pushed you past it.

– Thank you, she gasped, close to delirious. – Thank you!

They looked down on the city.

– Everything looks so insignificant from up here, she mused.
Then she caught herself, shaking her head.
– No, that isn't correct. – Everything looks great, looks so very significant.
They walked along the edge for a while, not really looking for a way down. They just walked, focusing on the experience. She was very conscious of how she experienced it with him.
– There used to be eagles, lots of eagles here, he said. – There's no one left.
She sensed his sadness, and marveled at the resonance it created within her.
– There is an emptiness, she nodded empathically, – a hole in the world. I could never… quantify that before.
And now, everything opened up to her, doing so with marvelous ease.
– Humanity is destroying nature, he stated, – making the animals go extinct at an alarming rate.
– They are, she acknowledged, – and we're destroying ourselves, the foundation of our own survival. It's completely insane.
She felt even closer to him then. It didn't seem like they were standing several steps apart, didn't feel like that at all.
They started on the way down, as if by an unspoken agreement. It didn't exactly bring less strain on her aching thighs. But she didn't really notice much, with the ongoing euphoria ravaging her mind.
The old, white house appeared before her like a mirage. It welcomed her yet again. They both stopped in the entrance hall and faced each other.
– You look so strange, she said, – as if there are no thoughts behind that mask of yours.
And then it struck her. He hadn't opened up to her, not really. She still didn't know more about him than what she had read in the paper, or her friends had told her.
– I find it hard to express emotions, he said, – at least in part.
She nodded. He didn't enjoy talking about himself.
– You should shower and have a change of clothes, he said.
That was so strange. He would most certainly know she didn't bring an extra set.
– I have quite a few clothes matching your size, he said.
She looked stunned at him.
– That is amazing, she marveled. – Weird, but amazing.
He did look a little awkward, then, evidently understanding her ambiguity. One more warm glow surged through her.
She walked to the shower on the ground floor, removing her soaking wet clothes while she did, inviting hm to join her with a sensual smile.
But he didn't. She couldn't stop the brief rise of disappointment,

resentment from manifesting.

Thoughts didn't really register in her conscious mind while she cleaned herself, while she enjoyed her hands on her skin. Impatience ruled her. She forced herself to calm down, to slow down, and she did enjoy the warm water on her skin, on her sore limbs. Later, not that much later, she loved the sensation of the large towel rubbing her skin dry. The temperature in the bathroom remained pleasant, not too hot, not too cold.

He had placed several selections of clothes on hangers in the dressing room, the fucking dressing room. She felt appreciated, wanted, and the cautious voice fell silent.

She tried on several combinations, not making haste, enjoying that, too, the very process of… of transformation. He appreciated her, treating her like a princess. She displayed herself in the full mirror. The clothes fitted her perfectly, and that thought made her suspicious again. She smiled at the pretty girl in the mirror, snarling at her gullibility.

Her body turned, and the pretty girl in the mirror did, too. She wore dark brown leather jacket and pants, and a green blouse, matching her brown skin exceedingly well. She heard him in the living room, and stepped into the space with even more antique furniture.

He was staring with an open mouth. She had to smile. It looked so gloriously undignified.

– Does My Lord find pleasure in my appearance? She asked, hardly recognizing her own voice.

– Extremely so, My Lady, he said hoarsely, practically choking.

She couldn't stop smiling.

– I guess you need to return to the apartment and your roommate, and to your studies.

– I want to be with you, she stated with confidence.

He nodded once, twice. She wanted to go to him, but hesitated.

– I want you to be honest with me, she said. – I want there to be nothing between us.

He walked to the record player. There was purpose to that walk. She recognized his moves, his shifting expression. He put on the record already there. Heavy drums, but from a film score, not a rock album flowed from the powerful speakers. It gave her an impression of ancient times. The sight of a glowing sword filled Lillian's vision. Tall, snow-covered peaks, the winter forest. And the words: «… you're all alone in this world, and only yourself you can trust».

The blade turned wet with blood.

– The music from Conan the Barbarian, she cried wide-eyed. – Where did you find it?

– At Virgin Megastore in London, he replied. – Records not found there aren't worth having.

His voice sounded extremely strained, as if he could hardly speak. A hum of thoughts rose in Lillian's ears. Martin's voice faded away. The entire room seemed to dissolve before her eyes. She had returned to her childhood, to the fair during the Bergen anniversary. The laughing girl held hand with her distant mother. She stared at the man with the long red hair, stared at Martin Keller with both long and short hair, recognizing him, both by and beyond appearance. She recalled the crystal-clear dreams from her early childhood, those her parents had rejected as childhood fantasies and made her forget.

– I remember, she said stunned, beyond stunned. – It was you I saw at the fair when I was only five, not your father or grandfather. But how can I be so certain? It doesn't make sense.

– You know, he said quietly. – You've always known. You've even researched the matter. But in spite of that, and that I've prepared you, it's difficult, always difficult.

She shivered like a leaf before him.

He pulled out a long shelf, one embedded in the wall, concealed, hidden. She spotted two objects, and both had a profound effect on her. *She knew.* She shook when he grabbed the hilt of the sword and raised it above his head. It looked so very familiar. She recognized the other shiny object as well. He threw it to her. She caught it easily, as if her reflexes had suddenly improved tenfold. It was a silver coin, very old. She had seen one similar only a few months ago, but this was far better preserved. It had an inscription in runes. It said Olavr Kunukr - Olav King.

Olav Kyrre, she thought in a rush.

– Where did you get this? She asked him, smiling to conceal the inner unrest. – I saw one like it at the University coin collection, the antique collection in Oslo. You haven't stolen it, have you?

She kept her voice light, casual. He handed her the sword. She grabbed the hilt and held the sword with awe in her eyes. The steel was grayish, but the edges were shiny and sharp.

– I've seen nothing similar at any museum, she mused, – and I've visited quite a few.

This was a lethal weapon. It could be used to effectively stab, cut, wound and kill. Lillian Donner shook even harder as she straightened and met the green eyes under the red hair.

– I was my father, he stated, – and my grandfather. I have now used the name Martin Keller for well over fifty years, longer than any other, except for the one given to me at birth. I used the sword during the battle of Bjorgvin in 1135, and I killed Tore Arneson with it in 1070. I'm 935 years old, give or take. In that timespan, I've suffered wounds that brought me close to death, but that would surely have killed most others. I will never grow old. I am as close to immortality I can possibly come.

The girl's lips shivered. She couldn't make them stop shivering. The sword and the coin slipped from her weak hands. He caught them the moment they did.

– I could have done more to convince you, he stated, – I don't have to. You know that your memories aren't your imaginations. You're a modern, truly enlightened human being. You *know*!

She stared at herself in the mirror, at the face shifting between several set of features, but two in particular.

– You're in transition, he said softly, – and thus vulnerable.

She stood by the window, looking out, seeing nothing, nothing at all. The grass, the leaves had not turned quite green yet. She could see, see everything. She looked at the blurry mirror image of the brown-skinned, black-haired young woman in the window. Pretty, pretty place, she thought. She started humming an old melody, one she had hummed as a little girl, and a few times later, but she hadn't had any idea where she had first heard it.

– It's such a nice, haunting song, isn't it, Gudrun, he said, using the tongue he hadn't spoken in a long time, and almost had forgotten. – I always loved hearing you sing it.

– My mother taught it to me before she died, she responded, speaking the same tongue. – I know I will never forget…

She started shaking hard again before she had finished speaking. She turned slowly around and faced the man she knew so well, knew beyond death.

– Kjell, she whispered.

She repeated it aloud. Her limbs turned weak as jelly. She almost fell.

– I've seen this happen several times, he said softly. – It is a shock. Your entire life is turned upside down.

He grabbed her and pulled her into his embrace.

– Who am I? Which one?

– You're both, and more than both, even more than the sum of the parts. What is a name? What is flesh? It's just the surface, not the real you at all, but just the superficial features you display to the world of flesh and phenomena. We're so much more. You're what remains after the death of the body. They call it the… the Shadow, the eternal self. I've seen it rise from the shell, from the ashes many times the last thousand years.

The shaking stopped. She looked up at his face and eyes. He was half a head taller than her. And she was tall.

– I don't really understand yet, she mused, – but I understand enough. I love you. Thousand years, or a million won't change that, and expressing myself like that sounds both so very strange and so very right.

All kinds of thoughts kept tumbling through her head, in turmoil and calm.

– I don't look the same, she said anxiously. – I'm not anything like that big blonde bombshell of a Viking girl. Do you still… like me?

She hated the whiny quality in her voice, but couldn't help herself.

– You look fabulous, he said without hesitation, – and never forget that you're the same beneath the skin.

She turned deep red.

Her mirror image did look strange to her, now. She would never view herself the same way again.

New thoughts opened up to her every moment, but she stayed focused on him, delegating the confusing thoughts to the backburner of her feverish mind. She began swaying, performing for him, and also for an invisible onlooker.

– I remember doing this long before Gudrun, she said coquettishly. – I danced for you in the dark halls and realm of the Dark Lord. I danced for him, too. We were sorcerers, and sought his favor.

Snippets, flashes she now knew to be memories kept revealing themselves to her. She watched the man with half the front skull visible sit on his throne, and study her with desire in his eyes, and she knew she would be his for the night.

– This is disconcerting, she giggled. – It isn't like remembering in the traditional sense, but like reexperiencing it. It's like I'm actually there.

She began removing her clothes. It didn't really feel awkward at all. Her sensuality, her performing for the male seemed perfectly natural. The recently reawakened memories of her unpleasant experience faded to the back of her mind.

The woman, the sensual dancer moved for the male, willfully enticing him, teasing him, making dark interest lit the fire in the green eyes. She started fondling herself, something she couldn't remember ever doing in this… this life. Her hands grew bolder. A gasp escaped her open mouth.

Gunnar should see me, now, she thought feverishly. Can you see me now, you prick?

A thought appearing one moment, gone the next.

He began undressing, too. A happy grin cracked her face. She pushed the pants down her thighs, all the way to her ancles and removed them altogether, staying down there with her upper body for a moment, displaying her further.

– I can be so free with you, she said throatily.

They were both nude. She closed in on him, evading him when he reached for her, teasing him. He stepped forward in a rush of air and caught her. She laughed pleased. He pushed her over the back of the heavy chair, making her butt stick up. She gasped, moving her lips constantly, attempting in vain to speak, to give voice to her need. He rubbed her cunt.

– YES, she shouted.

He grabbed her hips and entered her. She couldn't get enough air. The chair was rocking with each thrust, and so was she. Wild, it was so wild, a savage rutting, and she loved it, loved it, loved it.

She screamed when they both erupted in orgasm, in rapture. Her water splashed her face. She laughed in delight, in wild, wild laughter, as she hung on the back of the chair, breathing hard, her breath just slowly slowing down. Sweat kept soaking her sensitive skin.

– Throw me on your shoulder and carry me away, she mumbled. – I'm your game, your conquest.

He did, carrying her up the stairs. Her limbs dangled with no strength as he did. He carried her to the bedroom, and the old, giant bed. He put her down on her back. She smiled in bliss at him. He slipped down by her side. She turned on her side. They rested there, face to face.

– I'll be knocked up in no time with this kind of activity.

He looked uncertain at her. She rubbed his cheek. Then, she rubbed her body against his. His cock began twitching. She grinned pleased. They began exploring each other. It felt very pleasant and satisfying, notably different from how Lillian Donner, born twenty years ago had experienced it before. This man had extensive experience. He knew how to touch a woman. She felt how her arousal returned, burning on a low, but growing flame. He made her gasp when he squeezed a breast, when he rubbed her on a thigh close to the wet and warm hole. She knew it would happen, and excited anticipation surged through her.

She put her arms around him, and began kissing him, moving her body up and down his. Martin enjoyed it. She knew he did, when his cock returned to its full strength. That is a sign of his interest, she thought feverishly, and in his case, his compassion. It was rough, and she loved that, contributed just as much to that as he did. She put him on his back and mounted him, impaled herself on his… his sword. The loud, pleased moan rose from her throat. She giggled darkly. Her body moved on its own volition, sliding up and down on his shaft, his big and hard shaft. He squeezed her breasts hard. It didn't hurt. Pleasure and pain are the same, she noted, the very same. One of his hands and its fingers joined his cock in her steaming forest. Her dirty thoughts boiled over.

– I am your cunt, she cried, – your wet and dirty *cunt*.

Her father had not exactly appreciated her dirty mouth and given her several beatings over it. A teacher had discovered it, and attempted to put a stop to it, reported him, but it had ended with her losing her job, and him getting away with it, with that, too.

– On fire, she hummed. – My cunt is on fire.

And then, with the next up and down, it truly felt like that. Her entire body caught fire. She froze. He froze. And then, their motion grew even more volatile. She imagined herself to be a ragdoll riding on the rocky steed. She shook to pieces, there, on the rocky *steed*.

His hot load burned her cave. Her hot lava burned his loins. She collapsed on his strong and hard body, licking it with her tongue, kissing it with her lips. Two pair of lips stayed glued together. The two sweaty bodies collapsed in each other's arms on the rumpled sheets.

They rested in each other's arms, drifting away. His shrunken cock slipped out of her. She imagined it was still there.

– This was different compared to yesterday, she said, whispered. – You knew so much about me, and I almost nothing about you then, at least not in my conscious mind.

She kissed him again, kissed the wound on his shoulder. She had scratched a hole there in her fervor. Her hand was soaked in blood.

– I'm a savage, she said startled. – My nipples itched so much that I wanted to rip them off.

The wound was already healing. He had strong recuperative powers.

– It's Saturday today, she said brightly. – What action shall we undertake this late on this fine day?

– What do you want to do? He asked lightly.

He was asking her.

– Let's just stay here, she said sweetly. – Have a good time…

She climbed onto his lap. He sat on the bed, leaned against its back.

– We will certainly be busy… for quite some time, she giggled.

His cock had begun twitching again.

– My enduring Viking, she whispered.

He grabbed her and put her down on her back. She spread her legs. He fondled her, teased her.

– It feels so good…

She moaned pleased. Freedom grew within her yet again. It spread all over the soaking wet body in moments, and grew further from that point.

– You won't take unnecessary risks, he bid her.
– That's easy with you, my Lord and Master, she laughed, a bit uncertain. – I promise!

He reentered her. She bit her lip. He started moving. She was moving with him.

– We… have… such… fun, she gasped. – We… will… have… such… fun. We'll have an eternity together.

The last word shifted into a moan. She clung to him as he moved on her, as she moved under him. She had become warm again, so very warm. Her mind threatened to explode on her. At least that was what she told herself as she writhed and moaned under the large, muscular male.

There were thoughts, but they didn't solidify. They didn't actually form words or solid impressions. Lips touched and parted, and touched again. The scream worked itself up forever, until it finally expressed itself. The pain, the need made her twist and turn in his arms. He turned her around and pushed her down on the belly, and kept going. There was no thought at all anymore, just the overpowering pain and need. He pushed her forward, pulled her back. A dry leaf in the storm had more control over herself than she had.

It burned. Everything burned. They moved in ever more thrusts and pulls, and then they froze, shouting their release, and collapsing on the bed.

The smile lingered on her sweaty face. They rubbed each other's faces, smothering the other in affection.

– So good, she mumbled, – so happy, happy, happy.

They dozed off again, slipping easily into dreaming. It made Lillian anxious. But this night's dreams seemed totally ordinary. She noted that with a content sigh, both inside and outside the dreams, the many vivid, but pleasant dreams. They walked in a park somewhere. She frowned. There were tall buildings in the park. The very road was covered with growth. She looked around in the strange place. The two of them were accompanied by three red-haired children. She giggled in incredulous delight.

She woke up. He sat on a chair watching her.

– I sleep less than most people, he said. – That's one disadvantage of having a thousand years of memories cramped in your head, I suppose.

She grinned and stretched for him. The green eyes lit up like fire.

They shared the shower. That felt like an even more intimate act, somehow. She enjoyed that, even as she frowned. He looked closer at her. She pondered her response.

– Jonathan, a friend of mine feared the visions would completely supplant the ordinary dreaming. He feared for the consequences.

– It might have turned into a serious problem, Martin said, – but not anymore, not now, when you have acknowledged the truth. You can deal with it in a proper and healthy manner, the way people have done for as long as there have been humans.

She stretched pleasantly in his arms and kissed him on the lips. Her lips lingered on his, her skin staying close to his. Then, she stopped and grew timid again.

– She was so timid, so submissive, so weak. Lilian gestured hard with a hand. – Gudrun was. So obedient. I shrank to nothing in his care. He had such mastery over her, over me.

– Anyone can be broken, can become a slave under the right circumstances, he soothed her. – You fought. What more could you have done?

– I could have fled, but I never even attempted it. He, Erling broke me, and I let him. I made it so easy for him, so very easy.

They dried each other with large towels. She closed and opened her eyes. He touched her jaw lightly, made her look at him. It felt strangely comforting.

– You're strong, he stated with conviction, – physically, mentally and spiritually. Your suffering has made you troubled, but also powerful.

He squeezed her muscular thighs and upper arms a bit, making a point. She reddened, couldn't help feeling he was appraising her, pondering her value. She bowed her head.

– Don't mind me, she whimpered. – I'm just silly.

– You aren't silly, he stated. – There are people buying and selling others, and they would do stuff like that. I'm sorry.

– Don't be, she assured him. – This girl understands.

She knew what he was talking about, even though she couldn't match a memory to the conviction.

They dressed. She noted that the desire that had nearly consumed them earlier was burning on a low flame. They stayed close, within an arm's reach. That, too, felt pleasant. She stepped away from him and picked up the sword, and began wielding it, cutting the air with the sharp blade.

– She was never really into swords, but I am.

She straightened.

– It feels so good in my hands. It's like I'm improving with each stroke.

– It's like swimming, or riding a bike, he said. – You never forget it.

– This is a lethal weapon, she stated. – It can stab and cut flesh.

With each motion, a sensation, impression came to her.

– But this body doesn't have the muscle memory, of course. It still needs to learn everything from scratch. I should have started from early childhood.

– Your critical analysis serves you well, he noted.
– It does, doesn't it, she grinned somberly, feeling how both cold and heat surged through her. – I know things I've never learned, too.
So many voices spoke in her head, but she handled it, and felt stark pride.
– The voices will eventually coalesce into one, he said. – Some ignorant people claim that experiencing reincarnation will be confusing, with all those lives crammed into one, but it isn't. Clarity is growing with greater awareness, not shrinking.
She cast him yet another lovesick and grateful look. She kicked herself hard, in vain.
He found another sword. She knew he would attack her before he did. They had been sparring many times before. She blocked the strike with the strong part of the sword, the one close to the hilt, taking most of the force out of his attack. She pulled back and struck back. Two moments into the sparring, and she was already gasping for air. He kept attacking. She knew he didn't fight in earnest, knowing vaguely how he would do it if he had. His speed and agility kept staggering her.
That large and heavyset body, and he moved like the wind. She felt awkward and clumsy.
– You are lighter and physically weaker, but you can still become a lethal weapon. You can train yourself to be faster and craftier than almost any man, and that's your advantage.
She listened, even as she kept fighting. Sweat drowned her brow. She bumped into furniture, but hardly noticed. Thrust, defend, thrust, defend... This had quickly reached a completely different level compared to her previous sparse training. She heard his voice, heard her own, as a choir of voices spoken in ancient tongues.
Tongues, she thought.
She struck his blade hard, making sparks fly. He picked up his pace further, and she was forced to pull backwards, to doing pure defense. She knew he could overcome her easily if he so chose, but he didn't. He kept up the pressure, forcing her to dig deep into herself to keep going.
He lowered his sword, and so did she, hardly able to remain standing or holding on to her weapon.
– You could have disarmed me easily at any moment, she said.
– You would have learned nothing from that, he stated. – Now, each movement you made brought you closer to the shield maiden, the ancient warrior you can only glimpse, not remember.
She nodded in solemn joy, in breathless anticipation. He caught her excitement, and her anxiety, she knew he did, saw the concern in his eyes.

– All your various emotions come to the fore more or less simultaneously, he said. – I've seen it happen several times.

– And how did that go? She joked.

– It can cause all kinds of reactions, he said calmly, – from the ridiculous to the dead serious.

She nodded. He wasn't lying to her. A warm, warm feeling surged through her.

They walked to the extensive library.

– So many old books.

– I spent centuries collecting them. Many of them are first editions.

She wanted to say «get out of here», but stopped herself in time.

– I will eventually tell you what really happened in Europe and the new worlds the last nine centuries, he stated. – Your impression of it will probably stay jumbled for quite some time, while mine isn't.

She devoured his words like nectar, and kept kicking herself for acting like the typical young girl facing an idol. His advanced age and simultaneous youthfulness burned her. The certainty of what he had long since become smothered her being.

– Let's go dancing, anyway, she suggested. – I want to show off the new old me.

Her pronouncing changed midsentence into another accent. She noticed, but found it strangely reasonable. She chuckled and curtsied.

They walked down the mountainside to town. The late evening brought twilight, and eventually darkness.

– It feels so different, she mused. – All of it does.

The city center stayed packed every Saturday night, and this was no exception. The closer they got to the area around the main city plaza, Torgallmenningen, the more people filled the streets. Cars drove in endless circles around the central buildings. Loud music thundered from car speakers. They imagined they had stepped indoors. The music bombarded them from all sides, as if ricocheting from invisible walls. Lillian danced as she walked to the heavy rhythm.

– Everything used to be hard walls, like the bricks. Now, everything is fluid.

She giggled in stark euphoria. He looked concerned at her.

– Why don't we remember from birth?

– You did, he stressed. – Your parents, and your general surroundings made you forget. Without a culture favoring the notion of reincarnation, I guess it's difficult to maintain in a given society's collective consciousness.

She remembered. It took just his prompting to remind her of the countless concerned glances from her mother every time her very young daughter mentioned her disturbing dreams.

There was a queue to get admitted to most places, and in the end, they just chose one, more or less at random, but it didn't seem to Lillian like much time passed. She enjoyed the waiting, and the stares, and the whispers. Some of the others recognized both her and her date. She enjoyed that, enjoyed showing him to them.

The flashing lights on the dance floor supplanted the calm lights outside. The long hair of the girls whirled around their bodies. Lillian Donner let go, giving in to the rhythm in a way she had never come close to doing before. Black hair and red moved together. They stayed a pair on the chaotic motion bathing in the flashing lights.

They danced tight. She kissed him passionately on the lips. The surroundings faded again, returning to the mist and shadow they had always been. They stayed out there, on the misty field, never once venturing to the bar or the chairs and tables.

I'm high, she thought.

She had heard of people dancing for days after having ingested certain drugs.

But I don't need such crutches anymore.

She was laughing. The loud, repetitive sound echoed across the endless field. She could hardly handle the constant overload. A moment later, she almost lost her footing. He caught her, and kept her from falling.

– … dizzy… she mumbled, her voice drowning in the loud noise.

He brought her outside, to the fresh air.

– What are we? What are we humans?

– I don't know, he replied.

They walked a bit, reaching the small City Park, with the lake and its fountain. The shadows were even more pronounced and invasive here.

– You see, or at least glimpse living and dead spirits, he stated. – They're everywhere, but far more visible during moments of heightened emotions and stress.

She giggled, unable to help herself.

– *We* are Phoenix, he stated. – All human beings are, reborn time and time again throughout eternity from our own ashes.

Both a deep chill and a sizzling heat surged through her being.

– That sounds so right, she marveled.

They bought food from a street vendor. She giggled between the chewing.

– I love chili, she said, – love hot, strong food. I did from early childhood. I never knew why.

They sat on a cold bench and made out. She imagined she would never get enough. They headed home. She led on, wondering if they would reach the nice, quiet house before their passion got the best of them.

– It's a good thing we fucked to exhaustion last night, she said, – or things might have gotten interesting fast.

She noticed she was more mellow, relaxed. It didn't take much imagination to «guess» what would happen, would happen soon, but she could enjoy the lesser urgency, the gathering certainty. They climbed the mountainside. It brought a smile to both flushed faces. One blink brought them closer to… home. The next she experienced like a whirlwind, and the next after that, they had reached the house, and he had locked the door. Then, they had returned to bed, rocking on the rumpled sheets, and everything turned sublime again, wild, savage again.

We're lightning flashing in the storm, she thought in a moment of lucid thought.

It felt very much like that, during the next moment, when the beyond powerful need surged through her, from head to toe, and she lost all thought, and only savage joy remained.

She dropped on her back on the sheets, totally exhausted, totally exhausted again. The smile, the wide grin lingered on her face. She descended into sleep, into dream. She recognized this as a dream, a faint memory of how it was supposed to be, with its confusing imagery and sensations.

It made her frown. In her dream, she frowned, standing at the mountaintop, staring at a vast valley below, struggling to see the details of the vast tapestry.

The tapestry, she thought.

Something shifted. A dark cloud appeared on the bright sky.

Establishment symbolism, she thought and kicked herself, even as the anxiety persisted.

The dream quickly turned into a night terror. She writhed and whimpered in her sleep. The killer, a huge, shapeless shadow chased her through the modern streets. She ran, but feared she could never run fast enough. When she turned and looked for him, there was no one there. She kept hearing his loud steps.

– You can be broken, he hissed. – You have been several times. This time I will keep you forever.

He sounded so certain, so confident. She shook subjected to his certainty.

– God gave you to me, as an eternal gift. You are mine!

In her dream, that didn't sound farfetched at all. She believed it with all her heart.

2

Karin Torstad threw the wet towel on the floor. She straightened, and touched her back with both hands. Her back hurt. She had handled the hotel's dirty laundry all evening. It hadn't been enough to please her employer. He had wanted her to work faster. She had worked fourteen hours without break, and he wanted her to work harder, and doing so without overtime pay. Her lips curled in dismay.

She painted her face in front of the mirror, pretty much overdoing it in her own eyes. It still didn't hide the swollen skin around the eyes. She combed her smooth, fair hair, juxtaposed against the smooth, brown skin.

It was pouring outside. She made her way to the bus stop with a hard to handle umbrella. It almost twisted itself inside out several times in the strong wind. A car rolled up by her side. A door opened, seemingly by itself. A man stuck his head forward. He clearly offered her a ride. She shook her head. He didn't insist. She walked on. The car didn't follow her.

Four people stood at the stop and waited for the bus. She imagined they stared at her. She shook her head, rejecting her own anxiety. The bus arrived. Its doors opened. She stepped inside as the first, and sat down in front by the driver. She regretted that immediately. He seemed just as hostile as the others. Karin shrunk in her seat.

– She's black, a woman declared with a loud voice from the back of the bus. – Her flow of fair hair can't hide that.

Karin didn't show any signs of having heard it. She just sat there still and quiet. The long, dreary bus ride stretched on forever to her.

It had stopped raining when she stepped off the bus on Danmarkplass. No one else did. The bus drove off. She saw no people anywhere. She didn't walk through the subway, but rushed across the broad road above. A driver blew the horn, even though the car was far away. She could swear he was speeding up.

She reached the other side well before the car came close. The car roared past her, practically snarling at her. She passed the Forum cinema theater. The cold streetlights didn't bring much light. At least she imagined they didn't. She glanced around. Shadows seemed to move wherever she looked. She walked up the hillside, approaching the hilltop. The familiar route seemed strange and scary. She walked faster. There was a distinct sound of steps seemingly coming from somewhere behind her, but she couldn't decide whether or not it was the echo of her own steps or a true sound of someone walking behind her.

She turned in a fast whirl. She spotted the creature dressed in a dark coat immediately. Its eyes seemed to burn at her. She started running. All lights in the houses she passed had been turned off. She was tempted to scream, but resisted the temptation. Her street, her building, her home appeared in front of her. Relief flooded the paralyzed mind. She rushed forward. There was no one behind her, or within her sight now. She reached for the keys in her pocket. They weren't there. She searched the other pocket. Nothing. She searched her purse, swearing, and emptying the content on the ground. She spotted the keys. Relief flooded her. She grabbed them. The large shadow fell on her. She shook and attempted to scream, but the big cloth pushed at her mouth and nose reduced the potentially piercing sound to insignificance. She stared at the face covered by a mask, and spotted only the eyes. The cloth had such a… a sweet smell. The heart hammered in her chest. She tried freeing herself from the hard grip, but could hardly make an effort. Her limbs felt weak, so weak. The darkness blanketed her mind as well. Her vision blurred. Her entire body grew slack. She collapsed in the arms of the unknown assailant. A brief, nameless fear surged through her. The masked face dissolved in a cascade of gray.

3

– We BURNED, she shouted, practically screamed. – WE BURNED TO ASHES

She realized that she sat upright in bed, and was screaming her heart out.

He was comforting her, caressing her, kissing her, calming her down. It worked. She looked grateful at him, returning his caresses in boundless gratitude.

– I'm sweating like a pig, she mumbled.

He kept holding her in a light, comforting grip. Her heartrate slowed down. She stopped gasping for breath. They were having a shower together again. She enjoyed that, even as she wanted it to go further, but didn't really feel up to it, and neither, apparently did he. His cock stayed soft. She reddened a bit by that thought, but marveled far more over the fact that the sight of him nude didn't really affect her that much, one way or another.

They were having breakfast. She enjoyed that, too, even as her thoughts started drifting. She remembered ever more of Gudrun's life, her own earlier existence. It rose to the surface like pleasant and unpleasant memories. Gudrun Halvardsdatter and Kjell Gudmundson had looked at each other across the bonfire. The golden blade flashed in the dark, glowing red covered by blood. Erling's brother dropped dead to the floor, the blade having penetrated his vicious heart. It still pleased her. The fiery emotions hardly frightened her anymore.

Erling's face twisted in rage as he punished her in thousand inventive ways. The memory of that did make her cringe in fear, in the worst terror imaginable. He kept raping her, pumping her up, making her belly grow large and bloated. She had died like a broken doll, barely sentient, reduced to a semblance of a human being.

The twisted face she knew wasn't there kept filling her vision.

– You're worthless, a damn disobedient ruffled slut. You should thank me on your knees for my generosity, you, who are worth less than the lowest thrall.

And she had done so, many times, in deep gratitude. She had believed every word, even as she laid dying on the bed after having given birth to his progeny.

– You will never get rid of me. You're wrong if you ever believe you will. You belong to me forever. I'll be back. I'll always be back…

She crouched on the floor with wide-open eyes, seeing nothing. The arms around her felt like snakes. She stared bewildered at the kind features under the red hair holding around her, slowly calming down, calming down yet again.

– I remember, she whispered with her sore throat. – And I am Lillian, and I run through the streets of the modern city, and he keeps chasing me.

He brought her down in the basement. She marveled at the sight of all the weights and exercise equipment.

– This is far better than the training club, she said. – Between sweating hard here and long runs in the mountains, I'll become a mean and lean bitch.

They changed into training gear, and ran up the mountainside and far into the mountain plains. It felt easier, somehow. She kept up with him easier, and knew he wasn't patronizing her by matching her slower speed. They ran and kept running. Her legs and thighs did burn, but that was nothing new to her. The run did exhaust her. She still continued the workout in the basement. Her arms burned, too. Everything faded in the haze of physical prowess.

She braided her hair after the shower. The pleasant memories of the shower lingered. The smile stayed on her face. She chuckled softly. The color of the braids confused her. She imagined they turned blonde, that the skin turned pale, but then the familiar and unfamiliar features of Lillian Donner returned.

They sat down around the antique table and had dinner. She practically wolfed down the food.

– How did you find me? Was it just pure luck or a result of a deliberate search?

– I feared I would never find you at first, he said slowly, painfully. – The thought hardly struck my mind. I spent the first centuries without much deliberate thinking at all, hardly more than drifting from one war to another. It's all pretty much a blur by now. Slowly, painfully, I rose from the abyss of my past. I met witches, and the first people that knew for a fact that they had been reborn, that they had once died and lived again. With that came a better understanding of myself and my dreams and also my… my nature. I encountered my first fellow immortal during the Black Plague. We walked through streets of dying and dead people and didn't even get sick. I had my clearest vision ever in the Valley of Kings in Egypt in 1935. I saw the mountains around Bergen, recognizing them beyond doubt, saw you as Gudrun in the field of flowers. Tall buildings grew there, what I later would recognize as the modern Bergen. It was like a compulsion. I traveled there and scouted for years until I finally found you. Your looks, your eyes, your voice, your body were completely different… but the way you moved and talked were the same. I recognized your inner being, your Shadow, your true, eternal self. When you recognized me as well at the fair, I lost the final doubt, and I just needed to wait it out a few more years until you became an adult, and could make your own decisions.

– You had a precognition, she marveled.

I did. I faked a marriage and a child with a Norwegian woman, and arrived here in the late sixties. I met your father, Lillian's father, and recognized him as well.

– How could that be…

It dawned on her.

– He was Arne Einarson, he said, confirming her suspicion.

– That makes sense, she choked. – That makes perfect sense.

She knew he was studying her with concern in those unfathomable eyes of his, knew she crumbled before his eyes.

– What is it? He asked, no longer hiding his concern.

– We only have fifty years or so together, she said subdued, – if we're lucky. And you will stay young and healthy, while I will fade away like a rotting fruit. And then, it might be a thousand years before we encounter each other again. Humanity might not even exist anymore in a thousand years.

The pain within felt very much real. Her stomach twisted itself into knots.

Something happened, both subtle and not. A pale glow seemed to form and explode from the center of her body. She straightened, and looked incredulous at him when the happy, cautious smile cracked his face.

He rushed to her and grabbed her, and held on. She whimpered when he squeezed her arms, but that pain didn't seem to matter, as if they were fucking.

– I can recognize other… mutants, and also other immortals, he said excited. – I wanted to tell you, but I had to know for sure.

She looked incredulous at him, for several reasons.

– You mean that… that I…

It slowly dawned on her, her face an image of contradicting emotions.

– I've seen the process, the transition as it happens several times by now. I am certain, as certain as anyone can be about anything.

– That's great, she choked. – That's so great!

– You aren't like me, he said, – not exactly. I'm not born immortal. You are. More and more people are.

– Why me, and not my brother and siblings? She asked, instinctively understanding the process behind it, but still unable to analyze it on a conscious level.

– The randomness of genetics, or quirks of fate, he chuckled, he laughed out aloud.

He kissed her passionately. She returned it breathless, astounded beyond astounded.

– That doesn't mean you can't die or be killed, he stressed. – You just won't die of old age. You are more vulnerable, now, in your transition phase, but soon, as you grow physically and mentally stronger, as a certain threshold is crossed, you will be extremely hard to kill, too.

– Your words make me so dizzy, My Lord, she breathed, so warm and fuzzy.

Her voice and accent changed again, but not her appearance, only her impression of it. She studied herself in the mirror, the brown skin and dark hair and tilted eyes.

– So, what do we call each other? One of the names or both? Or both simultaneously?

He grabbed her hair, and began untying the braids. She understood and nodded to herself.

– Now, we're Lillian Donner and Martin Keller. Once, long ago, we were Kjell and Gudrun. Let's keep the memories of them, but be Lillian and Martin.

She nodded in happy agreement. He took her hand. They stepped outside, breathing the sharp spring air.

– I will never give up, she insisted. – I did that once. I never will again. I will keep fighting to my last breath.

That calmed some more of his concern. They stepped close, touching brow to brow.

– Forever, they choired.

Hand held hand, as they started walking down the hillside, down the twisted road, on the forever path, the invisible labyrinth they had both chosen.

Chapter 8

Lillian finally made her way to Lisbeth's birthday party. It was still going strong this Sunday afternoon. They stepped off the bus in the suburbs. Lillian knew the way, but she wouldn't have needed to do so. They heard the noise from far away.

The two of them crossed a long field to the house at the base of the mountain at its end. They spent considerable time delaying the crossing by stopping and making out. Lillian couldn't stop herself from grinning. They realized easily the futility in knocking on the door, and walked right inside. Lisbeth met them the moment they entered the hall. She did look like she had celebrated for two full days, with ruffled clothes and appearance, but she brightened notably as they watched. Lillian noticed that someone had turned off the music, and that a choir of excited voices reached them from the living room.

– I... changed my mind, Lillian grinned. – Better late than never, right?
– Dear girl, Lisbeth gawked, – you're officially forgiven. Your choice of partner more than makes up for your idleness.
– Congratulations, Martin greeted the birthday girl, and handed her the gift.
– Thank you, so much, Lisbeth kept gawking.

She turned and led the way to the living room.
– Isn't she great? Lillian whispered in Martin's ear.

They found themselves in a large, spacious living room. The other guests struggled hard to appear indifferent to the recent additions to the party, pretending to be engaged in eager conversations. Quite a few made room for the two. Lillian couldn't help feeling a bit of schadenfreude. She also caught Martin's ironic smile, imagining he had learned long ago to easily spot hypocrisy and similar.

She heard them whisper among themselves.
– So, she caught that big a fish, did she. How did she manage that feat? She hasn't wasted any time, that's for sure.
– I've heard she followed him from the lecture.
– I'm certain they've spent their time well... to get to know each other.

Lisbeth opened the gift. An envious choir surged through the room.
– So, I was right then, Eva said to Lillian.
– You were more than right, Lillian chuckled. – You were extremely right.

Very loud, unnatural laughter echoed through the room.

Lillian and Martin danced. She met the shimmering emerald eyes, and laughed happily. The others couldn't possibly avoid seeing their joy.

Everything, the needling, the envy surrounding her faded away during the dancing.

The party showed no sign of slowing down. Lisbeth joined the two lovebirds at the dance floor. She clearly displayed herself to Martin. Lillian, pondering her emotions, found that she didn't mind. She just didn't. There was no jealousy there.

Lillian recalled her conversation with Lisbeth about sharing Ronny, and she couldn't keep herself from reddening.

– So, this is the guy? Lisbeth asked, totally unable to contain her curiosity.

– This is the guy, Lillian nodded solemnly.

– I'm so jealous.

She didn't look jealous. She grabbed Lillian and kissed her on the lips. Lillian found herself responding. Lisbeth turned her attention to Martin and kissed him on the lips, too.

– Mmm, she grinned in delight.

She looked excited at them both.

– The guy in Scotland didn't remember me, no matter what I did. Even when my previous mother intervened, and told him she recognized me, he couldn't be persuaded. The inglorious fucker stayed in denial. I left frustrated and crushed. The two of you are far luckier.

She opened two buttons in her blouse, displaying her glorious boobs further, offering herself.

Lillian grabbed her and kissed her on the lips, kissed her hard.

– Happy birthday, she said throatily.

She pulled back. Martin grabbed Lisbeth, too. He kissed her. She started breathing faster.

– Happy birthday.

– Thank you, she whispered. – Thank you both.

– HI, GUYS, GET YOUR ASS OVER HERE, Eva shouted loud enough to wake the dead.

– We could run for the hills, Lisbeth sighed.

They joined the others around the long table. More bottles were opened, and more glasses emptied. Lillian, already drunk, in more ways than one, turned even more so. Ronny filled her glass again. It dawned on her in the distant part of her mind that still cared or could analyze that he and the others had set out to get her drunk.

She glanced to the side, and saw that they were just as generous with the drinks to Martin.

Get us, she thought. Get us drunk.

She giggled.

Good luck with that, she thought, with getting a Viking warrior drunk.

Loud and dark laughter erupted from her throat. She relieved Ronny of the bottle and poured more in both her own and Martin's glass.

– CHEERS! She shouted.

Glasses met and parted. The two of them drank, emptying the glass in one go.

This body isn't a Viking, she thought with dismay. Modern Norwegians suck.

Martin didn't get drunk. The others stared incredulous, almost pissed at him, insulted because he didn't fall into their well-crafted trap.

Lisbeth didn't get drunk either. She never drank much.

She supported Lillian out on the porch.

– Everything is whirling, Lillian giggled.

Whirling, she thought dumbfounded.

– I see the Southern Cross, she said incredulous.

– That's amazing, Lisbeth breathed.

There was no skepticism in her voice or expression. Lillian grabbed her head and kissed her lips in pure gratitude.

– The air is so fresh, Lillian marveled.

– You see and experience everything in new and exciting ways, Lisbeth noted.

They walked back inside. The party had begun deteriorating. Everyone that had attempted to keep up with Martin in their zeal to get him drunk had run to the toilet. There was a long queue, and most had to rush outside and puke their guts out on the stairs, or in the garden.

It dawned slowly on Lillian that she didn't get sick.

– Perhaps I am a bit of a Viking, after all, she mumbled.

– You are, Lisbeth insisted. – You always have been.

– The Vikings did get sick, Martin joked. – They ran outside and puked and continued partying.

He looked with contempt at the pale, greenish faces of the bodies crouching on the floor and on the lawn outside.

– These won't, he stated.

The party died for lack of steam. It lingered, but would keep fading away to nothing soon.

Tove entered the living room. She looked gloriously happy. Lillian knew instantly what she had been doing today.

– You came, the girl cried.

They rushed into each other's arms.

– This is Martin, Lillian presented. – This is Tove, my roommate.

He knew that, of course. He didn't say anything. They shook hands.

– He's a hunk, Tove said impressed to her friend.

Someone made the genius decision to turn on the television. Many wanted to point that out quite strongly, but the very first news report struck them mute, and someone rushed to turn down the music. The news anchors didn't appear at all. The program started at the main police station in Bergen, and stayed there for the rest of the broadcast.

There had been a new murder. A huge and bewildered crowd had gathered outside the building. An agitated press conference had started inside. A row of pale and serious-minded people faced the journalists.

– I'm asking the questions to the leader of the KRIPOS-team, they heard the voice of Erling Borgen, the reporter from the Norwegian Public Broadcasting. – What you think is the reason for these murders?

Oscar Haugli's face turned dark, and if possible, even paler, a noticeable departure from his usual joviality.

– As stated… it is self-evident that we're dealing with a sick individual. The way I see it, he wants to be stopped, to be caught. The remains of this murdered girl were so badly concealed that they had to be found quickly.

– Isn't it just that he likes to mutilate them, that he's a racist filled with rage against dark-skinned women of mixed origin?

Haugli's face turned red again. His sympathies were well known.

– We believe in our hypothesis, he said curtly, with a rigid expression on his red face. – We will keep working from that assumption.

– He's actually honest for once, Lisbeth said incredulous. – That is astonishing in itself.

The press conference continued along predictable lines. Nothing much was conveyed or learned or gained.

Lillian stood like frozen, there, on the floor. She stared at Martin and clutched his hand, without seeing much else around them. He returned the stare, making every effort to hold on to her eyes. It was like she was slipping away by the moment. He attempted with desperation in his eyes to hold on to hers.

2

They stepped out of Åsane Cinema Theater after having watched 2010 one more time.

– Why didn't you make yourself known to me before? She wondered. – You had plenty of opportunities.

– I wanted you to come to me, he replied, – wanted it to be your choice. I had waited nine-hundred years for you. I could wait a few weeks longer.

– But we could have experienced this movie together for the first time, she said, – and the Never Ending Story…

She choked a bit, kicking herself for her… her weakness.

They kissed some more, drowning in each other's embrace.

– Do you believe there is life out there? She asked.

– I'm convinced of it, he replied. – There have been numerous sightings of alien visitation just the last forty years, and also historically. I've seen quite a few of them myself.

– You've… seen them?

– I've seen their crafts. I've spoken to several people who was taken onboard those crafts, and experimented on.

– I've read about that, she said wearily, – read the UFO-experience by J. Allan Hynek and Missing Time by Budd Hopkins and others. The visitors haven't come here to save or aid humanity, I guess.

– I don't believe they have, he said lightly.

– They've crossed many millions of miles through empty Space, she said enraged, – and they're hardly any different from us.

They shared a laugh again. That always felt good, felt great.

The two of them sat down on a bench, reading each other's mood, enjoying that, too.

– All the victims are of mixed race, she eventually stated with frost in her voice. – I guess that's why the killings haven't made major headlines. That might also be why I feel personally threatened. The police and I seem to agree for once. They finally issued a general warning about it.

– Or it could be your ongoing visions, he joked, not joking.

– That, too, she nodded subdued.

She grew enraged again.

– All racists are scumbags, she shrugged, – and racist cops are twice scumbags. My only reaction to them attempting to claim even more power than they currently have is to spit them in the face, literally and figuratively. I guess they see a kindred soul in the murderer. It wouldn't surprise me at all.

Her voice turned a bit loud, loud enough for some people passing by to catch what she was saying. She ignored their weary and angry stares.

They watched Reckless. They caught it just in time at the Konsertpaleet Multiplex. The venue was packed on all performances, but it still just stayed on a few nights.

– I guess the managers realized how radical it truly was, Lillian said afterwards. – A rich man's daughter choosing a poor kid instead of a plush life. It's amazing that the movie was made at all.

She glanced around her. Everyone having watched the movie looked awestruck at each other.

– People want this, Martin stated, – want to be reminded that it's possible to actually have a life, if you choose it, instead of an empty career and existence in the establishment meat grinder.

She looked affectionately at him.

– You would have been a great boyfriend even without the perks, she joked.

Then, several times the next few days, they watched Terminator. People sat there absolutely stunned while the credits rolled on the screen.

– I identify so much with Sarah, Lillian said outside. – She goes through a massive growth as well, teaching herself to be lean and mean. It was such an exciting, original story. I actually had trouble breathing properly during the movie.

– I've seen lots of movies since the Great Train Robbery in 1903, Martin breathed. – Few can match this one.

They looked at each other with shiny eyes.

– And we share the experience, she said, totally mesmerized. – That made it twice valuable. At least that. I couldn't even be properly frustrated with the fact that the Norwegian Censorship Board has cut it, made it less than the director intended.

– It's like tearing up a painting or pull out pages of a novel, he snarled, – a despicable practice.

They did a high five, and couldn't believe how attuned they were.

– Supporters of the oppressive society have always blamed art for bad things in a given society, he added, – instead of blaming the true culprits, those in charge.

– That is so right, a boy standing nearby agreed.

The excited mood persisted in the crowd. Lillian grinned and played along.

– This is just a trifling matter compared to everything that is truly wrong, of course…

It turned into a riot, just alike that. Excitement rose within her like an inverted waterfall. They started marching from the cinema to Torgallmenningen. It was just approximately hundred meters, but they took it slow.

Lillian experienced the motion, the force of many feet marching in the same direction. It felt remarkable.

She jumped up on the Seafarer's Monument. She put a finger to her lips. It turned quiet.

– We've seen sinister rightwing forces rise in the western world in recent years, she shouted. – Those have also reached Norway. They've played upon people's greed, and gained their support. It's quite demeaning. Not that it was that great here before either, but this is clearly a step or ten in the wrong fucking direction.

She enjoyed immensely the fierce response from the gathering. It bloated her and encouraged her.

– Racism has also started rearing its ugly head. The Labor Party never truly challenged the racism in their own ranks, and we see the result, now. People like Ivar Garberg and Carl Ivar Hagen spout their hatred in public, and their public support swell. What's fucking wrong with this picture?

Unafraid, she thought, with soaring joy.

– «We», the Norwegians born here are what's wrong with Norway, she stated, - not the immigrants.

It caused a storm, one only growing in the coming days. Wherever she and Martin walked, people wanted to give them a piece of their mind, both positive and negative.

A caller to Ivar Garberg, the popular local racist radio host with his own station unloaded his feelings.

– The foreign whores are just getting what's coming to them. They should return to the country they come from, and stop bothering decent Norwegians.

Another caller with completely different viewpoint had a sore, angry subtext in her voice.

– I'm a mother of a brown-skinned adopted girl, she stated. – She knows no other life than this. She is Norwegian in mind and inclination. How can you attack these children and young people like this?

– Because she is a threat to my grandchildren, the uncaring, unrepenting radio host replied.

– You guys are nothing more than fucking nazis, the caller snarled, – and should be treated like that. You are the people that should be deported, not the refugees and immigrants. Jan Mayen, with its active volcano is too kind for you.

She slammed the receiver down hard when she hung up.

– I agree with her, Lillian snarled. – I agree with her so much.

They sat at a packed place in central Bergen. People cheered at her. Someone turned off the radio.

Lillian and Martin sat on a bench at the small rest area in the mountainside and relaxed, somewhat, getting a brief relief from the boiling cauldron the town below had become.

– Watching a movie or reading a book is like living an entire life during those precious hours, she mused. – I want to do that in real life, too. I want our life to be real, but just as exciting and meaningful as the best story.

They held hands. That small act felt so real.

– Are you certain you want to move in with me? He asked.

She looked incredulous at him.

– Are you kidding? She snorted. – I can tell you honestly, right here and now that I don't suffer a single stray thought of doubt about it.

They immersed themselves in each other, forgetting time and space.

Lillian and Tove stood in the apartment Lillian was set to leave behind.

– You don't need to pay more here, Tove assured her friend. – I can handle it, and I will probably get a new girl I can share it with before long, anyway.

She was clearly displeased with… something.

– Are you sure? Lillian asked.

– I'm sure, Tove replied.

The silence in the living room grew awkward.

They made their way outside. Tove locked the door behind them. They made their way through the streets.

– Martin and I are *whole* together, Lillian said brightly, staying upbeat.
– Sometimes, it seems like we're one single being in two bodies. I never believed I would experience anything like that.

Tove hugged her and kissed her on the cheek.

They walked up the mountainside carrying a few items in two bags each. When Lillian glanced back at the city, it was as if it shrunk in her gaze and returned to the small village it had once been.

– It's amazing that you don't bump into something and harm yourself when you zone out like that, Tove smirked.

– I see the path in front of me, Lillian said, still distracted. – I always do, no matter what I might otherwise glimpse.

She heard distant drums, and that sound really distracted her more than her waken visions did. She heard the cries of… of ravens, and grew immersed in them. Her feet kept carrying her forward.

They reached another plateau in the mountainside, and the old, white house appeared before them. Martin left the house through the open door and met them halfway.

– Let me relieve you of your burden, fair ladies.

Both ladies giggled and curtsied before him. They handed him the heavy bags. He carried them effortlessly to the house.

He's so strong, Lillian thought.

She saw no real straining of his muscles, and she had learned to spot such matters.

– He's so charming, Tove whispered.

The two women joined him inside. The three had dinner. Martin had cooked, and Lillian noted that he was indeed at his most charming.

– This is a most excellent dish, Tove noted.

– Indeed, Lillian remarked, as if she couldn't quite believe it.

– What are the ingredients? Tove wondered. – I've never tasted anything similar.

– It's spiced Guana, he said, – from South America.

– I'm confident that Tove is dying to know what a Guana is, Lillian joked.

– The Guana is a lizard, Martin grinned. – The spice is crushed bat wings.

– You're k-kidding, Tove stuttered.

The next moment, all of them were laughing.

– You're not kidding, Tove chuckled and dried her tears.

She had another bite, and another.

– It's delicious, she insisted.

She hugged them both a bit later.

– You impressed her, Tove told Martin. – It didn't even occur to me that anyone could impress her.

They stood in the yard and watched her disappear around the nearest turn.

– What do you say? She said seductively. – Shall we stay home tonight?

He turned serious then, and she froze, knowing he had something on his mind.

– Tonight is the night to May first, he stated. – The night of the ancient witch sabbath. All the murders have been inspired by such rites.

– But paganism is nothing like that, she objected. – That's just lies Christianity has invented to demonize the heathens.

– That fits well with what I said, he said. – I believe he is a Christian. He won't let an opportunity like that pass him by. We should go out, be seen as much as possible until dawn, in an effort to not end up as suspects.

– Who would… she began, before she froze. – The murderer?

She dug her nails so hard into his arm that he started bleeding.

– Who is it? You… *know* him?

– So do you, he said calmly.

– Erling, she breathed.

She shrunk in her tracks.

– All the evidence points to that, he said, – knowing what we know. I was there when he died. He vowed that he would come for me. I saw his vengeful spirit leave the body, and felt the truth of his words. I've waited for him as long as I've waited for you.

– But shouldn't we, wouldn't we… recognize him if we encountered him, the way we've recognized each other?

– Stine told me about him, he mused. – She recognized him then, from the truly old days, from ancient times. She said he had a protection of sorts, that he was an old enemy of ours, serving another, far more powerful enemy.

– But she recognized him?

Impressions and sensations rocked her, and she yet felt pride over her awareness.

– She couldn't remember herself, he acknowledged, – but she remembered bits and pieces of her ancient past. She believed that made it easier for her, for some reason to see through masks and masking and machinations.

– I remember feeling drawn to her, Lillian said. – I wish she was here.

They made their way down to the city, descending into its maw. It chilled and heated her. He looked at her again, prompting her to speak.

– I felt something when I stood up and spoke, she mused. – It was as if the wild emotions from the crowd… strengthened me. Does that seem presumptuous?

– I've felt something similar, he acknowledged. – Several times.

They walked a bit in silence, enjoying the other's closeness.

– You're right, she stated. – We need to get ourselves… alibies.

She shuddered again, and she didn't quite understand why.

– We don't know who he is now, Martin said with a taint of desperation in his voice. – We can sense him, know he's close to you, to us. That's his advantage. He recognizes us, but we don't recognize him.

His words hammered her like thunder.

– Yes, he knows me, she nodded. – He wishes to reach you through me. He's playing with me, like a cat would a mouse.

She understood now, why she in her gut had realized that the murderer was targeting her. She was mixed «race», now. Everything… fit.

They set out to stay visible the entire night, practically displaying themselves to the surrounding people. Many snapped photos of them. Lillian even overdid it occasionally, like a model on a catwalk or an actor on the red carpet. The dark giggle hit them all like soft hammers.

Her senses worked in a completely different manner than they had done during most of Lillian Donner's life. She caught so much more from her surroundings, from everywhere, from the flesh and blood giving her their praise.

– Look at them, he bid her. – Study them.

She did… and recognized some of them. Unfamiliar faces turned familiar and dear, familiar and loathed. She gasped soundlessly in the grip of powerful emotions, and wanted to act on them, go to them, reacquaint herself with all of them.

– Not, now, he stopped her. – We need to fight our age-old battle alone.

She nodded in more understanding. She couldn't believe how much more she understood, what horrors she could imagine.

The moonlight burned her. She spotted a face on the moon. She recognized Stine's wrinkled face. Its features turned young and smooth in a moment.

The cauldron faded from their eyes. The night faded, and dawn arrived. They stayed awake, participating in a small get-together in Sandviken. Lillian enjoyed herself. Some of the people she recognized were present. They spoke to her silent tales of longing and joy and strife and death. She was shaking, but also knew it wasn't noticeable.

Their eyes, their eyes spoke to her, telling the story.

– Morning cheers, a boy raised his glass. – We have survived another dawn.

– MORNING CHEERS, everyone in the room chuckled.

Glasses met and parted.

These were the most hardened partygoers. People had fallen asleep in bedrooms and on the kitchen and everywhere in the apartment. Others had long since started on the walk home. Those still up started yawning. Martin had also fallen asleep in his chair. Lillian cast him fond glances. Her eyes closed as well. The energy kept surging through her, delaying her falling asleep even a bit longer.

Some night, she thought just a moment before consciousness faded. Some night indeed.

The giant bird spread its wings and flew into the night.

3

Lisbeth had returned to her home after a long day at the office. She recalled having locked the door behind her. Then, she just remembered the glimpse of the sinister face, and the sweet, sinister stench.

She ran for her life through an unknown forest, nude, except for the remains of a stocking on a leg. Her feet had a thousand wounds. She hardly noticed the pain. Fear dominated her features and entire consciousness. She heard the hunter chase her, sometimes close, sometimes farther off.

The hunter had humiliated her, used her in all possible and unimaginable ways, broken her, reduced her to nothing. She recalled the patronizing voice, and the sword cutting her. Memory had shrunk to bits and pieces in her mind. She had managed to free herself, unable to tell how.

She sought down the slope, like a river flowing to its lower point. Instinct ruled her, ruled whatever reasoning remained in her feverish mind. Blind eyes cast a glance forward. The forest remained deep and dark. She saw no sign of it ending.

Logic suggested she was descending towards the sea. Thoughts worked in a way. Instinct worked. Flashes continued. She frowned, realizing that she didn't just saw the forest around her anymore, but a large field. People kept chasing her. She fled from them the fastest she was able. They were her enemies, and they hunted her like wild, two-legged wolves.

One more flash, one more blink, and she had returned to the forest. She spotted less tress ahead. The forest ended. Joy flooded her. The terror kept pushing her forward. She entered another field, one far more familiar, with a main road. The panic almost made her miss the hard and narrow gray surface. She stumbled and fell, and lost her breath.

She jumped on her feet and looked in both direction for a car, a single car. The fear paralyzed her. She hadn't believed such fear was possible. A distant, growing roar reached her ears. She spotted the car in the distance, and placed herself on the yellow line.

The driver hit the brakes. The sound of whining tires reached her straining ears. The lone driver pushed open the door at his side, and stepped out of the car. She heard him curse her in anger and astonishment.

– The sword killer… she gasped, – … abducted me… I escaped.

– Jesus, the driver exclaimed.

She ran into his arms, and grabbed them in her mindless fear.

– We must get away, she shouted. – The hunter is COMING.

– Don't be frightened, he soothed her. – I won't let him harm you. I almost hope he will come, so I can teach him a lesson.

– … coming, Lisbeth choked, – … coming.

– It's so strange, the driver mused, not really noticing her hammering his chest with her fists. – I didn't plan on doing a detour. It was a coincidence that I chose this one.

Lisbeth froze. The big man's body shook. Blood flowed from his mouth. The point of a sword stuck out of his chest. The point vanished and all the blood flowed from the hole. The large, dying body dropped to the ground. Lisbeth pushed herself at the car. The masked murderer looked at her with cruel eyes. The gaze turned her to stone. He slapped her, slapped her hard, almost making her lose consciousness.

– Naughty girl, he said. – You won't be naughty again.

She dropped to her knees.

– Please not kill me, she begged him. – I'll be a good girl, serve you well. Please.

– You show promise, he said. – You deserve a pretty collar.

He pulled one from his jacket, and slipped it around her neck.
– You sound so strange, she whimpered, – almost like a boy. Who are you?
– On your feet, slave, he snarled.
She obeyed like in a dream. Nothing seemed real anymore.
But she knew the blood was real. She choked in misery and terror.
He slapped her again. She hardly reacted at all.
– Walk.
She stumbled in front. He was right behind her, giving her repeated slaps on her butt. They all hurt. They all burned.
He pushed her across the field and back into the forest, to a place far from any population center. She made no attempt at resisting.
I'm an obedient bitch, she thought dully.
The forest swallowed them whole.

4

They couldn't carry the swords with them, and used wands instead. The balance was off, but Lillian quickly got used to it.
May sixth was the first real spring day. Lillian and Martin stood on the deck of the ferry to the island in the heat of the sunshine. They had traveled straight from a strenuous day at the university. Lillian's face was flushed in joy and anticipation.
– It never occurred to me that I would enjoy these trips, she grinned. – You're to blame…
It was a great day, the heat thick in the air. The breeze from the sea was just about right, not too hot, and not too cold. Martin wore just a leather jacket on his upper body. The hairy chest and flat belly and muscular arms were exposed. She pushed her nose at his skin and drew a deep breath.
– I'm so… dizzy, she mumbled, glancing around her.
– It's the spring hotness, he remarked lightly.
She struck him in the chest.
– Don't be so damn technical!
She rubbed herself at him, teasing him. She noticed how he hardened below, and her knees grew weak. Her mouth turned desert dry.
– … the toilet? He whispered in her ear.
She nodded fervently, unable to voice a response.
They rushed across the deck, and into the nearest toilet. The heavy steel door opened and closed. There wasn't really that much space to go around, but they managed. Lillian pictured it from the outside, the loud grunts and moans, the very recognizable sounds. She chuckled in double delight as the

two of them rocked the metal structure.

Her face had a pleased, lazy expression when they emerged from the toilet. No one watching them had any doubt what they had done in there.

The ticket master looked downright distressed at them when they paid him. They pretended nothing special had happened. He looked even harder at them.

The ferry reached the quay on the island. Everyone not local rushed into the awaiting buses. The two of them walked east on the main road. They walked through a short tunnel. Cars passed them in both directions. The exhaust made them cough in discomfort.

– By damn, cars should be banned, she swore.

– I've never gotten used to them, he agreed.

The couple continued on the main road until they reached the school at Florvåg, and then turned left and started their steep ascension on the more or less private road. They walked fast and continued north when they reached the top and the football pitch. Lillian did sweat a little, but didn't experience any notable fatigue. They walked through the wilderness and forest areas now, putting the populated area behind them.

Silence descended on them. They could just hear civilization's distant noise. Lillian pictured the terrain in her head, pictured the central trail of the island they moved on, and the coastland population centers on both sides of them.

– Askøy is like a Norway in miniature, she breathed. – It has coastland, farmland, forests and mountains. And the forests are shrinking, while civilization makes its destructive march everywhere. A mirror image indeed. Of everything gone wrong in human existence.

– The eagles aren't the only species that have gone extinct, he said. – More and more are, at an accelerated rate.

Sadness and rage surged through them both.

They made good speed north, even though they deliberately slowed down most of the time. The late afternoon turned to twilight, the twilight to night. They lit a fire and cooked food. She looked at him in the light of the dancing flames, and a catching formed in her throat.

– I'm sorry. I can't enjoy myself, she choked.

– It would be strange if you could, he stated.

And she looked endeared at him.

– They found the car, she said subdued. – They found the dead man that had probably seen more than he should have. But they searched the entire area, every possible hiding place, without locating Lisbeth. We don't know if she's dead or alive.

– My guess is that she is still alive, Martin said, – or they would have found her. He wants us to know.

They trained with the wands. It felt so very satisfying. Lillian reached another deep level of herself. She went at it, at him with abandon, even as she stayed alert and aware. Wood cracked against wood. Sweat poured from her brow, and she got it in her eyes, but she still saw well. She shouted in delight and triumph when they ended it, and her breath slowly returned to normal.

– It's almost like sex, she cried, her instant embarrassment not keeping her from enjoying that ferocious statement as well.

– The warrior is a fundamental part of you, he stated, – of who you truly are, beneath the exterior, the shell, the surface thoughts. It might not express itself in every life, but it's always there.

– Your warrior, she said hoarsely, – fighting by your side.

And that sounded so right. She imagined herself fighting with the sword for real, maiming and killing their common enemies.

She moved for him, and caught his instant interest. Her hands moved, removing her clothing. She touched herself, rubbed her large and firm breasts, imagining that the flame tongues licked her skin. The sensation felt so real. She had become so immediate, so instinct-based. Feverish thoughts grew even more so. She watched him as he undressed, and she grew weak in her knees again. The crisp night air didn't feel cold, didn't fell cold at all. She rushed to him, and smothered him in affection. He grabbed her, grabbed her hard below. She shouted short and sharp.

– Yes, she moaned. – YES.

She was ready already. The low-level arousal had grown to a storm in seconds.

He put her down on her back, and entered her, moved on her. She moved beneath. Everything turned so pleasant.

– I'm a hungry, horny cunt.

She scratched him on the shoulders. Blood jumped from his skin and hit her face. She turned completely savage. Strength flooded her limbs. She pushed him off her, and put him down on the back, and mounted him, pushing him deep into her. He rubbed her while moving back and forth within her. She was rocking up and down on top of him, shaking herself apart. Everything dissolved in a seemingly endless pleasure. She collapsed on top of him, and smothered him in kisses and caresses.

– … savage, she mumbled, – a horny, gratifying savage.

She rested in his arms, knowing there would be more, more, more…

They began fondling each other again. The desire, the craving returned fast and effortless.

– Some men can't handle active women, she said and shook her head.
– I pity them, he said.
She chuckled pleased, as she watched him grow hard again, as she felt herself grow wet and warm and wild. Thought faded, rationality slipped away, and then they were rocking again, dancing again, caught in the heat of the fire. She caught a glimpse of a feral creature in his eyes. A shifting, shimmering being seemingly out of sync with reality. Her happy laughter echoed through the forest.

They started walking again at dawn, and reached the mountaintop of Varden not long after that. Varden was one of the nine mountains surrounding Bergen. Lillian marveled as she looked at the view, the world below.
– I love mountaintops, she cried. – I just love them.
He turned soft-eyed. She noticed and snuggled against him. They kept heading north. On some stretches, the forest seemed endless. On others, they saw more horrible examples of «forest harvesting» and hillside removal.
– It looks so damn ugly, she said subdued. – It's such a depressing sight.
– We need regrowth, he stated, – need rewilding.
She nodded empathically, familiar with the concepts.
– The wilderness should overtake the cities, she stated, – not the other way around.
They were on the same page here as well. That did counter her despair.
The outer world faded further around them, even as it kept reminding them of its presence. The noise stayed with them, even in areas of seemingly untouched forest.
– It's like a drill at the dentist, she remarked. – Except that this burrows into your head and stays there.
They stopped at a hilltop at the center of the island, quite simply called The Queen, for some reason.
– I've always found this a breathtaking view, she marveled.
They could see lots of the western part of the island, all the way to the ocean. They stayed quiet, or mostly quiet for several minutes.
He pulled out his wand from its resting place on his back, and so did she. They began sparring again. Wood hit wood, hit flesh. She noticed the pain when the point hit her arm, but it just made her grin. Her handling the physical pain felt even better than everything else.
Better than sex, she thought. No, not that, but close.
She chuckled while attacking him, while he defended himself. She experienced it like a dance… one of fire and shadow. Yes, that was it. It was as if she could spot both in the air, and as a coating around the wands as

they slid through the ether.

They set out south again.

– Let's do the north another time, he suggested.

She nodded in agreement.

Her endurance seemed endless as they made their way back south. She listened to the sound, the thousand sounds of the forest as they rushed forward between the trees.

– I imagine I can hear everything, she said brightly. – You've done such a great job with shredding the shell of civilization choking my awareness, My Lord.

Speaking like that felt perfectly natural, not really formal at all, but quite casual.

They reached a water of some size when they approached the southern part of the island. Both pulled off the soaking wet clothes and dived into the chilly fluid. She shouted in delight. The nudity didn't turn them on, for some reason. They just enjoyed the bath. She floated on her back and looked up at the sky, watching the clouds drift. A sense of peace descended on her. The thousand sounds of the water entered her ears.

– My senses have indeed been sharpened to an uncanny degree, she noted. – To say I feel aware and awake is a gross understatement.

She chuckled softly. He rubbed her cheek.

Their soft intimacy pleased her, too. Everything about their time together pleased her. They were diving below the surface. Another world welcomed them. They floated above the bottom, experiencing little trouble in keeping themselves down there.

She enjoyed the sensation of them drying each other. The memory of the time beneath the water surface stayed with her. Everything seemed to do so, now.

They dressed in the last set of dry clothes, and took it slow the rest of the walk back to the ferry, hardly sweating at all. The walk seemed totally prosaic. The road was only the road, with cars passing them like buzzing wasps. She shook her head in dismay and wonder.

The ferry reached the quay just as they entered the large open space leading to it. The cars drove off the deck and onto the island. The two of them waited patiently by the land bridge as the passengers left the ferry. They walked inside when the final traveler from the city had left. The ferry crossed the bay. They enjoyed its slow pace.

– We used to play cards during the crossing, she grinned. – Fond memories.

Her father had beaten her when he found out.

It hadn't exactly weakened her resolve to stand up to him.

His strict upbringing had never really worked on her, not even when she was a little girl.

Those memories brought others, deeper.

– It's like some kind of Pandora's box, she said with the remote expression in her eyes. – I'm dreaming about myself having a dream about an even earlier version of myself.

– Yes, he said, – it works in similar ways for me. I believe it does for all of us.

All of us, she thought, knowing perfectly well what he was actually saying.

– The visions didn't really bother me at first. It was like watching a movie then. But now, it does feel real.

– It's like you said, he said. – You know they are real now.

She kissed his hand again. They sat there, in their own bubble of the world, except for the fact that they saw far more than most people. A girl sat on a seat across the room. Lillian watched her, noticed how her eyes flickered anxiously from point to point, and her hands seemed to wander aimlessly and unending back and forth on the table, how she didn't seem to be present in the room at all.

The ferry approached Bergen. The mountains towered above them on three sides. There wasn't a queue to get out on the city side in the afternoon. They left the ferry in a casual manner, and set out on their walk through the city to the eastern mountainside, heading home.

Home, Lillian thought.

– You chose such a great place to live, she said, as they were climbing the stairs of the mountainside again.

– It has recently gained one more attraction, he joked.

She struck him in the arm.

– It's so nice to just walk, she said brightly. – I don't miss riding a bus or a car. Walking is a seriously underestimated pleasure.

She was just talking, running her mouth off, like she had always done.

– We should start applying ointment on your body after hard exercise, he said. – It will make your limbs soft and functional the next morning.

– My great and useful witch, she chuckled.

– You will be an herbal witch and more, too, before long, he said lightly, – become what you're born to be.

More heat and cold flowed through her bones.

– I love that, she declared, – just love that.

The house appeared in their vision. A catching formed in Lillian's throat. They rushed it a bit the last, few steps.

It took only one step inside before his features froze.

– The stench, he mumbled distressed.

She could smell something, too, but couldn't identify its source.

– He has paid us a visit, hasn't he? She said startled.

She watched him, watched him become battle ready, and she did her best to emulate him. He sniffed the air, actually sniffed the air. She would have smiled if he hadn't had the tense expression on his face.

They moved through the ground floor. His eyes moved, focusing on every shadow, every corner.

– He isn't here, now, or I'm fairly confident that I would have sensed him, he stated, – but he has left us… a present.

He rushed up the stairs. She turned cold as she struggled to keep up with him. The light on the bedroom was lit, lit in quite an artistic way. Martin froze a few steps inside it. They could not help but staring at the antique bed. It was painted red. The stench of blood ripped into both pair of nostrils.

Lisbeth had been placed on her back on the bed. She stared at them with dead eyes. A sword penetrated her chest. Her legs had been spread in a parody of an erotic position. Everything had been covered in blood. The bed, the sheets, her body, her hair… But the worst in Lillian's eyes was the smile, a disgusting twisted grin of pleasure.

Lillian heard a scream of terror, despair and rage. It made them jump, and penetrated them to their very bones. She couldn't quite identify its origin at first, but then she could, and began shaking, shaking herself apart.

The scream shaking her to pieces was her own.

Chapter 9

The lights were lit everywhere in the house. The lights outside flashed in blue, only blue.

It makes sense, Lillian told herself. Norwegian police lights are only one color.

Police cars crowded the yard. There wasn't room for a single car more. The air had grown thick with exhaust, humidity and fear. Policemen and policewomen in anti-riot uniform circled the property to keep curious people away. Several of those that had ventured inside puked their guts out in front of the large gathering.

Patronizing laughter echoed across the yard. The stench of blood had mixed with another smell they eventually identified as garlic. That didn't exactly make them feel any better.

– I'm cracking up, a man in uniform shouted, the shout sounding more like a wail.

More shared his sentiment.

– I'm seeing things, a woman whimpered.

Some quite simply fled from the place. They didn't return.

– Why *garlic* of all things? A man in riot gear complained.

A pervasive mood lingered in the air, something going far beyond the stench and the death.

Martin sat by the window in the bedroom. They had removed the body some time ago. He opened his eyes, looking at the word scribed on the wall over the bed.

SAMHAIN

Some people outside had lit torches, and were humming, a dark hum reaching deep into his mind.

Haugli and Nielsen looked at him with suspicion. He acknowledged them, giving them his attention.

– Now, Keller, Haugli spat. – Any idea what this paint means?

– If you're talking about the writing on the wall, that is easy, Martin replied, and misunderstood deliberately. – It doesn't mean anything, not in this context. The Festival of Samhain is a pagan autumn ritual, celebrated in October, before the All Souls Night. This is more a desecration of that, a deliberate insult, if you will.

– That's right, Haugli snorted. – We intended to ask experts, but we already have one on the premises, don't we?

Martin more or less ignored the rhetorical question.

Nielsen held up the bloodied sword packed in plastic.

– I bet you can tell us a lot about this as well.

Gunnar Nielsen. Lillian had informed him of him.

– It's a common, modern sword, mostly used in motion pictures, Martin shrugged. – You can get them anywhere. I favor far older swords myself.

Lillian entered the room, pale and drawn. She sat down at Martin's side. He grabbed her hand and squeezed it.

– I'm okay, she assured him. – I can stand it.

She directed her attention at the investigators.

– You want to ask us questions, she said. – Well, ask away.

Haugli and many of his colleagues turned deep red.

– You can perhaps tell us again about your so-called alibi, one of the five other investigators said.

– The night she was kidnapped, we turned the city upside down, from dusk to dawn, Lillian said. – I bet you can get hundreds of witnesses on that, and even get many of your fellow cops to confirm it. We've been on Askøy for days. I'm confident hundreds of people observed us there as well. Before that several of our friends spent time in our house. Jonathan Mover, Marianne Beckman, Eva Cranner and Ronny Pettersen will be more than happy to testify. Our neighbors can also confirm it. The fact is that we can hardly go anywhere without being noticed. If we carried a body around, they would have seen that easily.

Her voice turned patronizing, very patronizing then.

– You arrived in the country… Haugli checked his notebook, … January third, Keller. The murders started in January. How do you explain that?

– I can't, Martin shrugged. – I can't explain why the murderer chose my place as the place of sacrifice either.

– What was that word again?

– Samhain, Martin said, very helpful.

– Can you elaborate on what you told us earlier? As a scholar, I mean.

– As stated, the word is used completely out of context, probably used to throw suspicion on pagan practitioners. Unless the murderer is a total amateur, and mistook Beltane for Samhain. Beltane, April 30 is also an ancient day of celebration, where all the gates to other worlds are wide open.

He spooked the cops with his presentation. They suddenly developed a very vivid imagination.

– My take on it is that he's a christian set to cast suspicion on heathens. Christians have perverted the old practices for two millennia.

Martin added.

– But the murder happened today, Nielsen said.

– As stated, Martin shrugged, – the man might be an amateur when it comes to paganism, not really being very familiar with it.

– I think you guys should leave, now, Lillian choked. – Lisbeth was one of my best friends, and I wish you good luck in catching the murderer. I find your interrogation of us revolting.

Gunnar stepped closer to her, and attempted to grab her arm. She pulled away.

– Don't touch me, she said icily.

– I don't like your attitude, young lady.

She stared incredulous at him. Was this guy for real? She once again questioned her judgement. She had actually fucked this guy, fucked him several times.

– I guess you want me to feel intimidated, then, she spat at him.

A violent rage threatened to overwhelm her, and she almost struck him, and turned sick and weak in the throes of the adrenaline rush.

– I guess you prefer me as doormat, she said sweetly.

All his colleagues glanced at him.

She studied him, attempting to get something from him, anything, but there was only the surface, the ordinary man, no matter how disgusting.

– Don't contact me again outside official work, or I'll get a restraining order.

He made no verbal response to her statement, but the expression deep in his eyes told her everything she needed to know. She had grown far more astute lately.

The house and the yard turned empty, desolate. Cars and people filed away. Two cops in uniform placed themselves by the road, watching the house.

– I guess we must accept that they're pretending to watch over us, she remarked. – Let them stand there as peacocks, and see how it benefits them.

The tears finally came. She struck her fist at the wall repeatedly. He let her do it for a while, until he grabbed her and hugged her. She kept sobbing hard, making numerous attempts at drying her tears, until no new supplanted those she attempted to dry off her face.

– What horrible human beings these uniformed people are, she said with a quiet rage.

It was like she… she caught something from the air then. She straightened.

– Death touches me, she breathed, speaking with a spooky voice.

She found herself falling into trance on the spot.

– I see you, she mumbled.

She saw a transparent figure levitating in the air and gasped. It wasn't Lisbeth, but someone she didn't recognize. The ethereal face looked startled at her, and faded away in a moment.

Her friends arrived. There were more hugging, choking and mutual comforting. They sat down and had a low-keyed conversation for a while, exchanging memories of the dead.

– She wasn't afraid of anything, Eva said. – I bet she gave the monster a hard time.

That made them laugh.

It did prove to be a catharsis. They sat there until all high and low words faded, and they just enjoyed each other's company.

They started on the extremely unpleasant cleanup. Lillian pushed herself far beyond endurance. Her muscles and limbs hurt. She kept going. They washed the bedroom several times. The stench and taint of blood and garlic seemed to linger no matter what they did. They cut the furniture and the bed into small pieces with a chainsaw. The loud noise settled in their distressed mind. Eva had to run to the bathroom. They heard her puke her guts out in there.

– I loved that bed, Lillian chuckled. – It's a priceless antique. It has belonged to Martin's family for generations.

They looked at her both good-humored and with pity. She felt bad for not being completely honest with them, but she didn't change her mind about it.

All the pieces were loaded into a truck and brought away. The chill surrounding Lillian persisted. Spirits kept displaying themselves to her.

– Do they do it on purpose, she asked Martin in a quiet moment.

– No, you're doing it, he stated softly. – Your heightened emotional stress has made your powers manifest.

– It's amazing that I can listen to that little piece of information without incredulity, she said. – Are you positive?

– I've witnessed it many times before, he said. – I am absolutely sure.

– I feel dread, she said. – From them.

– When you touch the dead, that's inevitable.

I can stand it, she thought.

The job was done. Her friends said goodbye. There were more hugging and caressing and comforting and everything.

– Be careful, Jonathan said. – Be ready.

He knew more than the others. Lillian waved to them as they walked away.

The summer twilight descended on Bergen. She felt it. It buzzed and burned within.

– I can't turn it off, she said, – but I don't want to do so either.

They returned to the inside of the house, to the fresh, antiseptic stench twisting her nostrils.

2

She rested nude on the table covered with soft carpets. Martin applied his ointment on her skin. It felt cold at first, then hot on her skin. She looked with dismay at the greenish stuff in the cup. Both the ointment and the massage worked on her, made her wonderfully relaxed and softened her limbs. She stretched drowsy and joyfully her body subjected to his pleasant treatment.

– Why did Stine want to die? She wondered.

– I'm not certain she wanted to, he replied. – I'm not even certain she did die. I remember seeing her after the ceremony, but can't say whether or not that was her spirit or her physical body. She kept stressing the necessity of the ritual to me. Anything else seemed secondary.

– Even her own life. Wow, that's what I call dedication. She wasn't that old. She had many good years left.

– We will be just as dedicated, he stated.

She nodded wide-eyed, sensing more than seeing the intensity in his words and pose.

– You will use this opportunity to Travel into your own past, he bid her. – You will go as far as possible, beyond as many boundaries and walls as possible. You will learn more of who you are in the glimpses of eternity revealing themselves.

He continued his massage, his oiling of her smooth skin and muscular body. She sensed his interest (his dark desire), and moaned in need. She rested on her belly, and wanted to turn, to face him, but he kept her from moving that much. He began humming. It reached deep within her from the very first moment. The hum turned to a chant. Archaic words she didn't understand caressed her ears, her increasingly feverish mind.

He's casting a spell, she thought startled.

– You won't sleep. You will stay awake. Listen to my voice, to my will. Obey me.

She moaned and complained. She wanted to beg him to possess her, but she could not speak, just reply dully to his command.

– Yes, My Lord. Please, My Lord.

Focus. Find a soundless sound within. Repeat that. Keep repeating that. You are nothing but that sound. Do you understand, vessel?

– Yes!

What are you doing? What are you doing to me?

She nodded, and kept nodding, until her emotions «slowed down» and eventually stopped altogether. The rhythmic movement of his hands changed slowly into something else. The echo in her mind became the same sound, not deviating in any way from the one before it. Her breath changed from panting to deep regularity.

– Lillian Donner. Lillian Donner, can you hear me?

She breathed the confirmation. The voice calling her came from far away, from the end of a long, long tunnel. She rushed towards the light, pulling, shaking the chains binding her.

– Think, Lillian, think far back, beyond your current existence. Even beyond the boundaries of Gudrun's life. Where were you then, human being? Who are you. Who do you want to be?

Can I be who I want to be? She wondered.

The ASC came unprompted with the drowsiness, the deep consciousness imposed on her. She returned to a light trance-like state. The wind seemed to pick up outside, to howl like a banshee in her ears, or in her expanding consciousness. The lights in the summer twilight started flickering in a ghostly glow. The endless twilight turned dark. The Storm gathered strength both within and without. She mumbled silent words in her trance.

I want to live as a witch. I want power beyond imagination. I want to keep rising from the ashes throughout my eternal existence.

She writhed on the table, twisting her body, straining her mind. She was Gudrun standing on the pier waiting for her beloved, but this time she looked in the opposite direction, at the infinitely high and impenetrable wall. She collided with it several times, as she attempted to walk through it.

It isn't there, she kicked herself hard. I have made it, and I can tear it down.

Eternities stared at her while she struggled and bled and burned.

Something happened. She was changing, not just in appearance, but within.

Her eyes grew wide and strange. She pictured herself in an ethereal mirror floating in the ether.

– I was here, she mumbled. – I wrote my name on the wall of Dust and Smoke.

We all did.

She faded before the mirror, and there was nothing there but the empty room, but she still looked into the mirror. The redhead male turned her around, and kept applying the ointment on her hot, glowing skin. She hardly noticed anymore. She writhed in dark desire in his grip, in his soft and strong hands, realizing instantly that his touch, his spell didn't really bring the visions.

She did.

The temple servants oiled the nude body of the young queen. The temple hall turned blurry in her hazy vision.

– Give praise to the ascending goddess, they choired. – Give her your all, and she will return everything.

The young queen was dreaming, twisting and turning in desire and anxiety on the slab covered by soft carpets. She saw herself as a hunter, a warrior chasing a large beast with her arm holding the spear ready to be thrown above her head.

A band of eternal ice stretched out left and right of her. Even Warm Daystar couldn't make it go away, couldn't melt it. A woman independent and proud froze in the warm sunlight. She rode a horse in the land south of the white band. The temple had faded for the young queen on the slab. New, startling sights revealed themselves. The wind tore at her skin, her vulnerable self. The camp around her was lit by tall fires. She found herself on her back on another slab, bound hands and feet, unable to tell how she had ended up here, here on the sacrificial stone. Nameless fear paralyzed her. A shaman chanted his wicked spell, cutting into her like the sharpest of blades. Erling stood by his side with his knife raised. She smiled in ecstasy, in eager agreement. She asked herself stricken how this could be the same fierce female that had been riding the horse.

Erling shouted in savage triumph. The sacrificial knife flashed as he pushed the knife into her hammering heart.

The flame reflected in the shining blade… had the shape of a bird, of giant bird Phoenix rising from its own ashes, and that small fact didn't sound startling at all to her.

Lillian Donner dreamed about the girl dreaming about the hunter, writhing and mumbling in her sleep. Her eyes slid open in the bright morning. She still rested on the table covered with soft carpets, waking up to the scent of fresh flowers. The happy smile touched her lips. She rose from the table, her limbs soft and malleable. She stretched all possible parts of her body. It dawned on her that she could move without effort. The smile lingered on her lips. The memory of yesterday didn't ruin that. The oil, the ointment kept her skin smooth and shiny. She shivered in simultaneous enjoyment and profound terror.

She caught early the heavy steps closing in on her. It happened in such a casual and natural way. She posed for him when he entered the room. She probed herself for signs of shyness, but she didn't find any.

– My King, she greeted him with a muffled voice, hardly recognizing herself in her mind's mirror.

She rushed to him and placed herself in front of him in a humble pose.

– Thank you for sending your untrained witch, your apprentice on a powerful vision quest. You strengthened her to no end. This girl learned so much, even though much remains hidden from her. She wishes to reward her master, wishes it beyond anything.

Heat rose between them, and rose again and again and again. Everything faded away into nothing.

She smiled in bliss at the breakfast table. She devoured the food and drink. She just kept devouring the items on the smorgasbord before her, and imagined she would keep going forever.

– Your witch is a sinner supreme…

Can you see me, father?

– Will we recognize Lisbeth when we see her again?

– I don't know, he replied quietly. – At least not until she has become four or five, when her personality starts emerging and manifesting.

– I thought as much.

She considered it.

– It's like I know the answers to the questions I ask before you reply, she said awestruck.

They returned to the living room. He turned on the television. There was nothing on. She looked curiously at him.

He put on a video. One more American preacher did his pompous speech. She got slightly peeved with him because he had chosen a religious program, but she realized quickly that there was a reason behind it.

He shook. She marveled at that, and wondered what could actually scare him like that.

– Stine warned me about a man, an immortal man. I believe it's him.

– Brian Garret? She asked incredulous.

– The same, he nodded. – The renowned, self-appointed Bishop of California.

– My… father made us children watch him all the time, she said with frost in her voice. – He always spooked me. I never knew why.

– I've followed his exploits for a long time, he said. – He had a different name hundred years ago, and five hundred years ago, but he looked the same.

He looked the same.

– He's like you, like us?

What had by now become a familiar chill passed through her.

Martin didn't have to voice a reply. His expression told the story.

– I believe he has been alive a very long time, he finally said. – I've seen him in my vision quests from ancient times on numerous occasions.

– He looks so familiar, she frowned.

And then she got it.

– He was Erling's master, the one presiding on the ceremony ending with the sacrifice.

– That does not surprise me.

He said.

– SONS AND DAUGHTERS OF LIGHT, Brian Garret cried from his pulpit. – WE ARE CLOSE TO THE FINAL DAYS, WHEN GOD SHALL DESCEND FROM HEAVEN AND GATHER US ALL IN HIS EMBRACE.

– He sounds and looks completely insane, she said, very frosty. – And dangerous, not the least that. I might have seen him as one more religious quack if you hadn't alerted me to his true nature, but I don't think so.

She watched him speak, no longer hearing him, hearing him better than ever, beyond the actual words, to what he was actually saying.

The world, her flesh seemed to fade away to nothing but a tiny heap of ashes, and it was all due to him.

They attended two funerals on the same day, Lisbeth's and Lillian's great, great grandfather. Ronny drove the guys around to both. Lisbeth's was first. Closed caskets were the burial of choice in Norway, and this followed the common procedure to the latter. The guys paid their respects to Lisbeth's parents. Lillian had never met them before. She pretended she had, kept up the appearances for her friend no longer in the coffin. She believed that. It no longer sounded strange to her.

– It must be bad for you, Lisbeth's mother choked, and hugged Lillian. – I admire your composure.

Lillian said something. She forgot what the moment she had spoken.

The priest held his ridiculous speech. Lillian turned it off. She had never been keen on funerals. She wasn't now. Even though her perspective had changed.

The old man's funeral was something else. Her grandaunt followed the script ordained by the dead man to the latter. One of the items on the program was the playing of the 1978 live version of Manfred Mann's Earth Band's Mighty Quinn, the entire long melody, with the extensive instrumental part.

– I've heard it's about *LSD*, a woman whispered to Lillian's mother.

It pleased Lillian to see how her mother turned pale.

Gunnar was there.

– You do need a restraining order, Eva whispered enraged to Lillian, – perhaps even several of them.

On the tombstone was engraved

HE LOATHED AMBIGUOUS STATEMENTS

Lillian started giggling, and she had trouble stopping. In the end, she didn't care.

– This is the funniest funeral I've ever attended, Ronny said brightly when they walked to the van.

There was a wake, which also had its moments. Grandaunt had Mighty Quinn played again.

– This is great, she marveled. – I feel positive that he's dancing happily on his own grave.

She was quite drunk, but not so drunk that she gave up the control of the wake.

– This is the FUNNIEST wake I've ever attended, Ronny shouted from the kitchen.

He was extremely drunk.

Lillian didn't drink much. She still debated with herself if she should until the moment everything ended, and everyone gathered in the library in the large house for the reading of the will. Lillian inherited half of the fortune, and a considerable part of his properties. Many in the family sent her ugly stares. She ignored them.

– You're independently wealthy, now, kiddo, grandaunt stated. – Have fun, do you hear.

– Have no fear, my favorite aunt, the girl replied. – I intend to catch the moment, cease the day in full.

– *Good* girl…

Lillian danced away on light steps. The guys, her friends followed behind her. Martin walked by her side. Her expression softened when she looked at him.

They went home to the house on the mountainside. The guys joined them. Lillian enjoyed that. They watched the news at some point.

The murders had finally grown to become the main story. Haugli's blown face filled the screen.

– I must say that the media's behavior in this case has become quite… questionable, he stated, clearly struggling to stay somewhat calm. – They should know that we can withdraw their privileges at any time if we deem it necessary to continue our crucial investigation.

He got a lot of criticism over that remark, and he apologized, not really apologizing a few hours later the same evening.

– What a pig, Eva giggled.

The days ahead stayed busy.

Lillian's bank account swelled.

– I'm loaded, she marveled. – It didn't dawn on me until now, until I saw the amount on my account.

There were more papers to study and sign. It became a pleasant distraction. Her new lawyer aided her, and Martin watched him like a hawk. The timid man made no attempt at doing anything fishy.

– I've made a list of everything I want to do, she said stunned. – I can hardly believe that I can do them all, now.

He studied her. She couldn't help smiling. He was so easy to read, at least to her. She didn't find that strange. They had spent thousands of years together after all.

– I want to travel, she said with longing in her voice and voice, – travel a lot, catching up on all my lives.

Speaking like that didn't feel strange, didn't feel strange at all.

– That's good, he said. – We need to get out of here, the sooner the better. You're ready. We've stirred up so much in this city that the situation has become untenable for us short term.

– It looks like you've given it some thought as well, she joked. – Where did you have in mind?

– London, he said. – It's so big that we can vanish in it, almost no matter how much we stir up. And it's a melting pot of cultures. You will learn more about humanity and yourself there than almost anywhere else.

A thrill fired through her synapses. She recalled the dream. The future. The unknown, known streets and alleys.

– Erling will most certainly follow us there, Martin said, – but he will more exposed, not less. Anyone familiar we encounter will strand out, and be easier to scrutinize, expose.

– The great tactician, she praised him.

She made a fist with her right hand.

– I will fight him, she swore. – I will kill him, vanquish him to eternity.

– You might just as well take your exam this spring, he shrugged. – We can stay long enough for that.

– It no longer feels important, she mused. – I can learn far more outside the school system, and can spend hundreds of years or more doing it, if I so desire.

She giggled again. She still did when she ran upwards through the crooked road to the top of the mountain. He ran where she always expected to find him, by her side. They ran far into the mountain plains, far beyond the point that had discouraged her such a short time ago.

They stopped and stared at the sunset in the western ocean.

– I see the Phoenix in the sunset, she mused. – I see it everywhere.

– You see it every time you look at yourself in the mirror, he stated. – Everyone does, even though they might not be aware of it.

– I believe that, she said, – but I also think it sounds too simple, that it can't be the entire truth, that there has to be more to it. It feels like a god, a true god to me. We all burn in its fire. We certainly do!

She squeezed his hand.

– Many have worshiped it, he granted. – Way before Ovid and others wrote down the legend. The stories are global, far more distinct than the much later Abrahamic religions. All religions started with one of two things, the worship of the sun and the moon, fire and ashes.

She shivered and couldn't stop.

– The giant bird flew out of the night, he chanted, – and humanity was born.

His voice sounded different. He looked different. She imagined she could see dark flames dance on his body.

And when she looked at her hand, she could see the same dark shimmer there.

They turned around and headed back west. Her limbs burned, and she knew that was a different kind of fire. At her core something far hotter burned.

– The fire is within us, she cried out. – It's worth any hardship to keep burning.

Her words, her proud cry seemed to echo in the air, and she almost stopped running in her astonishment.

They reached the forest of thick, tall trees. She imagined they had entered another world, another realm. The wind blew between the stems, and… and whispered to her. This time, she did stop running. She stood there with a remote expression in her eyes and listened.

– I wanted to write down my dreams, and show them to you, she stated, – but that could be used against us if it ever ended up in the wrong hands, so I remembered them instead. We must be content to keep them orally, for now.

She could measure… threats, picture them in their future, both from Erling and others. He nodded in acknowledgment to her, and pride coursed through her.

– Erling beat me, she snarled. – He beat me slowly to death, and enjoyed every minute of it.

She watched Martin, how rage filled him. She kept talking.

– I was more than a thrall to him. He owned me completely. I was his eager slave. There was nothing I wouldn't do for him.

They returned to the house. She couldn't enjoy the sight and the experience like she had before. The rage filled her as well. They walked straight to the exercise room, and started beating the heaviest sandbags. His hands started bleeding first, but hers followed not long after.

– It's… good that we know the reason for our rage, he gasped. – I've watched many be consumed by it, because they didn't know its cause.

He struck a sandbag hard. It cracked open and dissolved subjected to his boundless anger.

She wondered how any emotion could be worse than this anger, this hatred boiling beneath the surface.

He put herbs on her hands later.

– They feel so pleasant, she mumbled.

She put herbs on his hands. They were slightly worse off.

– I want you to teach me everything you know, she bid him.

– I will, he acknowledged, – but it will eventually be more like remembering than learning.

She understood his point.

– We will learn and remember together, she stated. – We will learn more than anyone before us.

And right there and then, that didn't seem like an empty boast.

– Dark passion burns me, she said. – Dark passion is human.

They had trouble falling asleep that night. It didn't matter how many times they mated. She lost count of that, too, like she lost sense of time itself. In the end, they just crouched there on the rumpled sheets, in each other's arms, unable to achieve more relaxation than a pitiful dormancy. They saw the bedroom, the world through half-closed, swollen eyes. They looked out of the window, as if they stood right in front of it, and didn't crouch on the bed, as the first stir of red dawn revealed itself on the northern sky.

3

People walking back and forth outside at the University Heights distracted Martin Keller as he watched them from Professor Ronaldsen's office.

– You shouldn't blame yourself, he told Ronaldsen. – Most boards manage to invent the proper pretext to fire me eventually. It happens almost every time. I'm interesting at first. Then, I become irritating, and eventually quite bothersome. I and Lillian had planned on leaving after the semester anyway.

Roaldsen looked clearly uncomfortable. He wanted to say something, but didn't. Martin set out to leave.

– Wait, he said. – What do I tell your students? You aren't even allowed to hold one more lecture.

– I won't be able to say goodbye in an official capacity, Martin grinned. – Rest assured I will do so unofficially.

He left.

Lillian Donner set out to have her exam. Martin aided her. He brought even more into sharp focus to her.

– To achieve your goal, you need to distinguish between what you know and what you need to know, he imprinted on her. – If you reveal your greater knowledge, they will judge you to know less. Modern education in a nutshell…

She got his point, sharing his strange grin. She had her exam, gaining her degree, not feeling much either way about it. The next day she, too, had her moment in Ronaldsen's office, when he asked her why she quit.

– I'm not really quitting, she shrugged, – just choosing different ways to learn. I want to travel, see and experience the world in all its beauty and horror.

– You shouldn't do so just because of Keller…

– I'm not, even though he's a great companion. I do it for myself.

The office faded for her as well, and the busy streets took its place. She met Martin outside, and rushed into his arms. They had dinner at a restaurant. She devoured the food, and had to order a second helping.

– It's the harder exercise, I guess, she mused. – I could never have eaten this much more every time and not put on weight.

She ordered desert without really pondering the issue. Martin looked at her again, and she frowned. Something was clearly on his mind, but he didn't offer any illumination.

– The celebration tonight should be fun, she brightened. – There will be an inevitable, somber quality to it, but I can handle that.

Nausea overwhelmed her in seconds. She rushed to the bathroom. His exalted smile lingered in her vision, as she puked her guts out in the toilet bowl.

She returned to him in a rush, a little pale.

– Three guesses what this is, she chuckled.

He hugged her, clearly relieved.

– You feared I wouldn't want it? She asked.

– I wasn't certain, no, he admitted.

– Silly boy…

They shared the happy news with the guys at another restaurant that evening. Everyone congratulated them.

– He didn't wait long before pumping you up, Tove joked in a private moment at the restroom.

Lillian looked closer at her to see if she actually was joking.

– The two of us together didn't wait long, she grinned.

None of those present drank much alcohol that evening, not to celebrate and not to forget. It was, like Lillian had surmised, a somber moment.

– They miss those not here, she told Martin as they walked home. – We will always do that, won't we?

He nodded serious-minded. She kissed him.

– And this was a farewell party, she added. – We won't see again some of them for quite some time. When they return from their holidays, we won't be here anymore.

His eyes flickered. This time, she looked at him. Both smiled.

– I like modern cities even less than those I visited in previous centuries, he admitted. – They're seemingly cleaner, but that's just on the surface, just deception. They're further removed from nature. I can never stop coughing during rush hour. Humanity is moving in the wrong direction, and never seem to get a clue. Even the Sixties, with its brief enlightenment didn't truly wake people up.

The streets and buildings seemed to dissolve around them, as they returned to the house in the mountainside. Memory took precedence over matter. She began lifting weights just a few moments later.

– I need to become stronger, she acknowledged. – I will be a mean, lean wolf when I'm done.

She watched as her body changed further.

– I was always tall for an Asian, she mused. – I guess one of my ancestors was a very tall Chinese, or something. It's so funny that neither the southern nor Asian genes manifested for generations, and then, finally returned with a vengeance. I was teased at school because the kids believed I was adopted, or my mother had played the field.

They rose early the next morning, packed their «camping gear», and headed for the hills. This time, they brought the swords. The walk, the frequent runs brought them far from the most popular trails and routes. They unpacked their swords and began their sparring.

She excelled at the fighting. Certain moves seemed to… come to her, either by instinct or by memory. The body caught up slowly to the mind, or rather to the Shadow, the eternal self.

– I probably should be cautious because of the kid, she mused.

– Not really, he said, – and not by several months. My daughter Jennifer had medical training and both modern and older education. She can monitor you closely.

– Your daughter? Lillian grinned. – I guess you've got numerous kids, huh?

– Too many to count, he admitted, a bit anxious. – Jennifer is the only one still alive that I know of. She's a natural born immortal, like you.

She searched her feelings, realizing that she didn't feel jealous or anything.

– I'm looking forward to meeting her, she said graciously.

He visibly relaxed. She grinned.

They practically lived in the mountains the next few weeks. Summer never seemed to arrive in Bergen that year. The chill kept lingering in the air. They brought a portable radio. There was no important news concerning the killings. The town returned to a kind of equilibrium. They noticed, even though they hardly visited, except by the proxy of the radio.

– It feels strange to experience the world through such a small device, she said.

– People used to gather in living rooms and do that before television, he said. – At least they needed their imagination then.

She looked good humored at him.

He taught her to use bow and arrows. She took easily to that, too. The different parts of the weapon rested comfortably in her hands.

She was riding, crossing a vast plain with an equal amount of male and female warriors. They were definitely Asian. Dust rose between the horses.

The two of them were moving without weapons, except their fists and feet. She remembered other fights. He hit her. She was shocked how little it shocked her. He hit her again. Something broke in her mouth. The taste of blood made her dizzy. The heavens opened op above, the depths below, the vast stretch in front and behind. They made the moves without fighting. He was extremely fast and agile. She struggled to keep up, as usual. The martial arts woke up her body as well.

He taught her to hunt. She followed tracks for days with him chasing behind her. She learned… or remembered. Everything kept awakening within her.

She froze, staring almost directly at a deer through the bushes. It was a young male.

– Do we… kill it? She whispered.

The deer didn't move. She put the arrow on the bowstring.

She raised the bow in a smooth and confident motion. There was a slight, temporary shiver as she was aiming, but not as she let go of the arrow, and it hit the animal in the heart, and the buck hit the wet ground and expired with slowly ending gasps.

– The body remembers, too, she stated with bright, shiny eyes. – That, too, just needed to wake up from its slumber.

They digested the meat around the campfire in the summer twilight. She gorged on it, almost beyond control.

– Your body is changing, he instructed her, – preparing itself for the transformation. The pregnancy makes it even more volatile.

She imagined she felt it deep inside, how bones and tissue changed and reset. Her limbs burned.

The breakfast the next morning brought no relief. The Hunger almost overwhelmed her in its extremity. The feeding ended, and she sat there full and content.

She managed just about to jump on her feet and do a few steps before the vomit flowed from her mouth.

– Fuck, she mumbled. – FUCK!

The morning sickness remained a problem. It continued the next day, and the next, and the next.

– I feel like puking has become my natural state, she mumbled in despair.

She kept up her hard exercise and learning. It actually helped, both as a distraction and in purely physical terms. He oiled and massaged her. The growth pain kept rearing its ugly head, too, making her twist and turn and moan in her sleep. She could now with confidence claim that her bones and tissue grew and rearranged themselves. Each time she put one foot on front of the other, it hurt. Every part of her body did, not merely the parts she was using at the time.

Time stretched on. She could hardly measure it anymore, and she found she didn't care. Other things concerned her. The moments, and the moments between moments concerned, or didn't concern her.

– It is like we have left the world, or at least the modern world behind, she mused. – Everything that used to be so important isn't anymore.

They hardly saw any sign of civilization, and when they did, she just shrugged it off, like dirt.

One morning, when she faced Martin. She had almost caught up to him in height.

– My Goddess, she marveled.

When they one day or one night returned to the house in the mountainside, she imagined they had stayed away for an eternity. Their surroundings outside and inside the structure seemed strange and alien. When she studied herself in the mirror, she saw a tall and muscular creature with enticing hips and curves. She could confirm it to herself further when she encountered old acquaintances and looked down on them from a vantage point.

– Is that you, Lillian? A boy asked incredulous.

– It is me, she replied sweetly.

– I didn't think people grew taller after turning eighteen or something.

– I'm an exception, then, she shrugged.

She noticed it in many ways, the physical just being the most obvious. Her senses had improved. The stench from a burger-joint nearby ripped into her nostrils. She feared she would puke right on the spot, but managed to keep it down.

Both she and Martin waved to the boy as they parted company, but he didn't wave back. She listened to conversation as they moved through the streets, even able to separate the voice from the noise. She turned giddy by the very thought, and feared she would go totally overboard.

They had breakfast at a cafeteria. They chose a table close to the toilet. Wise by previous experience, they ordered a double helping from the start.

– We can afford it, she shrugged and grinned.

She downed the first glass of milk in one go. A glass of orange juice followed suit. She started on the coffee after a few bites of the delicious sandwiches.

– I love coffee, she stated, – love it even more than I used to. I believe I might have grown dependent on it.

Her eyes moved as she fed, keeping an eye on the room, getting a «feel» for it, its layout and potential dangers.

The ancient warrior asserting itself again, she thought.

Every motion caught her eye. She kept listening to the conversation, even as she kept yapping herself. A man with a hat and dark glasses and a coat sat in the other corner. He didn't remove it either, but had his meal in a quiet, unassuming manner.

– It's a cop, Martin enlightened her.

She nodded slowly to herself.

– He could hardly be more obvious about it, she giggled. – At least as someone tailing people.

She turned more sober at the end of the meal, preparing herself for the inevitable.

– I'm so excited, she said subdued. – Is that wrong?

– No! He shook his head. – That can never be wrong.

Their meal ended, virtually at the same moment. She sat there apprehensive and waited. Ten minutes passed. She looked at her watch and confirmed that several times. There was no nausea, no sense of dizziness or anything. She paid for the food.

Half an hour passed. She started smiling.

– Let's go for a walk.

She jumped on her feet, an eager kid. He swallowed hard.

He watched her as she danced and jumped on light feet instead of walking in front of him on ancient ground.

– I feel a pressure in my back, he said.

She nodded, understanding what he was saying.

– Well, the nice policeman is still with us.

Neither of them turned and looked behind them.

– It isn't him, he insisted. – The source is clearly a greater danger.

– Of course, she shrugged, nodding again.

They walked hand in hand from the ancient fortress area, down Øvregaten (Upper Street), passing the Church of Mary, continuing down *Stretet*.

– Do you see anything familiar?

– I do!

She reexperienced what had happened almost thousand years ago. The eagles flew above the town, the small Viking village. Celebrating people ran down the only street there was to welcome the treasure from the sea. There was a mood, an excitement in Bjorgvin these days, a hope of a better life for everyone.

The gray, modern houses dissolved in their vision. The rock was once again covered by green fields. She saw it like that for a prolonged moment, until the modern city reemerged.

He had his head turned away from her, at the surroundings, and the dark, invisible shape following in their tracks.

The pressure in his back turned bad enough to hurt.

Part two: Cold Fire

Chapter 10
Valley of the Kings 1935 CE

Egypt in September. Dry. Quiet.

Martin Keller dried sweat from his brow. He struggled with the excessive heat, unused to it, to the desert. His notable anxiety made it worse. He had sensed it the entire morning, a stirring within.

He and his companion Arnold Monroe found themselves on the western shore of The Nile, a remote landscape with many names, close to the modern city of Luxor, the ancient city of Thebes. They walked alone in the searing heat. Martin regretted not bringing a hat, even though he doubted it would have done much good. He carried a medallion around his neck, an Egyptian pendant, an Ankh. He grabbed it and rubbed it a bit. It burned in his hand.

An old woman had rushed him in The City of the Dead in Cairo, and hung it around his neck. She had spoken a language he didn't recognize. The sight of her black eyes still burned in his eyes.

Then, she had handed him another identical medallion and chain. She had put it in his palm and closed his hand around it. That one, too, had burned his skin.

– She looked so familiar to me, he told Monroe. – Her eyes met mine, and it was as if I had known her my entire life.

He had turned around to speak to Monroe, joke about it all. When he turned his eyes back on the woman, she was gone, seemingly vanished in the very air surrounding them.

– She clearly wanted money from you, Monroe shrugged.

– But she didn't ask for any, Martin insisted.

– I guess she lost her nerve.

Monroe shrugged.

Martin walked fast, so fast that Monroe had trouble keeping up. He had his attention directed forward, and hardly noticed the man struggling in his tracks. There was a slight rise in the terrain. Martin stopped at its top, and had a great view of the valley below. He spotted the tomb of Tuth Ankh Amun.

Tuth Ankh Amun had reigned as pharaoh for a short period during Egypt's eighteenth dynasty. His last name had originally been Aton, one given to him by his father-in-law Amenhotep, a pharaoh worshiping the sun god. Tuth Ankh Amun put a stop to that. He moved his residence back to Thebes, a city that had long since been the seat of the Pharaoh. Amenhotep IV had resided in Amarna.

The tomb was discovered, excavated and plundered in 1922 by Lord Carnavon and Howard Carter and companions. Tuth Ankh Amun's mummy and many treasures were removed from the site, and brought to England. Kjell had read about the «remarkable find» in the newspapers, and had visited British Museum to take a closer look. It had become more than that, much more. He had stood on the floor, among the mummy and all the objects, and felt like someone... spoke to him. Not with words exactly, but impressions, sensations translating into words.

He had been pulled back to Egypt. all kind of emotions had surged through him, fear, longing, desire, boundless curiosity, all of the above and more. He had never quite experienced anything like it before, not in a thousand years. Contradicting emotions kept surging through him.

During the following years, he became Martin Keller, the archeologist. He had created his reputation from scratch with breakneck, but to him safe expeditions, like a true English «gentleman». He had approached the Carnavon expedition like a patient predator, diving beneath the surface, seeking behind the fame and glory and the official version.

Lord Carnavon had died under mysterious circumstances, not long after the excavation. That hadn't created much attention, but when others that had ignored the inscription by the entrance started dying one by one, the panic started spreading among the survivors. One strange death after another followed the first. Very few died what could be said to be a natural death. Almost all of them had died by now. Howard Carter was still alive, thirteen years after the breaching of the tomb. Rumors had it that he was hiding at an undisclosed location, scared to death by everything and everyone. Perhaps he had suffered the worst punishment of all, a living death devouring him with each new breath. He hadn't escaped the curse, the Curse of Tuth Ankh Amun.

Monroe kept gasping, never really catching it. Martin froze. He held up a hand.

– What is it, Monroe said, gasping like a fish on land.

– Quiet. Can't you hear them, the voices whispering in the wind?

– Is there any wind? Monroe frowned.

The Ankh seemed to glow in Martin's hand.

– Karama, Martin said.

– Huh?

– Her name is Karama. She's a priestess at the temple in The City of the Dead. I heard someone at the bazar speak about her in reverence.

– It will protect you, she had told him.

Understanding the ancient tongue seemed so prosaic, such a given, now, like no task at all.

– You're at an end of a journey that has lasted twelve-thousand years, she had told him, – perhaps even fifty thousand. I can't remember properly yet, but I know I will.

She had spoken to him with such elegance and rationality, not like a local crazed priestess wanting his money at all.

– I know you, he had whispered in the wind.

And that conclusion didn't feel far-fetched at all.

The man that would never grow old found himself west of Thebes, the high seat of the ancient kingdom, approaching what had once been Tuth Ankh Amun's tomb.

– I hear something, Martin said cautiously.

– You can't smell hidden treasures as well?

Martin didn't reply. He began making his way down to the tomb. It was quite the stretch. The sun had reached the horizon on the westside of The Nile when they reached the target. Large parts of the valley lingered in shadow.

They removed their rucksacks and set camp, lighting the fire.

– It looks like a ghost town without any houses, Monroe mused.

Martin stared at the dancing flames, at the flickering shadows on the ground. He sat down with his feet crossed. Monroe faded to him, as if the man had vanished from one moment to the next. Martin focused all his attention, all his enhanced senses in one direction, at the dangerous, irresistible awaiting him in there.

He had rarely used his abilities deliberately through the centuries. Now, he did. This, whatever it was, was personal. It concerned him very much. He was confident about that much, at least.

The wind began blowing in earnest. It seemed to start from nothing, come from nowhere. It hardly touched Martin, but practically shook Monroe. The man choked. It just slipped out of him.

– Come, Martin bid him.

The firehair rose, and started walking into the dark.

– I'll never believe in any hocus pocus, Monroe claimed anxiously. – No way! What do you expect to find? Everything has been removed long ago. Whatever is left has no value to speak of.

A sharp motion of Martin's left hand stopped him cold. He didn't speak again.

The inscription above the doorway seemed to fill their complete attention. Martin had no difficulties reading and understanding the ancient hieroglyphics:

«Death will come to those who disturb
the sleep of the Pharaoh».

The two men stepped inside, crossed the threshold with oil lamps in their hands. Monroe stumbled after the man leading on. He suffered major difficulties on the uneven ground. Martin didn't. His eyes stayed wide open. He saw quite well, both with his eyes and other senses. The tomb seemed empty, but he knew something both giving him pause and attracting him remained. The rock wasn't just rock. He had never experienced anything similar, not even when he guided by the old shield maiden had done the purification ritual.

The emotions, the lingering emotions he received from his surroundings hit him like a storm, exactly like he would imagine an overwhelming power resting in an ancient grave chamber. He heard Monroe's lamp hit the floor, and that the man ran off, fleeing the place in mindless panic, and it didn't seem important at all. Chaotic impressions and sensations assaulted Martin. They didn't just come from the outside, but also from within.

The flames rose from the floor. He believed they would surround him like they had done before. They didn't. But he sensed them, sensed the power and the glory, life and death, fire and ashes. The dark flames fought to grow bigger. Whatever rested here didn't give energy, but took it, devoured it like a sponge... if it was given the opportunity, if he allowed it by fighting it. He backed off. He didn't run, but returned slowly to the darkness outside. The moon and the stars had moved significantly on the sky, above and below. Monroe stared at him, and his skin grew from pale to transparent. It was almost funny.

The loud scream echoed many times back and forth through the valley.

Kamara waited for him at the end of the field.

– You know my kind, he said. – Have there been others here with the same impact?

– Others, yes, but not like you, she replied, speaking Coptic. – They found... nothing. They caused only tiny ripples compared to your waves.

Monroe caught up with him. Martin turned and faced him.

He turned back and Karama had faded away again.

– Stine, he said aloud. – Stine and so many others.

Monroe looked at him as if he wasn't in his right mind. He looked more than a little bit distressed.

They started on the long way back to the river's western shore.

– What did you see?

– I? Monroe replied with a shriek. – Nothing. Absolutely nothing. Not in that heap of stone, or when you returned to the outside. We're just imagining things, that's all. The so-called curse that supposedly struck down Carnavon and the others is just more bullshit, like I kept telling you before we traveled to this godforsaken place. I don't believe any of that supernatural shit. No way, I say.

Martin couldn't hold back a patronizing dark laughter. Monroe shrunk in his tracks.

They reached the western shore, and crossed the river by boat. They returned to Luxor, to Thebes and the Winter Park Hotel, an amazing structure speaking to Martin of both the near and ancient past.

– We're right in time for breakfast, Martin said excited. – Very good. I'm famished.

His companion kept looking at him with his glum face.

They had a shower, and a change of clothes.

– I always look so funny in a suit, Martin remarked.

Monroe didn't respond, hardly more than a pale shadow by his side.

Martin stepped out on the balcony, and something shifted. He didn't see Luxor, but saw Thebes, saw *Waset* in its heyday. It was an amazing sight. He saw, or rather experienced the Karnak temple. That was the vantage point where he experienced the city.

They walked down the stairs and had breakfast. Martin noticed the anxious mood and glances immediately. His expedition to the other side of the river Styx hadn't gone unnoticed. That did please him, somewhat.

His appetite remained something else. It had stayed insane since that walk through the fire in the Norwegian mountains. Monroe hardly touched his food. He consumed lots of wine instead.

The staff photographed the guests many times during a given stay. The giant flashes lit up the room almost constantly. Most didn't mind. This was a world-famous destination, and people found it appealing to have a chance of being a part of the future walls. Martin did, too, but his reasons were slightly different than most other guests. People might come here, he figured, and might recognize him. The very thought made chills and heat pass through him.

The two of them looked closer at the photos later. It was an amazing collection of famous and well-known faces.

– That's Aleister Crowley, a man told his wife, – «the wickedest man in the world».

She didn't say anything, but it was evident to Martin that she didn't share her husband's fascination with the man on the wall.

The two traveling companions did the walk through town, both the ruins and modern city, in broad daylight. It didn't seem to matter. Martin imagined there was always night here.

Monroe kept glancing at him, even more than the hotel guests had done. It dawned on Kjell Gudmundson that the man could see something strange when he looked at him.

– What do you see? He asked again.

The other didn't respond, but just kept looking straight ahead with an empty stare in his eyes.

Martin felt excitement. He had believed that the other wasn't anything special, now he realized that wasn't necessarily true. He wanted to speak about it, but held his tongue.

– My feet are killing me, Monroe complained.

He complained a lot.

Martin felt fine, felt better than good. His legs didn't feel like they had walked many, many miles the last week. It pleased him to note that he had stayed in shape.

He looked for Karama, but didn't see her anywhere, and he presumed he would have at this point.

They returned to the hotel early for dinner in the la Comiche Restaurant, one of the hotel's five dining spots. Keller wanted to be there, wanted the great experience even more today.

They entered the room at late twilight. A staff member snapped their photo just as they did. Monroe almost fell. Martin had to grab him to keep it from happening.

– I'm famished, Martin joked.

And he was. They sat down by the table and ordered the first course.

– I expect to have the full dining experience, and then some.

Monroe ordered wine, only wine. Keller shrugged.

Keller kept feeding while Monroe kept drinking. He emptied the first bottle and ordered another. It didn't seem like he could become really drunk. The alcohol seemed to dissolve somewhere within. Martin looked at him with envy.

– No way, Monroe mumbled. – No way I'll believe in ghosts and shadows.

– Do you recall the first time we met, Arnold?

Keller said, his fingertips touching.

– It was in 1912, Keller said, very helpful. – I wasn't Martin Keller then. Neither was I Russel Kellerman. I «died» in the accident, and you helped me transition into a new life.

Monroe looked very vexed at him.

– I know all that, he snorted. – I'm not stupid.

Aggression was also pretty common in these matters, preferable to admission of the truth, it seemed. Keller wanted to stop, but his rage kept building.

– Shall I tell you why I keep doing this? Because my acquaintances eventually start casting me long glances, and wonder how I can stay so youthful. The name I used until 1912, I had used so long that I had to color my hair gray at the temple. You read about him, right? You traced him back to 1870.

The voice had gradually grown more intense. It cut into the man across the table.

– Why are you telling me this?

– I want you to admit the truth. My patience has run out. You're the only mortal who has known me through three of my lives. Now, tell me what you saw.

The last sentence erupted like a quiet roar from his throat.

The bottle slipped from Monroe's hand, and hit the floor. It broke and the content floated across a vast circle, crossing the boundaries of several tables.

– I don't know, he mumbled. – A shape around you… emerging from your body…

He practically jumped from his chair and rushed out of the restaurant.

The staff approached the table. Keller put discreetly a bill in the head waiter's hand.

Martin sat there while they cleaned the floor, feeling both rotten and enraged. It pleased him that he had forced the other man to admit the truth. He realized that the consuming Hunger within had grown stronger.

He caught the loud sound of breaks and a crash from what he perceived to be far away, but just had to be right outside. He jumped on his feet, too, and rushed down the stairs and outside. The stench of blood already overwhelming grew even stronger.

Two cars had crashed front to front. Burned and broken bodies had been distributed all over the sidewalk. Arnold Monroe had been squeezed between the two cars. His body kept burning, displaying quite a bit of its skeleton. People began screaming in distress. Several women fainted. The collective scream seemed to spread through the streets of the modern city, and echo back in time between far older buildings.

Kjell heard the scream, saw the body long after he had removed himself from the site. He crouched on the bed in the hotel room. His eyes stayed open. He knew he wasn't sleeping, even though he was most certainly dreaming. What he saw had nothing to do with the room where he currently found himself. Its walls, floor and ceiling dissolved around him.

He had returned to the street. Gudrun was there as well. She sat in one of the burning cars, and couldn't get out. He attempted to save her, but the flame, the fire devoured her. He pulled back stricken.

The beyond chaotic site rearranged itself, reforming to Bjorgvin, to Kjell Gudmundson's place of birth and adolescence. Faces filled his vision. They were him, all him, in various forms. He couldn't believe how many there were.

– You will find her, Karama told him. – And you won't see her grow old and die.

He wanted to protest her ridiculous assertion, but knew the futility of that. She wasn't there.

He saw Gudrun suffer again, like he had done many times, until the memory of her had faded to the back of his mind. He saw Erling stand above her with the wicked smile painted on his face.

I WILL SIT WITH THE GODS AND LAUGH AT YOUR PATHETIC GRIEF. WHEN I FINALLY COME FOR YOU, YOU WILL BE AN EASY MATCH. YOUR HATRED IS NOTHING COMPARED TO MINE. I WILL WIN. I ALWAYS WIN…

Martin whimpered in his dormancy. The whimpers slipped from him in an even flow. The dreamscape shifted again. A modern city supplanted the small village. He saw a very modern city, and he realized that he didn't see the present, but the future. Large ships, or rather rockets pierced the sky. He had read about a crazy genius by the name of Robert Hutchings Goddard that wanted to send his rockets in orbit around the planet, and also to Mars. A smile transformed the features of the sleeper. He saw sea and land from high above, but it didn't move. He saw Gudrun in the modern Bergen. He had known its name for quite some time. He found it absolutely amazing that he had. He watched her rush to him with open arms, saw her run through dark, dancing flames.

And then he understood.

2
Madrid 1570 CE

Madrid in the fall was drowning in rain and strangled in heat and fear. Kjell Gudmundson dressed in front of Julia d'Abo. She rested in bed with a content grin on her face.

– You're such an enduring beast, Pietr, she said lazily. – You brighten my days and nights to no end.

He called himself Pietr van der Haart, now, a medical doctor, a practitioner of medicine from the Netherlands, a part of the giant, worldwide Spanish empire.

She was a widow of a high cleric at the imperial court, and enjoyed her new-won freedom to the max.

– Perhaps we should marry, she pondered. – We would be able to show ourselves together in public, and wouldn't have to skulk in the shadows anymore.

– Would you obey and submit to your husband in all things? He said ironically.

– I would be a humble and devoted wife, she said sweetly. – I would love my husband to be strict with me, and would cherish the many red-haired offspring flowing from my loins.

He walked to her and kissed her on the lips. She clung to him. He was prepared for her if she wanted more, but she was spent after yet another wild night and morning.

– Mmm. The witch wouldn't have to give me those horribly tasting potions anymore either.

He looked out of the window. It was still dark outside, dark enough to slip away unnoticed. He walked to the door and turned briefly.

– Will I see you tonight?
– It's very likely, he shrugged.
– You cruel boy, she pouted.

He walked out the door and closed it behind him. This was quite the high-standard house, large enough for the servants to live in the other wing of the building. The cleric had left his widow quite wealthy. Pietr walked down the massive staircase. The entrance door opened. Inez Velarde had her own key. They met hallway in the stairs. She curtsied before him with lowered eyes.

– Master Pietr, she greeted him subdued.
– Inez, he said, and continued on his way down.

She wore the pretty much common clothes of her family, her class. Her father was a fairly successful tailor from the lower nobility.

He turned. She noticed and turned, too.

– Have your father found a suitable match for you? He joked.

She was twenty-three, considerably older than the average wedding age. Her father had despaired of finding a proper suitor for her.

– No, Master Pietr, she replied and reddened.

Inez also came from a long tradition of Wise women. Pietr had sensed that the first time they met. Her father didn't know that his wife and all his children were witches. It was quite funny, or would have been, if the situation for witches weren't so dire.

– Too bad, he said.

He waved to her from the door. He closed and locked it behind him. He had a key, too.

It kept pouring outside. He put on the hood, and walked in stealth mode the first block, before putting on speed. On the low rise, the ground had turned black, covered in ash. The stench of smoke, of burned flesh still lingered in the air from yesterday's witch-burning. The House of Terror rose beyond it, the high seat of the Holy Inquisition, «The Hammer of Witches». Nausea did assault Kjell like a hammer. Terror and rage and a thousand other raging emotions surged through him. He almost lost it that very moment.

Madrid drowned in terror, in fear of the Holy Catholic Church. The entire continent of Europe did.

Pietr van der Haart walked along the river Manzanares to reach his abode faster, pushing through the labyrinth-like streets where everything looked the same.

Madrid had a population of 25 000 people. Philip the Second had made it Spain's national capital only nine years earlier. Philip was a strong supporter of the Holy Inquisition, and he would have been present at all the burnings in town if he hadn't been on an ongoing warpath of conquest.

Pietr returned to his modest home, locking himself in with a flickering glance at his surroundings. He opened his doctor's office for the day on the ground floor of the house. As a medical doctor, a practitioner of medicine, he balanced on the edge between respect and condemnation… or worse. He didn't need to prepare anything. He just left the door open, and that was that.

The night had been wild, as usual. Julia had scratched him, making deep wounds on his shoulders. They itched and burned, even as they healed prematurely. He had enjoyed a deep sleep.

The dreams, the nightmares had come, inevitably. He was burning, and he knew it wasn't a dream, but a vision, a memory. He had burned before, and he didn't understand that, since the first, official public burning of what the church now called witches, heathens and the servants of Satan hadn't happened until long after he had become immortal.

It didn't seem like the usual premonition either. It still left him sick as a dog.

He received his first patient, a man dressed in rags. He mostly got fairly wealthy patients that could pay for his services, those not having access to the royal court physicians or similar. He treated this man, and the few poor daring to venture here without charge.

He had learned the not quite acknowledged craft from some of the few and rare Dutch physicians before leaving the country, among them an empiric by the name of Margaret Kennix. She had taught him many useful things, both outside and inside the burgeoning profession, among them how to learn from experience, making him realize stuff he hadn't consciously considered before. It had proven useful many times, and that had given him a limited influential position here. Julia had certainly appreciated his services. A brief smile crossed his lips.

The man just needed an ointment for his open, festering wounds. It could be something far more serious, but Pietr's limited skills as an herbal witch had so far taken him in other directions. Inez was teaching him her superior skills, but they could hardly do that outside the dark, empty spaces of the city.

Other, fairly wealthy, influential men sought out him, in his worn office, on this rainy day. He went through the motions as they did, distracted, not really there. He pulled himself together. His patients didn't really care or notice, but he had learned repeatedly the danger of inattention during critical moments.

He sighed with relief when the day ended, and the darkness returned to the petrified city. He visited a tavern a few blocks away. Travelers and coachmen spent the night there, and Pietr was eager to hear unfiltered news from the world. He bought ale and sat down at a deep corner table, well aware of how certain people would interpret that.

Two Dutch coachmen had a merry conversation two tables away, and he had no trouble hearing what they were talking about.

– Spain is a worldwide empire, one muttered, – and it's a horrid place of the darkest fear. As enlightened as a man sitting alone in an unlit room at night. What a waste.

– Philip is busy with conquest, the other mumbled, – leaving his kingdom in debt and ruins.

The Spanish navy had conquered the Philippines, a major country far away five years ago.

– Perhaps we shouldn't be so accommodating, the first man mumbled with flickering eyes. – Perhaps we should consider other options?

Among other things, this was a frequent spot of sedition. Pietr felt anticipation surge through him.

A strong urge made him consider joining the two men. He held himself back.

Others in the room entertained similar ideas. The king wasn't really a popular man in Spain proper either, using an abundance of the country's finances on war, leaving large parts of the population destitute.

Pietr did encounter some acquaintances, and they had a few ales, more than a few ales together. They got drunk. He didn't, as usual. He needed far more and far stronger stuff to get drunk. It was an ongoing joy to him how he could ingest far more alcohol than most others without ending up under the table or similar.

The other two, those that had entertained each other with such interesting stories didn't either, and that told him something, told him that they were quite serious in their intentions, and wouldn't risk revealing themselves.

He stumbled a bit, just a bit, on his way home. The river looked dark and deep when he walked on the embankment. He almost lost his footing and fell into the deep, dark waters. His walk paused, and he turned, and looked closer at the dark river. It seemed different, somehow, as if it wasn't the same flowing waters he had looked at just moments ago.

His feet moved, even as his mind seemed to linger by the river. He had experienced such moments of dislocation before, but hardly this pronounced.

Inez waited for him in the dark alley by his home, just a dark shape in the night. He pretended not to see her, and just proceeded to open the door and step inside. She rushed to him the moment he did. The door slid close behind them.

They kissed and caressed each other slowly, tenderly, wild. They stepped back from each other for a moment. She had dressed in the best clothes her father could provide for her, and looked stunning.

She didn't really look like a Spanish woman, or Spanish at all. Her skin was significantly darker. Her features also resembled more of what he had seen of southerners further east, Turks and even beyond that, Palestinians. He recalled that men from the southern dunes, the Moors had invaded this land long ago, breeding with natives, turning their skin dark. A detail caught his attention.

– Your siblings don't have the eyes?

Inez Velarde had eyes glowing in dark fire. He had never seen anything similar before, but they still looked strikingly familiar to him.

– They aren't my siblings in blood, she said earnestly. – I and my brother Carlos are the children of a couple befriending my mother in her youth. Our parents are long dead.

– But your brother doesn't have the eyes?

– Not yet, she replied calmly, with pride in her eyes and voice.

She held up the hand with the ring, firering, with the eyes of a dead relative in the glass container.

– The eyes are a sign of our wretched blood, our rejection of the church and everything it stands for.

She chuckled when she saw his expression.

– You have heard about us…

He had. Whispers in the dark. Fearful voices and flickering eyes in daylight. Lillith's children. The demon children. The Janus Clan. The *ShadowWalkers*.

– We're hunted, she said subdued. – Our parents were killed defending us from the hunters, the riders at dawn.

– No wonder your father has trouble finding a husband for you, he joked somberly, the familiar catching forming in his throat.

She didn't take offense, but smiled sensually to him.

– I've been waiting for the right man, she said sweetly, blushing hard.

She had experience, but not that much. The young girl had been taught modesty with a hard hand, and much of that remained. He grabbed her and pulled her close. She started breathing faster. He kissed her. She returned the kiss.

– I won't use the potion this time, she declared.

– We must leave, he said, – as fast as possible.

She nodded in solemn agreement.

– I will follow you anywhere, My Liege.

Her hands moved, started removing her clothing. She displayed herself to him as she did. He started undressing, too, not taking his eyes off the enticing creature offering herself to him.

She stood nude and naked before him, rubbing her large, firm breasts, a bit distracted, keeping her attention on him. He noticed her gasp when he pulled down his pants, and exposed his cock. It did affect her, and she made no attempt at concealing it.

– I feel like I know you, she said, – like we've met many times. When I look at you, I don't see you as you are now, but countless other faces. It's disconcerting, delightful…

He had undressed as well. She set out to cross the gap between them. He met her halfway, and grabbed her shoulders, squeezing them.

– Yes, rough, My Lord, she moaned. – Please, *rough*. I'm not the typical, frail human female. I can take it.

He traced his finger on her muscular, curvy body almost as tall as his. She writhed in his grip, not content to leave it to him. She rubbed herself against him, teasing him, certainly not blushing anymore.

She grew notably more aroused with each new movement. There was no pretense here. She didn't make excuses for her desires. They fondled each other in what was to an increasingly degree automatic movements.

– I've never met anyone like you, she gasped.

I was going to say that, he thought feverishly.

Her stench ripped into his nostrils. He lost it, and pushed her at the wall, and grabbed her below. Her moaning turned loud. She was ready, more than ready, turning wild in his arms. He pushed her up on the wall with his hands on her hips, pushed himself deep into her. She started scratching him on the shoulder. He knew that, even though he didn't feel it, didn't feel the pain.

– Wretched Madonna, she cried. – That horny whore.

He had discovered that she loved swearing and blasphemy and had developed an entire personal range of vocabulary in that regard. It spurred him on.

– Mi hombre, she mumbled, – mi gran hombre.

The long black hair clung to her wet skin, even as it kept dancing in the air. She rocked as he pulled in and out of her, back and forth in her hole. Her limbs shook like that of a doll.

– Wild man, she moaned. – BELOVED WILD MAN.

Her words turned unintelligible, just an endless flow of screaming and moaning. The remaining reason left them both. He seemed only to push, push, push, and it grew so very pleasant for them both. They dropped to the floor, and smothered each other in endless affection. He rubbed her cheek. Her eyes both darkened and softened.

– I want more, she said softly, – much more, but I can't fall asleep. I need to get home before first light.

She climbed onto his lap, and put her arms around his neck, giving him slow, lingering kisses. He hardened, squeezed between her skin and his skin. Her eyes turned big and wet. She began rubbing her butt, her entire body at his.

– I'm such a sinful girl, she mused happily. – I've always been. I remember ancient times and us, all of us.

He grew to full size again. She looked at it with feverish, predatory eyes. Her features shifted in his vision. She impaled herself on him, and screamed short and sharp.

– The pain, she moaned. – The *pain*…

She began rocking up and down on him. He began pushing back. Her moans turned into wails. He pushed his palms at the floor, and used that as leverage. Her moans and wails drove him crazy. They rolled across the floor, while he stayed within her. He stopped them, and put her down on her back. She clung to him. He resumed the pushing and pulling. He lost sense of time, of his surroundings, seeing only her sweaty, shifting features.

They had mated many times. They rested totally spent on their back. Her eyes slid close. He slapped her on the butt. Her eyes grew aware again, and she sent him a grateful look.

She cleaned herself with water from the sink, rubbed herself, repeating it several times. He watched her. She reddened when she noticed. She kept displaying herself, signaling that she was his with every single glance and move.

They said their goodbyes. She wore the dress again, not exactly looking like the honorable young lady that had arrived here hours ago.

She kissed him on the cheek, and slipped out into the night. He pictured the route she would walk. It wasn't that far. She should be okay. He resisted the urge to follow her home.

He cleaned himself a bit, too, just removing the «worst» of it. The huge grin lingered on his face. He walked to the bedroom, to the made bed. Moonlight brightened the floor, brightened the city as he looked out of the window. He glimpsed the bed through half-closed eyes. He fell asleep before his head hit the pillow.

3

He woke up in bright daylight by hard, anxious hammering on the door. He recognized that sound, having heard it many times before. His feet and body moved, dressed on instinct, racing across the floor on bare feet. He recognized Carlos's breathing. Instincts polished through centuries of living dangerously woke effortlessly. Carlos was alone, even more beside himself with each new breath.

Kjell opened the door.

– They took her, the boy gasped. – They took her to the Dungeon.

Horror beyond words ravaged the seasoned Viking warrior. He put on his shoes, and they were on their way.

– They will torture her and burn her at the stake, the boy cried, hardly able to keep his voice down.

He was six years younger than his sister, not quite an adult, or at least not fully grown.

They made their way through the streets. The fairly short stretch seemed endless. The turning of each new corner seemed to repeat itself, as if they were not making any progress.

The castle seemed to appear in front of them, towering above them like an unsurmountable mountain. It was as if Kjell saw it for the first time, the massive guard duty, the extreme security measures. He imagined there was no air, no space between each soldier.

He stopped. Carlos did, too. He shook his head. The boy understood. His expression grew even more naked. They kept going, pretending to have business elsewhere.

They returned to Pietr's house. He grabbed the boy and stared at him, making him pay attention.

– They will torture her in a room with a window, he stressed. – They want everyone to hear her. Do you understand? Can you stay calm?

The boy shook. He nodded with wet eyes.

The long, dreary and horrible days began. They walked there often, deliberately. The Viking warrior kept studying the defenses around the castle. He heard even more soldiers march inside the giant, fortified structure.

They heard her scream, heard her horrible wail. He certainly did. He practically experienced her torture as it happened, and didn't know if it was due to him or her.

He closed his eyes halfway, suspecting it was both.

Frustration kept riding him, as he kept prodding the defenses, looking for any chink in the armor, in vain. He made a plan where he took the place of one of the guards, but realized quickly it was just one more fool's errand. The soldiers knew each other. Their faces were quite visible. They didn't wear helmets. There were frequent inspections. Only small rodents could get inside without being spotted.

They had drugged her with an extremely effective variant of the Hammer of Witches. They had chained her. She could hardly move without help. Her wounds burned, clouding her mind further. It was one of the times he cursed his extended awareness.

He studied the boy. He seemed to handle it somewhat, in spite of the occasional peak in emotions and the tears in his eyes. There was something stoic over him. And then it wasn't. Pietr rejoiced when he spotted the flares of dark fire in his eyes. Even if he should be the last of the Janus Clan, he wouldn't be for long.

Every new morning and sometimes even at night, the people living in central Madrid woke to the horrible wails of pain and desolation. Kjell slept even less than usual, hardly slept at all. He looked with dismay at the pale swollen face in the dusty mirror.

The final day of the Burning Court arrived. Soldiers in heavy armor left the Castle of Terror, and started building the bonfire on the rise nearby. The ground stayed dark, stayed black, stayed a sick, ashen color. Excited people gathered around the rise. They saw this as a day of celebration. Anticipation filled them. They began chanting.

BURN THE WITCH, BURN THE WITCH, BURN THE WITCH…

Kjell brought his sword to the burning. It was pretty much customary, and didn't bring much attention. He watched the twisted faces with a contempt he could hardly conceal. A shift in the crowd caught his attention. The procession approached. The nuns and priests walked first, then the executioner with the convicted. The crowd shouted in anticipation and excitement. The holy men found their seats under the black sun. The archbishop raised his hand and silenced the crowd. They had learned good behavior through many other courts.

The wagon left the castle. The woman doomed to nourish the fire had been chained to its roof. One hundred soldiers accompanied her.

– The heavy presence of soldiers has become mandatory after several unfortunate escapes and assisted liberations right in front of his holiness the archbishop and his priests, a man whispered to his companion close to Pietr.

Inez stood tall and proud, even though she couldn't help crouching a bit in the pain brought on by her wounds and general ill-treatment.

– This is a great day, the same man whispered. – Inez Velarde is a wretched witch with access to the royal castle. She used her satanic powers to poison members of the Court.

Pietr wanted to strangle the man on the spot.

Inez looked with cold contempt at the crowd, and her eyes didn't waver when she passed the Burning Court, the men who had convicted her. Pietr saw how she shivered, but doubted that anyone else saw it. She had been brought low, but they hadn't been able to break her.

She hadn't made a confession beyond the rudimentary. She hadn't snitched on anyone.

The thought brought instant shame and even stronger rage to him. He cursed his helplessness, his inability to help her, to even give her basic comfort in her beyond horrible suffering and terror.

He had watched other young girls in her position. They hadn't really been present in their skin. She very much was. She had retained her dignity. And he knew she would spit in his face for him thinking that.

A big soldier began beating a big drum. It vibrated in the air, in flesh, in the Shadowland.

They brought her to the stake and tied her to it, tied her so hard that she could hardly breathe.

Pietr made fists so hard that they hurt. He stood still.

His Holiness, the Archbishop raised his hand again. The drumming ceased. The crowd turned quiet.

– This is a holy deed, the man shouted with pompous holy wrath in his voice. – A witch, a servant of Satan is receiving her well-deserved punishment. GOD IS GREAT!

– GOD IS GREAT! The crowd echoed.

His Holiness turned to the witch.

– Inez Velarde, you've sold your soul to Satan to gain earthly power. You've spread his unholy teaching on earth, and spat on The Lord and his creation. Do you regret your actions?

She stood there, gasping a bit, struggling to speak.

– I will track you all down and slice your throats, she said hoarsely, – torture and kill you a thousand times.

She began speaking in Spanish, but her speech changed during the sentence, and when she repeated her statement, it sounded archaic, ancient.

He watched them, their stricken faces, how her curse impressed itself on them. They knew, even though they wouldn't admit it to themselves.

– BURN THE WITCH, the archbishop *shrieked*.

– BURN THE WITCH, the crowd echoed with equally vicious tongues and laughter.

They had enjoyed themselves, but now, they suddenly didn't, and they turned spiteful and scared.

Kjell shook.

No more, he told himself. No More!

The executioner and his apprentices rushed to the heap of wet wood and lit the fire. It caught on immediately. People gasped in awe. They didn't know there were ways to make wet wood burn. Inez kept chanting while the flames started licking her frame. Her voice turned loud and powerful.

I can kill twenty of them, Kjell thought feverishly, perhaps even thirty, maybe as many as fifty.

He choked in his deep helplessness and shame.

Inez's scream grew to a louder pitch, changing to become that of a wailing banshee as the flames started devouring her. Kjell stared at her. He didn't look away a single time. The chains fell off the shrinking body, the body hardly even visible anymore. A loud cheer rose from the spectators. He heard music. It both distressed and comforted him.

His feet moved. He hardly saw the path in front of him. The music kept ringing in his ears. He began humming the melody, as he made his way through the streets.

He ended up in front of the Velarde house. Determination lit his emerald jewels. He knocked on the door.

Carlos opened the door, a little tense, brightening when he saw who it was.

– You need to come with me, all of you. They know what you are, now. They will enjoy letting you sweat a little, and then drag you kicking and screaming to the Burning Court.

He saw the father and mother and the other children hiding out in the dark part of the entrance.

– We need to leave, now. Don't bring anything except the most necessary items. We will start over elsewhere, make a life for us where no priest has power. If we encounter any of them, we'll force him to devour his own entrails.

They got it. It took half an hour, but then they were also more or less ready, ready to leave their lives behind.

All of them made their way through Madrid's streets. The heavy smoke lingered everywhere. The wife threw up. The husband held her, keeping her on her feet. The children looked calmer, anxious, but determined. He spotted the fire, the fighting instinct in their eyes.

– I will teach you, he told them, – making you fierce warriors taking shit from no one.

The oldest, the girl looked brightly, darkly at him, and nodded in something resembling understanding. He had seen that expression before, and knew she would learn.

– We're all of the People, Carlos said with a remote expression in his eyes.

And everyone shook. Powerful emotions surged through them.

Pietr stopped outside Julia's house.

– Wait here, he bid them.

He stepped into a quiet house. He could hardly believe how quiet it was. The music had also turned quiet. He kept hearing it as he walked up the stairs.

A sigh went through the house. It seemed so potent in its insignificance. He imagined he felt Inez close, so very, very close and choked in misery and longing.

He found Julia kneeling on the floor.

– You're angry, she whimpered.

He just kept looking at her.

– I did it. I turned her in. I saw how you looked at her, looked at her in a way you never looked at me.

He didn't move, not a single finger.

– I'm a bad girl. Please punish me.

She crouched there like a scared animal, having lost the slightest will to fight.

– I punish you the hardest by letting you live, he finally said.

She collapsed on the floor, shaking in shame and horror and wicked triumph.

He turned and left.

They met him with relieved smiles. He choked again.

– You loved her, the mother said softly. – She was that kind of girl, too good for this world.

He could have told her more about her adopted daughter, taught her a thing or two she didn't know, didn't have any idea about, but he chose to stay silent.

They reached the stable. Their horses waited for them.

– I know you can ride, he said, – but you will probably need to ride harder than you have ever done.

He pondered returning to his house to burn it to the ground, but resisted the temptation.

That thought made him grin as well.

They rode in a relaxed mode through the streets, leaving Madrid, leaving their old lives far behind. He pictured himself crossing the Spanish high plains. They were already there.

– Deep dissatisfaction with the empire is brewing in the Netherlands, he said. – People's rage is growing to rare heights. We'll go there and join the resistance. We will strangle every priest on our way with his own entrails.

– We will! Lyta Velarde, the oldest girl stated passionately, ignoring the shocked expression her mother sent her.

Madrid, the city of fear and hatred and horror and inhuman two-legged dogs faded in their wake.

Chapter 11
Europe/Egypt 1985 CE

Chaotic impressions and sensations haunted him. He twisted and turned on the bed, coated in cold sweat. He kept stabbing what he believed was Erling, but it was Lillian every time. She stared at him with hard, accusing eyes. Lillian the witch was a prisoner in something resembling a medieval torture chamber. Erling was the executioner. He grinned triumphant at Martin. The frozen images Martin had seen had been photographs. Erling would attack Martin through Lillian. Erling would torture her, break her and make her his property.

Again.

AGAIN.

AGAIN…

Martin was wide awake. He rested on his back, alone in the large bed. Lillian wasn't there. Brief panic grabbed him. He looked at the sliding door to the balcony, at the beach outside. She ran to the shore from the shallow water, ran to him fresh and happy.

– Come, she called him. – The water is great.

He stepped into the bright sunlight, glancing at the cloudless sky, the illusion. They had rented this house outside Padstow, Cornwall, currently Southeast England in a week, now. Time to move on.

The photographs of planet Earth. They had heralded both a joy he had never dreamt of experiencing, and the nightmare he knew too well. They had kept their promise.

He chased her into the waves. The warm saltwater closed around him, challenged him. When he returned to the surface, he saw her at the top of a wave. She enjoyed the power and the magick, too, enjoyed it to the full, enjoyed the freedom she had fought for her entire life. They rode the same wave, and were carried far into the beach. She brushed the thick, black hair off her face in a motion where the entire body seemed to follow. Her moves, her entire stature seemed so natural that he was confident everything was intuitive, more instinct than conscious thought.

– I love big waves, she chuckled.

She seemed unaware of how much she had changed. There was something… immediate over her, something not learned, and certainly not in the current society of advanced technology and stilted emotion.

He noticed that she studied him, and he realized that he had revealed himself, his concern.

– You carry with you nine-hundred years of struggle, she said softly. – Perhaps getting reborn occasionally can be an advantage.

She stressed that she was teasing him, good-hearted, slipping into his arm and kissing him on the lips.

– This wasn't this expensive, she mused. – Almost anyone could afford it. I think most people travel too little, have too little change in their lives. The rigid capitalistic society doesn't exactly encourage idleness, of course, but still.

She pondered things constantly. A grin broke on his face.

They walked and ran on the shore until the sun dropped into the ocean, and daylight faded away. They studied the people they encountered on the way, with both casual interest and in an inevitable somber manner.

– I feel him, she said subdued. – It isn't just the itch in the back, but far more. We're connected with unbreakable bonds. He will come for us.

– He will! Martin confirmed.

– We are ready for him, she stated, and grabbed his hand. – I feel ready enough to burst.

They ventured into town, what little remained of it. There were ashes and ruins everywhere. Black and green dominated wherever they walked.

– Methinks it isn't strange that we got the beach-house cheap, she marveled.

She recalled the owner's words.

– The place is cursed. No one will go near it anymore.

They received so many impressions, shaking in their onslaught.

– Witches? She finally asked.

– Christians, Martin replied dryly.

– I heard about it, she said astonished. – We don't really get such news on Norwegian Public Broadcasting, but we got this. My father was livid. He blamed the… The Janus Clan, of course, like all good Christians.

It was like a filmset. Everything looked like burned-out props.

– I saw Ted Warren's photos, too. They're *amazing*. If my father had known I visited that exhibition, he would certainly have spanked me good.

The fact that she could joke about it felt twice great. She looked around her, at the dead place with curious eyes.

She heard a wicked laughter, or imagined she heard it in the wind. The frown appeared on her brow. She glanced at him to determine if he had heard anything, but nothing suggested that he had.

– I believe I just heard the Satan of Cornwall, she giggled.

She sensed a much stronger malevolent presence then.

– Look, he bid her.

She looked at the overgrown streets and scant remains of the buildings, of every single structure within city limits.

– Only two years have passed, he said, – and nature has practically reclaimed the city.

– You're right, she said brightly. – That is so very encouraging.

The presence, whatever it was seemed to lessen a bit, but she kept sensing it.

Every detail seemed to burn itself into her vision, into her cerebral cortex. The photos she had seen mixed with that. She saw a man impaled on a stake. A cross hung around his neck. The haze lingering in the air turned into mist. The malevolent laughter echoed in Lillian's mind.

The ruins stayed with them as they left, as they returned to the house, and their car.

– How long time did we spend there? She wondered. – I can't tell.

– It has become a pocket in time, he responded, – a place outside time and space.

– That's remarkable, she breathed. – That's absolutely remarkable.

They drove the car to another small town nearby, and a pub there. Bodmin looked like the typical, unremarkable Cornwall town. People recognized Martin. His reputation preceded him. They looked weary at him and his companion. She had a field day studying them, easily spotting the fear in their eyes.

– Christians burned witches, she stated, – and the Christians have the audacity to blame the witches.

The other guests couldn't avoid hearing her. She cast them a wicked, challenging grin.

– The world hasn't changed, he said unusually subdued and enraged. – Beneath the surface, it's exactly the same.

They didn't stay long, but just returned to the car and drove on.

– There are quite a few interesting historic sites here, he noted. – We could drive north, and experience the sights.

She knew what he was saying. She felt so aware and awake.

– Perhaps another time, she shrugged.

They drove on east. The mist, the smoke, the stench of ashes seemed to follow, chase them across the country. Lillian stared at everything. They had come this way a week ago, but it still felt new and fresh in her eyes.

They stopped at the stone circle at Avebury, a lesser but bigger and different version of Stonehenge. She circled within the circle. They circled each other, mumbling words they didn't understand. Ghostly flames danced on their skin.

– There is a connection here, she marveled, – one notable and undeniable. I can't express how it makes me feel.

She imagined hands grabbing her, and shaking her, and she glimpsed the spirits closing in on her. They whispered to her words of rage and awe, repeating one specific word she couldn't identify. She fell into trance fully awake, not really fighting it, uncertain if she could have if she had wanted to.

They experienced the circle at its heyday. A choir rose from the circle to the sky, from all the people facing her, and now, she understood the word.

– GODDESS

They chanted it, over and over and over.

Power surged through her. She couldn't contain it. Their worship strengthened her beyond belief. She suddenly wanted this, all this, and focused on staying in trance. New doors opened in her mind, waiting for her to enter.

– We were gods, she marveled.

– We were, he nodded.

But she was unable to sustain it, and the scene stayed out of context, hardly more than flickering moving images on a wall. Everything returned to the gray, pale present.

They reached Kent, and drove on, driving onboard the ferry crossing the channel. Her excitement persisted. She spent the entire crossing like that, like a battery unable to overcharge. People studied her with the same uneasy looks most did. She studied them back, and several faces twisted and shifted and changed while she did. They spent some time in the bar, some in the restaurant, where she once more indulged her appetite, and some on the deck. She stared at the waves.

– I can sense the currents, she said with her put on voice.

It made another dark giggle rise from her throat. She couldn't believe the constant euphoria surging through her.

She cast him the occasional uncertain glance to see if he approved, and she saw that he did. She kicked herself because of the remains of her childish insecurity.

The two travelers crossed the European continent in the car, taking it slow. Each new place, city or country he brought her just added to her joy. They drove through the Ruhr Valley in West Germany, just to remind themselves what was at stake. What little forest they saw was sick and miscolored. The smog alarm had sounded here in January. The air had become even more poisonous than it usually was. They didn't stay long, and continued south and east.

The heat grew stronger as they passed through the alps and reached the other side of the mountains.

– It's like everything is burned into my mind, she mused. – I can't believe how astute I've become.

And that word didn't feel even remotely sufficient to describe her rampant emotions.

Wood clashed against wood and flesh. They used any opportunity to spar and train. It had become an integrated part of their life. They never forgot. She knew every time he slipped into trance, recognized her own experience in him.

She pictured the two of them as an arrow in motion racing through the air. The car became an expression of that arrow. They paid with cash. There were no tickets, no flight plan. They had become nearly impossible to trace. The arrow in motion arrived in Athens during sunset. They spent days in the city and on the mainland and sailing between the Greek islands. They stuck to the ancient Greek sites, Acropolis, Epidaurus, the Poseidon temple, Mycenae and others, all over the country…

The Oracle in Delphi…

They stepped into the temple, and the moment they did, everything seemed to shift, to change. People stared at them, and whispered among themselves.

One blink of an eye, and reality shifted in front of her. She spotted the Oracle, as the woman received her visitors, those seeking her favor.

Lillian recognized the woman, not as herself, but one almost more familiar.

– I know her, she stated with her hollow voice.

Another blink, and the vision faded, lingering forever in her consciousness.

People stared even harder.

– The Mediterranean climate is so dry, Lillian stated. – The erosion is slow. All this would have been long gone in most other places in the world. But now the erosion has speeded up because of the pollution. Both the past and the future are going away for us, for all humans.

People listened to her even there. Some rejected the experience, while others were drawn to it. She learned to distinguish between them, to tell which was which, who was who. More than a few of those she encountered seemed eerily familiar to her.

I've gotten around, she thought.

She studied the statues, and they spoke to her, too, as if they were flesh and blood. They shifted in her vision, and suddenly, they didn't look like stone anymore, but living, dreaming people. It dawned on her that she remembered, and didn't dream.

– We were indeed gods, she mused. – People worshiped us, and we gained power from their worship.

She looked stunned at him.

Some of those standing around them looked stunned and shocked at her. She wanted to do something about it, to probe her experience, but lost her nerve.

They rented a boat. Martin spoke Greek just as fluent as he had spoken German, French and countless other languages, tongues on their path. They sailed between the Greek islands. Almost anywhere on their travels, they found pieces of themselves, of their ancient past. It hardly surprised her anymore.

When she looked at herself in the mirror, she saw another woman, dressed in ancient Greek garb. He, too, looked different, with dark hair and dark skin. She spoke silent words.

– I do feel like a goddess, she marveled. – I feel… powerful.

Her smile looked so different, so confident.

She returned to her own image, and noticed that she had begun to show in earnest. It just added to her earlier statement.

A woman approached them, but clearly changed her mind as she did, and walked off in another direction. Lillian confirmed that to herself with a casual glance.

They crossed the Mediterranean. The voyage stayed enjoyable, uneventful. The warm, pleasant air pushed softly at their bodies. The night brought no notable change from that. Both of them moved effortlessly to handle the sails. It didn't make Lillian even close to breathless. They enjoyed the sailing even more when they entered the port in Cairo. She breathed the air and the scenery of the ancient city. The chuckle rose from her throat when Martin began speaking Coptic to a man on a pier. They walked through the modern streets. The heat struck her and made her gasp, but she didn't really had trouble handling it. The heat was merely one more challenge to… to *conquer*.

The streets changed, subtly at first, then pronounced.

– Al Arafa, The Cemetery, The City of the Dead, he informed her.

Her eyes grew wide in stunned wonder, even more so as they penetrated deeper into the ancient necropolis.

– People live here, she stated with the remote look in her eyes. – It's amazing, so amazing.

– An old woman named Shayara lives here, he said. – She's crafty and knowledgeable. I've always suspected she knows more than she's saying.

Lillian nodded to herself. He had come here to meet her.

The tombstones looked like houses, and the houses like tombstones. Lillian shivered with emotion.

Martin led on, clearly with a goal in mind, bringing them deep into The

Cemetery. Her unprompted visions began again. People, faces paraded before her eyes. She feared for a moment that the experience would overwhelm her, but it really didn't, and she realized she quite simply operated on a higher, or at least different level of consciousness.

They entered a hall, or a space large enough to be perceived as one. A woman stood on a podium and spoke to a curious and excited audience.

– The Raven birthed the Phoenix, she cried with a powerful voice, and the Phoenix will birth the world.

Her words affected the travelers from the north deeply, on more levels than they could imagine.

– She has waited for so long for the wind to blow. She, Thalama, Goddess of Destiny has waited patiently for her destiny to be fulfilled.

A thrill surged through Lillian. A face formed in her mind, one she knew wasn't her own, but still was of enormous importance.

– Her story has been told down the generations in our family for many centuries, the old woman told the gathering. – It has become an integrated part of ours.

The mood picked up further, as she became more agitated, and the audience, participants grew even more receptive.

– We gather here tonight, and many nights to remind ourselves of the past, of our story, and to speak about the present and the future, how we live in a fundamentally unjust and inequal society where there must be vast improvement and true change. And when I say that, I mean the whole world.

She ended her speech. The loud applause echoed between the ancient walls. She froze the moment she stepped down from the podium, and rushed to Martin.

– Ancient Ones, she curtsied.

Everyone saw that and wondered.

– This man, and this woman, she cried, as she turned towards Lillian, – are our honored guests tonight, in this tomb of the dead.

People looked intrigued at the newcomers. Several of those who had considered leaving stayed behind. Eyes locked on Martin and Lillian even more than usual.

Everyone gathered around the worn long table. Lillian noted that she and Martin was placed at its head, and that Shayara had placed herself on their left side.

– I don't see Assaf here, Martin noted.

– He traveled with *them* on their path east, Shayara said. – I asked them to take him under their wings, and they heard my prayers.

That statement spoke to something in Lillian.
I know what that means, she thought.
She enjoyed the simple setting, the spicy food, and the sour wine.
I haven't been spoiled yet, she thought, cautioning herself.
– Cheers for the wandering couple, Shayara cried and raised her large cup.
– THE WANDERING COUPLE, the others choired.
Lillian blushed deeply.
– They heard your prayers? She prompted.
– Aye, Shayara nodded. – My grandson was deeply troubled, and the wanderers in the wilderness took him under their wings.
Suddenly, she spoke English, but sounded Irish.
Lillian heard music. It rose slowly, until becoming loud.
– Someone is playing a violin, she remarked.
And everyone looked stricken at her.
– The young goddess is correct, Shayara said. – Someone is.
The young goddess, Lillian thought.
Kicking herself for her arrogant presumption again.
She enjoyed herself immensely among these strangers. They didn't really seem like strangers at all, but like kindred souls. At least that. She suspected even closer connections, and couldn't believe all the paths her thoughts chose in the semidarkness of the tomb.
Her attention shifted back and forth around the table, and there was a delightful randomness to it she couldn't help but appreciate. Light and shadow and fire danced in an endless flow, both inside and outside her mind.
The meal ended. The conversation, the engagement continued. She couldn't tell how long. Even when it clearly approached its end, she couldn't measure its length.
– You found her, My Lord, Shayara said softly just as the couple was about to depart. – I'm so happy for you both.
Stunned wonder passed through Lillian Donner.
She could hardly contain herself, in any way when they walked through the darkened streets of the dead.
– That was so… so cool, she practically shouted.
She struggled to say more, but found herself unable to do so. The catching in her throat had grown hard and big. She kissed him on the lips, knowing action spoke louder than words.
They visited Memphis and Heliopolis and Giza the next day, returning to Ra Atum's hot sunlight. They walked among the pyramids of Giza, looking up at the Great Pyramid.
– I can see, or at least glimpse them in their heyday, she whispered. – Four

thousand five hundred years seem like nothing.

She snapped her fingers.

– The value of my education has improved to a downright uncanny degree, she giggled happily.

They traveled south, upriver. The wide delta immersed itself on them. Lillian almost bubbled over with excitement, as they lost sense of time as they rode on the deep water of Styx, the river of time. They couldn't sleep while sailing, and when Lillian started getting sleepy, they camped on land. There was no trouble getting there, no trouble staying there. They lit a fire and cooked their food.

– This could be thousands of years ago, she mused. – The boat would probably be wood, but that's the entire critical difference.

She undressed, displaying herself to him, giving him a sweet, seductive smile. Her screams and moans echoed across the river of time.

She recreated the mating in her equally feverish dreams. They seemed endless. She awoke with a content smile on her lips.

They reached Luxor, Thebes, Waset. Lillian's excited eyes kept moving incessantly. There were some more stares when they stepped into the reception lobby of the Winter Palace Hotel.

– They've seen your likeness on the wall, she whispered.

– Welcome, Mister Keller, the receptionist greeted him. – Your grandfather had quite a memorable stay at our hotel, and I hope you will, too.

– I'm confident I will, Martin grinned, making the man uneasy.

They walked to the photo section on the walls later. His photo was featured prominently. They looked at the newest color photos, those of Ted and Liz Warren, and those following them on their travels. More excitement surged through them.

– Look at those eyes, Lillian said with shivering lips. – I can hardly believe they're real. I remember them. They're burned into my eternal memory.

They were shown to their suite. Others carried their luggage.

– This is an old-fashioned hotel, she stared. – I love it.

Her eyes grew even wider when they entered the giant apartment.

– It's even quite inexpensive, she marveled. – Virtually anyone with a basic income can afford it.

She rushed out on the balcony and stared at the city below.

– Luxor, Thebes, Wasat, she mumbled, as she slipped into ancient Coptic, and even pre-Coptic without noticing. – We lived and reigned by the mighty river of life, death and knowledge, and Power beyond imagination.

She turned and realized that Martin was as excited as she was. She had woken him up just as much as he had her.

The huge full moon rose on the sky.

– ISIS, MIGHTY HUNTER AND GODDESS, Lillian Donner cried, and didn't feel awkward at all.

They crossed the river the next day, to the Valley of the Kings. There was transportation available at the other side, but they chose to walk.

– It's pulling me, she mumbled.

She led, now, and he had trouble keeping up, and that realization felt remarkable in itself. The terrain seemed the same everywhere, and the path endless. They crossed the barren land of the west with many names. The West Bank, West of Thebes, The Great Field, The Valley of the Gates of Kings, The Valley of the Queens, The Valley of the Kings.

– I feel lost, she mumbled. – I've been searching for so long, and there seems to be no end in sight.

– We're endless, Martin told her.

– That's so true, she marveled, – and I love that, love it so much.

They spotted several sites on their way. She hardly paid attention to them at all. She pictured in her mind where she was headed before she actually saw it with her eyes. Then, she did. A long queue had formed in front of its entrance.

– Your ankh is glowing, she said hoarsely.

He looked and a ghostly glow reflected in his eyes.

They placed themselves at the back of the queue. People glanced and stared at them again. The queue didn't really last that long. Some of those ahead of them even stepped aside. Lillian found that absolutely remarkable. The notable, potent energies from the tomb reached her. There was no denying it. The inscription above the entrance seemed to glow in her eyes. She translated the hieroglyphs effortlessly.

«Death will come to those who disturb
the sleep of the pharaoh».

She spoke it aloud. The unrest in everyone gathered outside picked up further.

They stepped inside. There was a notable threshold. Incalculable energies filled her. She knew everyone noticed. Those that had stepped out of the queue dropped to their knees.

– All the old gods came here to die, she mumbled, – but we're two of the old gods, and we're still here. We will always be here.

Everything shifted around her. She found herself at a different place, at Thebes, Waset the eighteenth dynasty of Egypt. She looked at a royal procession reaching the river.

Ankhesenpaaten had a holy bath in The Nile, surrounded by temple priestesses and guards. She was to become the Great Royal Wife of Tutankhamun and take the name Ankhesenamun.

She turned at some point and looked directly at Lillian.

– Ah, there you are. I knew you would come.

Lillian looked around her, but there was no one else here, only the two of them.

– We're invisible to most people, Ankhesenpaaten said, – even to our brethren.

Lillian wanted to speak, to say something, anything, but couldn't do it.

– The past beckons you, one young girl told another. – You've grown up ignorant, but aren't anymore. You have entered your Long Walk, your Journey of Mystery, and this time, there will be no end to it.

– I look at myself, Lillian breathed.

Ankhesenpaaten nodded exalted.

– Your world fills me with sorrow, but also with joy. It will return to what it once was, and become greater than ever before. I envy myself. I'm finally fit to reenter my rightful position of power. I've waited so long. I will probably not battle the Enemy again. That burden and honor fall to others, but I will reap the benefits of his ultimate defeat.

– I have so many questions, Lillian gasped.

– You already have the answers.

The powerful experience faded away, but lingered. She stood outside the tomb. Everyone except Martin and those having not fled in panic knelt around her.

– She created the curse, she marveled. – *I* created the curse.

Her voice changed then, turning deeper and more menacing. The dark grin formed on her face.

– This is such a thrill.

She looked at Martin in a completely new light. She saw the horns on his head. The sight didn't frighten her, but excited her beyond words.

– Horned God, walk with me.

He shook, but followed her across the valley, and so did all those who had knelt, and bowed their head. Her surroundings, the very world around her kept shifting around the group making its way back to the riverbank.

– I know you, she told those following in her shadow. – I know you all.

The vivid memories and the supreme confidence faded, as she had known they would, but they lingered, and kept burning within. The dark laughter kept bubbling in her throat. They returned to Luxor, to Thebes, to Waset. The ruckus and mayhem followed them there. People shook in terror and exalted joy when she walked near them.

They see me, she thought, see me as I really am.

Chaos ruled the modern streets in a matter of minutes. The modern city would never forget this day, when the past had returned in unimaginable and undeniable ways.

2

September 2, the same day as the hurricane «Elena» ravaged the American states Louisiana, Missouri and Alabama, they returned to England, and finally arrived in London. They arrived by train from Dover to Charing Cross Station. Lillian looked around her at the old train and tube station with bright eyes. Everything, all impressions and sensations had become such a powerful experience to her.

Other major news of the day included the discovery of the wreck of the passenger liner Titanic four thousand meters below the surface. It had broken in two parts, and rested in the deep for seventy-three years. Gold, diamonds and jewels of enormous monetary value had been found onboard.

They traveled on with the Tube, the Underground to Baker Street Station. It was yet another station with a distinct design. Lillian's childish excitement prevailed, both inside and outside the station. Baker Street looked fairly similar to most other old London streets and architecture, completely different from Bergen and other cities Lillian Donner had visited.

They walked along a major, seemingly infinite green area. She saw no end to it.

– That is Regent Park, he said. – The house is at the end of it, by St. John's Wood. It's quite a stretch.

He said that as if it meant something. She grinned.

The grin faded a bit when the high heels started giving her problems.

– Yes, you warned me not to wear high heels, she shrugged unconcerned.

She removed the shoes, and walked barefoot the rest of the way. It felt better, much better.

The house, and the surrounding estate with many trees and a *wild* garden pointed to itself. Both the house and its surrounding property were considerably larger than the one in Bergen. It looked both common and magnificent.

– Our home, she whispered and grabbed his hand.

– One more brief home in eternity, he said.

She nodded to herself, understanding very much what he was saying.

Its interior spoke very much to her like a museum. Martin closed the door behind them. Sunlight through the windows revealed the dust in the air.

The architecture looked different, very different, a mix, she assumed of styles spanning a thousand years. The entire floor was one single room or hall, except for an octagon-shaped space big enough to be a living room at the center. Two of the walls had no windows. They were covered by bookshelves filled with books. The staircase and the windows reached to the top floor. A large glass dome made even more light reach all the plants. A wonderful peace flowed through her.

He showed her around, not without a certain pride, but one far from that of a boy.

All the floors had valuable stuff displayed. Books and various pieces of art, weapons, antiques making the collection in Bergen seem cheap. But in spite of that, she realized quickly that this was not… it.

– This is just a public display, isn't it? She stated. – The best is yet to come?

She had become so perceptive. Her mind had grown so sharp that she could hardly believe it.

At the top floor, in one of the large, giant rooms was the giant bed. It was even more of an antique than the one in Bergen.

– The double or triple bed, she chuckled scandalized.

They entered the room with the dome, with a great view of the surrounding town.

– He won't be able to enter this place without working hard for it, he stated. – Wicked spells and modern alarms make it an intruder's nightmare.

She could sense the spells easily, like waves in the air. She had grown so astute, and she had lost count of how many times she had noticed that the last six months.

He opened the door to the octagon room. Another, smaller bedroom revealed itself. It dawned on her that there had been no doors inside on the two other floors. He stepped inside. She joined him there. He bent down, and reached under the bed. She spotted a switch there. He turned it. A small part of the wall slid aside, and revealed a panel with numbers. He rushed to it and punched a code. She heard a hum, and had a sense of motion. The entire octagon was an elevator.

It stopped. He opened the door. They walked through it. She couldn't help staring. The bedroom was gone. Surrounding her was something resembling a… swimming pool. In a circle around the octagon, there was a tiled floor. That aside, there were deep waters everywhere.

He pushed a special place on the wall, and another panel with numbers revealed itself. He pushed the numbers with confident moves. The bedroom moved up again, and another door appeared. He opened it, and stepped inside. She joined him. The door closed behind them. The muted lighting revealed the treasures.

– These are your personal treasures, she mused, – stuff you really appreciate.

It felt almost redundant to say that aloud when she took a closer look.

Two glass cases caught her eyes. One was empty. The other contained an ankh in a chain, a twin to what he carried around his neck.

He opened the glass and removed the ankh, and put it around her neck. It started glowing immediately. She felt the pulsing rhythm.

– We've worn these many times, she breathed. – We'll wear them many times more.

Memories from the two of them in the temple of Isis flashed before her eyes. They knelt before a tall woman with black eyes.

Lillian could see forever when looking into those eyes.

– I still haven't caught up with you, she told Martin, – but I'm getting there.

There was so much to see that she once more lost sense of time. Things both of great monetary value and beyond precious items. There was a lock of… Gudrun's hair. She had given it to him when they were children. There were original writings from the Middle Ages. Various weapons. An original edition of Copernicus's book about the motion of the planets. Système de la Nature by Dietrich. Writings and letters from Newton, his masterworks Principia. An early edition of Hamlet by Shakespeare. A microscope used by Kjell in the Netherlands. Old Dutch ocean-maps. Ancient coins. Among many a Carl XV coin from 1861 with a B under the portrait. There had only been thirteen of them. Now, there were only two known coins left. There were complete sheets of the first stamps, including the Norwegian. A banner from the Russian revolution. One of the red caps from Paris uprisings. A mug from the pub Four Oaks…

The room moved again, moved further down. Far more time passed. They went far deeper. Her anticipation grew even stronger.

– I can't read this, she said with regret. – What is it?

– It is Latin, he replied. – Atlantis by Platon. I saved it from a convent just before the Inquisition burned it down.

The mere mention of those names made her both hot and cold.

The door opened, and yet another world appeared to her.

– Welcome to my fortress of solitude, he said. – It can withstand an atomic blast, and contains years of supplies, and the knowledge of the world saved for posterity.

This place was much larger than everything above. There were far more books, movies and film-rolls here. It was chilly and dry down here, but not cold, the best possible place to use for storage.

– I had it made just after World War 2, he said. – I hired older people from other parts of the world. I rented machines for a completely different project. I stole or procured all public drawings in existence. No outsiders alive know of its existence. I made the last modern modifications myself a couple of years ago. There are several secret passageways that can only be opened with a strength you will gain when your Time of Change is completed.
– I wonder what you haven't considered, she teased him.
She looked at him with lowered eyelashes. Both cast their attention on the bed.
– I feel like I've awakened so much already, she marveled. – I can't imagine how it can grow even stronger after the Time of Change has ended.
– It is hard to explain, he said. – Both subtle and momentous.
They undressed, both slowly and in a hurry.
– I've lost count of how many times we've fucked, she giggled. – I can't even tell how many times we do it each night and day.
It felt very much like that this time, too. Every measure, every count grew meaningless. There were flesh and heat, and nothing but. She descended into one more feverish mire of pleasure and pain.
It kept burning and warm her the next day when they wandered through the seemingly infinite streets of London. The sense of ancient times kept surging through her body and mind in equal measure.
– This is an ancient area, she said. – I can feel the energies. It was populated long before even the Romans arrived.
– The St. Paul's Cathedral is built upon an ancient pagan ceremonial spot, Martin said.
– I knew it! She exclaimed.
They found themselves there, already there. And they already had been, before she had spoken about it.
She looked astounded at him (again). The visions began unprompted. She stood there with half closed eyes and saw wild men and women dance around the campfire inside the temple.
– The Christians have defiled it, she snarled. – They defile everything.
The overwhelming sense of revulsion made them leave, made them walk west again. They had already crossed Central London on foot. Now, they did so again. They arrived at Piccadilly Circus in the late afternoon, with sunrays casting its ghostly glare at the Eros statue and its surroundings. People had gathered around the monument, and enjoyed the dry weather, and having a conversation, both one on one, and in groups.
She imagined that people looked at her again, knowing that it wasn't her

imagination playing tricks on her. Some of those looking had that remote expression in their eyes.

The two of them moved on, through Coventry Street to Leicester Square, yet another crowded place, and further on, to Charing Cross Road. The short walk took quite some time. Lillian practically stopped every single step, and admired the surroundings. She grinned mischievously.

– Everything is moving, she frowned, – is constantly in motion. It's remarkable!

They dined at a small, intimate restaurant. Her gluttony hadn't diminished any. She suspected strongly it had grown. A brief touch of gloom and incredulity didn't keep her from enjoying the meal.

– Your body is storing energy for the final transformation, he said lightly.

She looked at him. His casual tone didn't fool her for a minute.

They had red wine to the spicy food. She devoured that, too.

– I could never afford having wine while eating out, she giggled. – It was way beyond my wallet.

That, too.

– A la vida, he had said and raised his glass.

– That's Spanish, isn't it? What does it mean?

She could almost, but not quite tell.

– To life, he said, even more intense than usual. – It's a greeting. I've loved it since I first heard it in Madrid four hundred years ago.

– To Life, she said softly.

Glasses met and parted. They drank.

– I feel such joy, she breathed. – Where does it come from?

– From you, he stated. – Don't let anyone tell you otherwise.

She softened further subjected to the glow in his eyes.

The dining ended. She leaned back in the chair and patted her big belly.

– I'm stuffed. I feel confident this will last the whole night.

She giggled darkly again.

– I've always loved gallows humor…

They reentered the dark, enticing, sinister streets. Their mood entered her as easily as her breath. Every corner, every shadow and bright spot brought new impressions and sensations on a full scale. She saw it as it was, as it had been. The West End and Soho areas around Leicester Square stayed packed with people. They walked through Chinatown, and the impression of being in a foreign land grew even more distinct. The visuals changed further, but beneath that, she sensed even deeper differences.

– A brick isn't a brick, she stated good-humored, – but a wall of mist and smoke.

A bell struck midnight somewhere. It seemed to be too early. She couldn't imagine that time had passed so quickly, but when she looked at the clock up there, it did show midnight.

– We enter the hour of the dead, he said.

A shiver passed through her.

– Isn't there always the hour of the dead somewhere on the planet?

– Yes, he replied.

A black woman, a shimmering figure studied them with an even stare from the other side of the street. Lillian returned the stare, even though she had trouble keeping her eyes on the spirit. The woman stood in front of a door, but the door was very much visible through her transparent body.

The woman faded away. The wicked laughter echoed in Lillian's ears.

– She laughed at me, Lillian said subdued.

– She would, Martin said. – She isn't very nice.

– That's soooo funny, Lillian snorted.

Even as she knew he hadn't been kidding.

– I've always sensed the spirits, she stated, – but I believed they were a figment of my imagination, of course, like any stupid cow or bull. Now, I know better, and the world has grown so big.

The street theater began in Covent Garden at three o'clock at night.

– It is funny, she chuckled. – This is almost too much of a good thing...

The performers played Shakespeare, but very much their own version of it, disregarding all the experts that would have vomited hard if they had watched it. Lillian applauded hard and shouted her praise. Several others joined her.

– Is this everything we are? A young man said while holding up the skull. – Is there nothing more than this slow decay turning to dust?

Dust, Lillian thought.

And then, it was as if she saw it, saw shimmering dust in the air in front of her.

– It is Dust, Martin said, – not dust.

Her excitement flooded her again.

– Move the Dust, Martin bid her.

She focused on it, on the shimmering substance she knew wasn't material.

It moved. She pulled it close. She drew breath and it entered her. She gasped in pain and joy. Her hand turned transparent. She couldn't stop the anxiety rising within.

– It isn't turning me into a spirit, is it?

– On the contrary, he responded completely relaxed.

Her senses expanded. They seemed to cover the entire plaza, the performers and the spectators in front of the church. Some of them turned and glanced at their surroundings, and some of those again looked at her. She sensed how the effect faded, and she returned to normal, or close to normal. It had been brief. Ambiguous emotions of loss and relief flowed through her. She realized startled that both were meaningless.

Several of those there cast her more curious looks, but they couldn't determine if there was anything solid, quantifiable to their suspicion, because they couldn't do that with anything or anyone. She didn't have that problem. More chills and heat surged through her.

– I created the curse, she stated with a dark voice and laughter.

And now, they noticed her, and grew sore afraid.

The dark girl and the man with firehair moved on in the night, one seemingly endless.

– I didn't know what I wanted, she mused, – but now I do. The world beyond is within me, and I want it to bloom there, to grow to full strength.

They kept walking until dawn. They watched the sunrise with all the birds in St. James's Park. The birds… touched her every time they flapped their wings, and it seemed so very familiar. The two of them rode the Underground home. They slept until the late afternoon, and after one more gluttonous meal, they returned to Soho and West End. She remained restless, hardly able to sit or stand still. They walked with the pigeons by the fountain on Trafalgar Square. The pale sun hovered low on the sky, just above the Canadian Embassy. The weather stayed dry and hot. Lillian wet her arms and neck. She noticed his glance and the catching in his throat, and smiled. They watched the pigeons. The males paced back and forth, displaying themselves to the females and rivals alike.

– Look at that one, she grinned. – His main interest is certainly not food right now.

Even that, she shared with the other people nearby. Even that strengthened her.

They walked up Charing Cross Road. A young boy sitting by a tree caught her attention. He was drawing and painting on a white canvas. She decided to approach him on the spur of the moment.

– Can you do a portrait of me? She asked him.

– You don't beat around the bush, he acknowledged. – Most people tell me they love my work before asking.

– I do like what you do, she shrugged. – That's why I want you to draw me.

She felt so mature then, felt positively ancient then.

He nodded and put aside the drawing he had worked on. She sat down in the chair opposite his. He began drawing lines with pencils and colors with a remote expression in his eyes. He was just as immersed in his work as she had hoped.

She studied the people passing them, beyond fascinated.

– There is such variety of people and races here, she marveled. – I love that. It must be heaven for an artist.

– I lose myself in it all every day and night, the boy agreed.

The boy had completed the work. He looked shocked at the result and her. She looked incredulous at it.

He had drawn her with long, red hair and green eyes. She glimpsed Martin's features there in addition to her own, features strange and twisted, as if it didn't belong to a human being. But it was. It was her.

– I'm s-sorry, the boy stuttered. – I don't know what I was thinking. I'll draw another.

– I like this, she declared. – You've done what I wanted you to do, drawn my inner self.

And she saw that he knew what she was talking about.

– It is yours, for free, he stated.

– Are you sure?

– I am!

He handed her the drawing, and she accepted it.

– You will become quite renowned, Martin told him.

And infamous, he thought.

They walked a bit further north. Lillian stopped and immersed herself in the drawing. She imagined it caught fire, imagined she caught fire. The red hair turned to flames. She saw herself in a store display window, and she saw the being, not Lillian Donner.

– Is this me?

– It is you, Martin replied. – He drew your inner being, the way you are beneath the flesh, your eternal self.

– That's... amazing, she said faint.

A being surrounded by flames walked ancient streets. She saw it happen right in front of her. It flapped its wings. Fire spread to the entire street and all its buildings. Terror and discord walked in its shadow.

It faded like a mirage, and she couldn't decide whether or not she felt disappointment or stark relief. She imagined she kept burning, body and mind, as they made their way north.

Chapter 12

More strangeness immersed itself on her when they stepped into the Virgin Megastore in Oxford Street. She saw everything there in immaculate detail. What was in motion, people and objects seemed to slow down and speed up alternately, and to slip in and out of reality. It dawned on her that they weren't, but that she was.

– It's enormous, she breathed. – I can hardly believe it.

The store sold vinyl records, cassettes, CDs, comics and similar stuff part of the modern entertainment culture.

– It started off as a perceived counterculture project, she remarked, sobering, – but is hardly anything like that anymore. Too bad.

Did she catch a flash of relief in his eyes? She grinned.

She still had blushing cheeks when they returned to the streets. She shrugged deliberately.

– What happened between me, us and the artist was truly remarkable, she mused. – Our subconscious interacted and bloomed.

Blooomed.

– London is such a shock to the system of a poor provincial girl, she chuckled. – I can hardly believe it.

She couldn't stop talking. The words just kept flowing from her mouth like air.

Oxford Street was quite a stretch, and they made many stops on their path. She bought fruit at an outdoor venue, tried on clothes, shoes and everything under the moon, really, but found out that she hadn't bought that much when they reached the end of the stores. It had turned dark when they passed the Marble Arch monument, and the shopping street slipped into Bayswater Road. The road was packed with cars during the peak hours in the morning and the afternoon. Now, it had turned somewhat quiet and dark. Lillian looked up. She could see the trees in Hyde Park against the skies brightened by the city lights.

They stopped outside The Swan, a pub in the tourist area. It was packed outside, so they stepped inside, and bought two glasses of pint. People made room for them at already full tables. Cheers echoed from dry throats and mouths. Many glasses met and parted. They drank. The noise reached deafening proportions. They could only communicate with gestures. But that suited Lillian and Martin just fine. They could read body languages far better than the others. Everyone spoke to them without knowing it. She heard the music. It changed slightly with each person she looked at, but it never went away.

She had a few, quite a few Guiness. The fat, dark beer flowed down her throat like a waterfall. She laughed aloud. The males clearly desired her. Some of the females did as well. It created a pleasant buzz in her mind. Her intoxicated mind and body sat there, swaying in the chair. More time went away. The two of them left the company of strangers at some point, saying their goodbyes. She walked without support, but noticeably unsteady on her feet.

– The night embraces me, she said, she called…

The Night.

The full moon rose above the city buildings, as they walked (stumbled) home. She started getting sober after a while. She noticed it as her dull senses slowly turned sharp again.

– The Horned Man was the god of the forest, the hunt and celebration, she mused, amazed by how easy the words and the thoughts rose to the surface. – The word spread long and far about his wild parties. He is an older, far more primitive version of Dionysus. It was said that he loved his drink.

She frowned, aware of the fact that she used both her modern education, and far older knowledge simultaneously.

– My mind is an endless well, she sang.

They walked north, closing in on their house in the small forest.

– This is the last time we indulge ourselves, he stated, – until our urgent matter is solved.

She nodded serious-minded, easily catching the somber meaning of his words.

They reached Regent Park, choosing the eastern side this time.

– For variety, he said.

But she knew that wasn't it, not completely, knew he wasn't completely honest with her, and sent him an angry stare. He got it.

She knelt on the dry ground, and raised her arms above her head, looking up at the bright bulb in the sky.

– The werewolf of Locus Bradle is howling at the moon, she said.

She threw her head back and howled. He shook, and she knew she had done it right. She repeated it, even louder, piercing the very firmament around them.

It's my power, she realized startled. I must just learn to access it and utilize it properly.

She noticed it before she had the house in her sight. She saw that he did as well. There were people ahead. They turned the corner, and had a direct line of sight to the house. A small crowd sat or crouched by the entrance. She recognized several of them from Luxor, from The Valley of Kings. Excitement surged through her.

Several of them were sleeping. The others shook them awake. They all rose, practically jumping on their feet.

– Welcome to our home, she greeted them. – It's so great seeing you again.

She could name them without effort. Elijah, Monique, Annabelle, Francois, and six more, a diverse group of colors and creeds.

Martin opened the door, and everyone walked inside.

– We've got more than enough room, Lillian said brightly.

And she did catch worship in their eyes.

– You will train with us, she stated curtly, – until you become weapons, until you are weapons. You will be the Guard of our temple, the conveyor of our desires.

The no longer put on voice shook them.

– You will kneel for no man.

She understood herself. They understood. She smiled.

They looked so open to her. She imagined she could see right through them. But she knew she could just catch surface emotions and intentions, not those experts in hiding themselves, in concealing their true self.

She and Martin spoke their private hand language, and no one was the wiser.

– We suspected a few of you would follow us, she said. – Things will change even more from now on. All of us will take several major steps further on our path.

Our destined path, she didn't say.

Everything seemed so clear to her. She could hardly believe how much.

– I'm dirty, and I stink, Monique whimpered. – I hardly cared about anything but reaching you. I'm sorry, Goddess.

– Don't worry about it, Lillian shrugged.

The girl, older than Lillian brightened.

– You can all shower together, Lillian said. – It's a big shower, with room for us all.

Monique turned deep red.

– Just leave your clothes here, Martin said. – You don't need them anymore. We'll dress you up tomorrow.

There was hesitation, but not really that much. The ten began undressing. Martin and Lillian began undressing a bit after that. The ten followed the two up the stairs to the top floor, and the bedroom.

– We need only one bed, Lillian stated.

– It's more than big enough, Annabelle said eagerly.
– I see what you're doing here, Elijah said, slightly agitated.
– Good boy, Lillian grinned.

She and Martin entered the large shower with ten hoses. The ten followed them, both shy and bold. Martin pushed a button. Water began flowing from all the ten hoses. Lillian walked to Monique and kissed her on the lips. Monique gasped, but responded eagerly and returned the affection.

Martin and Lillian began applying soap on each other's sweaty bodies, and the others did as well.

– This feels so good… Annabelle said sensuously and displayed herself to them all. – I love how the water is caressing us from all sides.

Twelve people did fill the space. They moved tight together, but it didn't feel awkward or wrong.

It felt right.

– The Goddess is with child, Monique said shyly.
– Don't worry about it, Lillian responded. – I don't.

Monique kissed her on the lips.

I was right about her, Lillian thought.

Monique set out to pull back, but Lillian grabbed her. Monique fell into her arms. Lillian kissed her, and began fondling her breasts. Monique moaned.

Everyone washed off the soap. They turned off the water, and dried each other. Anticipation grew slowly as they did. It was a dance, a dance turning wild. Everyone started breathing faster. Lillian observed that, all that, even as all her senses failed her. Lillian Donner had never done anything even remotely like this, but the powerful being resting within her had done so many times. When Lillian moved her hand and caressed Monique's thigh, that hand moved with confidence and abandon. When she led them into the bedroom, there was no hesitation, no shame. Some of the participants displayed some awkward moves, but they caught up as their fervor grew. Everyone moved as one, as they caressed people back and front and to the side. Elijah grabbed Annabelle, and she gasped happily. Some climbed onto the large bed. Others fell like ripe fruits. Lillian and Monique kissed and fondled each other. Other bodies surrounded them. We flow, she thought, flow like waves on the beach.

They stretched and bent in an ocean of flesh, flowing from one body to another in an endless series of waves. Elijah put Annabelle down on all fours, rubbed her a bit, making her cry out in need and entered her. That was the signal, the start of the deluge. Lillian found herself on her back, with Monique licking her. Francios fucked Monique from behind. She slipped back and forth while having her mouth buried in Lillian's cunt. Faint incredulity kept up its presence in Lillian's feverish consciousness, but not enough to bother her, or keeping her from doing anything or enjoying the… the ride. Her wild laughter rocked them all.

It descended into incoherent moans and swearing. All eyes slid close. All minds closed down, except for those pleasant dreams of tonight, yesterday and tomorrow.

2

The training of the recruits began. It was a grateful task. They were so eager to learn. Lillian found herself enjoying the role as a teacher. She and Martin moved with the swords, showing them how it was done. The recruits used wands and tree swords. The training filled their days and feverish passion their nights. So much remained unsaid between them. The distant past stayed with them, whether they spoke about it or not.

Francois bit the dust, literally. He crouched on the ground and spat soil from his mouth. Lillian towered above him with her expressionless mask in place.

– On your feet, she bid him with her cold rage voice.

It seemed so easy, such a casual act. She didn't remember on a conscious level, but deep down, she did.

They took the train to Brighton and its beaches and piers. Lillian wore a short, tight top. She displayed proudly her growing belly, her mean and lean body. They kept exercising, swimming far into the ocean. She dived beneath the surface, to one more world, one more realm. They followed her. White and brown bodies twinkled in the deep darkness. They rested on the beach. People walked back and forth in front of them. They seemed to shimmer in Lillian's vision, making her frown.

Twilight arrived with mist and dark clouds. People passing back and forth kept shimmering in Lillian's vision. The twilight beach itself seemed to shimmer. She had become somewhat used to stuff like this by now, but it still brought a tingling down her spine and in her frontal lobe. A hand sought her head. She turned and Martin's face appeared in front of her.

– The frontal lobe is the seat or at least a conduit for our powers, he said. – Our extraordinary perception and expression stem from that.

He had seen her touch her head, and he had known exactly what that signified. She smiled to him, grateful for his presence, for him being there for her in her time of transition.

Thinking about the time of transition no longer seemed that strange either.

She recalled other times she had transformed, in ancient places.

– I fear losing myself… losing Lillian, she said hesitant.
– You don't lose yourself with higher awareness, he stated. – You find yourself.

And those words echoed true within her.

The twilight beach faded in her senses, but not in her consciousness. She kept glimpsing the world Beyond, the other realm, the Shadowland. Sometimes, she did lose herself, and stared straight ahead with a remote expression in her eyes, but she had no trouble finding herself when it happened. She just grew distracted, that's all.

She woke up in the morning with unblinking, aware eyes. Yesterday's events mixed with those the last few weeks and brought a smile to her face. Nude and warm bodies surrounded her. The smile turned wide.

The others woke up, too. Everyone exchanged relaxed kisses and affection. Lillian sat up in bed. The birds rose from the roof outside. The flapping of their wings echoed in her ears.

– What day is it? Someone asked.
– Thursday, I think, Monique frowned, – the middle of the day. My Goddess!

The last was an exclamation, not directed at Lillian. The girl bowed her head and reddened. It looked good on her.

– Time is immaterial, Francois shrugged.

The bell chimed. It sounded both sharp and far away in Lillian's ears. She dressed at a languished pace, and walked downstairs. Monique followed her with the tree sword concealed behind her back. Lillian made out who was standing outside with a little effort. The door didn't really block her view. Joy and anxiety mixed and turned interchangeable in her mind.

She opened the door.

– SURPRISE, Marianne, Jonathan, Axel and Tove choired.

It seemed profoundly strange seeing them again, like they were from another life, and in a very true sense, they were. She went through the motions, embracing them, playing the happy reunion girl and all. They gathered on the ground floor.

– This is an amazing place, Marianne said with wide eyes.

Lillian studied the four with her extended awareness, doing so in the unobtrusive manner she had taught herself, but didn't really catch much, except for the usual flashes of other features. Marianne's features looked familiar. The others didn't.

She had recognized something in Marianne when they first met. Now, she saw more, saw two farmgirls carry hay bales.

Lillian brightened visibly when Martin entered the room. She made no attempt at holding back her delight, her joy.

– We have all managed to get one exchange year at various London universities, Axel stated. – We're here to stay.

– We talked about it among ourselves, Tove said, – and decided to do it to support you in your plight…

Lillian giggled, failing gloriously to hide her appreciation.

I have become so immediate, she thought.

She also appreciated the notable irony in Tove's voice and wording.

The ten walked down the stairs, cleaned and dressed.

– Welcome, Annabelle greeted them sweetly.

She kissed all the newcomers. The other nine did, too. It caused more than a bit discomfort. Lillian grinned wickedly.

Everyone sat down on the sofa, and on the numerous chairs around the large table. Lillian enjoyed the strange mood, and incredulity of her four friends.

– This is such a nice area as well, Jonathan said. – The outside actually reminds me of the inside.

He looked a little flustered then, unable to give voice to his nagging thoughts.

The sixteen people had breakfast together, even though the four newcomers already had enjoyed one breakfast that day. Everyone helped carrying plates and food to the table.

Lillian watched Axel and saw how awkward he was. He was used to women doing the chores inside the house.

– This is what I call an open interior solution, Marianne marveled.

– You stink of body juices, Tove whispered to Lillian as they passed each other.

– We don't care about such stuff here, Lillian responded unconcerned, drawing an incredulous look from her friend.

– Can I talk to you? Marianne asked Lillian anxiously.

Lillian nodded. They stepped outside, far enough from the house to not being heard by those inside.

– Remember what we talked about? What I didn't want to come out? I've stopped worrying about it, and have long since talked about my belief in reincarnation openly. I just wanted to talk to you to see if you feel the same before talking about it here.

– I do, Lillian said. – I have come out of the closet, too. So have the others living here. Feel free to talk about it anytime.

Happiness transformed Marianne's weary face. Lillian felt good about that. They returned inside. Everyone looked inquiringly at them as they sat down around the table again.

– The two of us have had some shared experiences about… reincarnation, Marianne stated.

The ten and Martin didn't really react to that news at all, of course, but Jonathan, Axel and Tove certainly did.

– That's remarkable, Jonathan said. – You found what you were looking for then?

– I did, Lillian said and took Martin's hand. – There is still so much to explore, though.

Tove and Axel didn't say anything, but Lillian knew they wanted to.

– The last time we met, we were Vikings together, she said. – I've experienced many lives since then, but it doesn't really feel long ago at all.

She wanted to see their reaction, but couldn't catch anything suspicious.

– I feel more like Lillian again, now, with the arrival of you guys.

– That's how it goes, Martin said, – in an ever-shifting cycle.

– Yes, she acknowledged, – you've witnessed it many times.

– I remember the two of us being sisters on a farm in Norway in the eighteenth century, Marianne said.

– I remember that, too, Lillian said.

– Is there anything you can do to make us remember? Jonathan wondered eagerly, meaning himself.

– There are quite a few things we can try, Martin said. – It doesn't always work. We need a quiet place, without distractions.

– I'll pass, Tove and Axel choired, and grabbed each other's hands.

– I'm looking so much forward to it, Jonathan said. – I can wait a little longer.

The four stayed the entire day. the sixteen shared dinner as well. Lillian didn't hide herself, but devoured the food in her usual manner.

– I feel so prosaic saying it out aloud, she munched, speaking while eating, – but it isn't really. Finding out who and what you are is a profound experience.

– You look… good, Axel said.

– I'm free, brother, she said brightly, – liberated beyond confines.

– I've broken with those at home, too, he stated with a certain pride. – Tove helped me do that. I believe we're great for each other.

– I'm happy for you both, Lillian stated.

She watched him, and saw more signs that he wasn't that liberated from his upbringing. She caught him frowning when everyone helped out with the food and the setting of the table, and the dishwashing.

Rome wasn't built in one day, she thought optimistic.

The mere thought of Rome brought bad memories. She remembered Rome.

She hung on the cross on Via Appia. The slow torture could easily compete with that of the Burning Court. Her smile turned strained, no matter how much she fought to conceal that.

They looked at her. She relented.

– It's both good and bad memories, she revealed. – You can't get away from any of it. But that is a good thing, too. When you accept it, you embrace everything you are, the totality of your being. Every single human being should do that.

The ten had that look of reverence in their eyes again. She ignored it.

– London, steeped in ancient memories, is a perfect place to start our final journey towards a truly enlightened and just society, Martin said. – We've waited so long, but now the final days are here.

– He's so intense, Marianne whispered excited to Lillian.

Flashes of memory assaulted Lillian again, even though she remained unable to access them properly. Frustration inevitably followed.

– We need to embrace dark passions, she declared in a moment of zealous inspiration. – If we don't, we'll just remain lambs to the slaughter.

The four glanced at her, sensing, seeing, catching easily her notable change.

– She's a Goddess, Elijah said, – an ancient teacher of us all.

His statement didn't embarrass her, no matter how hard she probed herself.

– You recognize me? She wondered. – You're not just saying that?

He straightened, closing his eyes halfway.

– I stand in the Valley of Kings, he said. – I see you as you emerge from the desert. You are not visible, but we see you still. Then, you turn visible, and we're blinded by your brilliance, blinded by your shifting light and Shadow. We kneel in pride before you. There is no shame, no sense of humiliation or enslavement, but the exact opposite.

Light and Shadow, she thought.

Frustration rode her.

– I don't remember, she said.

– You aren't yet complete, he stated earnestly, – but you will be. You and the other ancients will lift us up, making humanity what we always should have been.

Ancients, she thought.

Humanity, not just the ten.

A traitorous joy filled her, and she made certain to kick herself again.

He could use that to seduce me, she thought. Play on my insecurities, my longing.

Rage shook her, rampant paranoia shook her, and made her gasp in her weakness.

They hadn't noticed anything, at least not the particulars. She gasped in relief.

The stench of her body juices suddenly seemed to rip into her nostrils. Monique was there and dried her brow.

– My grandmother told me about the transition, she said softly. – It's always hard on the powerful.

She sounded totally casual about it. Lillian did feel comforted.

Martin played the flute. He hadn't done that before, for some reason, not nine hundred years ago or during their modern companionship, but he could clearly play. It was both different and not compared to the music Lillian remembered. It evoked more memories, which was clearly his intention. She heard easily that it wasn't exactly like the music she remembered, but even older. She remembered before Gudrun again. A horned man stood on a hill and played his pan flute. It evoked all kinds of emotions in her as she crossed the valley below. There was a dark water ahead of her. She walked to it, and met a women with tattooed features face to face.

– Yes, this is you, the woman stated. – This is the goddess you once were, and will be again.

She had dark hair, dark skin, even though she was dressed in warm clothing. Martin and she walked a mountain trail with many others, and some of them had fireeyes. A jolt shot though her limbs. She knew her eyes had turned white, that the eyeballs had twisted themselves in their sockets. She couldn't see anything of the cozy living room, only the dark waters and the long trail in front of her.

– You've grown even more powerful, the ancient version of her told herself. – I didn't believe that was possible. Clearly, those of us fearing that the blood would be diluted with time were grossly mistaken. I salute you, my future self.

The face in the water mirror frowned.

– You've got questions, of course. I will give you one answer. You chose this body. You could have chosen several others available to you, both before and after this one, but you picked this one from the smorgasbord available to you. Yes, you are a Goddess, a non-material force of being reaching beyond time and Space. You can do that.

Lillian collapsed on the sofa. Martin stopped playing. She could see her surroundings again.

He's pushing the change, she thought.

She sat up.

– I need to go to the bathroom, she said.

Everyone chuckled. She joined in, as she rose and stumbled to the bathroom upstairs. Tove joined her. Tove smiled. They reached the bathroom simultaneously. There were several toilet bowls there.

– Do you believe this shit? Tove asked her.

– I do, Lillian replied calmly, ignoring her friend's patronizing tone.

Tove didn't say more, even though she clearly wanted to do so.

Lillian stopped on her walk down the stairs, and looked out the giant window. Twilight and mist had descended upon St. John's Wood. Lillian had become distracted again, dreaming herself away. Tove grabbed her arm and shook her. They returned to the gathering below.

– Can you tell us more about your travels? Marianne wondered. – The physical travels, I mean

She gets it, Lillian thought.

Everyone looked attentive at her. She appreciated that.

– Everything was… different, she began, searching for words. – We visited Cornwall and Padstow…

– You visited Padstow? Marianne gasped.

– We did. It was calm after the storm, but we could still sense the deeper echoes of what had happened there. The spirits had not left the place. It was a remarkable realization when I sensed them, when I sensed their eyes on me. Any sensitive person visiting would feel the same, and acknowledge that the world is completely, totally different from what we're told it is.

She grew passionate in her storytelling, practically glowing in the chair. Her hands turned transparent. The four stared. She smiled.

– Greece was amazing. All those old places there spoke to me as well. But Egypt was even more remarkable. I met myself there, my ancient self. She spoke to me, and shared her experiences. It felt so… so natural, like the most natural thing in the world. I was carried away, up The Nile, down the River Styx, the river of knowledge, life and Death…

She talked herself to exhaustion. The dark night descended outside. She finally ran out of words. The ten and Marianne and Jonathan hugged her and caressed her, making her calm down, even as her inner unrest and fire continued burning.

The four left somewhere during the late evening.

– I'm so interested in hearing more, Marianne said.

– So am I, Jonathan said.

Tove and Axel didn't say anything.

The four waved goodbye as they vanished around the nearest far corner.

Martin and Lillian, and the ten remained. It felt peaceful, but also quiet, too quiet. Lillian remained energetic, unable to sit still or relax.

– You did public performances in the seventies, Lillian said abruptly to Martin. – The time is overdue to return to that. I'm so impatient. I can hardly wait.

Her visible energies made the ten gasping in awe. She paced the floor, and those energies grew even stronger.

She rested in Martin's arms.

– Something will happen soon, she stated. – I'm certain of it.

– London is a melting pot, a cauldron, he said. – Something will most certainly happen. It has been brewing for decades. At least that long.

– I'm looking so much forward to that, she mumbled, mentally fatigued, emotionally drained. – I need an outlet. I need…

– I know, he soothed her.

– You're so kind, she choked.

He rubbed her back. They sat there for a while. He signed for the ten to leave them, and they did, retreating to the bedroom on the upper floor. She yawned. Her eyes slid close. She attempted to keep them open, but failed.

She slept.

2

The Hurricane Gloria had swept the American east coast and ended a long dry spell there, but London experienced an Indian Summer, a heat stronger and more enduring than people could remember.

They noticed it the moment they reached the more populated streets the next day, the anxiety, restlessness in the air.

Lillian knew it wasn't the weather that made people walk around with flickering eyes.

– London is like a vibrating string, Martin said, – so sensitive to changes, and now, the string vibrates much, much stronger.

Lillian made one glance at people, and saw how they glanced at each other, how they whispered among themselves.

– Something is happening, she mused. – It's impossible to tell what it is, but the natives are notably restless.

She glanced at a newspaper at the kiosk they passed. It was September 28.

They boarded a Tube train at St. John's Wood and headed south. The twelve of them stood out as usual, but they were no longer the sole center of people's attention.

– The Underground is such a great Swiss Cheese, she grinned.

The surrounding chuckle pleased her.

– It's true, Annabelle said. – If you want to ditch a stalker, he or she must struggle hard to keep up with you. One change of trains at a busy intersection, and there are several directions to consider. Two changes, and you might be anywhere in town within half an hour. It's a nightmare to those doing surveillance.

– They will probably install an extensive camera surveillance eventually, Elijah said.

They were strong individuals, Lillian noted. They might have an inflated view of her, but they weren't sheep.

Relief surged through her again.

They took the Victoria Line to Brixton, the end of the blue line.

– I haven't seen Stuart Elliott in ten years, Martin said. – He will probably start wondering about my enduring youthful appearance soon.

More chuckles.

– They should celebrate your longevity, Honored One, Monique said, – not fear it.

She was such an innocent soul, in spite of her cruel memories. Pondering the issue, Lillian found herself different from her.

Lillian noticed the decay the moment they stepped off the train. It was notable at the station, and even more so in the streets outside.

– He's a community leader, Martin added, – well respected in the community, the typical pain in the ass for the police and authorities.

Everyone in his group snickered.

Lillian was sweating, in spite of her dressing light. The pervasive heat was just that, and she was unused to it, in spite of her brief time in Greece and Egypt. She knew she was in excellent shape, knew it went beyond the muscular arms and thighs, the broad shoulders, the athletic body she spotted in the store windows. Pride filled her every time she did.

Brixton was a derelict, long neglected area of London, quite different from the tourist traps West End and Soho and certainly Mayfair. Lillian could picture all the places they had walked the last month, and this was a far cry from that.

– All cities have… slums, she remarked.

– It is an integrated feature, he said.

– I love hearing the wrath in your voices, Francois said.

So do I, Lillian thought.

Her rage burned on a low flame, but it burned. It spurred her on.

Whatever they had noticed far north, they noticed even more here. Lillian heard angry shouts from several directions. The unrest grew by the minute.

The building didn't look any different than the other buildings in the street, but Lillian could tell that was their destination when she studied Martin. She had become so astute, sensitive to minute changes in features and body language.

They walked inside, and up one floor. Martin knocked on one of the doors. Lillian heard the footsteps grow louder. A black man in his forties opened the door.

– I knew it wasn't the cops, he grinned. – Their knocking is significantly different. This sounded very much like a Martin Keller knock.

Stuart Elliott hugged Martin, fiving him an extensive hug before pulling back.

– Come inside, all of you. There isn't much physical space, but lots of room for those with a heart.

A poet, Lillian thought. That sat well with her.

Calling the apartment a dump was too kind. To top it off, the place was already packed with people. The newly arrived slipped into the tiny spaces left.

All colors, all creeds were present here. More excitement surged through Lillian.

– We were just about to start, Stuart said.

A thin layer of sweat covered all his visible skin. Lillian saw with a glance that he was angry. He was practically fuming with rage.

– The police have shot Cherry Groce, he said. – She has six children. Whether or not it was yet another «bungled operation», or deliberate is, as always hard to say. They invaded her home, looking for her son, and shot her.

Shouts of rage filled the closet of a studio apartment, matching the growing roar from the outside. More flashes shook Lillian. She remembered other meetings like this, many more.

They heard a shot being fired outside. It sounded extremely loud through the walls. The noise rose to a roar in her ears. It sounded like that for a while, but then it started… changing. She started hearing the music beneath the noise.

– A few thousand people, a few groups control human society, Martin stated. – They might not agree or cooperate about everything, but they're joined in all ways that count, against the rest of humanity, and all life on the planet. This is the society their kind desire and has designed.

Lillian gasped soundlessly as the implications of what he had said dawned on her, and she pondered what it entailed, what it actually meant for humanity.

He enjoyed great respect among these people. She could see that with half an eye. When they looked at him, they didn't see a wealthy or successful man, but a kindred soul sharing their view on the world. He had overcome what had certainly been their initial reluctance.

She had heard that about him from others, in other groups of poor or destitute people as well. Many had scolded him for it, but she knew him, and knew it was genuine, that he wasn't playing poor rich man. A warm, warm glow filled her.

– Let's go outside, she heard herself say. – We shouldn't be couped up here a minute longer.

They looked astounded at her, as if they had just noticed her.

She knew they glanced at her belly, but she ignored them.

– We should poison the constables, she said. – They will probably drink from the same coffee machine or machines, or get food from the same kettle during such a major operation. It should be a small matter to put something there. I read about a potion that is very effective for such matters. It will probably take some time until it starts working, but it should eventually put quite a few of them out of commission, and do so for days.

They stared at her. She smiled sweetly.

– I carry some important ingredients on me. The rest, like salt and stuff are easily found anywhere.

Martin looked both stunned and pleased at her.

She made the brew in the kitchen sink in front of everyone, grinding and mixing the herbs. It didn't really feel awkward or difficult, but casual, easy. The dark giggle worked itself up her throat again. Words she had read, the flashes of a long gone but not forgotten distant past flashed before her eyes. She knew how to do this. It was practically instinctive.

– I'm a wretched witch, she hummed.

It wasn't just the mixing of the herbs. She… spread to the entire room, to everyone in it, to those passing by outside. The potion boiled. She looked pleased at the process.

She filled small bottles with the brew, doing so with casual, confident moves, as if she had always done so.

– Some of these are poisons, she informed them. – Others are more explosive stuff. You just throw it at a wall or hard surface. It blows when it breaks.

They walked outside as a group, moved through the streets as one, cohesive unit with a singular mind or at least mindset. She found it remarkable. They walked to the police station in Brixton Road. The station was being refurbished. A new, temporary building had been constructed to the rear for the public to use.

– Strike me, she bid Martin.

He hesitated for a moment, but did as she asked, hitting her on the jaw, making the blood flow from the mouth. She staggered, but stayed on her feet.

– Wait here, she bid them.

They looked at her with respect. She couldn't help but enjoy that as she stumbled toward the entrance. Two constables guarding the door caught sight of her and froze.

– I was assaulted, she mumbled.

They heard her.

– He tried pulling me into an alley, but I fought him off, and he ran away.

She dropped to her knees and on her side. They rushed to her.

– I'm okay, she mumbled. – I'm just dizzy. You don't need to call an ambulance.

They grabbed her and carried her into the station, past the reception area. Several constables stared at her. Her two heroes put her on a coach in a quiet hallway.

– Stay here, one of them said. – We'll get back to you.

They rushed off, and disappeared around the corner.

She waited ten seconds and rushed further down the hallway. Finding the kitchen, and the large pots of coffee and the giant kettle with food weren't really that hard. She rushed to empty one small bottle into each of the pots and the kettle. The heart hammered in her chest. She kept looking around her. No one appeared. She rushed back through the hallway. There was no one in the reception area. She heard loud voices from a room nearby.

Her comrades in arms gave her a warm welcome. Martin hugged her and kissed her, clearly relieved. Poor bugger.

The activity picked up outside the station even as they left it behind. Three vans filled with constables arrived. The constables practically ran into the building. Five guarded the entrance.

– They prepare for war, Martin said.

That did bring a chill to Lillian's bones.

They encountered a large crowd of people. Dozens gathered outside Dorothy's house. Rage shifted and burned between them, a palpable seething of emotions making Lillian shake and burn with them.

– They did it again, a man shouted. – Damn those trigger-happy arseholes!

– They must have had a reason, another stated with a conviction. – What had she done?

– Done? The first snarled. – Nothing, aside from being in the wrong place, her own, fucking home with her children.

– They're fed up, Martin told Lillian. – They've been run over so many times, and won't stand for it anymore.

The gathering headed for the police station. A large contingent of constables waited for them there. A roar of rage rose from the approaching crowd. They spread out in the neighborhood, and began smashing store windows and doors.

– They see those stores as part of the occupation, too, Stuart explained.

Martin and Lillian stayed back a little with Stuart and a group of people slightly bigger than those from his apartment. The number of people ravaging the area around Brixton Road grew significantly. The shouts of rage made the walls shake.

The night fell, and everything exploded in massive chaos. Reinforcements arrived. At least fifty constables wearing black uniforms and helmets, carrying and holding shields, weapons, dogs, water cannons and teargas were added to those already there. They placed themselves opposite the protesters further down the street. The protesters threw bricks and rocks at them. They shouted enraged at the advancing troops without face:

– GESTAPO, GESTAPO.

A well-known name of shame from recent human history.

The troops started the attack with teargas and steel bullets coated in rubber. Then, like mad dogs they started assaulting the unarmed crowd in earnest. The crowd was dispersed, and screamed in terror and rage. Some of them began fighting back. They gathered in smaller groups and continued the protests. The constables turned notably more desperate behind the masks, and even more violent. They began assaulting people passing by that hadn't been a part of the original crowd. It was at that very moment they lost all control over the situation.

– They assault those they claim to protect, a man with a bleeding head shouted stunned.

The constables kept raising their sticks and hammer vulnerable flesh and skulls. Two of them hammered an old man crouching in pools of blood and guts. Others held people, and encouraged their dogs to bite them. Several of the four-legged creatures complied. The screams of pain turned even louder.

Lillian and Martin stayed back, as much as they could. He and the ten focused on protecting her from the worst of the violence. A mix of gratitude and frustration surged through her. She understood his position. She wasn't exactly fit to fight in such a cauldron this had become.

Some of the constables began exhibiting strange behavior. They ripped off their helmets and began gasping and choking and puking their guts out. They dropped to their knees, weak as kittens.

Finally, she thought with glee.

People chuckled incredulous. They began hassling the sick constables, and giving them a touch, just a touch of their own medicine. The chink in the uniformed armor grew huge. Several constables stumbled off, fleeing the scene. Most of them didn't get far before dropping on their knees and puking their guts out.

– BAD FOOD, one constable whined. – BAD FOOD!

Their own dogs started biting them. A loud WAIL rose from the still armored people on the ground.

Lillian cheered when four protesters held up a constable and started beating him, tearing off his armor, giving him, as one of the few some tiny payback. She could hardly contain herself, could hardly stay back. One constable squealed like a pig. The dark laughter rose from her throat.

The constables more or less unaffected by the ailment striking their colleagues kept beating up protesters. They struck the protesters to the ground, and dragged them into the black vans. Protesters fought them, and cut the tires, keeping them from driving off. More and more pigs dropped to the ground with a downright unhealthy skin color. When the protesters set out to liberate the prisoners, there were only a few left to defend the black vans. All the prisoners were liberated.

It turned quiet for a moment. Lillian sensed it, experienced it in slow motion. The few pigs still standing pulled back.

– Let them go, people, one man chuckled. – We've got work to do.

They ran to the police station and rushed inside. Several people came with torches and petrol, and set fire to the building. It didn't look like it would take at first, from Lillian's pulled back position outside, but then it did. She looked awestruck at the spectacle, as the flames began licking the walls.

People began pulling back, as if by solemn agreement. Lillian and Martin did, too, along with Stuart and others from the small apartment.

– The two of you are awesome, he chuckled. – You made it all far more memorable, made it something to remember for *ages*. But you better get the hell out of the neighborhood. The repercussions of this will be quite something, and they will come down even harder on those not living here.

Hands clasped hands, and waved goodbye. Lillian and Martin, their charges, and others headed north. They ran through a street with burned-out cars and several buildings still on fire, ashes covering the ground and ripping into their nostrils.

They saw burned, abandoned police barricades, heard distinct moans interrupted by screams of pain from the houses they passed.

– Everything looks so different, Monique marveled. – I see everything in a blinding light.

– The police will get away with it again, Lillian remarked. – They always do. Some of the others looked shocked at her. Most nodded in agreement.

– They always have, she added.

They reached their home early in the morning, in a seemingly long twilight between shadow and light. The long fast walk hadn't really tired them.

– I could have run the whole day, Annabelle stated with confidence. – I could have stayed awake for weeks.

The impressions and sensations from the previous day and night burned within them. The fire burned, and didn't make ashes.

– I can't remember ever feeling more aware, Lillian said. – There is no contest.

– I can with confidence say I've enjoyed a few defining experiences lately, Francois said, – but this one is definitely one more.

They couldn't sit down, sit still, but kept pacing back and forth on the floor. Lillian caught the motion of them all according to herself. A pattern revealed itself. She saw it from above, and it felt so familiar. The sun rose in the sky, and brought the strange white light, lots of bright shadows into the room, the hall. She imagined she could see everything in that shifting glow.

She could recall feeding, devouring food with her extreme appetite.

– I do four full meals a day, now, she munched. – It doesn't really affect my figure. That doesn't.

It was supposed to be funny, but they didn't laugh, and she didn't hold it against them. Monique grabbed her hand, and squeezed it softly.

– We are different from baseline humans, Lillian said. – We enjoy a series of skillsets they can only dream of. We're everything they dream of being, and they envy us beyond insanity.

Martin turned on the television. The others looked curiously at him.

It was the news. They covered the «riots». The spokesman for the government blamed the protesters, and praised the police for their «heroic fight against the mob rule». The entire coverage supported that, and gave the retouched version of the events. The shooting of Dorothy Groce wasn't mentioned with a word.

Martin turned off the television.

– It looks and sounds like Not the Nine O'Clock News, Annabelle snorted.

She referred to a satire program that had been running on BBC a few years ago. The others chuckled by the very thought.

– The establishment media is totally unsurprising in their usual deliberate denial of reality, Elijah added.

Everyone nodded. They were all on the same page. Pride surged through

Lillian.

   Lillian and others started yawning after dinner that day, and decided to go to bed, in an effort to get some hard-needed sleep. She did feel emotionally drained, and she recognized that in the others, too. Martin didn't exhibit anything like that. He had been hardened by centuries of vicious struggle.
   She could understand that.
   They undressed in an unceremonious manner, and dropped down on the bed. Lillian twisted and turned on the pleasant surface, unable to fall asleep. Monique had her back to her. Lillian could hear on her breathing that she wasn't sleeping either. She began brushing her lips on the skin of the girl's neck.
   – Are you alright, little one?
   Monique turned, and smiled.
   – I'm so excited, My Goddess. I can hardly close my eyes. I thought I was sleepy, but I'm not. Thoughts keep churning in my head.
   She hesitated a bit. Lillian prompted her.
   – I was so encouraged by your decisive action, My Goddess. It felt so great seeing the thugs receive their just reward. They would have done far more and worse to all the protesters if you hadn't.
   A warm, warm feeling surged through Lillian. She kissed the other girl on the lips. Moniqe smiled happily.
   – That was just the modest start, Lillian stressed. – There's so much left to do, so many years of neglect to repair.
   – When I look at you, I don't see the young girl, Monique said in a hushed voice. – I see… the creature.
   – Very good, Lillian shrugged.
   She saw it, too, in glimpses. She saw the demon, saw it burn.
   – My father, Lillian's father scared me with tales of Hell and damnation since I was a little girl. I learned to discard and reject it as the bullshit it is, but I guess some of it stuck.
   – Monique's did, too, the other giggled.
   Lillian put her arms around her, comforting her a bit. She noticed how it relaxed her, how her breathing slowed down, and she closed her eyes. She fell asleep.
   The wind was blowing outside. Lillian heard it, sensed it. She made one more attempt at falling asleep, in vain. The wind blew harder. She slipped out of bed. Someone had turned on the television again. Lillian had no trouble hearing it. The sword killer had struck again, in London. They spoke about the case in the news studio, bringing the viewers through the case from the first victim in Norway, and to date. Lillian froze, and feared that

she wouldn't be able to move.

She remained nude, and stepped into the octagon. The two main swords twinkled and burned in her vision. She made three jumps, and grabbed the handle of her sword, and slipped instantly into fight-mode. There was no opponent here, but that didn't matter. She moved as if there was, picturing shadows with swords, as she turned and moved. She had learned to fight against an imaginary opponent, but this one did feel real. His stabbing and cutting felt real, and so did hers. She remembered battles, fights and people bleeding. It was an extreme type of shadow fighting.

The sense of time faded away. She lost herself in the sparring, in the stabbing and cutting. The world changed around her. The air grew crisp and a thick haze of red.

One of her bodies, her shells rested on the wet ground, leaking blood, leaking heat, dying. She waited for death as she gasped for air, as her heart stopped beating, and she drew her final breath on a battlefield covered in blood and torn-apart flesh.

Chapter 13

Another black woman Cynthia Jarret suffered rough police treatment. She died as a direct result of it. London exploded in rage and explosive violence.

Lillian visualized it in her feverish mind, glimpsing details from the beyond excessive and deliberate Police brutality. The uniformed and armored troops attacked in rows. It hardly looked any different from Brixton, or any other place where the police assaulted unarmed people.

– You can see because you have access to the Shadowland, he said, while drying her brow. – Distance becomes less and often even meaningless when you can do shortcuts like that.

This was in Broadwater Farm, in Tottenham, North London, far from Brixton. It didn't seem like that when Lillian, Martin and the guys arrived for the public protest meeting after the explosion had somewhat subsided.

– Michael Randle pushed my mother, Patricia Jarret shouted from the platform. – He and the other constables knew she had trouble with her heart, but he did it anyway.

A roar rose from the massive crowd. Members of the heavy police presence looked shitty, very shitty.

– This, all this has happened so many times. Each time, we're promised that there will be changes. Each time, it repeats itself, and we're treated with the usual contempt and scorn.

She kept raging on, and Lillian, standing by her side found herself riled up, her rage and determination growing by the second. She hardly managed to stay still.

Patricia ended her speech. Lillian's began.

– First of all, I'm honored to be given a platform here. I'm a foreigner, and I'm confident that will give even more fuel to the white supremacy hatred dominating Europe.

The crowd cheered her. The cheering strengthened her.

– Let's be clear. What we're facing is the institutionalized racism inherent in the entire British and European society, like there is in all countries where people of European ancestry are dominant… where the gross notion of white supremacy is dominant. Nothing ever changes, unless we take it all in our own hands, and reject the very idea that those ruling us will ever treat us right. We aren't small children begging favors from our parents. We're adult human beings, and we're fed up with living in a tyranny treating us like lambs to the slaughter.

She paused a bit, the cheers and applause picked up.

– Stuart Elliott and activists, like Stafford Scott were arrested in Broadwater Farm during the heat of the street battles. Those having participated in the killing of Cynthia Jarrett face no charges or jail time. There are those of us daring to call «our excellent police corps» for what they are: paid thugs and murderers for the oppressors and the privileged classes. ENOUH!

The cheers and applause grew to a roar. The crowd grew wild. The uniformed thugs beating their shields drowned completely in it.

– Western leaders have committed the worst war crimes and crimes for many decades, both foreign and domestic, and have the gall to criticize people standing up to them, having the gall to criticize leaders in foreign countries for being «undemocratic». Each accusation from our proud leaders is a *confession*. People belieiving them are not mere sheep, but mindless, brainwashed puppets. New thoughts are killed every second, in this thought-killing place. We're supposed to be living, thriving beings, but are slaves under the yoke. ENOUGH!

She stepped back. It took time, but the roar eventually faded.

– Lillian Donner, Ladies and Gentlemen, Patricia cried. – Don't forget to attend her and Martin Keller's upcoming public performance. Listen to the grapevine and the word of mouth for the time and the place.

The ten surrounded her, protected her, guarded her as she stepped down from the platform and rushed into Martin's arms.

Watching the news on television that night was a downer, but they had expected that, prepared for that. Prime minister Margareth Thatcher, during the Conservatives' annual conference praised the constables, «our excellent police force» for their «resolute action against the street bullies».

Martin started laughing. He couldn't stop. He was literally rolling on the floor laughing. Lillian and the others looked good humored at him.

The twelve exercised together. Lillian enjoyed that even more, now, when she had ten struggling to keep up with her, ten to teach. The big belly didn't seem to impede on her physical prowess in any notable manner.

She and Martin floated in the pool down below. They had given the ten some meaningless tasks to perform.

– We're keeping secrets from them, she frowned. – I guess that makes sense.

– When the time is right, we'll share all the secrets in the world with them, he stated.

She floated on her back, looking at the flickering pattern of light and shadow on the ceiling. It worked on her. She noticed how it encouraged her ASC, her ESP, putting her in a trance.

Eyes opened wide. The big body shook. She turned limp and almost dropped below the surface. She fought herself back on shallow water. He stood there and watched her. It was like he faded away before her eyes.

– I don't know, she said distressed. – I don't know what…

She died on the battlefield again and her spirit «rose» from that discarded body and entered the Shadowland. She caught a glimpse, one with a million indescribable impressions and sensations.

Wide eyes stared at him. She struggled to talk.

– How long was I out?

– You were hardly out at all, he said.

– It was unbelievable. In one tiny moment, I saw infinity and eternity squared. I saw everything worth seeing. I was an enormously powerful entity roaming the void. Is that how every visit to the Other World is like?

– It is pretty much how many aware beings describe it, he said.

– I faced… myself, not just a shard of myself like before, but me, my eternal self, and it was like a massive amount of pure information downloaded itself into my mind, and now the memory of it is already fading. This is who we truly are beyond the flesh. It's… indescribable.

She stood there and repeated the last word several times.

– Most people believe they encounter God or Satan, or the equivalent in other religions, he said, – but they aren't. Like you said, they encounter themselves, the complete entity, and all its memories, all its experiences, from every single life it has ever lived.

She rushed to him and kissed him, smothering him in kisses. They stood like that for a while, while she slowly calmed down, and felt both good and bad about it.

They returned to the top floor and walked down the stairs. The others returned. She noticed that they noticed.

– Something has happened, right? Annabelle said, unusually solemn, unsatiable curious.

– I faced myself, Lillian said.

And they knew what she was talking about. They dropped to their knees.

– Ted and Liz Warren say that people doing that a lot get sore knees, Lillian said lightly. – It seems appropriate to us as well.

They had jumped back on their feet before she had finished speaking.

– I may inspire you, may lead you, but never make you crawl at my feet.

They got it. She was the one they listened to, not him, not so much him. The interaction between them puzzled her yet again.

The October heat never seemed to end. When they took repeated strolls though the streets, it was there with them, all the time. They watched some great movies, like Starman, Crimes of Passion, Cocoon, Lifeforce and Mad

Max Beyond Thunderdome.

Lifeforce directed by Tobe Hooper was about space vampires draining life force from people. The story echoed strangely familiar through her mind. It was shown at Leicester Square Theater, and was packed on every presentation.

– This will never be shown in Norway, she giggled. – The content is way too controversial for weak souls. And to think the British also complain about their censor board being too hard on movies.

It was also packed at Warner Westend, during the presentation of Mad Max Beyond Thunderdome. The sixteen were there at the premier performance, on one of the matinees. The queue reached through the square and Coventry Street, all the way to Piccadilly Circus.

– This is quite something, Francois beamed.

Lillian had dressed in a short skirt and violet sweater. She displayed her shapely legs with pride, not shy because of all the stares at all.

She had picked everything herself, except the heels. She sent Martin a wicked glance.

– You will seem clumsy, helpless, he had told her. – Perhaps that will encourage Erling to take a stab at you. His frail ego might not be able to resist the temptation.

– It isn't a bad plan, she grudgingly admitted.

He was a warrior. He didn't need to pull that from his depths. She nodded to herself.

October 18, 1985, was a hot day, even hotter than most. She still felt the chill touch her bones.

They stepped into hall 2.

– This is enormous, she gasped impressed. – I'll bet there are at least two thousand seats here.

– The goddess' wild heart makes her easily impressed, Annabelle noted. – I love that, just love that.

Lillian shook her head in wonder. She seemed to impress her charges, no matter what she did or said. She pretended not to notice Tove's caustic look.

The music thundered through the speakers. The hall had turned dark. Tina Turner's voice echoed through the room and people's ears and imagination. The dark canvas shifted to the desolate, desert-like landscape supposed to be Australia after World War 3.

It felt very much like it. Her imagination brought her there, to the dry sand and vehicles running on pig shit. She descended into the story, the moving images, like she always did with an engaging movie. The entire earth had become an endless wasteland, and only a few survivors remained.

It stayed with her afterwards, in soft impressions, easily discerned from her visions.

– It's like you told us, Monique said. – A good movie or book are like living an entire life in a few hours.

They stepped out on the street. She froze, and he froze the moment they did. They all felt a… a presence, there in the shadows. The dying daylight looked far weaker than it was supposed to in her eyes. She glanced at Martin. He nodded imperceptibly. The murderer was here, was nearby. They didn't see anyone, anyone pointing to themselves, but they felt him.

Both tensed and prepared themselves.

Minutes passed. Nothing happened.

Saturday night, they rewatched Cat People and The Hunger at Roxie Cinema Club in Wardour Street. Lillian loved both movies, and the mood in the small, intimate theater made it an even more intense experience. Most of those in the theater had clearly watched the films before, even several times before. They, like Lillian enjoyed the details and the mood more.

– She was so sensual, Monique said about Nastassja Kinski. – I can't believe how sensual and beastly she was.

– The story reminds me of Ted and Liz Warren, Annabelle breathed. – They've been called the wild men in the modern world. Such performances and people are so very dangerous to those in charge, because they can't be controlled.

Those two names kept coming up. An excited trickle ran down Lillian's spine.

– A standard to uphold, she said lightly.

Yet another movement seemed to stretch out, to last forever. The sinister presence returned, non-localized, all around them, and faraway. A draft hit them in the dark, narrow alley, causing a different kind of chill to surge through her. She acknowledged the difference, acknowledged the sight and presence of the first yellow leaves on the trees.

2

Martin frowned. Lillian frowned. Monique frowned. They floated in a landscape of mist and shadow, light and darkness. The twelve, and also Jonathan and Marianne knew they were dreaming, dreaming together, and the dream was lucid, lucid enough for them to know that, and many secrets were revealed.

The hunter was tracking snow, crossing a strange, rocky prehistoric landscape. The snow melted fast, and it got harder, much harder to move. He reached a few ruins, everything left of what had clearly been a considerable city. Lots of footprints appeared before him. A cruel grin grew on his face. Martin saw, like Lillian only Erling like Erling, not as he truly looked or should look in the vision. He couldn't penetrate the haze surrounding the blurry figure.

One arrow penetrated the man's chest. One more hit him a moment later. He dropped to the ground, releasing a splash when his body hit the wet slush. A snarl of frustration and despair rose from his throat. He began gasping as death approached. The group of people surrounded him. He spotted the fire in their eyes.

– You will never catch us, the woman with black eyes stated, – never truly beat us, no matter how many times you try.

He snarled at her in atavistic fear, as the final gasp worked its way up his throat. He stared at her with dead eyes.

Martin recognized the woman. Lillian and several of the others did, too. A happy grin spread on their faces.

Stine, Martin and Lillian breathed.

Prometheus, Monique breathed.

They looked stunned at her. Lillian witnessed as the woman with the black eyes caught fire, as the flames surrounded and embraced her, and it was a remarkable sight.

A bit to the right of… of Prometheus, she spotted herself. She wasn't hard to recognize at all. Lillian marveled at the sight of her, of the hardened warrior witch.

Everyone woke up. Lillian kissed softly Martin's cold and sweaty skin.

The prolonged flash of lightning blinded them momentarily. The thunder sounded strangely muted in their ears.

– I'm alright, he assured her.

– Bad liar, she said softly.

Something was… off. It had turned cold. The weather had changed completely in a few hours. They noticed that beyond doubt the moment they left the warm bed, and no longer was surrounded by all the warm bodies. Everyone rushed to dress. The Indian Summer had made artificial heating unnecessary. All of it were turned off. They rushed to correct that. Martin lit the fireplace. Elijah and Annabelle carried the dry wood to him, and he put it in the right place and lit the fire.

Another lightning brightened the large floor, all the three floors. The thunder followed almost instantly this time, and was considerably louder. The various heat sources slowly made the air warmer. Martin stayed close to the fireplace, as if he couldn't get warm soon enough.

– Something happened, he stated. – The fourteen of us combined our resources and experienced something we probably wouldn't have experienced alone. One of you is clearly a telepath, or at least a sensitive of some kind.

They knew what he was saying and turned both encouraged and anxious, the latter mostly because of his visible anxiety.

A loud crack practically shook the house and the flesh within it. Something heavy had hit the door. Martin signed to them. They spread out on the floor, keeping their attention on the door. Francois approached it cautiously. There was no new sound, except the rain against the windows, and the thunder.

He walked far enough forward to peek outside, at the short stairs.

– I can't see anyone, he reported.

Annabelle walked to the other side.

– I can't see anyone either, she said.

Together, they could see every spot in front of the door, and most of the outside front area of the property.

Elija opened the door. He looked around and up, notably anxious.

– There's a box with something attached to it two steps from the stairs, he reported. – I guess that was what hit the door.

– Pick it up, Martin bid him. – Be ready for anything.

Elija stepped outside. They saw him well enough, but he still seemed to vanish, to fade away in the darkness. He picked up the box. They watched him as he froze.

– A fresh scalp is tied to the box, he choked. – The blood is still wet.

– Can you open the box?

It was no trouble. He hesitated briefly before finding the simple lock, and pulling the lid off the box. He held up a video cassette.

– There is nothing here that can possibly be a bomb or anything, he stated.

He sounded perfectly calm. The others couldn't believe how calm he seemed, and he couldn't either.

– Bring it back inside. Close and lock the door behind you.

The young man did, fast on suddenly shaky feet, as if the very darkness out there chased him.

Everyone's attention was drawn to the scalp with black hair attached to the box. They stayed on their guard, but rushed to put the video in the player.

The video started with Lisbeth walking nude in the room where she had been killed. Welts from hard whipping covered her back. She walked with a bowed head, and looked at the floor, never raising her head, very cowed and timid, broken.

– Please, be kind to me, she whimpered. – I'll be a good girl.

257

Lillian forced herself to watch, to listen.

There was a loud crack. A whip hit her back. She screamed and choked in anguish, and rushed to the bed, rushing to lay down on her back. The camera was left on the floor. It showed only the wall. The recording continued. They heard easily the sound of the girl's gasps, and her moaning, and the flat hand hitting her skin. Lillian rolled her hands into fists, attempting in vain to stop her vivid imagination from working.

A muffled scream. They heard the knife cutting flesh.

– It's just like on film, Monique choked.

The camera was raised from the floor and directed at the mangled, unmoving body on the bed. The final frame was a frozen picture of Lisbeth's twisted, frozen features.

The video reached its end and stopped by itself.

– We must report this, Martin said.

– The establishment media will have a field day, Jonathan joked, or attempted to do so.

They watched the video one more time with Inspector Burke Adams from Scotland Yard. Lillian sat unmoving and pale in a chair and forced herself to watch and listen once again.

– There has been a murder in London, too, Adams mused. – I'm certain you've heard about it. We read the reports from Norway. Without saying too much, I can say that the cases have striking similarities.

They didn't comment on his musings.

– And now there is another. The scalping is new, though, but that is more than suggesting that there will be another dead body soon.

– She's dead, Martin said evenly, – probably nearby.

– The murderer seems to carry a grudge of some kind against you, Adams remarked. – I have to ask this. Do you have any idea who the murderer is, and what is the cause of all this?

– I have no idea who he is, Martin replied, visibly frustrated.

Adams frowned, perhaps catching the nuances in Martin's reply.

The police, after a tip from the public, found the body less than two hours later by one of the exits of Regent Park, found it nude, scalped and stabbed to death, and buried in mud and blood. Lillian's vivid imagination, or her esoteric powers, she couldn't tell which, made her see everything.

Adams returned alone to Martin and Lillian and the guys later that day.

– The girl was of mixed race. She was raped. There was no semen in her vagina. She was stabbed many times with a swordlike blade.

He didn't spend much time there, clearly anxious to get going, to begin the investigation. He shook hands with Martin and Lillian.

– You're still persons of interest in the case, in spite of your alibies and stuff, he informed them. – Some of my superiors would love to see you arrested for the murders, for anything under the sun, really. Stay alert.

He walked off. They watched him as he did.

– Was that a policeman? Annabelle wondered incredulous.

– I've heard about him for quite some time, Martin said with a solemn grin. – He started off as the typical conservative policeman with respect for law and order. Something happened ten years ago, during and after his first major case involving Mark Stewart and a very young Ted Warren. He turned into a radical, someone they would have booted off the force if he hadn't been untouchable. He kept solving strange cases, making him practically impossible to remove. He's such a glorious anomaly…

3

The fourteen woke up in the bed on the morning of October 31. They stretched and hugged each other.

– Today is Samhain, Martin said at the breakfast table, – the day, the All Souls Night the bold and sensitive and skilled and powerful might reach beyond the veil to the Other World.

– I can hardly wait, Marianne cried, with both anguish and anticipation in her voice.

The mere thought of it made Lillian's skin tingle with excitement, no matter how much the horrible experience the other day kept lingering in her gut. Determination made her roll her hands into fists again.

They watched the news as Oscar Haugli and Gunnar Nielsen were filmed when they entered Scotland Yard. They were interviewed in all major newspapers and TV-stations. When Lillian studied Gunnar, she didn't really feel much, one way or another.

– I'm so done with him, she told Marianne and Jonathan.

The fourteen started experimenting with biofeedback after breakfast. Jonathan brightened when he saw the machine.

– I have used it before, he mused, – and not getting satisfying results, but I might not have been in the right mood then. Everything is different, now.

Everything is different, now, Lillian thought.

The machine was basically a blinking light, and electrodes attached to skin and head. The point was to make the blinking slow down. The moment it slowed down to a crawl, the subject had reached an altered state of consciousness.

Lillian was first. She demonstrated the apparatus to the others. The blinking slowed down almost immediately.

– I feel strange, she reported, – like I'm not here.

Dislocation, she thought.

Her hand turned transparent. The shock made her lose control, and the light blinked faster again. She regained control.

– I sense the spirits…

She fell silent. Her eyes grew distant.

– Hello, she said with her strange voice. – Is there anything I can do for you?

Annabelle wanted to say something. Marianne hushed her up.

– She isn't speaking to us.

Lillian smiled. A chill entered the room.

– I can do that, she said.

She tilted her head, as if she was listening.

The dead girl stood in front of her, a black female with Asian features like herself. Lillian probed herself. She didn't feel frightened. If anything, she felt excitement.

– He will attempt to break you, the girl insisted. – Don't let him. You were given to him, in a moment of bad circumstances and weakness. You've beaten him so many times. You can do so again.

This time a chill passed through Lillian as well, but it didn't feel bad.

The girl faded away, leaving only an encouraging smile.

Lillian removed the electrodes, and turned off the light.

– She knew me, she frowned. – She remembered something I didn't. Erling's… master gave me to him as a gift, as if I was something to discard and throw away, as if I was nothing, and in that moment I was.

– What do you think it means? Monique asked, intensively curious.

– I don't know exactly, but it certainly shows that this is much bigger than just Erling and me. There is a… a tapestry vast and wide we can't yet see or fathom.

More chills and excitement surged through her. She could almost picture it in her buzzing mind.

The others tried out the machine. They did get some results, but nothing like she had done.

– It will come to you, she said softly to a frustrated Jonathan. – I know it will.

She pondered something unfathomable for a moment.

– Yes, Erling is so skilled that he knows how to better harm me, to rock me to the core. He knows what makes me tick, after our many encounters, while I can still only see him as Erling.

– It isn't enough to remember intellectually either, Martin stated. – You must remember emotionally, all the bad and good. Then, it will become real.

Real, she echoed in her thoughts.

It was real to him. She could tell that by a glance. But he had had nine-hundred years. She could not quite hold back the flare of resentment.

– Let's have a walk through London Town, she declared brazenly. – Let's take its measure, and enjoy every taste of nectar on our tongue.

She didn't quite sound like herself then. An unladylike giggle shook her throat.

They started walking and kept going. London's seething cauldron embraced them. With their heightened awareness, they sensed that even better than others. Lillian certainly did.

– This spread is so big, Jonathan said and shook his head in marvel. – Not even thousand lives will be sufficient to cover it all. A friend of mine growing up here keeps telling me that he hasn't become familiar with it.

Everyone chuckled. The shadows comforted and encouraged Lillian, didn't scare her. The walk made her feel better. They hadn't even walked past Regent Park before it had. The sights, the impressions and sensations licked her like…

Like flames, she thought startled.

– Samhain is our Lord and Master, Monique stated. – He's one of you, one of the gods walking the earth.

Lillian couldn't quite relate to that, even though she felt strongly that she should have. Frustration kept riling her.

Samhain… Lillian glanced around. The very air seemed alive, seemed to shimmer around her. This was a special day. They spotted far more drawings on the walls than what was common on any given day. The figures seemed to gain flesh, gain substance, gain life in her vision.

– The All Souls Night is the anniversary of my rebirth, when I was purified by the fire of his kingdom, and gained physical immortality, Martin said. – I will be at my most powerful.

Their temple guards bowed their heads in awe.

The fourteen moved in accordance with each other, with Martin and Lillian at the center. The group shimmered like the air. The surroundings darkened in Lillian's vision. The day seemed to turn to twilight. A man played the violin. He stood on a corner across the street. The music still sounded loud in her ears.

A woman and a boy approached the city wanderers on their side of the street.

For some reason, Lillian noticed the boy, eight or nine of age. He looked perfectly ordinary, there, walking at his mother's side. She did, too.

– Hi, the boy greeted them.

– Hi, Lillian said good humored.

She frowned and noticed that Martin and several of the others froze around her.

– I know you, he stated, frowning as well.

She looked puzzled at him.

– You know me, too.

The chill trickled down her spine. Her frontal lobe itched. His presence awoke something in her. She knew that for a fact, even though she couldn't identify it.

His mother hushed at him, and pulled him with her. Lillian wanted to cry out to her, to implore her to stop, but cat, or rather tiger got her tongue.

The boy turned and waved, and she saw one half of his face disappear, and only the naked skull remained. She blinked, and his face looked ordinary again.

She met his eyes. One moment, and she was lost.

– I'm falling, she said with her spooky voice, – not through space, but through time.

She wanted to move, to give chase, but was frozen on the spot. When she finally got going, the boy and the mother entered a cab. The cab drove off. Lillian kept seeing the half-skull and the sticking eyes.

– I do know him, she told the others.

The twelve looked awestruck at her, and this time it didn't seem awkward.

– But what is he doing here, in that body? Monique wondered in puzzlement.

– He has been reborn, like all of us, Lillian said. – That was his current body. Did any of you recognize him or her, their faces?

Everyone, Martin included shook their heads.

– She did look familiar, Jonathan mused, - but I can't place her. She wore expensive clothing.

The urgency stuck in Lillian's gut, but she couldn't put names on their faces either. She shook her head in frustration.

They turned as one and looked north. The street was packed with people. The fourteen people living in St. John's Wood headed home. They had a late dinner there. Marianne was shaking. Lillian felt strangely calm.

– The boy was… scary, she mumbled. – In one way, he looked completely ordinary. In another, he looked like something from another world.

They sat around the long table. Martin put one extra set of plate, knife, and fork on it.

– Who is coming to dinner? Monique asked with her naïve curiosity.

– We will have one more guest tonight, Martin replied lightly. – At least one.

Lillian heard the sound of the octagon elevator. It went straight to the top. A bit later, a tall, athletic black woman with black, curly hair descended the stairs. She didn't look older than Lillian, but Lillian suspected strongly that she was.

– Hi, I'm Jennifer Woodstone, the young woman greeted them. – It's so nice meeting you all.

– You are…

– His daughter, yes. Can't you see the resemblance?

It was a good joke, but they did look similar, if you looked past the obvious.

She had dressed in the latest fashion. White slacks and blouse, and a light green coat reaching her to her knees. The modern clothing didn't hide her wild nature.

Martin met her with a kiss. She returned it.

– Greetings, papa, she greeted him. – Best Samhain wishes.

– BEST SAMHAIN WISHES, the others returned.

She smiled.

– We're officially siblings, Martin explained. – Her mother was a Mameloi, a Voodoun priestess I met in the Caribbean hundred-and-fifty years ago, give or take.

– My mother was very powerful and very evil, Jennifer said softly. – But papa broke her and crushed her to dust, made her less than a grain of sand on the beach.

She stared at them with the glowing green eyes. The effect was quite remarkable.

– You're hundred-and-fifty years old? Jonathan gasped.

– Give or take, Jennifer said lightly.

– She's probably my only living child, Martin said, – and the first natural immortal I, and others in my circle of immortals, am aware of. I and her mother didn't do anything to make her that way, except conceiving her.

Jennifer looked a little peeved then, but stayed quiet.

She sat down, and the dining continued. She devoured the food in a manner matching Martin and Lillian. She was hard on the wine, too. Lillian and the others studied her with an excitement they couldn't hide. She revealed a patronizing taint she didn't bother to hold back.

– Someone has been stalking me lately, Jennifer said to Martin. – It wasn't easy to be positive about it. The feeling was so fleeting, and the stalker in question stayed cautious, but on our organic farm last week, I spotted the flash of binoculars reflecting the sunlight. I didn't know him. He realized that he had fucked up, and vanished before I could even come close. What does it mean?

– Just that we need to stay the course and do it a bit earlier than planned, Martin replied unconcerned.

– It's dangerous, Jennifer protested. – Erling can't do anything substantial to us. We can merely wait until he comes for us, and deal with him then. Why should we care about a few humans?

He slapped her so hard that she fell off the chair and hit the floor. Lillian and the others stared shocked at him. They hadn't really seen this side of him before.

– You will not contradict me this way, he told his daughter in a very strict manner. – Do you understand?

Jennifer bled from the mouth.

– Yes, papa. Of course, papa.

He nodded curtly, and she returned to her chair.

– You should ponder this very carefully, he instructed her, – and finally learn that all life has value. Nothing says you're a better person because you have powers and live longer. On the contrary, your outburst is more than suggesting that you're an elitist, and therefore a lesser being.

She stayed quiet and timid during the rest of the dining. She participated in the cleanup and dishwashing the same way.

– This girl was stupid, Goddess, she told Lillian humbly. – It won't happen again.

And that was the moment Lillian realized that Jennifer didn't see her as a young, inexperienced girl.

All cups, cutlery and plates were returned to its place in the drawers and cupboards. It happened in an effortless, flowing motion they couldn't help noticing. They exchanged more happy smiles.

Jennifer regained her good mood surprisingly fast. It was as if the event at the dining table hadn't happened.

– You should pay a visit to the organic farm, she said brightly. – You won't believe everything we're doing there.

– Thank you, Lillian replied. – I would love to.

The darkness entered the town from the east, from the dark horizon untouched by the sunset. Inspector Adams left his home to supervise the patrols through the streets of London.

– This is All Hallows Eve, and there is a full moon, *and* an eclipse, he instructed his men and women. – It's a special night, and we should do our best to not step on celebrating people's toes. I trust I can't trust on your discretion in this matter.

The constables mumbled their reluctant agreement. He settled for that. He had been forced to settle for far less.

Shifting clouds revealed and hid the moon in a constantly changing pattern. Thunder rolled in the horizon. The fifteen moved upstairs. Martin drew effortlessly a perfect pentacle on the floor with room for them all.

– This has been the night of the dark witch sabbats since long before they were called that, he said. – It's older than the church, older than Christianity, than religion itself. According to ancient mythology, the All Souls Night is the night where Samhain, the ruler of the kingdom of death calls to him the souls of the condemned.

Lillian placed big, black candles at each of the five points of the pentacle. She lit them, and they burned with a ghostly flame.

– Bring the gift, he bid Jennifer.

Jennifer brought the snake, the Black Mamba she had carried in a cage. She held the big animal with ease.

Martin prepared the brew in one large cup. Fifteen small cups had been placed around it. He worked fast and effective. The spells rose from his throat, a guttural speech hardly reminiscent of language, or any language Lillian had heard. She saw him in a strange light, as if her eyesight had changed, but he was the one who had changed. He did look very much like she had pictured a true sorcerer, a strange and dark creature of the myths.

The brew began smoking when he applied cold water. It began boiling when Jennifer made the snake release its venom into the cup. Everyone except Martin and Jennifer stared fascinated and apprehensive at the process. It was more than evident that the two of them had done this quite a few times before.

He emptied the cup, pouring the brew in the fifteen small cups. He offered the content to each and every one of the fourteen. They drank it empty. They gagged. Lillian drank the bitter brew, and she was gagging. He began chanting. The fourteen froze, their eyes staring straight ahead at nothing. Lillian could still see, but her view grew distorted. The entire room and its flesh and bone seemed to change dramatically. All her senses worked differently. Her ears picked up a silent discord. She wanted to giggle in excitement, but couldn't do it, couldn't move a muscle or an eyelid or anything. She had become a motionless statue. The venom, the brew moved, flowed through her veins, roaming her body and mind equally. Her eyes opened wide, looking like huge windows in the night.

Martin moved, deliberately, his hands painting gossamer lines in the air.

The lines danced like flames. He stretched his arms, stretched his mind, his very Shadow. It filled the building, reaching outside, all the way to busy streets. The four winds blew around him, and he decided their course. His voice grew louder, grew loud, matching the thunder. Who could stop the wind?

Kjell Gudmundson could.

He... drained the others, as if he had been a psychic vampire and touched them. Their energies filled him. The snake slipped out of Jennifer's weak hands and coiled around her body. It didn't bite her, not a single time. Her arms raised themselves above her head, sliding like the snake. She hissed like the snake. A loud moan rose from her open black mamba mouth. The body rose into the air. Demballah, the snake god took her as his. They glimpsed a demonic face. Her body writhed and twisted in ecstasy. His blood flowed hard through his veins. He started bleeding from the nose. It flowed into his open mouth. The taste of it ripped his tongue.

The enemy was here, was close, not necessarily in this house, but not far off, and certainly in the town.

The first level, the first on a steep rise had been reached.

He... let go. Everyone dropped to the floor, Jennifer included. They crouched there, grasping for air, fighting to stay alive. Then, in the blink of an eye, they recovered, and power, and then some returned to them, bloated them.

The Thunder seemed to grow louder, to expand within him, within her, them, and in the air surrounding them.

The color of his hair changed from red to black. Two pairs of emerald eyes started glowing.

Night turned to day, and bright day. The bird with the beyond wide wingspan flew above London. The city below him changed to Bergen, no, Bjorgvin. He reexperienced his early days. Kjell and Gudrun played with each other under the moon. The fishing boats passed Fenring the island. It was the dream again, but clearer, more detailed. The eagles faded from the mountains, from all mountains. Soon, no eagles would remain anywhere. The human being that had once been Kjell Gudmundson walked in a field covered with blackened and bloated corpses. The dancing, wicked Mameloi in the Caribbean with a big belly crouched before him. He had learned to appreciate his power there, by sheer necessity. She had challenged him, and made the power burn within him. He had vanquished her, and his daughter had survived. The Egyptian and American pyramids, their startling similarities flashed before his eyes, his inner eyes. He had sensed the immense power within the tiny body that was his flesh and blood, and he had brought her with him when he departed, when he moved on yet again.

He walked through London, even as he knew it wasn't him doing it. This body was smaller, physically weaker, a woman. He was riding her, had become a passenger in her body, her mind. She looked at her reflection in the window of the Burger King hamburger bar near Plaza Cinema Theater in Regent Street right before she stepped inside, seeking shelter from the rain. He recognized one of the victims of the sword killer, and frowned in confusion. He realized that this was no dead spirit. This was Anthonia Stephenson, not her dead twin sister Roberta.

She ordered a burger, but didn't eat much of it. It turned cold, and she pushed it away. She sat there for a while. The sadness was engraved on her face. A tear dropped from her eye. A couple of males studied her, but it quickly dawned on them that she wasn't in the mood. Even they, boys filled with hormones and as considerate as a rock saw that. She choked by the thought.

Toni Stephenson looked around, frowning. He knew she had sensed him, his presence. She had been convinced that someone had been sitting on her left side, but there was no one there. She was a sensitive, but her untrained mind couldn't make more out of it.

She and her sister had always been close, hardly spent any time apart. She choked again. Every piece of music, every glance and sound reminded her of Roberta. Martin sensed her surface thoughts. They were pretty grim. She had left the apartment tonight in a deliberate attempt to get some relief, to move on. It didn't work.

One step outside, and the darkness seemed to swallow her. Twenty steps or so, and she reached the Piccadilly Circus Underground access. She walked down the stairs. It was crowded down here. Her claustrophobia kicked in hard. She gasped and rushed back to the street the same way she had entered the station. A couple of cabs passed by. They were unavailable. She found a phone booth and called for one.

– It's an emergency, she said, while she kept gasping. – I'm in Coventry Street. Could you hurry, please?

She didn't hold her breath. Her hand shook when she put the receiver back on the hook. She stepped back on the sidewalk and leaned against the wall, at least partly protected from the rain. She watched people as they rushed past her, in both directions, on both sides of the street. They didn't look good. She could see such things. It almost made her feel better.

The claustrophobia had not really been a problem before, but now everything was. Just the low number of people in the street caused her to flinch. She bowed her head.

Minutes passed. She kept glancing at her watch. The cab would probably not arrive the first half hour. She kept looking to her side. Martin knew she sensed his presence. Time hardly passed for him. He found himself on the outside, looking in. It was a completely different perspective he had not really experienced before. He wanted to comfort her, but held himself back.

She imagined that people stared at her. Her sister's face had been shown in the media as a victim of the sword killer. Toni had changed hairdo, but feared it wouldn't be sufficient to anonymize her.

A cab approached. It didn't really make her react. It was unavailable. It slowed down and stopped close to her. She brightened, and opened the door.

– You're early, she said brightly. – That's a first to me.

She sat down in the cold seat, looking forward to the conversation with the man. The London cab drivers were usually great at conversation.

– I'm new, the man said. – I want to make a good impression.

She giggled softly.

– Hammersmith Odeon, she told him. – By the bus stop.

– You're lucky, then. You don't need to walk far in the dark.

Martin saw Erling's face in the usual haze. He was pretty certain the man wore a mask, but he remained protected, and couldn't be exposed through magickal means. Erling grinned triumphant at him. Martin shook in frustration, doing it to such a degree that Toni noticed.

The rain hammered the windows. The windshield wipers couldn't keep the window free of water, even at full speed. Toni experienced the world outside in a haze. Someone had left a wrapped-up package on the floor. She pondered what it would be, before shrugging indifferent.

She bent forward, with her head in her hands. She pictured the small apartment in her mind, pondering what she would do the rest of the evening, and subsequent days. She couldn't think of anything.

– You forgot switching on the taximeter, she said.

The shock surged through her. Her suspicion, everything else not right here, suddenly made sense.

She tore off the canvas wrapping, and revealed the sword. The breaks screamed as the car stopped at high speed in a dark street. She pushed opened the door, and attempted to get out, but he was already there. He struck her and slapped her several times. She choked and stopped resisting. He gagged her, and tied her up, hands and feet. It happened so fast, in such an effortless, casual manner.

– You should thank me, you know. Why should you live on when Roberta is dead? You certainly don't deserve to do so.

He threw her on the floor in contempt. It hurt and she started crying. He returned to the driver's seat and opened the windows between the compartments, before driving on.

Don't be fooled, Martin told her. He destroyed and killed Roberta. You had nothing to do with it.

The ropes were so tight. Her arms and feet had already turned numb. She rested her cheek against the sword with the ongoing dull expression in her eyes.

The sword, woman. You know how to use it, dammit.

Her head raised itself again, and she was looking at the smooth and sharp sword by her side. It was so hard to move. Cry, she had to keep crying, keeping him complacent. She wanted to live.

The numb fingers grabbed the handle. She pulled it out, enough to expose the sharp edge. It could cut tissue… tissue and rope. She had been such an easy prey to him. The blade sliced the rope without her needing to apply much pressure or effort. Her hands and arms were free. She rested on her side, unable to move…

… drowsy. Martin blinked or imagined he did. The gag was poisoned. It drugged her, making her sense of helplessness grow. But it didn't make her unconscious. Erling wanted her to be awake, aware of what was happening.

Martin rolled his hands into fists. Toni did, too. He made one more effort at getting through to the young woman. She kept sobbing. Very good, since her body was moving. She didn't have time to free her legs. Ignore that, she told herself. Kill him. She wanted to LIVE.

She fought herself up on her knees, glimpsing his face, his masked face in the mirror. Her hand moved, her fingers stretched like claws. She scratched his face with her long nails. The face vanished. His mask, Martin thought. Before Erling could react, Toni jumped through the open door. She screamed in pain when she landed on the hard road. She crouched on the ground with something feeling very much like a broken arm and foot and clutched the mask and red wig in her hand.

The car had stopped a few meters off, with the engine running. People approached her from all sides. She watched as the flow of exhaust thickened in the humid air. He drove on. She couldn't believe it.

He didn't want me to see his face, she thought.

She pulled out the gag. People reached her. The car was gone. She would live. The strange, soft smile made people wonder, wonder even more.

– The sword killer, she stated with a loud and clear voice.

– You… escaped? A man gasped.

– I did, she replied with a proud voice.

– How do you feel? Are you in pain.
– I'm fine, she said, – better than fine.

She kept looking for him among those standing around her, but was confident he hadn't returned. She kept herself battle ready, or as battle ready she could be.

Martin let go. He returned in full to his own body. He couldn't quite make it work. The others struggled as well. A long time passed. They recovered slowly.

– That was amazing, Jonathan cried.

They sat up. Eyes opened wide.

– The pain and lethargy will fade in a few hours, Martin said.

They seemed pretty awake and aware already. They stared at him with their wide and aware eyes.

– She fucked him over, Lillian snarled. – She fucked him over good.

The others shared her euphoria.

– Congratulation, shaman, Jennifer greeted him with shiny eyes. – The evil one's days are numbered.

– She pretty much did it on her own, Martin noted. – I was merely the catalyst.

They fought themselves up, standing on shaky legs.

– She will thank you forever, Lillian said happily.

That sounded very much like a true statement. They still sensed her nearby, as if she was right there, among them.

Dawn arrived. The night seemed like ages ago already. The wide-open eyes stared at the world undiluted.

Chapter 14

Martin and Lillian walked on Victoria Street, just the two of them. She jumped and danced by his side, the euphoria still very much there.

– Tonight was remarkable, she exclaimed. – I can't wait to do more of it, to lead a ceremony on my own. I feel so ready, so abundantly clear-headed and capable.

She jumped on his shoulder and sat there. It was a little awkward because of the big belly, but she experienced no serious trouble. He walked with her like that for a while.

– Everything looks so different from up here, she giggled.

The slight difference in viewpoint did matter. It also helped that he was moving, and she wasn't.

– It's like riding a horse, she said wickedly.

People they encountered looked anxiously at her. It didn't help that she looked back with a pointed stare.

She jumped back down, landing on light feet.

They walked north on Victoria Embankment. The polluted, very polluted Thames River flowed quietly on their left.

– You should have seen it the first time I saw it.

– Huh? She shook, pulled from her deep thoughts.

– The river, he said good humored. – It was clean and full of life.

– This is still an idyllic place, she remarked, – in spite of all the shit.

She was still brooding. He knew she was pondering something.

– Why did you strike Jennifer? How could you?

– That's easy to answer, he replied lightly. – I quite simply treated her the same way she treated you. I've told her several times I won't tolerate anything like that from anyone. She needs to be reminded now and then, every tenth year or so.

– I like her, Lillian decided. – I think we will be good friends.

They sat outside one of the restaurants in Covent Garden. She drank a soda through a straw. She pondered something again.

– The other immortals… where are they?

– Two are currently live in London, he said. – If you turn slightly and glance at the street theater, and look at the audience, you will see one of them, the man wearing a black suit and a suitcase.

He didn't point, just kept talking. She got it, and bent down and scratched her ancle. She spotted the man in a black suit and tie.

– That's Tom Farrett, she said stunned. – The Tory parliament member.

– The first time we met, he called himself Henry Lamont and was a trader.
– We didn't get along.
– You knew he would come here today, she nodded. – I guess you wanted me to take a closer look at him.
She giggled roguishly.
– That's a fair assumption, he acknowledged.
Farrett kept heading south. The two lovebirds started eating. They toasted with the glass of soda.
– I love everything you reveal to me, she stated, – even the unpleasant. The world is such a great place.
The excitement sometimes, like now, felt like a living thing within her.
A shadow fell on them. They looked up. She saw a man of medium height, incredibly muscular, with black hair and equally black eyes.
– Keller.
– Thorn, Martin grinned. – Long time no see, man.
– Turner, the other corrected him. – Thorn had a fatal accident a few months ago. A distant relative inherited his wealth.
– I see, Martin said. – Well, I guess congratulations are in order, then.
The cheerfulness didn't seem to impress Turner much. To Lillian, he seemed cold as ice.
– Our eager politician had you followed, Turner said. – I slowed him down a bit on your behalf.
– Thanks, Turner. I appreciate that.
Turner stared at Lilliam.
– She has already turned?
She pondered telling him that he shouldn't speak about her as if she wasn't there, but decided not to.
– She was born like this, Martin shrugged deliberately.
Turner's eyes grew wide.
One more flash of shadow, and he was gone.
– Such a cheerful guy, Lillian joked.
– For as long as I've known him, Martin noted.
The fourteen visited Jennifer at the organic farm, an enormous area once again challenging Lillian's perception of London. She listened to the wind above the water, between the trees. This was a quiet place, a reservoir of silence in the big city noise.
– There isn't much activity here, now, Jennifer said, – when the harvesting is done outside, but we still look after the soil. Organic farming is about planting a variety of different plants each year, giving the soil time and energy to recover. The yield is lesser and doesn't look so good, cosmetically

speaking, but the taste and content are far superior. We don't use fertilizers. Factory farming is strangling the soil and nature. Much of the «progress» of the industrial agriculture quickly turns out to be gross mistakes, and downright unhealthy. The soil is ruined after just a couple of years, and needs a break. Fertilizers are an unhealthy way of keeping that going.

– I'm so impressed, Lillian said brightly. – I had heard about organic farming, but only in limited, general ways. This is a completely different ballgame that might even mean a true difference in people's lives.

– Thank you, Lillian, Jennifer said, clearly awkward, even embarrassed. – I appreciate that, appreciate it a lot.

She led on on the guided tour. Lillian watched her, the effortless way she moved, the way she handled any given uneven ground or hurdle on her path. She moved like an animal. Lillian found herself emulating her. The baggage made it difficult, but she managed. Pride surged through her.

In fact, the baggage hardly felt like a burden at all.

They had the usual farm animals here… and more. Lillian spotted dogs and cats and more.

– As you know, humanity has kept and domesticated what used to be wild animals, Jennifer related, – adapting them to human needs. We do the opposite here, attempting to turn the forced evolution around, to return them to their natural version.

– I love that, too, Lillian grinned. – I want to laugh hysterically every time I see a dog, a domesticated wolf.

– We're also investigating how pollution is destroying all life on a fundamental level, how our immunity against diseases is seriously weakened, how it even weakens our ability to breed. Diseases that shouldn't affect healthy individuals do in ever stronger ways. The fools running the inhuman society are totally and willingly clueless. They don't even know what an ecological system is. And their horrible lack of basic knowledge about everything important, including nature has beyond dire repercussions on life on earth.

– You do such great work, Lillian said, and struggled to not go totally overboard in her admiration. – Could you do a full… checkup of me?

– I am a medical doctor, too, Jennifer shrugged. – I can and I would.

Lillian noticed, a bit distracted by the other's speech, how deliberate it sounded, fitting her intensity.

The two of them left the others. Lillian waved with a sweet smile.

They reached the laboratory. Lillian spotted no people.

– We keep this part private, Jennifer said. – The research I do will never be shared with outsiders.

– I understand what you mean, Lillian said. – I understand it quite well.

She sat down in a chair, and Jennifer started doing the bloodwork.

– It's fortunate that you want to do this, the «girl» said shyly. – I haven't had the opportunity to study immortals in their infancy. I haven't had much access to mutants in general either. I know we have a distinct genetic marker, but I haven't been able to study it much.

– You should study all of those available to you, now, then.

– Thank you, Jennifer said. – Thank you, Lillian.

– They might not be willing, Lillian mused, – but we should at least ask them.

– They will do whatever you ask of them, Jennifer stated.

Lillian knew once again what she was talking about, and pondered the implications with an excitement she could hardly conceal.

She studied the proceedings when Jennifer did her examination, and could hardly contain herself.

– The full result won't be available for a few days, Jennifer told her, – but you're clearly a typical mutant phenotype.

– You said mutant before as well. I thought we were witches.

– Those are merely two different names for the same thing, Jennifer replied calmly. – We've had hundreds, thousands of designations throughout history and the world, really. But mutant is what we *are*. The genetic markers are definitely different enough from Homo Sapiens to mark us as another species, or at least a subspecies about to become a species, one that will soon be unable to have common, breeding progeny with humans. We are at the cusp, if you will, of our ascension.

– So, we are indeed like the Neanderthalensis and Sapiens, then? Lillian half joked.

– Very apt, Jennifer solemnly replied, and Lillian was taken aback.

It seemed to Lillian that she had an appointment with every single machine in the laboratory, but her thoughts kept drifting, busy with pondering the new and exciting information.

– The implications are… staggering, she said.

– I would say so, yes, Jennifer agreed.

– We didn't use to be immortal, the lot of us, Lillian mused. – We were mortal, in spite of our godlike powers.

– That's a fair assessment. But now, that is changing. More and more of us are born immortal. You are, too.

– Is that a fact? Lillian asked anxiously.

– As close to a fact we can come, without being absolutely certain.

Jennifer did a prenatal testing, ultrasound, the works, more than Lillian had ever imagined could be done. They watched the tiny fetus on the screen.

– It's healthy, Jennifer declared. – You are, too. That's pretty much how it goes with us, but better safe than sorry.

– Thank you so much, Lillian said. – It has the same… genetic marker?

– Everyone with at least one mutant parent has, Jennifer said. – There is no return to what we were.

– That means Axel also might be…

– And either one or both of your parents.

Lillian couldn't hold back the giggle.

– My… Lillian's father would so appreciate that…

– You could be the first in your line, of course, Jennifer said. – That happens with growing frequency, as well.

– That would be okay, too, but I don't think so. There are many stories, going back centuries only my grandaunt would share with me.

Jennifer had completed the testing. She prepared to pack down the equipment and leave. Lillian grabbed her arm. Jennifer froze and attended her, giving her even more her full attention.

– Martin keeps hiding something for me. Do you know what it is?

– He… trained me well, Jennifer said softly. – He will do the same with you. That should be enough to comfort you, and ease your fears.

– I want to know, Lillian stated curtly, – and I want to know, now. Why won't you tell me?

She saw how the other woman froze and turned uncharacteristically insecure.

– Because I believe he wishes you only the best, the girl said with shaking lips.

– You fear he will… punish you if you tell me? That seems unlikely. You are his daughter.

– He's had many offspring, Jennifer said subdued. – He has always kept us on a tight leash.

Lillian felt something move within. It boiled and burned.

– Impertinent godling, Lillian snarled.

And slapped her on the cheek. The girl, and now she looked very much like a girl, froze like a statue.

– Please, Goddess.

Lillian slapped her again. Something dark and mighty rose from her depths, and she welcomed it. The girl shrunk to a timid creature before her.

– He wants to t-test you, to harden you, for the further t-trials.

Lillian smiled, and she knew the smile to be wicked, her appearance to be fearsome.

275

– Go on.

– He will risk your life to make it happen. He will make certain that you're well suited to survive the far greater trials to come, and live forever, even without him.

She stood there with her head bowed, humbling herself.

– That's my girl, Lillian said with her Voice, and petted the cheek of the other woman. – Your father was very much correct. You need a correction every ten year or so.

Jennifer collapsed in her arms, and started sobbing. Lillian held her and comforted her. She imagined they stood like that pretty much forever.

2

The word went out to the land. Excitement rose like steam on and off the streets of London. The grapevine, the word of mouth reached everyone, both those who wanted to hear it, and the rest, including those that absolutely didn't want to hear it.

They constructed the small stage in Hyde Park in less than half an hour. The performance began at twilight, just as the glowing disk in the sky set in the west. All colors turned darker, turned dark.

Fifteen large torches started burning on the stage, casting an even weirder light at the gathering, the large crowd gathered there for the performance. Someone beat a drum, a powerful, steady beat. They couldn't see the one doing that, couldn't see anyone on the stage, but felt each beat hitting their body like continuous waves. A hum reached everyone's ears. It seemed to rise from the ground itself. Fourteen people clad in hoods and robes appeared from the deep darkness at the back of the stage. They seemed transparent, like spirits.

Three solidified, turning flesh and blood. One of the dark-skinned women seemed to be glowing. Her big and bare belly was quite distinct in the pale light of the dancing ghostly flames.

The red-haired man and the other dark-skinned woman turned tangible as well.

The gathering heard a buzz, glimpsing a deeper shadow in the shadows.

– Welcome to his place, this moment of night and fire, he said with a loud voice, without aid from mechanical or electronic means. – This night will stand out in your memory. You will never be the same again, never return to your meaningless existence.

He paused, grinning. A collective cheer rose from the audience.

– You might ask how I can with such confidence claim that you are coming from that unbearable state of affairs. By taking one single GLANCE at the current mainstream society. Some individuals listening live to Jim Morrison didn't like him calling them slaves. It pleases me that you're different.

The cheer rose to an even higher level.

– All establishment politics since the late 1970s has been about putting the working class back in its box. Closing those horizons that had been forced open by hard struggle, through blood, sweat and tears. It wasn't that great before either, but now a brief reprieve of the brutal tyranny is at an end. Six years of Thatcher and less Reagan rule has already had dire implications for humanity. Neil Kinnock, the esteemed Labour Party leader sided with the police instead of supporting the people in Brixton and Tottenham Hale. The Labour Party is becoming Tories as well. Social Democracy all over Europa is deliberately failing. We need true, lasting change. We must become that change, those brave and bold agents of change.

The anticipation in the gathering grew.

– I've attended his gatherings before, a man told his buddy, – but I suspect he will surpass himself tonight.

– The rumors have it that he has found love, his buddy responded.

Lillian heard them. The buzz and the ruckus didn't seem to keep that from happening at all.

– Others from all over the world will join us, Martin cried, – but we must keep acting as if we're alone. Those currently ruling us have no God-given right to do so. No one has. They have on the contrary shown themselves totally unfit to lead anything short of a garbage heap. We must regain our connection with nature, with the earth itself. Those currently in charge are only a distraction we must leave behind. Oh, they are dangerous, never doubt that, but they don't have our respect, and never should have.

He pulled back a little. The drum began beating again. Jennifer stepped forward. Everyone saw that she was bleeding from both arms. She handed him the full bucket. He accepted it, and with a mighty show of force, he moved, and emptied the bucket, and the blood rose sky-high in the air. Every saw what happened next. Something struck and caught the blood, seemingly making it levitate, and distributed it unevenly across the big crowd. Everyone realized what happened with a collective gasp.

The swarm of flies descended, and touched everyone there, each being bathing in blood, and bringing some of it with them, as they ascended and flew to the stage and everyone there.

– Lord of the Flies, one woman said stricken.

– LORD OF THE FLIES, many shouted in ecstasy.

The buzz grew to a storm. It stayed quiet, and everyone heard the voice.

– Don't be afraid of Nature, the man reaching out to them all from the stage called. – Respect it, but don't fear it. These creatures are large. The building blocks of life, of nature, of reality are far smaller, though we should all recognize that scale is an illusion. We live in an illusion, not in the sense that what surrounds us in our daily lives isn't «real», but in its importance. Our perception is formed by propaganda far older than those men in the ridiculous costumes. And today that propaganda is developed to a razor's edge. Joseph Goebbels would have been stunned, been practically ecstatic to see what is under way today.

And the stage dissolved, and he seemed to be among them, among his beloved tiny creatures. And they seemed to speak in his voice, telling everybody about the wretched kingdoms.

Lillian stepped forward, and raised a fisted hand. The stage returned.

– Yes, Blood is the Life, Life is the Blood, she cried. – And blood shall set us free.

Their energies... strengthened her. She cried out in unadulterated joy.

– Yes, I'm in the mood, she cried. – One reason, even though it's far from the only one, is that I'll give birth to a red-haired kid in a not-so-distant future...

They cheered.

– Thank you so much, she grinned – I appreciate it. I'm so happy to be here tonight. I'm so happy you're here tonight. This is a night set in infamy, and it makes me so proud...

She touched her big belly, and she yelped in cheerfulness.

– He's kicking, she choked. – That's a first, too.

They hummed at her, strengthening her further.

– One of the reasons I left Norway was its pervasive, systemic racism. Then, I came here and found it to be just as bad... My guess is that it is like that all over Europe. Few of us have any reason to be proud of the country of our birth. Much is very wrong here, and has been for a long time. Taking decisive action against it is long overdue. We will return humanity to nature, return us to ourselves. Magick, witchcraft and spirituality will once again become an integrated part of our daily life, and by that sacred act, we will save ourselves, leave the horrid path of collective suicide we've walked so long.

She raised an index finger. The buzz faded. The storm grew hot.

– But tonight... tonight... we give birth to ourselves, now and forever. Our existence is ashes and fire, ashes and fire in an endless cycle, and they're equally important.

The fire burned even stronger, and the shadows grew deeper. Dark flames touched everyone on the ground, and on the stage. The fifteen stepped down on the ground. The ten surrounded Lillian in a very subtle manner. She sensed them around her, a soothing presence, a stark reminder of the ongoing threat. But the crowd stayed very considerate, and didn't impose. A few approached her and Martin, paying their… their respect, knowing more, remembering more than the others.

– You can feel it, Jennifer nodded, – feeling their energies strengthening you. Their worship is both subtle and obvious.

Lillian didn't voice any comment. She didn't quite know what to say.

– I feel so connected to you, a boy gasped. – Why is that? How could I?

– You worship her, Jennifer said curtly, – and why shouldn't you? She has stepped down from Mount Olympus to live among her subjects.

Lillian wanted to say something then, to contradict the girl, but she stayed silent. Impressions and sensations and glimpses of ancient times kept coming at her like a wave, staying more obtrusive than clear, more confusing than illuminating.

She and Martin danced, even when it wasn't obvious, moving according to each other, and the others. The connection was self-evident. It went beyond pure emotion, into something… something else pushing into the strictly rational. Even if she had felt little or nothing for him on a personal level, the age-old connection would still be there.

He nodded to himself, and she did, too.

– Feel free to help us carry the equipment, she cried.

Many did. It felt both prosaic and not. Lillian imagined that Jennifer had her eyes on her all the time.

She walked in front and most of the crowd followed behind her, like warriors on a battlefield. On one level, she marveled at it. On another, it didn't seem unusual at all. She saw herself move with other sword-carrying men and women through a forest, and she suddenly choked with emotion. A tall and athletic woman with black hair and black eyes led them, and Lillian had to stop, choking so hard that it hurt.

Right there and then, Lillian Donner imagined she could see forever.

3

Thick fog, and a heavy rainfall that never stopped followed her no matter where she ran. It poured so hard that she had difficulties breathing. Yellow leaves floated in all the many pools forming. All trees turned naked and barren. Lillian kept running, slowly not giving a damn about the bad weather. She had pushed past it, and once she had, it no longer mattered, and the triumphant grin formed on her lips.

She stopped by Marble Arch, at the corner of the northern and eastern side of Hyde Park, and started bending and stretching. The rain splashed in her face, and the grin stayed on. Martin kept an eye on her and the surroundings. She ignored him, ignored Jennifer at the other side of her. Lillian resumed her run, and ran even faster than before. It didn't really tire her anymore. She wanted to test herself, test herself thoroughly, but the thing growing in her belly stopped her.

There were others running in the rain. She knew they were good runners, well trained, but she passed them easily. The hard breathing didn't stop the chuckle from erupting from her sore throat. She turned and headed back toward the two waiting for her together. Jennifer grabbed the ankh, but it looked like it hurt her. She pulled her hand back, as if she had burned herself.

Martin grabbed the ankh, and it seemed to release a flare, ghostly but very much real. Lillian felt her own pendant flare as well. She stopped for more bending and stretching, raising her feet high above the ground. That hardly felt like an effort either. She grabbed the ankh, and gasped in wonder. Another physical body grabbed it in ancient times, and the connection reestablished itself in an instant.

She ran to the two waiting for her. The father and daughter looked so similar to her. She could easily look past the obvious differences. The glow of the green eyes burned her again. They were soaked, as she was, but it clearly didn't bother them. She wondered briefly if anything bothered them, even as she instantly corrected herself.

It felt twice great to bend and stretch in the underground swimming pool later. Gravity didn't exist below the surface, and she placed herself upside down, and attempted to stay balanced. She just floated away in the streams of water and reality. The other two roamed the pool as well, but they kept their distance. So many thoughts of fire and shadow roamed her head. She couldn't possibly keep track of them all. Much time had passed when she emerged from the trancelike state. She swam to the two relaxing in shallow water.

– So, the two of you play brother and sister, she said, slightly ironic. – How is that working for you?

– It's actually working out quite well, Martin replied cheerfully. – No one doubts us.

– They even insist on telling us how alike we look, Jennifer said lightly. Lillian studied her openly.

– There are those that don't bother, though, Jennifer shrugged. – A rich racist prick commented about my lineage in quite the patronizing manner. Papa spent the next twenty years taking him down, dismantling his entire extensive business and successful life in slow and agonizing ways.

The implications made Lillian shiver and burn more, but she looked at Martin with admiration in her eyes.

– I can't wait to take them all down, she shrugged, pretty much like Jennifer had done.

Three throats filled the hall with dark laughter.

She and Jennifer, and the other women of the household spent an evening shopping. They kept their eyes open, but had no trouble with enjoying themselves in each other's company. She had no trouble catching the anxiety in people's eyes either. The presence, the behavior of the wandering group of women, even though it wasn't overt, made others antsy. She studied herself in the mirror in the stinking toilet in the subway by Centre Point, attempting to gauge what made people so worried. Strange, Martin and Jennifer's eyes were quite accessible, easy to look into, but she didn't really see anything when she attempted to gaze into her own. They were just endless wells of darkness, just like those of the other woman she had walked with through the ancient forest.

The guys visited the health club. The stench of sweat and sight of bulging muscles met them the moment they stepped inside. They stopped in front of the desk by the entrance.

– Yes? The muscular man looked at her with doubt in his eyes.

– We would love to try the place out for a few hours, she said calmly.

He couldn't quite hide the grin when he showed her the various weights and gears. She went straight at it, working out effortlessly, without visibly straining herself. His tongue practically hung out of his mouth.

– These are too easy, she told him after a few minutes. – Can't you make them heavier?

There was hardly room for more weights on the barbell.

– I could go to the men's section, of course, she shrugged.

– Shouldn't you take it easy? The man asked dumbfounded.

Lillian's companions laughed openly at him by now. He didn't handle it well. She saw how he resented it and her. He walked away with one last angry stare.

The woman by her side smiled to her.

– You took him down several pegs, she said, very smug. – Congratulations. He can't stand it every time he encounters strong women. It's like it is personal to him, as if our strength diminishes his.

– His loss, Jennifer said very loud.

– We're having a party at home tonight, Lillian told the woman. – You're welcome to attend.

The woman's eyes grew wide.

– Thank you, she half whispered. – I believe I will.

They paid a brief visit to the wardrobe and changed to their training gear, and did walk to the men's section, and tried out the heavier weights. Lillian and Jennifer had no trouble with them. The woman, Annette, hadn't either. Monique and Marianne could handle it, too. They did spend a couple of hours there, straining hard, making themselves sweat. Lillian had a strange experience every time she pushed herself. The moment she pushed the barbell up, her vision turned dark. She couldn't tell what it meant, only that it meant something important, a conviction only growing when she noticed how Jennifer studied her even harder than she usually did.

Eventually soaked in sweat, they chose to have a shower. They enjoyed the hot water on sore limbs. Lillian noticed by a glance how different they appeared compared to the other females, far more athletic and muscular. Annette would probably get there, too. Lillian once again pondered the obvious implications.

They emerged from the showers and wardrobe fresh and clean. A man waited for them in the hallway. He looked at them, at her with a pointed stare.

– What do you say, sweetie? Do you want to party?

– I'm afraid not, she replied. – We're all heading home.

He stared at her bigger breasts. They had grown lately and pushed against her tight T-shirt. He… got to her, made her feel vulnerable, and she hated that.

The girls walked past him. He didn't try anything. They left the place, and walked directly down the subway stairs to the Tottenham Court Underground Station. Lillian didn't need to turn and look, or Jennifer's warning to know that they were being followed by Bulging Muscles and Pointed Stare and buddies. The girls boarded the Central Line heading west. The men entered the same car, but sat down far from them. They wore elegant clothing, suit and tie. The sight looked so far out there that Lillian shook her head, realizing that her expectations of the world was wrong in this regard as well.

– Be calm, Jennifer said. – But don't be fooled by them being well dressed. We all know what their intentions are. Let's wait until we get them where we want them.

Her companions looked incredulous at her, feeling both anxiety and anticipation.

– We want this, Lillian heard herself say. – We want to teach them a lesson.

Now, the girls looked awestruck at her, and she felt hot and queasy.

They changed train at Bond Street Station and headed north on the gray Jubilee Line. The same repeated itself. Their stalkers entered the same car, and sat down far from them. When the girls left the train at St. John's wood, the men kept following them, slowly catching up with their perceived prey.

Jennifer led them into the dark park. The darkness engulfed them, devoured them. The girls stopped and turned. The men stopped a few steps away, so damned smug.

– What do you say, sweetie? The leader, Pointed Stare chuckled. – I've always wanted one with baggage. There is more to touch, get it.

– I like screamers, another said.

– She wants it, Bulging Muscles said hoarsely. – They all do. Look at them. They didn't even put down the groceries and made a run for it.

– They will beg for it before we're done with them.

The girls burst into laughter.

– Are all men so stupid? Annabelle wondered?

They put down their groceries, but stayed put. The males cast them angry stares, and rushed them. The girls moved as one. Only Annette looked visibly anxious. Lillian grabbed the hand of the man reaching for her and squeezed. Pointed Stare yelped in pain, and she struck him in the face. She pulled him closer and struck him on the jaw with the palm of her hand. He received the full brunt of the stroke. Blood flowed from his mouth, and he dropped to his knees. She let go of him and kicked him in the head. He dropped to the ground and stayed put. She kicked him in the belly. He crouched and screamed.

She kept moving in an uneven flow. The next man attempting to grab her was a bit more cautious. She assaulted him, kicking him in the belly, and when he doubled over, she struck him on the neck. He dropped like a stone.

Monique and Marianne did a one, two, one, two on one of men, moving like one person. Jennifer hammered Bulging Muscles to shreds, poetry in motion.

All the six men crouched on the ground, beaten and helpless.

– Pussies, Annabelle spat, – pretenders to manhood.

She stamped on a hand, breaking it on several spots. The man released a loud whimper. Jennifer broke a leg with a single kick. The loud crack echoed through the forest.

– We will be kind to you tonight, she stated softly. – We will teach you a life's lesson.

– You will always think of us, Annette snarled. – Every time you even consider resuming your stalking ways, you will think of us with terror on your mind.

They kept going for quite a while. Monique found a loose iron bar by the fence and struck an arm with it. The men started sobbing, huge, loud sobbing. Lillian knelt by Bulging Muscles.

– You will think of us every night, when you twist and turn lonely and terrified in bed.

She struck and broke his nose. She twisted his arm, making him scream some more.

She stepped on his shoulder, and twisted his already twisted arm some more on its socket.

– I didn't strike a single punch before they were beaten, Annette marveled. – You gals are wonders.

– You will be soon, too, Lillian informed her. – You will remember, and you will be poetry in motion.

One of the men reached for her, not as an act of dominance, but of submission. She stamped on the arm and broke it, easy as pie. A loud wail rose from his throat. The loud, triumphant laughter echoed between the trees.

– They aren't savages, she told her charges. – We are!

Savage pride coursed through them all.

4

Lillian, Jonathan and Marianne visited Tove and Axel at their student apartment in Hammersmith. Lillian felt a bit under the weather, having vomited a few times the last few days.

– Are you alright? Tove asked concerned.

– I am. Jennifer did another checkup, just to be sure, and everything is fine.

She kept devouring the food and drink, and enjoyed the puzzled look on Tove's face.

Jennifer had explained it to her.

– Your nausea is more about your Transition than your pregnancy. All powerful adepts experience it.

It sounded so right. She was changing, changing even more, almost to the point that she hardly recognized herself. Her thoughts returned to the battle, «battle» in Regent Park. It had been a massacre, really, and she had been both so feral and so deadly calm. The mere thought of it strengthened her further. Her reoccurring dreams of Erling chasing her hardly seemed relevant anymore. She kept telling herself that they were, no matter how real

the threat was, how skilled her fighting had become.
– You should take it easy, Axel said, concerned as well. – At least easier.
– As stated, everything is fine, she shrugged. – In the primitive tribal societies, the females kept doing their daily chores until they gave birth. During marches from camp to camp, they kept walking, stopped for the birth, and resumed the walking when the birth was done. I don't plan on being quite that frisky, though.

The fire burned within her. She could hardly sit still. Her energy levels reached insane heights. She rose at uneven intervals and paced the floor. In spite of how the high-energy level kept distracting her, she could, by casting a glance at Axel and Tove that things weren't good between them.
– I love London, Tove said reluctantly.
– I love it, too, he said, – but that doesn't mean we should spend the rest of our lives here.

The dichotomy stayed so obvious that anyone would have noticed it, but she still wasn't certain her old, limited self, the serious but flimsy girl would have noticed.

Martin had explained the significance of the ongoing distraction, what it could mean. Her extended senses could sense something in the air, something unpleasant.

The telephone rang, loud and with a distorted sound she easily caught.
– I'll get it.
She picked up the receiver.
– Hello?
The silence sounded just as distorted in her sensitive ears. Ten, fifteen seconds passed. She hung up.
– It was him. He knows where I am.
You don't know that, Tove objected. – It could have been a miscall, or a typical crank call. We've had a number of those.
– It was him, Lillian stated calmly.

The three walked through the dark London's streets on their way home.
– The entire visit felt strange, Marianne mused, – like revisiting the past with a time machine, or something. We don't really have anything in common with them anymore.
– We never had, Jonathan stated, – and I guess that's the point.
Lillian nodded to herself.

She held on to the handle of the long two-edged knife under the coat. Lots of stores remained opened. They passed countless store display windows. The great darkness struck her, and she beamed in joy, drowning the anxiety, the fear, the ongoing terror. Her senses grew even sharper.

They passed the seemingly eternal construction work at Piccadilly Circus. She looked at her watch.

– It looks like you're reluctant to head home, Jonathan observed.

He was right, damn him. They had walked and moved in circles since they left Tove and Axel. They could have reached home long ago, but had taken the train further south. Lillian stopped outside the burger joint by the Plaza Theater. She pictured Toni there, the girl that had not been a defenseless victim, pictured the taxi stopping in Coventry Street not that far off. The cold draft made Lillian close the coat in front. The heat from the blade warmed her skin and her heart. She led on south, past the Canadian embassy. They approached St. James's Park. She turned abruptly, and led them up the street again. They passed the South African embassy. Protesters stayed outside it, like they always did. She spotted Jeremy Corbyn, the MP for Islington North. He carried his already iconic sign, «defend the right to demonstrate against apartheid, join this picket». The three of them approached the protesters and struck up a chat.

– We support you, Lillian told them, – support you all the way, and will join you at some point.

She felt shitty because of the evasive statement, but Corbyn and the rest only smiled.

– Thank you, he said, – we appreciate that.

The three walked on up Charing Cross Road to Leicester Square and the black trees. They walked through the dark passage to the Odeon Cinema Theater. Her eyes kept moving in a constant flicker. They emerged on the other side. «Emerged» felt very much as the right word. She spotted him immediately through the iron fence, even if he stood far away, all the way up in front of the Empire Cinema. It was Erling, alive, exactly as she remembered him. The shock froze her completely. She could hardly breathe, breathe, breathe.

When he moved, she imagined it happened extremely fast. He grabbed a brown-skinned woman, and pulled her close. The blade flashed in red as it penetrated her. Blood splashed several of those nearby as he pulled the sword out. Loud, panicked screams filled the square. The man threw the body on top of the iron fence, and impaled her on it. He dropped something on the ground, and smoke surrounded him, and many of those standing closest. People fled from that central point. Lillian lost the sight of him. She pulled the knife, and held it in front of her, moving, turning in the land of confusion ruling the place. A man appeared by her side. She almost stabbed him, but recognized Turner just in time.

– Stay calm and focused, he stressed to her. – If he comes for us, we will take him, will kill him.

She nodded with numb lips. She and the other two moved with Turner then. They looked like they had never done anything but moving together like they did.

– It was him, she choked, – was Erling, like he was.

– It wasn't, he corrected her calmly. – Remember, thanks to his enchantment, his protection, we can only see him as he was, not as he is. He isn't a vengeful spirit, but a man of flesh and blood.

She nodded to herself. His words made sense.

Erling didn't come for them. She cast frantic glances in all directions.

– He didn't know about you, Lillian said, – but he does, now.

– It can't be helped, he said. – We had this advantage, this element of surprise, but it didn't work.

She looked at him.

– You know him? She stated startled.

– I know of him, he acknowledged. – I guess he might remember me, even if I can't properly remember him.

She heard frustration in his voice, saw it in his twisted features.

He had treated her like an equal. A pleasant heat surged through her.

They pulled back, retreating to the darkness, the pale shadows. They heard the sirens, saw flashes of blue lights, as they made their way north. The sight of the red tiles stayed in her vision.

– I saw her spirit leave her body, Lillian stated. – It's such an amazing sight. I felt her anguish.

– You will vanquish him, Turner said curtly. – You will make him pay, making him return to his master in dishonor.

His words sounded… so right.

His master… A deep chill passed through her, far more pronounced than all others, she, Lillian Donner had previously experienced.

– I want to kill him, she said, – and I want him to suffer. I will vanquish him.

Turner acknowledged her words with one more appreciative look. It turned her on, and that… pleased her.

They caught the Tube and traveled west and north. The excited buzz of the other passengers accompanied them everywhere. Everyone's world had been shaken up. The emotional buzz felt even louder than voices in Lillian's mind.

Then, something happened to make all in the car fall silent. Toni entered the car. She set the course straight for Lillian and her companions. She stopped in front of her.

– I followed you, she said shyly, subdued. – I wish to join you. I felt you all, but especially him and his encouraging, passionate thoughts. I wanted to speak to you first.

She waited with lowered, stubborn, needy eyes.

– Sit with us, Lillian offered. – Feel free to join us at our house. You are, after all one of us.

And those words sounded so right, so extremely accurate.

Toni choked and sat down by her side.

They left the underground at St John's Wood. It dawned on Lillian that Turner has vanished at some point, without her noticing. She chuckled in delight. The others did, too, understanding why, understanding her.

– He's a shadow in the brightest day, she said, – and so will we all be.

They understood that comment, too.

– The darkness brings little or no fear, Toni remarked.

– The darkness is our friend, Marianne said, – our sister and brother.

And Toni brightened like the moon.

They reached the house. Lillian could see them in there. Everything looked fine.

She rushed into Martin's arms before the door had closed behind her.

– We found another stray, she grinned, – or she found us.

Toni looked shyly at him.

– You saved me, she said. – I will do anything for you.

– You saved yourself, he stated. – Welcome.

Everyone gathered around her. She found herself within the group, the circle, found herself home.

– You and Turner weren't talking about what you seemed to be talking about on that spot in Covent Garden, were you?

Lillian told Martin. She did not require his vocal confirmation.

It had been a remarkable performance by the two of them. Lillian saw it in a different light when she replayed it in her head.

– I woke up as if from a dream, Toni mused. – Everything suddenly made sense.

She sniffed and smiled simultaneously.

– I feel my twin. She speaks to me undiluted. She says everything is coming together, not just here, with us, but everywhere. She says the Great Fire is coming.

The Great Fire, Lillian thought.

A well of emotions passed through her and lingered.

– We've all sensed it, Jonathan said. – But what does it mean?

– It means exactly what you fear it means, Jennifer stated curtly.

The truth they could only glimpse burned between them.

– It doesn't frighten me, Lillian said. – Quite a few things frighten me, but not that.

– She calls you the Goddess of Mist, Toni said, and curtsied. – She knows you from old… and so do I.

Lillian acknowledged her with a pleased nod. The words didn't merely sound right, but rose like fire from her own depths, not really from Toni's throat.

– I can't sleep, Lillian said. – I'm not tired, not tired in any meaning of the word. Everything seems so clear, even I know intellectually that it isn't.

She led them upstairs, to the training room.

– This is far better equipped than the lousy gym under the Centre Point, Annette said.

– Martin has picked every single item, Lillian said with pride in her voice. – He knows what it takes.

She began working out. The sweat came fast. She didn't hold back, but pushed herself from the very first moment. Annette gaped.

– You're so strong, she whispered, beyond impressed. – Those jerks should have seen you, now. They would have peed on themselves.

Lillian put on one more heavy weight. Annette looked wide-eyed at her.

– You're stronger than most men exercising, she said. – That is remarkable.

Lillian got sweat in her eyes. It burned. She kept going. This felt really heavy. She struggled now. Jennifer and Monique guarded her, ready to act if she failed to keep pushing and risk that the barbell would slip from her hands and harm her. They grabbed it and put it back just before it did. Lillian looked a little vexed at them, unable to see the rationality between their caution. She bent and stretched a bit, doing some biking as well. Her legs didn't really grow tired. She was breathing hard, but the legs just kept going.

She resumed the weightlifting, the pumping of iron. They looked at her with the usual mix of concern and awe. She disregarded it, disregarded them, and kept going. Her muscles burned. Caught in her own world, she hardly noticed the others in the room.

Then, something amazing happened. She pushed the weight up without trouble. The strength surged through her body. She cried out as the pain began, as she almost dropped the weight. She managed to put it back in place before her body dropped to the floor, and painful spasms surged through her body. Her limbs burned, *burned*.

Then the pain, the true pain began. She heard the others speak, but couldn't tell what they were saying. Something happened, something happened to her… her arm. The flesh stretched as she watched. No, the bones stretched, and the flesh stretched with it. She watched astonished as her bones and sinew grew and reset. Her mind… expanded.

Tears flooded her cheeks.

– Play for me, she gasped, with sweat pouring into her eyes. – Play anything.

Martin played the flute. It did have an effect, soothing the pain, the anxiety, the hammering heart. The hammering sounded so loud in her mind, like her tympanic membranes were bursting. She was screaming, screaming her heart out. Her clothes seemed to shrink on her body, even as she incredulous realized that her body was growing.

The pain grew even worse, if that was possible. Her scream grew to a wail.

The growth stopped, the pain fading. She gasped for air, even as she felt air was denied her. Her body, or rather her mind attempted to catch up with the changes. The body turned limp. She stretched out on the floor, her breathing and heartbeat slowing down.

– Your eyes have turned black, Annette said stunned, unable to keep the taint of fear from emerging.

Lillian, contrary to her new friend, grew calm, calm and centered. A smile, a grin grew on her sweaty face. She jumped effortlessly on her feet, towering over almost everyone else in the room. She had grown just as tall as Martin.

– Everything seems alright, she reported. – I feel fine, feel better than fine, feel amazing.

The room, the very world changed around her, to something even stranger and more remarkable.

Chapter 15

The Christmas decorations in the streets had gone on in early November. The sales and shopping started growing slowly from that point.

London changed in imperceptible ways in the coming weeks, but it still changed, in ways that had very little to do with Christmas. An anxious mood settled among its people. They walked around with flickering eyes, and didn't quite feel at home in their skin.

– Look at them, Marianne said. – They look so... lost.

It didn't require a stronger sensitivity to spot their distress, but it helped. Lillian and her brethren spotted it with a casual glance everywhere they walked.

– It's so funny, Marianne giggled. – Other students have started asking me about anthropology and paganism and goddess knows what of both academic and esoteric knowledge. I've suddenly become their encyclopedia of all things perceived as occult.

They noticed a bigger interest in such matters everywhere, both on and off specialty stores selling such items. It was packed in one store when they visited to buy herbs.

People stared at them. Their presence in the store caused an instant sensation. People stopped doing what, whatever they were doing and stared at them.

– Welcome to our store, the man behind the desk greeted them. – What can I do for you?

Lillian handed him the long list of items.

– One moment, he excused himself, and were off.

The long queue in front of the cashiers grew even longer, but most customers didn't seem angry. They even moved reluctantly forward. Lillian felt their... energies. They strengthened her.

The man returned with the items.

– I found everything, he said. – I also added more volume and a few more alternatives, if that's alright, in case you must make a second attempt.

She nodded to herself, acknowledging the truth of the man's statement.

– That's so kind of you, she said sweetly. – Thank you.

He blushed hard.

Quite a few people joined them when they left.

– That was a bizarre experience, Tove whispered in Lillian's ear. – It still is, for that matter.

– The man clearly has knowledge of such matters, Lillian said both good

291

humored and somberly, teasing her friend a bit, – and is a far cry from the usual quacks running stores like these. He recognized a fellow practitioner.

– Speaking of which, I met Professor Ronaldsen the other day, Martin said. – He told me he would start a tenure here in the new year. We would all be surprised, I guess. He seemed to have settled well in Bergen.

Lillian looked closer at him. «Btw, I met Professor Ronaldsen the other day».

– Perhaps he liked them sacking you even less than he let on, Jonathan said.

– He did express some modest reservations about it, Martin acknowledged.

They cooked dinner at home. It had taken some effort to learn to cook for sixteen people, but not anymore. They had grown with the challenge.

All of them lived here, now, and all of them looked like it. One glance at them distinguished them from the average person on the streets.

– We're a good match, Monique remarked with a happy sigh.

Lillian nodded in agreement. Marianne and Jonathan had quite simply stayed one night, and not left the next morning. It had felt like a perfectly natural turn of events.

Axel and Tove had arrived earlier that day, too, making eighteen for dinner. Lillian suspected that they wouldn't move in, though.

There was a knock on the door. Everyone froze, and started moving in a predetermined pattern. Two stayed with the dinner. The others approached the door. Lillian knew who it was and smiled. She opened the door. Eva and the boy stood outside.

– SURPRISE! Eva shouted.

The two hugged each other.

– This is Lars, Eva presented the boy. – We've booked two weeks at Park Court Hotel.

– Hi, Lars greeted her.

– Please, Lillian said, – come inside, both of you.

They did. Lars looked impressed at the interior of the house.

– Some place, you've got here, he marveled.

– Thank you so much, Lillian said. – We're making dinner. You're welcome to join in.

The couple's eyes grew even wider when they looked at all the people gathering around the table.

– We're having a family dinner, Lillian joked.

– So, what happened to you? Eva wondered. – Did you gobble vitamins or what?

– Something like that, Lillian replied lightly.

Her old friend looked miffed at her. Lillian ignored the pointed look.

– And what has happened to your *eyes?*

– It's part of the transmigration, Lillian said lightly. – Some of our age-old traits are passed along.

Eva didn't really deal with that statement at all. Lillian suspected that she disregarded it without consideration.

Twenty people joined around the long table. Lillian and Martin sat down after everyone else had chosen seats. Eva looked curiously at her again.

– The Lady and Lord of the manor always choose last, Lillian grinned solemnly. – It brings great variety to the table.

– I can imagine, Eva said.

– We've started on something big here, Lillian said eagerly. – Something that is so very necessary, but that we can't possibly see the end of.

Eva cast one glance at the others present, and saw that they sat there nodding. She was frowning.

Everyone served themselves steaming stew from the giant kettle. There was no queue or rush. They enjoyed the slow pace. Martin stood up and raised his glass, the glass filled with wine twinkling like blood.

– Cheers, he cried.

Everyone stood up and raised their glass.

– CHEERS!

Glasses met and parted. They drank. The wine burned in Lillian's throat and stomach. When she started devouring the spicy food, the combination burned even harder. Her appetite had grown to astronomical proportions after her latest growth. She laughed when Eva told a silly joke. Her emotions stayed volatile, her hormones free flowing. She dried a tear from an eye. They looked concerned at her.

– It's like an endless wild ride, she said, – like they say high dosages of LSD works.

– Adepts have struggled with the Transition for times immemorial, Jennifer shrugged, – far more than ordinary teenagers. And now, in its final stages, it's reaching its highest peak.

– Thank you for sharing your knowledge, priestess, Lillian said solemnly.

Eva stared curious at her again, not getting it. Tove and Axel did get it, but pretended not to do so. Lillian giggled, seemingly unprompted, and this time they did get it.

– This city is something else, Eva said, deliberately changing the subject. – There are so many potential experiences to choose from that I've difficulties deciding what to do tomorrow.

– Anything a human being can desire, Jonathan said lightly.

– And the world has turned out to be strangely small lately, Tove chuckled.

– Others traveling here from Norway I've talked to have hardly met a single acquaintance from home here, but we encounter them all the time.

– Coincidences, Axel said curtly, making her look hurt at him.

– … and Lillian, do you know who I bumped into yesterday? Our admirer from the apartment upstairs.

He has red hair, Lillian thought.

And as if on cue, the phone rang. She froze, unable to keep it from happening. Monique walked to the phone.

– Hello?

There was clearly no answer. All those living under this roof froze. There had been quite a few such calls. Monique returned the receiver to the hook.

– What an asshole, Tove swore.

Lillian shrugged and resumed her gluttony. The others looked relieved at her and resumed their dining as well.

– I know what we should do tomorrow, she glared.

They looked attentive at her.

– We should show up at Carter Wainwright's speech, she said.

– «The new Oswald Mosley», Eva said. – I don't know…

– We should make our presence known, Lillian glared, – tell him and his thugs exactly what we think of them.

And everyone displayed their most dangerous grin.

2

– Everything is in order, Jennifer informed Lillian. – The fact that he keeps kicking is just one more of many assurances of his good health.

All of them prepared themselves for the day, the confrontation ahead.

– I recognize Wainwright, Martin cautioned them. – He was the archbishop of Madrid in 1570, during the Burning Times.

– It's fitting, I guess, Elijah mused, – that he's something like that.

– He's even worse than he seems, Martin added. – He's The Stable.

An atavistic fear grabbed many of those in the room. Eva looked puzzled at them.

– He's a mutant hunter, Lillian explained.

Eva and Tove looked incredulous at her.

– They've lost much of their worldwide membership and influence after the Janus Clan took them on and out in earnest last year, Martin said, – but they remain dangerous. They know us, and know how to counter our powers. The best way for us to counter that is doing what we have been doing, honing our bodies and train our minds to resist brainwashing even more than we're doing.

They put hard, protective pads under the clothes on the shoulders, elbows and knees, and a Kevlar vest around the upper body. The vest didn't fit Lillian, of course.

– This can protect you against various blades and even bullets, Jennifer instructed them, and might save your life even in the worst of circumstances.

– Looks like we're going to war, Axel said.

– We are, his sister told him.

They left the house and stepped out into the daylong twilight. The group in motion made its way to the Underground station. They descended its depths yet again. The Jubilee Line brought them to Green Park. They left the Underground there, not bothering to change trains. Stuart Elliott and acquaintances, lots of acquaintances met them outside.

– Well met, Stuart and Martin choired and chuckled, clearly sharing a private joke.

The two mingling groups walked on to Hyde Park Corner. The racist public meeting had started. So had a much larger counterprotest. Martin and Stuart's groups joined that.

– The blacks, the immigrants and our immoral, godless society are responsible, Carter Wainwright, an old man with a goatee and well-done hair cried from the platform.

Cheers and boos mixed and burned together. Stuart and Lillian took their place on the platform with the other speakers. The massive police force present had placed themselves between the two groups.

– Oswald Mosley and his thugs were confronted by compassionate human beings at every turn, Stuart shouted. – So should this man and his like be.

They spoke simultaneously. Sometimes people heard one, sometimes the other.

– I'm sick and tired of bigots, Lillian shouted enraged. – I'm sick and tired of humanity tolerating them.

Her voice rose and completely overwhelmed, drowned Wainwright's. Everyone looked stunned at her.

– We pretend to acceptance in a meaningless effort to serve freedom of speech, while forgetting completely that harassment got nothing to do with freedom of speech. No one has the right to bully others, and the contemptible racists do that every time they open their mouth. So, no, if they are so desperate to speak slurs, they can do that in the confines of their own private spaces. No one has a right to be a bully, to spread hatred of people not like them. They insult the very principle of freedom of expression. They are the individuals limiting others freedom of speech when they don't like to hear what others think of them. They accept only their own «speech». They turn to violence when they don't get what they want. ENOUGH!

Thunder seemed to roll across the field. Her rage diminished others' rage.

Most people at the other side of the line scowled at her, but not all. She smiled.

Wainright looked at her with sick hatred in the small eyes.

– If looks could kill… she giggled.

The announced in advance meeting ended by lack of steam. Most of those who had sought this place to listen to the hate monger slinked away like lizards, and those few remaining left together soon enough.

– SATAN'S HARLOT, a man shrieked.

– Everyone is a critic, Annabelle joked.

Loud laughter rolled across the field.

– Goddess of Mist, Jennifer greeted the woman with black eyes as she stepped down from the platform.

Deeply content, and with boiling blood, Lillian Donner took a deep breath.

– Let's spend the day away from the dreary mansion, shall we?

They chuckled, pleasing her to no end.

A large crowd made its way away from there. The silent buzz in Lillian's mind rose to insane heights. They dined by the Serpentine. The water and the surrounding faces shifted a thousand times in her vision. Her transformation had brought greater awareness. It pleased her. She enjoyed herself on the shore of yet another dark water. The memory brought her many more such occasions.

– Humanity can't continue like we have, she mused. – Something must give. The change will come, whether or not humanity as a whole wants it. Make no mistake, if it isn't voluntary, it will be forced, one way or another. Our current existence is completely unsustainable, bordering on impossible.

Everyone paid attention, and while she would probably have found that strange earlier in this life, she no longer did. They noticed something unfathomable within her. They couldn't explain it, but it was clearly there.

She did sense it, boiling even stronger beneath the surface, still waiting to fully express itself.

Most of them left during the next hour, waving goodbye, paying their respects as they did. The smaller, but still big group made its way into the dark streets, and flashing neon lights.

– Let's enjoy a mundane night, the young girl suggested.

Most of the seemingly unfamiliar people joined her on that venture as well. She found it more than a little disconcerting, but the happy smile kept lingering on her lips.

They watched several movies, and discussed them passionately afterwards.

– I loved Emerald Forest, she said eagerly. – Even though the movie was more about the idea of the noble savage than a true savage.

– It made me dizzy, Marianne brightened. – It was such an optimistic, far too optimistic view of a horrible reality, but it still brightened my day.

– Your sense of reality is reason for pride, Jennifer joked.

Everyone laughed.

They earned a brief respite from a looming horror lurking in their neighborhood.

– I love this, a boy stated.

Most of them nodded astonished to themselves, also because they actually knew, or at least had a pretty good idea of what he hinted at.

– Most people are full of themselves, with no reason to be.

The jungle, also the jungle from the movie seemed to surround Lillian. She ran, ran with a black panther, and there was no fear.

They stumbled out of a pub at closing time at eleven. Everyone hugged and kissed like old friends before parting company.

– This is the dream, she conveyed to her companions on their way home.

They nodded. They understood.

People on unsteady legs descended the Underground, floating down the dark river's deep waters. The companions from St John's Wood stepped onto the train, minded the gap, and stepped onto the train. They chuckled some more, as they sat down in their seats. The door closed, and the train started moving.

Something, an itch made Lillian turn and look out of the window. Erling stood there with his scornful grin in place. The train left the station. She kept seeing that grin.

– I see him everywhere, she said distressed. – I'm not even certain he's really there all the time anymore.

Her companions looked at her with understanding and concern.

– He will slip up sooner or later, and then we'll get him, Jonathan swore.

She squeezed his hand in gratitude, squeezed it so hard that it hurt. He didn't cry out. The rest of the train ride seemed unreal to her. She knew he probably couldn't be there waiting for them when they exited the station, but she kept sensing him.

– He could be like… us, she stated, wondered.

– He could be, Martin agreed.

She watched him. He held back a little.

– I've got an errand, he said. – I'll return soon enough.

She kissed him goodbye, and when she let of go of him, he was gone in a jiff.

– I've complained about him being overprotective, she told the others, – so I can't complain when he isn't.

– Passion is weird, Eva chuckled.

They returned to the house. Lillian caught and amplified its mood, and it caught and amplified hers.

– It looks different every time I enter it, she explained. – I guess it's I who have changed and not it.

Everything seemed darker and the air seemed colder, as if both heat and light were fading away. It persisted, even as they closed the door behind them, and switched on more light and heat.

Marianne pulled her jacket closer around the body, Marianne who had strange dreams. Aside from the obvious, she knew less about the reason for her unrest than Lillian and some of the others.

They began making the late evening meal, hardly acting on a conscious level, just going through the motions.

– Little me feels even smaller here, tall and big Eva said lightly. – And extremely dumb. He can't possible have had time to read all these books, especially not lately.

She looked at Lillian and her big belly. Lillian reddened.

They began devouring their spicy food and drink, but nothing with alcohol, staying away from that by a unanimous decision, their communication deeper than words.

Lillian put on music, Pyramid by Alan Parsons Project. That, too, sounded different, heathen. It reminded her even more of ancient Egypt, its golden halls and dark, dirty basement, and of the Dark River flowing beneath it all. She walked to the drawer and found the loaded and oiled gun. She held it up, and pointed it at those sitting in the sofa, looking for a revealing reaction. There wasn't any. Some of the faces changed to how they had once looked, but she spotted no obvious danger. She returned the gun to the drawer.

– You looked really dangerous there for a moment, Lars joked with a shaky voice.

– Excellent she stated. – It has to stop. I'll put the bullet right between his eyes.

Or slice his throat, she thought, and touched the shaft of the blade concealed in her jacket.

They didn't speak much, and only in hushed voices.

– I mostly remember Egypt, Monique said, – and other deserts and dry places in the Middle East. Why that, and not so much elsewhere?

– It isn't strange that you do, Jennifer said. – I do as well. I would venture it's like that with most of us, and also with many other humans. Humans grew numerous for the first time there. North Africa, the Middle East and Asia had major population numbers and countless ancient cities while the Europeans still lived in caves and small tribal societies.

Her words, her passion prompted more memories. They crouched in pain and wonder.

– You will usually remember the violent memories first, she added. – They make the strongest impact, and follow you like a wet blanket through your eternal existence.

They shivered in the heat from the fireplace.

– No wonder we're violent then, Tove whimpered. – It's who we are.

Lillian wanted to speak, to correct her friend, but stayed silent.

The music ended. The quiet silence began. She rose and rubbed her poor, sore back. A loud and long yawn rose from her throat. She shook her head in bewilderment.

– I guess humans are made to sleep eight hours a day, she said, – no matter our inclinations.

She and her brethren turned the lights off and withdrew from the first floor. The large bed seemed to be glowing, and she realized that she might already be sleeping and dreaming, already stretching on the soft ground of moss and soil.

The dreams began in earnest. The visions began, too. It was difficult to distinguish between them at first. The surroundings rushed past her, as if she was running, or her vision had turned blurry. She found herself levitating above a burning city, two burning cities. Then, something pulled her elsewhere. It happened several times, and she had trouble holding on to the fleeting impressions and sensations.

Then, they solidified. She found herself surrounded by fighting warriors of both sexes. A far greater number of enemies surrounded them all. They fought, fought hard and relentless, but the males were slowly killed, and the females slowly overcome and taken away in chains. She and the other female with black eyes were among them.

They were marched off in the searing heat, subjected to the most horrible torture and repeated rape by their enemies. The flash of memory seemed to last forever. The story was short on details beyond the march, but Lillian Donner remembered her own horror and deep shame. She had Fallen, and feared she would never rise again.

They hung in ropes on the city plaza, relentlessly whipped until their skin turned raw, screaming so long and hard that their throat turned sore. She imagined she hung there forever. Guards brought them to a dark, dank cell. She imagined she crouched and whimpered there forever.

Lillian was brought before her future husband, before Erling.

– You're the second of my new men, the man which face she couldn't see instructed her curtly. – You belong to him. You are woman, the inferior. He is man, the superior. Woman will crouch in man's shadow for all time.

And she did. He treated her like shit, and she didn't even resist him. Her existence had become one single ongoing, endless nightmare.

She woke up with tears flowing down her cheeks, shaking with sobs and shame.

3

They had a picnic in Regent Park. The park had turned dirty yellow and black, but they still experienced it as a respite from the cruel city. They walked through a tamed wilderness, but its echo remained strong. The sound of a single drum reached Lillian's ears. On the way to the water, they passed the nude man beating the drum, the jungle drum. It didn't look like he was freezing or anything. The dark skin was soaked in sweat.

– That's some tough guy, Lars noted. – Brrr…

The youths made camp by the small wood bridge. They sat down on the nice and dry ground. The light from the daystar warmed them more than it should have. They enjoyed the peace and quiet. Lillian Donner grew drowsy, even though her thoughts stayed remarkably astute. Her eyes threatened to slide shut. She slipped into her visions, even as she knew her brethren guarded her and would protect her viciously. The scenery shifted around her.

She found herself around a campfire. They cooked the meat the hunters had brought back to the camp. She knew she would have been one of those hunters if she hadn't carried new life in her belly. The raging river reflected the shine from the daystar. She spotted Erling across the dancing flames. He didn't look threatening to her, now. He had once been one of them, just like… like the other one that couldn't be named.

She returned to the here and now, if there ever had been anything like that. She heard that Tove and Axel quarreled again. She didn't hear the words, but knew what it was about. A few minutes passed before both of them approached her.

– We'll return to the house, Axel said curtly. – Is that alright?

Lillian wanted to say no. She merely nodded, and handed Tove the keys, as if to make a point. The thundercloud hovering above Axel's head grew even darker.

The young woman with the black eyes sat there, lost in her own thoughts for a while.

A couple approached them. The female carried a baby. Both the mother and the little girl had red hair. No longer lost, Lillian spoke to them, making them stop.

– May I hold her? Lillian asked softly.

The male seemed skeptical, but the female smiled and nodded. Lillian took the tiny female in her arms. A tingle passed down her spine when she gazed into the girl's green eyes.

– My son is kicking, she chuckled.

Both the male and the recent mother looked puzzled at her.

– Please, join us, Lillian bid them lightly.

They did, their initial skepticism evaporating as time passed, and Lillian's enthusiasm won them over. She found herself using that enthusiasm, that storm of emotion to win them over even more. Exerting her will felt so… natural.

– You are *kwaiala*, she told the woman, – and so is your offspring.

She watched the woman as she spoke, and the woman looked stunned at her, and deep down, Lillian saw that the redhead with green eyes knew what the woman with black eyes were talking about.

All kinds of feverish thoughts surged through Lillian.

Memories asserted themselves. She was an infant resting in a woman's fawn, and the woman had fireeyes. When she looked around, she saw several others, children and adults with red hair and green eyes.

– The Horned God will return to us, her mother told the youths. – He just needs to be elsewhere right now. Do not fret, kwaiala.

– Yes, Goddess, one of the young redheads said both humble and excited. – No, Goddess.

Lillian knew then that Kjell had left them not that long ago, before she was born, and that they would never encounter each other.

The woman with fireeyes put her daughter's mouth to her nipple, and Lillian sucked eagerly. The milk strengthened her like pure energy inserted into her tiny body.

Lillian rose. The woman followed her in an instant. Lillian felt so uplifted that she could hardly contain herself.

An otherwise cheerful bunch made their way back to the house.

My brief home.

The thought prompted a rush of other thoughts in her mind. One brief home in eternity. A fortress of solitude in the midst of the raging storm.

The drums no longer thundered in the giant park, but…

– Can you hear the drums? She asked the others.

They shook their head.

I do.

She hummed the old song as she led them out of the park.

– Such a strangely beautiful and haunting song, the woman said startled. – I can't identify its origin, but…

– Some people would claim it's an old Viking hymn to the gods, Lillian replied, – but I'm convinced its origins are far older.

One more turn, and they would be home. Thoughts and time flew like birds in the dark, bleeding in the night.

She didn't catch it at first, didn't look at the house, but at Marianne. A loud scream of terror overloaded her sensitive ears. Everyone heard Tove's wail, her death scream. They spotted her behind one of the windows. She knocked her fists at the glass, in vain, until she just seemed to collapse and push her palms at the cold surface. They watched as a creature with red hair rushed her from behind. A hand grabbed her hair. The blade flashed on the cloudy day. The point of the sword penetrated the girl, doing so several times. Tove froze and turned limp in the murderer's grip. The death cry mixed with Lillian's shout of horror. Lillian's feet moved her forward at raging speed. She watched as the murderer pulled the dying body back into the room. The blood painted a red cross on the window.

No! NO!

– You're dead, she shouted like a fury. – I'll make you eat your entrails.

She knocked on the solid door, kicking it hard. It didn't budge in a notable way. She kicked even harder at the window. It proved equally useless.

Suddenly, she found herself surrounded by armed constables. They fired at the windows. The bullets didn't even leave marks. Two giant bruisers grabbed her and held her. They were strong. She couldn't free herself. The detectives fired at the lock, shot it to pieces. The door opened. She kicked down the two holding her, and ran ahead of the civilian dressed constables.

She caught the sight of him standing at the center of the floor. He held the sword in one hand, and Tove's hair in the other.

A blurry motion, and he had pushed the blade through his own chest. The body hit the floor hard. Lillian froze to a statue.

– All that blood, a detective remarked offhand. – The blade penetrated the heart. He doesn't stand a chance.

Lillian walked forward in a daze. She knelt by his side.

Axel rested on his back. The red wig had slipped off his head. The sword kept sticking out of his chest. She couldn't decide whether or not she should remove it. He attempted to speak.

– Why? She heard herself ask.
– He… forced me… made me do things. I wanted to resist him, but he was so much stronger than me.
The constables mumbled between themselves.
– Split personality disorder. His inner voice told him to do it.
– Isn't all that just bullshit?
– I've seen it before. You don't believe it's the same person, and it isn't, not really.
– … poor sick fuck…
– … completely nuts.
Dead eyes stared at Lillian. She struck and kept striking the dead man. The blood splashed her. The room started spinning. She started screaming again, and this time, she couldn't stop.

4

Martin entered through the open door.
– She doesn't want you to go to her, Gunnar said, and blocked his path.
Martin pushed him aside like he would a feather.
– Marianne is with her, Jonathan said. – They're in the bedroom.
Martin seemed to fly up the staircase, climbing four and four stairs.
The two sat on the bed in tight embrace, Lillian dissolved in tears. Marianne just seemed lost. She rose, kissed him on the cheek, and left the room. Lillian didn't move. Tears kept wetting her drowned cheeks. She knew he was there, and eventually, she also focused her eyes on him.
– What's the meaning of it all? She choked subdued.
– The only meaning is that there is no meaning, he said, struggling to speak, to respond to her. – It's only when you realize that, that you see the meaning of everything.
– That is so funny, she joked with dead eyes.
She looked pointedly at him again.
– Did you know?
– I suspected, he said, equally subdued. – I had nothing to base my suspicion on, really.
– This will be one of the highlights of my immortal existence, she snarled. – It will always remind me of how life sucks.
He closed and opened his eyes. All the fire seemed to have left her.
– Will you be alright? He asked cautiously, kicking himself for being a jerk.
– Yes, I will make it, she spat, caught his concern easily. – You don't need to worry. I'm not ready for the grave yet. I wish I was. But then, everything

303

would just start all over again, wouldn't it.

She wasn't asking a question. She had accepted the truth. Relief flooded him.

– I need to leave again, he said. – You need time for yourself.

– Yesh, time for myself, she scorned him. – Do you recall how full of myself I was, claiming that he would never get to me? He certainly got to me, that slick bastard.

Martin left her. He hesitated by the stairs, as if he was turning back, but he kept going.

Adams waited for him in the garden outside. Kjell appreciated his presence, his mundane qualities right now.

– Meaningless, isn't it?

– Isn't it always? Kjell shrugged.

– The young man was obviously disturbed, the inspector mused. – You were wrong when you believed he killed with pure malice. That makes it even more tragic, of course.

– Tragic, Kjell agreed and left.

He left St. John's Wood, anything that could remind him of his brief home the last forty years, setting course south. He reached Bayswater Road. There was still daylight. He stood still for a moment, looking at the children in the playground in Kensington Gardens. He listened to their happy cries and smiles. He stayed for a moment, before continuing eastward, to Oxford Street, and all the people, all the Christmas shoppers.

They didn't comfort him. Even here in London, they were lightyears away.

That also held true in the intersection at Oxford Circus. Ghosts and ghostlike beings rushed past him in all directions. He froze, then, sensing the first chilly flare from the channel wind. He knew the wind wasn't really there. It was his powers, his sensitivity acting up. It originated with one of the people across the street. It didn't affect him as much as Tuth Ankh Amun's tomb, but it was closely related. He watched, as a figure covered in clothing, another immortal turned and vanished into the Underground. The feeling was unmistakable. But that was incidental compared to what the presence made him feel. He had met quite a few immortals by now, and they didn't make him feel anything like this one did.

Kjell crossed the street and rushed down the stairs, but the tall creature was nowhere to be found. Several trains left as he watched. The creature could be on any of those.

The chill down his spine grew pronounced. He turned. She stood there, leaning against the wall, displaying herself to him. He took a closer, much closer look at her. She had her plain brown hair in one braid reaching far down on her back. He found her sweet and pretty, even as she knew it was an illusion. She did redden under his close scrutiny.

– Aren't you… aren't you Martin Keller? She wondered sweetly.

– I am, he confirmed, playing the game.

– I recognized you immediately, she said brightly. – My name is Elanor Brenton. I'm so pleased to meet you.

– I'm having something to eat, he said curtly. – Feel free to join me.

He retraced his step up the stairs, up the escalators, and she joined him. She seemed young, hardly older than Lillian. Her eyes told a different story.

They walked down Wardour Street, to the heart of Soho, and to Leicester Square. The familiar place looked totally unfamiliar to him. They had dinner at Len Ho, one of the oldest Chinese restaurants. The girl spoke with her mouth full of rise.

– Do you know what, she said with bright eyes. – You made me study ecology. I had almost settled for economy before that.

– You have my sympathies, he joked.

– I know what you mean, she giggled.

They had a toast with glasses of soda. She kept behaving like the typical girl in her early twenties, practically begging him to pluck her, and he was tempted.

– It has meant so much to me, she said eagerly, – as if I felt alive for the first time. I found others sharing my passion. You mean so much to so many, Martin.

She glanced shyly at him, clearly aroused.

– I know I talk like the silliest girl with a crush, but I can't help it.

– I love it, he said. – I certainly appreciate it.

– That makes me feel positively giddy, the young woman with a crush said.

She displayed herself again. She wanted him, and he was tempted.

– You've done such a great job with our daughter, she said, changing in a moment to an older, experienced woman. – I couldn't ask for more.

He tensed, unable to stop it from happening.

– So, what do you want, Ashanti?

– I don't desire vengeance, she stated calmly. – On the contrary, I want to make peace with you. I would be very stupid if I didn't. I didn't know who you were. If I had known, I would have knelt in the mud before you, and begged to be your humble toy and servant.

She knows, he thought, knows more than I do.

– Take it from me, you and the Goddess will wake up soon, and you will be a force to be reckoned with.

She reached out a hand, offering it to him, careful not to overstep her bounds.

– I have a gift for My Lord, if My Lord will indulge me.

He knew what she was talking about. He fought to contain himself. He nodded.

She touched his brow, and he experienced it like he would an electric shock, not of matter, but of spirit. The visions began in an instant.

– Your humble priestess greets you with her love, Master.

She rose, curtsied and pulled back, leaving him alone.

The room shifted in his vision to something instantly recognizable.

Kjell and Stine crossed western Norway on foot.

– You are her, he cried.

He watched her, watched how the old woman froze.

– You remembered something, didn't you. Who am I?

He lost the moment, the brief memory. It returned to the murky depths of his mind, and he shook his head.

– I don't remember, she complained, – don't remember much more than you do, and I've had an entire life to dig.

His training was in its latest stages, and the ceremony could and would soon begin.

– Everything isn't clear to me yet, even though I know it will be. But I know we can't allow him to perform the ceremony of light and darkness on you. That will gain him one more undue advantage. *I* will do it. I remember enough to do that, at least.

He didn't understand. He did, in fast-fading flashes of insight.

The flashes slowed down again, and he was able to catch details. He was traveling north to the Netherlands with Carlos Velarde and the extended family. They made good speed, but never stopped turning their heads and looking behind them. The high plains of Spain changed to the lowland of the Kingdom of France. They stayed out of sight, out of populated areas as much as possible. He had always remembered it well, but now he seemed to recall with burning clarity. The drums of war between Spain and the rebellious Netherlands had begun beating the year before. They beat stronger, now. Kjell Gudmundson alias Pietr van der Haart heard them easily, like he had done every time since his rebirth.

The small group of people arrived in Antwerp early in the new year. His memories raged on in a condensed form, but he still recaptured them easily. They stayed in Antwerp for years. Even beyond the Spanish Fury in 1575, where eight thousand people were slaughtered by Spanish soldiers and enormous amounts of damage was done.

The two men did fight in the war, or served as medics when they felt there was no choice. They returned to their extended family with scars, but somewhat whole. Their ancient fighting experience surged through their mind, both on and off the battlefield.

He remembered catching Lyta's lovesick look and realizing its significance for the first time. They mated that night, and he had several children with her, all with red hair and green eyes. Carlos had children with the two other sisters, and his children were born with the fireeyes.

Antwerp became the capital of the Union of Utrecht, the Dutch revolt in 1979. They stayed there until they had to flee again, when the city was recaptured by Catholic forces in 1585. They moved to Amsterdam, the new capital of the seven northern provinces.

– Are you at peace, My Lord? Lyta asked him again in his mind.

And he replied in the same manner he always did.

– As much as I can be.

The children, all the children of both fathers had notable powers from early childhood. He and Carlos had discussed that, and agreed to foster and encourage the use of those powers.

– Call me Carl, the other man told him one day, – Charles Wharton.

They had talked about moving on to England, no matter how much Amsterdam seemed like the center of the world right now.

– I'm Peter Hardy, Kjell said, and hand met hand.

The second generation of children began dropping.

– The Janus Clan has returned, Charles stated in wonder. – They didn't get us this time either, and we probably aren't the only ones, anyway.

– I'm confident we're spread across the sphere, father, Leslie, his daughter said with thick pride in her voice. One of our males alone can spread our seed to thousands of females.

She was like most Janus Clan females, brave and bold, not taking shit from anyone.

They did thrive in the Netherlands, in the progressive environment there, even as they prepared for it to end, and also were impatient to move on.

The nomadic life was in their blood. And Peter knew that, even though he couldn't tell how he knew.

Charles and Lyta, and the others of their generation still alive turned gray, turned old. Peter prepared to depart.

– You should wait until the young one is born, Charles offered.

– I've seen enough friends die.

The men shook hands. The old ladies hugged Peter fiercely.

– Until we meet again, Lyta said.

Kjell repeated that, like a penance.

And like a brief draft from the open door, he was gone.

The neon lights began shining stronger in the waning light. He walked the streets of London. Everything flashed around him. He knew this was real, that she wasn't playing a trick on him again. She might not have been completely sincere, but she hadn't been lying. She had wanted him to remember, to experience some kind of clarity.

He heard the tones of a lone saxophone. The man playing it had placed himself at the base of the escalator. The naked music of despair and longing echoed between the walls. Martin put a ten-pound bill in the man's worn suitcase.

Martin Keller returned to the quiet darkness of humanity.

5

Lillian Donner woke up in the late morning, surrounded by warm and pleasant flesh. She looked for Martin, but he wasn't there. That always felt strange to her. Monique rubbed her cheek.

– The Goddess is sad, she said, – but she will grow from that low point to once more become the mighty creature of mist and shadow she has always been.

That sounded so right, even as it failed to comfort her. Lillian returned the affection.

They enjoyed yet another hearty breakfast. Lillian couldn't quite free herself from the lethargy lingering in her gut, her sore, sore gut.

– She, too, loved you, in spite of her superficial appearance, Jonathan said.
– She will love you again the next time you encounter each other.

He had embraced his new life. Everyone here had. The smile grew on her lips.

– She will know who she is the next time, Marianne insisted. – She will know herself and us.

They made their daily tour through town, visiting house occupants residing in several houses. They were received with honor. Their reputation kept growing.

– London is a crucible, Monique told the gathering, doing the talking for her clan. – It will attract many great and fierce spirits doing their part to transform human life into what it should be, what it always should have been.

Lillian studied all the eager, excited faces before her, feeling the stirring of interest and joy. She sat with her housemates, her temple priests, and allowed herself to be distracted, to be moved. Monique exceeded in her performance, her teaching. It was nice not being at the center of attention, but retreating to the chorus line.

Leslie, the redhead and mother had her eyes on her all the time. The emerald eyes had started glowing. The excitement made Lillian's skin tingle.

It kept tingling as she stood up in the circle, and began talking.

– You need to learn self-defense, she instructed them, – also martial arts. We will teach you, and teach you to teach yourself.

She watched them, and saw how they grew even more attentive, aware of how she communicated with them without words, and even without thought, on a level deep beneath the surface, or any surface.

– The establishment will always turn violent when their lies and deception no longer work. We must prepare for that, prepare for so much. But more than anything, we must return to what we once were, in a faraway time we still remember deep down. Yes, we are deep wells of power, ancient beings weakened by many generations of regimentation and oppression.

Her passion burned them, lighting the fire within. The smile broke on her face.

They spent a couple of days in the various communes, all of them filled with both star eyed and angry youth. Lillian felt positively cynical in comparison. She found herself distracted again, and refocused her objective.

– We have an obligation, she told her charges, – a sacred trust.

They nodded in happiness, noticing that she had returned to her intense ways. They noticed, and thereby she did as well. Her heart beat harder in joy and anticipation.

– We need to be patient, she stated, – but we can't be idle.

They listened to her. She knew they did.

She didn't really doubt that when she pondered the issue. She kicked herself because she did ponder it.

– I will be ready when the time comes, she stated with confidence, – and so will you.

Everyone nodded eagerly. She kept her face in an impassive mode.

They didn't understand. How could they?

Dark flames burned on her hand. They made the air darker, not brighter. They made her ponder impossible questions and issues. That had become her life, now.

– It has been almost a year, now, since life started changing for me. I can hardly reach back to that time and remember. It is like it doesn't exist anymore.

– That time is considerably shorter for most of us, Elijah said. – You came to the desert and fetched us to our new life, and we're so very grateful for it.

– We lived empty lives, Monique said subdued, – convinced we were having the time of our life.

– Are you alright? Marianne asked Lillian anxiously. – Is there anything we can do for you? Anything?

– I'm better, she assured them. – It was so very comforting and invigorating and darn *inspiring* to visit all those communes, sharing with them, see what they've made of their lives outside mainstream society. We will build on that, and take them and ourselves a step further. We will show them, show all the people in the stale, oppressive inhuman society that the human spirit is still alive.

And she saw how she lifted them up, and subsequently lifted up herself, and she felt the power. Her hand faded away, and this time she didn't fear it, didn't fight it. The others stared transfixed at the spot where the hand and the equally invisible lower arm should have been.

– Touch it, she bid Monique.

Monique tried grabbing it, but there was only air. Lillian focused and grabbed Monique's hand. The invisible hand stayed invisible, but was suddenly there after all.

She focused on holding on to the state of being keeping it like that. She managed for five, ten seconds until it reappeared.

– That's remarkable, Jonathan breathed.

Lillian let go of the hand. Everyone looked even more awestruck at her.

London didn't really seem to be there when they returned to the streets. Or perhaps she misunderstood? Perhaps London was more there for her than ever before?

She stood a bit away from the others, by the water with the many different birds in St James's Park. She noticed how Jennifer approached her, without watching her do it.

– I must leave, too, Jennifer said. – I'll be back soon enough.

– Can't you stay? Lillian implored her.

– Papa has given me a mission.

Lillian knew that settled it. The old young girl was strangely loyal to her young old father.

She watched as the black woman pulled back and faded away in the twilight of the park.

Chapter 16

December 21, the shortest day, the longest night, the Winter Solstice arrived, another age-old time of celebration. Lillian sat up in bed, distancing herself from all the warm, pleasant bodies. She walked to the window and looked out at the dark, remote landscape of naked trees and wet, brown ground.

– I can feel it, she said aloud.

The words rose unprompted from her throat, not formulated on a conscious level before she had spoken. The city stretched out in her mind, reaching out to suburbs and surroundings areas.

– I recall… long ago, she said. – The cities were so small. I could only reach a few people compared to these modern metropolises.

– Your memories enter my mind, Goddess, Annabelle said, unusually timid and humble. – I see myself in them. Thank you.

Lillian smiled. A small part of her wanted to correct the girl, chastise her for her worship, but she didn't.

This breakfast quickly turned out to be yet another gluttony. The young woman with the black eyes hardly remembered any of them being different.

– I won't ever return to Mount Olympus, she stated curtly between the mouthfuls.

They nodded, and she knew they understood.

Everyone participated in the dishwashing. It pleased Lillian to no end how smooth the process had become. There was no resentment, nothing of the destructive processes she dimly recalled between the sexes when growing up. They sat in the sofa and the chairs around the living space table later, having a low-keyed conversation. The words didn't matter that much right now, only the sense of community they all experienced.

There was a hard knock on the door. Another hard knock followed the first. Lillian's brethren exchanged anxious glances.

– It's alright, she said, quite relaxed. – I know who it is.

She still tensed a bit as she walked to the door, with Elijah and Annabelle by her side.

– I'm confident I'm reading the situation correctly, she said, – but we should stay cautious.

She opened the door. Eva stood there, looking like a wet rag.

– He left without a word, she whimpered, visible distressed.

– Come inside, Lillian offered her, feeling very adult and kind.

Eva rushed into her arms. Lillian kissed her and rubbed her back.

– You knew it was me? Her friend said. – How could you know?

– I sensed you.

– You couldn't see me, Eva rambled on.

Lillian slapped her on the cheek. Eva stared stunned at her.

– No more of that modern-day bullshit, Lillian stated curtly. – I'm fed up with that. Do you understand?

– Yes, Lillian, Eva said meekly.

Lillian led her back to the sofa.

– You're among friends and like-minded people, now, Lillian said softly. – You no longer need to pretend.

Eva grabbed her hand, and smothered it in kisses.

They welcomed the distressed girl, smothering her in affection. She choked hard. Lillian knew she took her words to heart.

Lillian had developed what she, in a distant past of Lillian's life would have called an uncanny ability to read people's motivations and desires.

They made their daily excursion into town later, moving like they always did, like a flow of motion. All of them noticed. Today was a special day. The fire burned even stronger within. One casual glance at the others, and Lillian could confirm that to herself yet again. She had the ability to look within people, as if their skin and the invisible mask covering their face were nothing but air.

Today's meeting was at a pub where pagans met. She noticed easily the special quality of most of those in the gathering. The pub didn't look that different at first glance, but then one began noticing the various pentacles and herbs and paraphernalia exhibited in the room. It did change both the general and deeper impression.

– Some people say that the protestors should be blamed for the unrest, Lillian said, – that they should indeed be blamed for the police attacking them and cracking their skulls and bones. The victims are appointed the perpetrators again. The perpetrators are appointed the victims. We do indeed live in an upside-down society. We shouldn't buy the establishment propaganda, of course. That is against our very nature…

They still did. They looked at her with skepticism in their eyes because she challenged their rigid perception of the world.

– Time is long overdue for us to reject this inhuman society, and do so in all things. It's time for us to live again, and not merely exist, and we can never truly live in this dead world. I've given this speech many times before, and you didn't listen then, but now, you must. We don't have much time left.

– We just want to live our lives in peace, one man said.

– That has never been a valid option, and it's even less so, now.

– They know, Eva said with contempt in her voice. – They just don't want to face reality.

But they did listen. Lillian knew they did. And got that confirmed fully as the group stayed as the shortest day turned to the longest night, as the celebration of the Solstice began in earnest, and quite a few people approached them, and cautiously expressed their support.

– You got to them, Eva said with a shining face. – You got them good. They can no longer hide behind their smug façade.

She spoke so loudly that most of the people in the room had to hear her, but she didn't care. Lillian and her companions grinned even wider.

– She has become so fierce, hasn't she, Annabelle chuckled.

She stressed that she was teasing the girl when she hugged her and kissed her on the cheek. Eva choked in joy.

– You've become so emotional, Annabelle said softly. – That's good.

– We are creatures of passion, Lillian stated, – and we need to be.

The people around their tables nodded empathically. So did several others throughout the room.

Lillian rose, and she knew she imposed her presence on the gathering.

– Bring the furniture and the curtains, she bid them. – Come with us.

Several people looked like they would object, but they didn't. Almost everyone grabbed a piece of furniture or ripped down a curtain, and stepped out in the dark streets. The glowing Goddess of Mist led them across several blocks. It had become a procession, and it attracted lots of attention.

– That's some moving load, a guy exclaimed.

– You come and help us out, Marianne cried.

He looked startled at them, and his buddies.

– Bring your buddies, Lillian cried.

All of them joined in, relieving the burden of those already there, glancing uneasily at each other, as if they couldn't quite believe what was happening. The extended number of people pushed on through the dark streets. A hum rose from Lillian's throat, and soon from everyone walking with her.

It dawned on Lillian that the man playing violin had joined them. He was playing, now. The music penetrated everyone's soft surface and changed them, changed them further. They reached Hyde Park. Everything, every gate had been locked for the night. They threw everything into the darkness of the park, and jumped the fence. Lillian had no trouble with it, and neither had most of the others. They penetrated the great darkness of the park.

A spot in there pointed to itself. She slowed down long before she reached it. She saw it in twilight, in summer twilight. Many fires burned in the ground. People celebrating the Summer Solstice swam in the water. People played instruments, and removed their clothing.

In her vision, Lillian spotted many people with fireeyes, and then, she spotted herself, wild and free.

The people celebrating the Winter Solstice built their single bonfire in the darkness, and put the curtains there with the furniture, all the dry items they had brought. It happened fast, like a hurricane. They lit the fire. It spread like a whirlwind. Its heat touched them all.

It felt like summer then. The cold wind faded. The dancing flames seemed to reach all over the open space.

– All human beings are on a long walk, a long, long journey of learning and discovery, Lillian cried, – and it's amazing, in spite of all the horrors and suffering.

She spotted acknowledgment and joy in their eyes, a flash of fire that might not have been there a moment ago.

The street musician played his violin, its brittle tones spreading across the water and field. He played slow and Lillian danced slowly to the haunting music. Her big belly didn't seem to obstruct her motion at all. The others joined in. A pattern of motion formed on the dry ground, one easily discernible from above. She pictured it like that in her mind, easily shifting her viewpoint.

The street musician had grown old. He would die soon. Sadness and a startling joy rocked her. She pictured him as a young man playing on a beach by a lake with a castle at its center. And she spotted more fireeyes, and herself, and also the other woman with black eyes.

– Lillith, she breathed.

And the name meant something to her, to them all. A surge of awe struck them all.

The dance brought awareness, brought magick. It flowed from her like waves. She gained contact with everyone nearby, intimate contact with her brethren. Everything old became new again, and more. What hadn't been there long ago, was here, now. It kept sustaining her and empowering her.

They moved through the streets again. No one had made the decision to move. No one had suggested it. It just happened. They moved through crowds of people at Leicester Square. They were bathing in the light from the neon signs at Piccadilly Circus. The Eros statue seemed to gain life, turning to flesh. They seemed to walk endlessly. It didn't tire them, but invigorated them further. Lillian noticed a pattern eventually. They were circling in on something, walking in ever-smaller circles, and it dawned on her that she had an idea, a notion of where they were heading.

The derelict building looked so very familiar to her, even though she couldn't tell why.

– It's where Ted and the others were squatting, a girl cried with noticeable enthusiasm in her voice. – I've seen the photos.

And then Lillian got it. The so very familiar shifting features appeared in her mind. She led on into the abandoned building. They entered an entrance hall with a concrete floor covered in dust. It looked considerably different upstairs. Lillian spotted personal items, among them a photography of a young man with fireeyes, and a young woman with red hair.

– This is amazing, a boy marveled. – I was convinced this place was recaptured by real estate agents and entrepreneurs long ago.

– We'll stay here for a while, Lillian stated. – It will be our new brief-home.

All beds, all furniture remained pretty much intact. It seemed like a ghost house, a relic from the past waking up. The next minutes felt like days.

– It's like removing a coat, Lillian mused. – Do that, and the past comes alive again, within and without. It's both such a casual and profound act.

Candles and torches lit up the rooms, casting its dark light on flesh and walls alike. She sensed how the fire awoke in them all, sensed no exceptions. They made an open fire in the remains of an old stove. The smoke drifted a bit, but basically rose straight up, through a hole in the ceiling. They found all the available normal-sized glasses from the kitchen. There were just enough of them for the entire gathering. Lillian began mixing a brew in a large bowl. Everyone in the room watched her with curious eyes.

– All the necessary herbs are still available, she said. – They've been cultivated through the ages to grow in more accessible places. I remember searching for days in the wilderness.

Her voice changed in notable ways. Her appearance did as well. The flames dancing close to her turned to pale, cold fire. She didn't feel their heat.

– Our journey begins tonight, she stated, the cold fire very much present in the black eyes. – We might have made a few steps before this, but this is the moment we begin.

The words echoed within her, within them, and she nodded to herself. They got it.

I get it, she thought.

– It's like a dance, one fluid and true. It's happening just as much in our mind as in our limbs, and both are equally valuable, a dynamic cycle, just like life and death. Yes, we rise from the ashes like we would any sleep or dormancy…

She had their complete attention, the strongest yet.

– It's a powerful unity, non-opposing, dynamic states of being. We need both in order to be complete, whole.

The brew in the bowl began steaming, then smoking. They looked transfixed at it, at her. She began emptying the bowl, and put the content in the small glasses.

– Drink and be merry, she bid them, – and experience what it's all about.

All of them stepped forward without any queue or stress, grabbed a glass and emptied its content in their mouth. Lillian watched as it flowed down their throat. She watched as their tongue turned numb first, then the rest of the body. She emptied her glass, and she chased her brethren down the rabbit hole. Her lips and throat moved, virtually by itself.

– I speak the silent language, she chanted, she hummed. – I burn the true midnight oil. I grow like a tree in spring.

The first began dropping to the floor. Lillian sensed the growing weakness in her limbs, in all their limbs.

– You dance before your queen, the Goddess of Mist in times long past, and all the moments suddenly seem so very recent. The memory burns your Shadow, your soul.

Monique, or she who would one day become Monique, danced before the queen watching her from her throne. She had dark skin and dark hair, like all the dancers performing for their queen, their Goddess of Mist with a hammering heart. It empowered Lillian further, strengthening her resolve, her desire to continue on her chosen path.

One blink, and she hung suspended in chains. Her husband, as decreed by the Lord stood behind her with the stick in his hand. He started beating her on the butt. Each stroke made pain surge through her body and soul.

– The Lord gifted you to me, he snarled. – You will be compliant and pleasant, or you will suffer.

Each new stroke hurt worse than the previous. She knew deep down that she had broken long ago, that the very thought of rebellion or even resistance stayed far from her feeble mind. Her butt burned, hurting even more than the strokes. The punishment seemed unending. She didn't understand. She had made every effort at accommodating him, but she kept rising his ire. She didn't know the reason, but she knew it didn't matter. He had become her entire world. He decided what was right and what was wrong.

She hung in the chains. He was finally done.

– I'll be good, husband, she sobbed. – Please, husband. I'll be an attentive and obedient wife.

She knew it would not be the last time he would punish her. Her suffering stretched out endlessly before her, and she could see no way out.

Death was the way out. She kept shaking hard far into the Shadowland, unable to let go completely of the sorry existence she had suffered, even as strength and power and memory returned to her undiluted.

She was reborn into the wandering tribe fleeing from the army of the riders at dawn. She recognized many of them, and they recognized her before she had reached her fifth birthday. She spotted joy and concern in their eyes. They asked her what had happened, and she told them, without holding anything back, without obfuscating in any way. They comforted her and cared for her in her distress. She had indeed come home.

The safe haven at the Forgotten City was long gone. Their Long Walk had begun, and it already seemed endless to them. She relearned the way of the sword and battle as she grew to womanhood. It was like slipping on an old coat. They fought, on and off blood-soaked battlefields. The sword, the various tools of war and steel, long since an integrated part of their hands, became even more so. Bloodied faces kept flashing before their eyes. They fought and died and were reborn in an endless cycle. They became the sword, the blade, the steel, the red, wet, shiny metal…

She woke up alone on the floor. Monique and Elijah slept soundly not far away. She recalled having pulled away from them after they had fallen asleep. Her silent motion brought her to her clothing. She dressed in fast, economic moves. One glance confirmed that everyone was sleeping. She sat course for the entrance. The streets imposed themselves on her as she rushed through them. Each face imprinted itself on her mind.

The train raced through the dark tunnels. She spotted countless faces there as well, both in the car and on the black tunnel wall. Her thoughts threatened to go everywhere, to spread themselves thin as gossamer strains. She focused them into a narrow path, a gray and dark red band growing ahead of her.

Her hands stayed closed as fist. She had to bend them open. It hurt, and she snarled to herself. Her eyes closed to slits. She was falling, not through space, but through time, and she experienced it as just as real.

She exited St. John's Wood Station tense and prepared. Nothing happened then, or as she made her way north. The familiar path became even more familiar as she approached the brief-home. She suppressed the warm feeling within when she caught sight of it. Everything seemed to be in order. She rotated once and surveyed the terrain. There was no suspicious motion anywhere. She approached the building. A single lamp lit the first floor, and cast a weak glow on the upper floors. The front yard left very little to the imagination. Her imagination still ran wild. She found her keys, and unlocked and opened the door. Her five mundane senses and numerous esoteric senses worked in unison. There was no one there. She stepped inside.

Her sight worked well in the scant light. She could gaze into the shadow, and see far more than most could in the brightest day. There was nothing even resembling motion nearby. She ran up the stairs on light feet. The big belly didn't really slow her down. Her balance was off, but that was it. She smiled when he turned energetic, when he started kicking harder. She once again ignored the warm glow within, steeling herself further for what was coming. The two swords hung on the wall. She grabbed hers, and retreated to the stairs. A very distinct sound of someone stepping on the floor reached her from below. The cold air reached her from the open door, from every side of her body. She noticed the weight of both the gun and the knife in her jacket, hardly noticing the heavy sword in her hand.

He stood on the floor, just a few steps from the entrance. She noticed his anxiety when he caught sight of her. He looked like Gunnar, now, almost only like him. She had no trouble reading him, reading the mundane, the normal human being.

– I knew you weren't Axel. I recognized him as one of your brothers from Bjorgvin. It wasn't hard at all.

– Your time has come, he spat.

– Do you really think so? Have you chased me, or have I chased you?
She teased him.

– The Lord promised you to me for all time, he boasted.

– Your Lord is just one more phony shit, she giggled.

It enraged him and baffled him. He couldn't fathom that anyone could ridicule his Lord.

– I've been waiting for you, she said huskily. – Why did you wait so long?

All his confidence had been exposed like the pretense it was. The big, muscular man look uncomfortable in his skin.

– You don't really believe I forgot to lock the door, do you?

He drew his sword. They started circling each other.

– I can see through you, now, as if you are empty, as if there is nothing there, beneath the shell. Your Lord has reduced you to a shell of a man.

Her voice changed, turning coarse, turning stronger, powerful.

– You remember, don't you, remember the last time I taught you a lesson? You're nothing but a naughty little boy fearing punishment. Thank you for volunteering as the sacrifice. I had despaired of finding a suitable candidate.

They struck simultaneously. Blade hit blade, hit steel. He faltered and staggered backwards. She did not. The physical and mental strength was like a song within. She had to contain herself to not grow overconfident. She knew what this was, what she was in truth fighting. Sweat poured on her brow. It pleased her that it poured even harder on his.

You move constantly, she heard the voice of a distant teacher. Your feet and you never stand still. You're a whirl of motion, a living lethal weapon.

Small and big pyramids grew up around them, and cast them in shadow, in pale fire and night, but she didn't allow that to distract her. The sound of metal hitting metal kept her astute. That sound, echoing thousands of times kept her aware and ready.

– The Janus Clan is born with metal at their side, she stated. – It's in our blood.

He struggled, unable to give a verbal reply.

You bastard. You abysmal bastard.

Pure rage filled her, and she had to watch herself. She used the rage, but didn't allow herself to become overwhelmed by it.

He made a charge at her belly, but she easily evaded it, and laughed it off.

– You're such a clumsy oaf, Sterark. You always were.

She watched herself from above, watched poetry in motion. The belly didn't slow her down at all. She turned her back to him. He attacked her. She rotated on one foot and blocked his attack. He almost lost the sword. She cut his free arm, just enough to let the blood flow. It hung down his side, useless. He struck at her, but she had already stepped out of range.

He struck her sword again. His blade hit the strong part of hers. She hardly felt the impact. Her feet moved. She kicked his knee, and it broke with a loud snap and his loud scream. He jumped back on one foot. His back hit the wall, and he broke several ribs. She struck the sword out of his hand, cutting off two fingers in the process.

She grabbed his jaw and squeezed. He grabbed her, and held on. She stuck the knife in his chest, and he gasped. She struck him on the head, and he slid down the wall, leaving a broad stroke of blood.

– That could have been your heart. That tiny hole won't kill you.

He produced a needle with a nasty content she recognized as the Hammer of Witches in an instant. She stamped on his arm and broke it. He shouted short and sharp, as the blood started flowing from the stump.

She kicked him in the belly, and kept doing so, kept roughing him up.

He crouched on the floor, unable to move. She spat at him, and the special wicked smile crossed her lips.

– This small thing?

She picked up the needle. He looked up at her with feverish eyes.

– I thought I would need my powers to deal with you, but I didn't. You were an easy target. You believed you were the cat, and I was the mouse, but you were the mouse. You always were. Only your master's protection made you anything more. I feared you for a thousand years because I didn't know myself. I will laugh myself silly many times because of that.

She stabbed him with the needle and injected the content into his veins.

– I know this won't really work on you, but it will certainly made you feel confused and dazed, making you feel my punishment even worse.

She turned invisible, completely invisible, from head to toe. Fear filled his feverish eyes.

More impressions and sensations flooded her being.

– Every thought, every act, she whispered.

She heard a door open, and watched as a part of the wall slid aside. She didn't really have to look at Martin and Jennifer as they appeared from the dark, secret hallway. He looked with concern at her.

– I'm fine, she assured him. – Our son his fine. I believe he just enjoyed the spectacle.

– Goddess of Mist! Jennifer greeted her awestruck and curtsied.

Lillian acknowledged her with a nod. She fetched a bundle of rope from a drawer and began tying up the very reduced Gunnar, the shaking Erling, Sterark of the ages. He whimpered in pain. It pleased her.

– I remember him so well, she mused, – but I still don't remember much of my own lives.

– It will come to you, Martin said, – as the ages pass.

She bent down and picked up the half unconscious man, and put him on the shoulder. The big, heavy man wasn't really heavy at all, not to her.

– The tide is low, and the tide is high, that's just how it is, but now, it's high, sky high.

And her two companions knew exactly what she was saying.

She carried her light burden into the dark hallway. The other two followed her. They walked down a staircase lit by torches on the walls. The visions kept assaulting her as she walked, but her walk stayed firm.

– She's an adult, and she has grown taller, the accuser accused.

The witch shook before the ridiculous man in the ridiculous costume. He burned her with the hot iron. She screamed herself hoarse. And this was just the beginning of the days-long torture.

Lillian, the Goddess of Mist shook her head in horror and rage.

– The impressions and sensations don't really frighten me anymore. They just make me go livid with rage.

She found some wires and tied them around his body, and strung him up on the wall. The metal ring on the wall seemed to be made for her purpose. He hung in the ropes, the constant pain making him moan in distress. She grabbed his jaw and squeezed, and not being at all gentle about it.

– The Goddess will punish you, so you never transgress against her again.

She will make you shiver with the very thought. There won't be a single moment when you don't think of her.

She heard commotion from the living room upstairs.

– Go fetch them, she bid Jennifer.

– Right away, Goddess, the old young girl said eagerly.

The anxious voices picked up as they made their way down the stairs. Their eyes grew wide as they caught sight of the man strung up on the wall.

– This isn't our eternal enemy, Lillian told them, – but one of his most dedicated servants. His master gave me to him as a gift, as a wife he could dominate and abuse. The master wants all women to be submissive and obedient. We will show him and his «new men» that such desires and actions have consequences.

– My arm hurt, he whimpered.

She struck the arm, right at the fracture. His scream sounded so pleasantly in her ears.

– You big BABY, Monique taunted him, her face twisted in rage, spitting in his face.

Lillian began cutting off his clothes. She did it in a fast, effective manner. He was nude in less than a minute. She examined his wound. It was hardly bleeding.

– You will survive for days…

She grabbed his balls and squeezed. He screamed again.

– I should rip them off, and let you live your life like that, she hissed. – That would at least approach a proper punishment for your millennia of vile crimes.

He shivered in terror. She cut his skin on several spots. He screamed again.

– You're the typical misogynist, a sniveling coward when you don't have all the odds in your favor.

She lit the fireplace, and placed the iron in the flames. He knew what she was going to do. Her vicious grin shook him further. She waited patiently, not rushing it, waiting until the iron was glowing in one end. She tied lots of fabric around her hand, and grabbed the iron in its hot cold hot end. She rushed him and pushed the glowing end at his toes. He began SCREAMING. She held it at the toes, burning them off one by one. The screaming stopped and he lost consciousness. She put the iron back in the fireplace.

– Fetch water, she bid her charges. – Let's wake him up.

Eva and Marianne rushed to do her bidding. Lillian slapped him on the cheeks several times. There was no visible reaction. Eva and Marianne returned with two buckets of water. Marianne splashed the water in his face.

Eyes slid open. Lillian burned his other set of toes.

Her charges watched, pale and queasy. Martin and Jennifer looked quite relaxed.

Lillian watched Gunnar, watched Erling as he woke up, as he became more and more Sterark, how it didn't make him stronger, but weaker.

– Perhaps, I'll let you live your life as a cripple. You're strong. You can survive the removal of your limbs.

His words cut into him like knives.

She kept going. Her strength kept surging, and she imagined there was no end to it. She felt neither physically nor mentally weary. The energy seemed to flow to the surface from some deep reservoir within. Some of her companions dozed off and even slept, but she didn't.

His screams eventually grew weaker, more like whimpers than screams. He had no toes, and no fingers left. She started on his left foot, and kept going.

He hung in the ropes. There was no motion, no motion at all, except his shivering lips.

– Please, he begged her. – Please, kill me, Goddess. Please, grant your servant this boon.

She scratched his cheek, scratched it deep, practically ripping the skin from his face.

– You swear allegiance to your Goddess?

– Yes, I swear allegiance to Lillian, to the Goddess of Mist, now, and for all time.

She began casting her spell, burying herself deep within him, transforming him at a base level.

– You're mine, she swore, – mine for all time. You're nothing but a speck of dust in my presence, but you will do. You will crouch at my feet for the rest of your sorry existence, as this will feel like an eternity every time you reexperience it.

It did. She experienced it with him, time and time again.

Again. *Again.* AGAIN.

He didn't fight her, but embraced his new existence at her feet. Something akin to pleasure surged through her. The vicious grin darkened her face.

– There will be no more Burning Times. Do anything like that, and you will face our wrath. Tell your former allies that if you should encounter them, before you viciously go for their throat.

– Yes, Goddess, PLEASE, GODDESS.

The broken man whimpered like a mouse at her feet.

– The reckoning has just started.

And she slit his throat.

2

She imagined she stood there forever, until she felt Martin's light hand on her shoulder, and turned to face him. She smiled and kissed him softly.

– I feel great, she stated. – I feel fucking great.

The others came to her, and paid their respect, their awe and their worship. They hugged her, and bared their neck to her.

Gunnar's body was strung up on a wall not far from Scotland Yard, impaled on his own sword. On the wall above him was a message written in his blood.

THE SWORD KILLER
YET ANOTHER COPPER
GETTING HIS JUST REWARD

Burke Adams stepped forward and held a press conference.

– We feel confident that this man was the sword killer, he stated. – We found more than enough discriminating evidence. So did the Norwegian police, in his home and cabin, found proof that the murdered girls had been held there.

– But you were confident with the previous killer, too, a journalist commented.

– We never said that. We never closed the case. We just pretended to do so, in the hope that the real killer would get sloppy. It looks like it worked…

He actually looked smug then. They watched him, as he paused and hesitated a bit, just a bit.

– We will look for the person burying his own sword in his chest, of course, but we don't really have much hope of success. Any one of his many potential victims could have done it.

– Can you confirm that he was tortured?

– I can. Most of his body had wounds and burns and marks from torture. It looks like his killer didn't like him very much.

– Based on the message left on the wall, it doesn't look like his killer likes coppers very much either, a journalist commented.

– We're certainly looking into that as well, Adams confirmed.

And that was that, really.

The case caused a sensation. It was one of the most covered cases in news media all over the world in the new year of 1986, Common Era.

The coven walked through the large park again. They even visited the local zoo. Lillian's belly had grown very big, and they took it easy.

– Are you certain you aren't carrying twins? Eva asked.

– He's just big, Lillian marveled, – just like his father.

Eva had changed further from the rather arrogant and obnoxious girl she had been the first few years Lillian had known her. She had turned deep, like all of them, had gained a new outlook on life.

Lillian studied the tiger, like it studied her. He roared at her. She was very tempted to return the roar, but, feeling generous, she held back.

The animals did show their anxiety in notable ways, so the coven kept their distance.

– We're apex predators, Jennifer noted, – and they're very much aware of that. Their instincts aren't that dulled by the imprisonment.

– You don't mean humans when you say that? Monique asked/stated.

– I'm not, Jennifer confirmed.

And all of them knew what she was saying.

– The tiger's roar sounds so good in my ears, Lillian mused.

The subsequent laughter did, too.

– I feel a bit empty, she added abruptly. – There's no immediate danger anymore, and I feel like I've lived with it forever.

And I have.

– And it isn't true, anyway. The danger may have shifted a bit, but it's very much still with us. One casual probe ahead of us, and it's there.

There.

London, one of the largest urban spreads on the planet, stretched out infinitely around her. She noticed at the back of her mind that they left the zoo, and that the heavy traffic picked up around her, and that felt extremely imposing and bad. She noticed the exhaust better with her improved senses. The cough worked itself up her throat.

– Damn, cars are such a horror, she swore. – I wish they would all just go away.

Everyone in the group nodded in solemn agreement, and she sent them all a grateful look.

They walked south. Her elevated awareness didn't leave her, in spite of the ongoing distractions.

Two males had a conversation, or rather a heated discussion.

– Older people have built the land, the idiot said.

– They've built the wretched nation, she retorted, butting in as she passed them. – Destroyed the land.

Both looked stunned at her. She almost broke into laughter.

– It was funny, she grudgingly admitted a while later.

There was a soreness in her voice and expression, one she didn't bother to hide.

– The system is wrong, she solemnly declared, – and thus everything is. The world is wrong. The inhuman society humanity has created on the ashes of mother nature is wrong on all counts. Leading the field of destroyers are the western countries, where most of the population is so brainwashed that they don't have a clue about anything.

She crouched, as if to confirm that.

– There is something…

She gasped, and crouched again.

– I think it is… I think it's coming.

A dozen smiles cracked around her. Martin wanted to support her.

– You're sweet, she said, – but it isn't happening for hours yet. I can walk home.

She turned around and started on the long walk back to St. John's Wood.

– Shouldn't we get you to a hospital? Eva wondered, retracting her statement the moment she made it.

– We have the best possible midwife and physician and witch available to us, Lillian breathed. – We don't need a stinking hospital.

She rubbed Jennifer's cheek.

– Can I just make a cursory examination? The young old girl asked nicely.

Lillian nodded. Jennifer bent down and checked her out.

– You're right, she said. – Nothing major is happening yet. We've got more than enough time.

Jennifer rubbed her cheek.

– You're pretty much on schedule, she assured her. – Everything looks fine. Everything has for as long as I have examined you. And you walking is actually good. You will even pace the floor several times before the boy pops out.

– That's some expression, Annabelle giggled nervously. – I guarantee a male invented that.

The anxiety grabbed them all. Lillian imagined they were actually more nervous than she was. She had no trouble walking. Both Martin and Jennifer looked perfectly calm. The next contraction did hurt a bit, just a bit. They were still far apart. She focused on breathing right, even though she knew it was pretty useless at this stage.

– Few pregnancies are the same, Jennifer kept talking, revealing her anxiety. – It's a very individual thing. Each would-be mother experience it completely different.

Everything seemed to have turned silent around her again. Lillian imagined she sensed a strange heaviness every time her feet touched the ground. She caught easily sight of the spirits as they gathered around her.

– They're curious, Jennifer said, – and they pay their respect. An ancient Goddess is giving birth. Both the father and mother are powerful beings. The offspring will most certainly be as well.

Lillian nodded in acknowledgement, but remained distracted. She had become so astute. She could hardly believe how astute she had become. Each new contraction brought another wave of awareness. The terrain ahead of her seemed alive, like an actual living being. She saw the house before her eyes caught sight of it. They turned a corner, and there they were.

– You've got hours of hardship ahead of you, Jennifer informed her in her straightforward manner.

– I remember our cat, Lillian said. – She was pacing the floor forever before she finally settled down, and got on with it.

Marianne ran ahead and opened the door. The doorway glowed in a pale light in Lillian's vision. Marianne gave the cautious signal of no danger. The others kept surrounding Lillian in a protective bubble. It got awkward when they reached the door. A few of those walking ahead stepped into the house first. Then Lillian did, and then the rest.

She walked up the stairs. She had to pause halfway up, during another contraction. They received her with honors at the top of the stairs, and began undressing and dressing her. She surrendered herself to their care. It felt good, not a cause for anxiety. They supported her, and she allowed it with a content smile. She rested in bed. She paced the floor. Jennifer checked her cervix.

– The dilation has begun in a satisfactory manner, she reported.

Lillian hardly heard what she said. The sense of time, always an issue for her went away completely. She began pacing the floor with notable anxiety, very much like her cat had done. Her groin turned wet. The water broke and splashed the floor, leaving no doubt what was happening.

It turned dark outside. The pale light, the cold fire inside prevailed. Lillian Donner imagined a blurry face in the haze lingering in front of her. A harder than before contraction rocked her and she screamed. They occurred more and more often, now. Each scream sounded louder in her ears. Each contraction hurt more. She stood on the bed. Eva and Marianne held her and supported her, whispering calm messages in her ears. Jennifer checked her for the hundredth time, giving her yet another smile of assurance.

The floor actually looked worn under her feet when she paced back and forth on it. She chuckled, just before she released another loud scream. Her entire body was soaked in sweat.

– The cervix is fully expanded, Jennifer reported. – It should happen any time, now.

It didn't. Lillian's sore throat released yet another loud scream. She shook and almost fell. The two midwives caught her just in time.

Marianne dried her forehead and kissed her cheek, comforting her as much as she possibly could. Lillian, totally exhausted, looked at her with gratitude in the hazy eyes.

– He's coming, Jennifer said excited. – Push, PUSH

Lillian screamed and pushed, screamed and pushed forever. One final horribly loud scream or rather wail emerged from that very sore throat.

She hung in Marianne and Eva's arms. Jennifer held up the tiny human being in front of her. He screamed, too. Everyone started laughing in relief and joy.

Lillian Donner rested in bed with her redhead son in her arms. She looked into his glowing green eyes. More time passed. He had begun sucking on a nipple. It felt so good. She closed her eyes halfway. The infant let go of the nipple and yawned, and fell asleep, and so did she.

She looked with dismay at the sagging belly a couple of days later when she emerged from the shower.

– I still look pregnant, she complained.

– It will take considerable time before you have a flat belly again, Jennifer explained with a cruel streak. – It takes three months with mundane females. Perhaps, you will get away with two, if you're lucky…

Lillian threw the towel at her.

She looked down on the sleeping Joshua in the crib, overwhelmed with emotion. One blink and she reexperienced the totality of herself as she tortured Gunnar. That really didn't bring very strong emotions. She nodded to herself.

Martin approached her from behind. She turned and welcomed him in her arms. They left the bedroom, and joined the others on the ground floor. Martin connected easily with them, but she couldn't quite do it. They felt out of reach somehow. Everyone welcomed her with kisses and caresses, and then she did connect, and choked in relief.

She and Martin sought a bit of joint solitude later. Lillian still sensed the others, as if they were still hugging and comforting her.

– Your powers are still nebulous, he said. – They will stay that way for years.

– I believe you are correct, she said calmly. – They will grow as I grow, grow with me.

They looked out of the window, at the green area, at the massive gray beyond.

– He could have killed me many times before I bloomed, she said.

– He didn't want to kill you, but to break you. He failed in both.

– He waited so long that I grew beyond him, she giggled, – beyond his meager ability to handle me. What a fool!

– Intelligence was never his strong suit, Martin shrugged.

That made her look closer at him.

– I remembered what Stine told me, he said. – I remember so much more. You've helped me bring the other memories back, too.

– They will all come, she stated fiercely, – and we will be whole for the first time since forever.

– She said «fire», he said, a bit distant. – I think she would have used «energy» today, even though I'm not sure.

She recognized herself in him, and was drawn even stronger to him, if that was possible.

– I don't really care whether or not he comes for me again in a twenty-years-time or so, she stated calmly. – I'm ready for him, for them all.

For them all.

They joined the others in front of the television again, and it seemed at just the right moment.

Jennifer turned up the sound.

– Ted and Liz Warren have returned to the American continent again, after years in exile, the news presenter informed the viewers unfamiliar with that event, – and they've brought lots of unknown relatives and associates with them. Vancouver is quickly becoming the hub of rebellion London, New York City and several other cities have long since become. This is certainly bad news for US president Ronald Reagan. He has criticized the couple for years, and lost a lot of the popularity he once enjoyed by doing so. Many, both political commentators and others, ask themselves what it means.

Everyone turned to Martin and Lillian with excitement in their eyes.

– We'll go there, right? Annabelle asked.

– We will go there, Martin confirmed, – and we will help out, and we will thrive and grow.

And the mood in the room grew tenfold, from its already high point.

They started packing, preparing. They didn't pack much, really, aside from a few clothes.

– It feels like we've spent such a long time here, Lillian pondered, – but we really haven't.

– You haven't, Jennifer pointed out. – I'm just happy every time we take a vacation. I've never been to Vancouver before. I haven't met any of the Janus Clan either. I'm so happy I finally will.

She was joking, but not really. Lillian nodded.

– We will land right in the middle of it all, Jennifer stated. – We've waited so long.

She looked at the young girl with boundless excitement in her blushing face.

Lillian and Martin met Burke Adams one final time, the day they left, just before they headed for the airport.

– You took care of him, he stated. – Thank you! He would have gotten away. I couldn't have touched him.

Burke Adams was a man with many secrets, and now one more had been added.

He watched them as they faded away in the mist.

They closed and locked the house, closed all access points, including the secret subterranean passages.

Lillian looked at Martin, at Jennifer and all her other companions. They looked quite ordinary. They looked so special and precious. A catching formed in her throat.

She carried Joshua in a rucksack. Her few traveling belongings, she carried in a small bag.

– We might never return, she mused.

They turned and walked away.

They didn't look back.

Author's word

I wrote the first draft of this in 1985, and then abandoned the project. This is a far cry from that. So much has happened to me since then, and the characters have grown and developed in major ways in my mind.

It took a while before I realized why I was unsatisfied with that version, why I left it alone for so long.

It's the only novel I've written, the first and only time where I caved to censorship, in the hope of increasing my chances of getting published. I was so disgusted with the result that I put it in the drawer and let it rot.

I've most certainly fixed that with this version. I spent six months rewriting it. I usually spend eighteen months on average on a novel of this size.

The rewriting is extensive. I'm practically doing everything from scratch, just keeping a few lines here and there. My writing and my understanding of storytelling are far more developed, now, compared to then, of course, and it shows. My understanding of everything is far more developed. It's the same story, but told with far greater detail and analysis and knowledge behind it.

It is a Janus Clan companion book, an introduction of sorts, and was always meant to be. But in those forty years, I've pretty much written the Janus Clan in its totality. I know the story far better, including the story behind the story not included in the books.

The tapestry has become so much bigger and better.

It can easily be read on its own. There is no backstory you need to know. You discover that with the characters.

I've always been fascinated with Vikings. It's one part of my Scandinavian inheritance I haven't disowned. I find all the stories I've read extremely fascinating, and the people living in Norway a thousand years ago far more real than today's sorry lot.

The story takes place more or less in the present, in the eighties, before cell phones, Internet and stuff. I've kept that, deliberately, also because it fits with the Janus Clan series. It is kind of funny. The story took place in the present when I first wrote it. Now, it is happening in a time that has already become history.

But all the pieces I chose deliberately at the time remain. All the details on where and when the various movies mentioned were playing for instance is true. Everything is still there, but while the first version was woefully superficial, this is nothing but. The first version was practically a children's book. This most certainly isn't.

The real-life events in Brixton and Tottenham Hale in London in late

September and early October 1985 are covered in far more detail. The police maimed and killed lots of people, acting very much like the police always do, and none of those involved have ever been charged with anything, far less convicted.

The police eventually did apologize for shooting Dorothy Groce, but not until March 2014, well after her death in 2011, when a public commission stated that her premature death was due to the bullet wound. They've never apologized for subjecting the protesters to abject brutality.

I hope the story will pull you away from the mundane human society, and into a world most people know very little about, and that it will have a profound effect on you. At least some people are changed in the right way by the act of reading my stories, and I just love when that happens.

To learn more about the Curse of Tuth Ankh Amun and also the ancient city of Thebes, read my novel The Valley of Kings.

I've kept the paper manuscript in my possession all this time, with a lot of moving around, so I guess I did see a future for it.

Rewriting the story also made my fond memories of my time in London return in a much stronger way.

The events in this book take place before the start of Eyes in the Sky, book nine in the Janus Clan series. The story of Lillian, Martin, Jennifer and the rest continues there, and in The Iron Cage, ShadowWalk and Phoenix Green Earth.

One Sherwood Forest 2024-06-13
Print version 2024-09-09

Eyes in the sky

UFO-sightings are suddenly increasing all over the planet. Both in cities and remote areas the sightings are exploding in numbers and detail.

The eyes in the sky have been here for a very long time, studying the world and its ants. They've been many things to many people. They might have been the origin of the gods of ancient Olympus. The chariots of fire depicted in many a religious text. Some claim they built the pyramids of Egypt and America, that they were the originators of human civilization, that they in fact created humanity from beastly origins.

Many have wondered why they're here, if they're here, why they haven't revealed themselves. Many claim that this is a ridiculous question.... Since they're clearly here and have been showing themselves for a long time, a very long time, and that they keep doing so during this our modern age.

So why are they here? Why do they work in clandestine ways (they do)? What is their agenda? Is humanity nothing more than beasts to them, something to study under a microscope like we're studying ants and other animals? If they have an agenda, what is it?

Or perhaps that isn't important. Perhaps the only important question we should ask ourselves is if they *are* here, and if so, what it means to the human species. As one thing becomes abundantly clear:

They're here.

ISBN 978-82-91693-38-5

The Defenseless

The two rivers meet and join in the city of Denver, becoming one…

   The two dark brothers, growing up with their sister Linda in a mundane, average suburb, a place well entrenched in modern United States and the world, have since their moment of birth been at odds with the world… and with each other.
   Mike and Ted Cousin are not who they are. There is a mystery here, one of birth and upbringing, one of fate. Violence and death, blood and fire are following them all the days of their lives. The fire is resting somewhere inside… waiting for the Spark.
   Their parents know something, but are not telling. The policeman Mark Stewart and their aunt Trudy do, too. Everybody knows something, pieces of the whole, but nobody knows the whole truth, nobody telling it.
   The ancient power is returning to the world, a world massively suffering from physical and spiritual poison, on the brink of collapse and a collective tailspin suicide run without peer in human history. Magick is returning from its long exile. Thus begins the story of the wild beasts rising from their ashes.
   The Spark is struck, horrible and terrifying.

   Hardcover ISBN 978-82-91693-08-8
   Paperback ISBN 978-82-91693-26-2

Other published and upcoming novels by **Amos Keppler** from **Midnight Fire Media**:

The Janus Clan - (twelve chapters about the Wild Man in the modern world, forty years of wandering before the Phoenix rises from the ashes):

The Defenseless
The Slaves
Birds Flying in the Dark
At the End of the Rainbow
Lewis of Modern York
The Werewolf of Locus Bradle
The Valley of Kings
From the Ashes
Eyes in the Sky
The Iron Cage
ShadowWalk
Phoenix Green Earth

www.ingramcontent.com/pod-product-compliance
Ingram Content Group UK Ltd.
Pitfield, Milton Keynes, MK11 3LW, UK
UKHW030625171224
452439UK00019B/174/J